Counterspell:

Guardian of the Ruins

Volume 1 of the Counterspell Chronicle

Robert C.A. Goff
and
Micah M.A. Goff

Dreamsplice
Christiansburg, Virginia

This book is a work of fiction. All characters and events are purely fictitious. The content of Appendix 1, though fictitious, was inspired by the extant fragments of Herakleitos of Ephesos as cited by John Burnet.

COUNTERSPELL: GUARDIAN OF THE RUINS

Dreamsplice Fiction
3462 Dairy Road
Christiansburg, VA 24073

www.dreamsplice.com/books

ISBN-13: 978-0-9761559-8-0
ISBN-10: 0-9761559-8-2
Library of Congress Control Number: 2017918453
Second Paperback Edition January, 2018

The Counterspell Chronicle

Counterspell: Guardian of the Ruins
Counterspell: the Second Law
Counterspell: Age of Fools (upcoming)

From the world of Counterspell

Ternaria: Legacy of a Careless Age

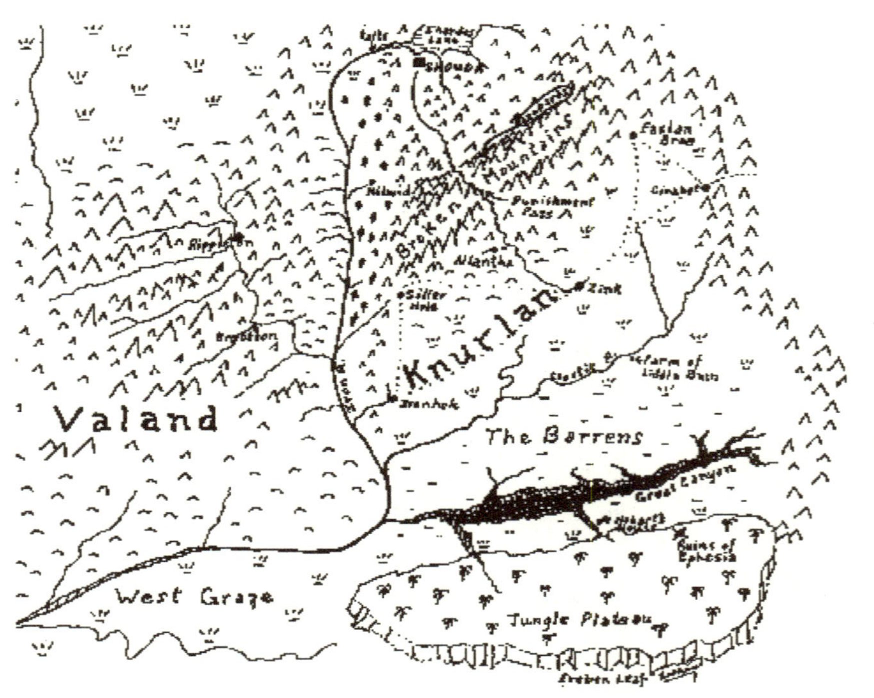
Valand
Knurlan
Broken Mountains
Punishment Pass
Zink
The Barrens
Great Canyon
Ruins of Ephesia
Jungle Plateau
West Graze

ꙮ

I take upon myself the task of recording all the events that brought us to the brink of extinction, and from there to the precarious balance by which we yet survive. Our posterity must not suffer the pain and horror allowed by the ignorance of my generation.

Ereben Leaf: Chronicle of the Counterspell, preface.

"Again, Grandpa?" Ereben asked.

"Again, yes. Until this burr at the base of the blade is gone." Chrysanthus replaced the dagger onto a small leather pad on the workbench and returned to his shack.

With an audible sigh, Ereben hefted the dagger. Although it was slightly longer than the distance from his elbow to his fingertip, its weight was that of a weapon half its length, and perfectly balanced. He smiled as he studied this product of his labor. The subtle waves of parallel lines, hundreds of lines, trapped within the blade bore evidence of its unique forging. Nine times he had forged the blade, only to fold it upon itself and return it to the fire. On its tenth forging, Ereben had shaped it to its present form and ground it to a razor along both its edges. *Five hundred and twelve layers of steel forged by my own hands.* "Steel," he whispered.

Its crowning touch was the handle of translucent green stone, capped with a smooth brass pommel to match the brass guard. Grandpa Chrysanthus always engraved a symbol of praying hands into the handle of each knife, then filled it with tin to leave the tiny symbol a glistening silver color. Except for Grandpa's personal dagger. Its symbol was filled with gold. Since Ereben's dagger was to be a gift to his own father, to be presented to him this very evening, it likewise bore a gold filled symbol of praying hands.

But there was that stubborn burr at the base of the blade. Grandpa's way of removing it would mean another hour with the polishing stone, and maybe still not get rid of it. Ereben glanced back to the doorway of the shack, to be certain he was still alone, then sat at the grinding wheel. His foot gently engaged the treadle to rotate its abrasive stone wheel. As he touched the blade to the moving wheel, the metal chimed in protest. His heart sank. He examined the base of the blade. The wheel had removed the burr, substituting a small notch.

Ereben hurriedly returned to the workbench, took up the white hand stone and attempted to smooth the new blemish before Grandpa returned. After three strokes, the stone slipped from his hand. Ereben's instinctive effort to catch the stone brushed the little finger of his right hand against the blade. The thud of stone striking the dirt floor coincided with a welling of blood from his injured finger.

"Press the sides." The voice came from behind him.

He spun around. At arm's length stood Grandpa Chrysanthus, his face encircled by a white fluff of beard and thin white hair. His rheumy eyes bore an expression of tenderness that Ereben had not seen during the past year of training.

"The cut. Press the sides of your finger to stop the bleeding," Chrysanthus repeated.

"The sides?"

"Blood moves through the fingers along its sides," Chrysanthus continued. "Press the sides until I wash away the blood and dress the wound with balm. We don't want it to fester."

As Chrysanthus dressed the cut, Ereben studied the fine wrinkles around his grandfather's green eyes. They echoed a life of wisdom and kindness and worry. And since Ereben's older brother, Caris, had died a year ago, his grandfather's eyes seemed to have added fear to their repertory. Grandpa Chrysanthus was a difficult mentor, but at least he had been willing to train him despite Ereben's failures at other trades. Since Caris had been Grandpa's apprentice when he died, Ereben suspected that his grandfather's determination to train him had grown solely from his brother's death, and would have never come about had Caris lived.

An earthy odor rose from a small, shiny bag that Chrysanthus held before him. His grandfather gently dabbed milky yellow paste onto the cut. Ereben winced. The stinging subsided. Chrysanthus tied it snugly with a band of linen.

"You go home now and clean up for tonight," Chrysanthus said. "I'll finish up the edge on the dagger." He smiled. "Your father will be proud of you, Ereben. You've made a truly superb knife, even with the new...variation on its blade."

Ereben hugged his grandfather. "Thank you, Grandpa."

"Now, go," Chrysanthus chuckled.

Ereben looked at the two daggers resting on the far end of the workbench. These two, with their tin-filled decorations, were to be offered for sale in town tomorrow. They would earn him his first profit from his newly acquired trade. *Ereben Leaf, Bladesmith.* Each had been folded and reforged five times—thirty two layers of steel in each blade. He looked back at the dagger he had made for his father, and the ancient, identical dagger always cinched to his grandfather's hip. Those were in a realm of their own.

As Ereben watched, Grandpa's pet mouse, Titus, sprinted across the workbench. Titus stopped at the edge closest to Chrysanthus. From beneath his robe, the old man produced a tiny cube of bread, which he placed ceremoniously before Titus. Titus gratefully gnawed at the feast.

His grandfather noticed him still standing in the smithy. "Ereben, go!" Chrysanthus said again.

Exiting the smithy, Ereben's eyes slowly adjusted to the late afternoon sunlight. Forested hills rose steeply above him on either side. Their autumn secret still successfully masked itself from the casual observer by a canopy of dulling greenery. Ereben absorbed the lazy warmth of this waning summer day, even while noting the yellows emerging from the north facing slopes. He recalled how strangers to these parts were never impressed by the height or ruggedness of these worn and ancient mountains until forced by circumstance or curiosity to climb their precipitous slopes.

Twenty paces brought him to the creek. A single hop carried him to the opposite bank. Not enough rain, he thought. Its scarcity had diminished the otherwise robust creek to a mere trickle no deeper than his finger. Ereben's soft leather boots crunched over the dry duff of the trail as he ascended the western rise of the hollow. At the top, he knew, Phaena would meet him. The thought of her transported him upward. *I am an artisan. A maker of fine blades. Lord Corban, I bring you this gift. I offer you this token of my artistry. I offer you this gift.* Nothing sounded right. *I ask for the hand of your daughter. I seek.... I wish to marry your daughter. I am an artisan who wishes to ask the hand of your daughter in marriage.*

Just over the rise, he approached a rocky overlook. A light, westerly breeze rustled leaves of several stunted oaks, which seemed to grow directly from the rock. While he caught his breath, Ereben seated himself on the loftiest boulder and absorbed the vista of round shouldered mountains and shadowy green valleys beneath a cloudless sky.

A click to his left drew his attention. In the periphery of his vision, Ereben was aware of a tiny object falling into the valley below. He spun his head to look behind. There he saw the diminutive figure of Phaena, standing with arms innocently folded. Her smile filled his vision. His heart swelled at her perfect, soft form, the cream folds of her linen gown, the lavender embroidery about the open neck. Orange light of the swelling afternoon sun illuminated cascades of tousled golden hair. And the subtle tilt of her head. It pulsed a wild warmth through his arms and legs.

Ereben rose to his feet. In silence, he approached Phaena, brushed both hands through her hair, and drew her to him. They kissed. *Almonds and strawberries.* He stood back a pace, straightened his shoulders and affected a posture of superiority.

"You are now looking at an artisan," he said proudly.

"You finished the knives?" she asked.

"Yes," he answered. "So your father has run out of reasons why we can't be married. All the bad luck is history now. I feel it in my bones. I'm nearly seventeen. I can earn a living, and maybe find a little respect in Rippleton."

"Maybe Father just doesn't want his grandchildren to have red hair," Phaena said, playfully tugging the hair behind his ear. She looked at his bandage and frowned. "What happened to your finger?" she asked.

"Just a little cut." *Grandchildren.* His ears grew warmer.

"I'm proud of you," Phaena said, kissing him again. "Can I tell father?"

"Well, maybe you should wait until I've actually sold the knives. I have to go now." He lifted her hand to his lips, kissed it many times, then folded her in his arms. "I love you more than all the world."

"All the world?"

"All the world."

Ereben skipped his way along the path, leaping to slap overhanging leaves, and singing softly to himself, as he headed home. "Perfect!" he said aloud, on viewing a patch of coltsfoot. He swept over the slope, picking handfuls of the fuzzy green leaves and stuffing them into his leather pouch. After harvesting a delightful supply of the leaf, he reached beneath his tunic, brought out his applewood pipe and a small pouch of dried coltsfoot. With deft strokes of flint against steel, he coaxed glowing embers from a tiny spark within the packed bowl. Sweet smoke filled his mouth. He puffed out a sphere of gray, then extended his neck forward to sample the rich aroma.

He hadn't felt such joy for as far back as he could remember. He lay down in the coltsfoot, propped himself on one elbow, and spent the bowl blowing smoke rings. *How can mother complain about something so wonderful?*

That thought woke him from his reverie. He remembered the ceremony tonight. He would be late if he didn't hurry home and get ready. Tonight he would present his special dagger to his father.

Moving quickly down the trail, Ereben pondered the mystery surrounding the dagger and the ceremony. To his questions about the reason for the presentation ceremony, Grandpa Chrysanthus would only respond, "You will understand later." Phaena had never heard of such a tradition. *I'll find out soon enough.*

Ereben reached the top of the ridge above his home. In the valley below, he could see his squat, stone house, surrounded by plantings of vegetables and fruit trees. To the East, slopes of ripening grain rose gently to meet the forest edge. And just to the

West stood houses marking the edge of the village of Rippleton. Forested slopes hid the rest of the village. Only the very top of the tower guarding the palace of the High Protector reached into view. This valley had been his home all his life.

The third house in toward the village deserved his special animosity. In it lived the tinker, Yarnish Blen, with whom Ereben had apprenticed for nearly two years. Each day that Ereben reached this point along the ridge, he would recall how Blen had berated him frequently, and eventually dismissed him publicly, accusing him of stealing. This day was no exception. He paused, drew up his hatred, and spit as far as he could in the direction of Blen's house.

It was at that moment that Ereben heard, or felt, a dull rumble to the East. It lasted for less than the span of a single gasp. He cocked his ears, but the noise was gone. Dark foreboding gripped him. The sun was passing below the horizon with shameless beauty. Uncountable realms of hill and forest spread out in every direction beneath a canopy of blue. But he knew that something was terribly wrong.

Ereben looked about him. To the East, over the second ridge, a column of dark gray smoke rose into view. Fear caught his throat. He knew there was only one thing in that valley. Ereben had just come from there. That hollow was where Grandpa Chrysanthus lived in solitude and created his knives.

Fighting panic, Ereben looked quickly down toward his own house. *Father couldn't have heard the sound from there.* He could not see the smoke from there. Quickly, he guessed that it would require a quarter-hour to reach his house, and another to climb back up to where he now stood. *That's too long.* He pivoted and sprinted toward the column of smoke.

Dread lightened Ereben's body, quickening every step. He knew these hills too well to expect to maintain a sprint the entire distance to Grandpa's hollow. Soon, exhaustion dragged at his legs and slowed his gait. The column of smoke seemed darker each time it came into view. When the terrain blocked it, his imagination conjured the smoke to a still darker, oilier hue, which held true at its next sighting.

He wished he could pray to Dragomin for strength, as he had done so often as a child, but his belief in Dragomin had faded. The way in which the Protectors dealt with him following Yarnish Blen's accusation had dowsed the glow of faith in his heart. Now, when he needed strength from beyond himself, there was none.

In a blur of fatigue, Ereben reached the ridge above his grandfather's home. The valley was filled with smoke. It billowed from charred remains, which lay scattered where Chrysanthus' house and smithy had been only an hour before. From the ridgetop, Ereben saw no movement other than the lapping of flames and the sickening smoke. His nostrils filled with the smells of burnt wood and flesh. And a strange odor of lightning. He looked up to the cloudless, darkening sky, then began the smoky descent to the valley floor.

Ereben knew as he careened downward through brush and vines that Grandpa was gone. The house and smithy were barely identifiable within the surging smoke and flames. Pieces of smoldering wood had started small brush fires about the ruined buildings. He hopped over the creek. Heat from the burning buildings stopped him short of the smithy.

What happened? The walls were flattened and burning with an intensity that reminded him of the forge. *The forge!* Maybe the forge had set fire to the building. The sweet smell of burned flesh was overpowering. Through the flames he saw what appeared to be a solitary charred body lying contorted among the flames. Benches, tools, everything had been destroyed.

The shack that served as Grandpa Chrysanthus' home lay collapsed and burning as well. The privy, a short distance up the hill, was all that remained of the home and smithy of Chrysanthus.

Ereben wandered over the smoldering brush. He stopped at the creekbed and sat on a polished boulder, facing away from the fire. In the darkening evening, the flames cast his silhouette as a lurid shadow across ripples of water. Crystal rills had become a thousand mirrors in which to see reflections of flame.

A sound of hoof beats caused Ereben to rise to his feet. Approaching him along the path of the valley floor, the roundabout way to Rippleton, were two horsemen, wearing black leather armor beneath a crimson cape, the garb of the Protectors. Ereben immediately recognized the medallion of Phaena's father, Corban, High Protector, who rode the lead horse. Corban seemed surprised to find Ereben there.

"What has happened here, boy?" Corban asked, as if speaking to a complete stranger.

"I don't know, Sir," Ereben replied, still dazed by the magnitude of his loss.

"How long have you been here?" the High Protector asked.

"A few minutes, Sir. I heard a loud noise, then saw the smoke. I ran all the way." Ereben began to cry. "I think Grandpa's dead. I can see him there." He pointed into the flames.

"I see one man," the second Protector said. "The flames are too hot to search, Lord. Perhaps we should return at daybreak."

"Yes," Corban agreed. "I will speak with you concerning this matter tomorrow, Ereben Leaf." Without further conversation, the two riders spun their horses around and returned in the direction from which they had appeared.

Ereben stood numb for some time longer, he wasn't sure how long, then started the ascent of the trail leading home. *Everything is gone. Grandpa, the forge, my knives.* He looked back at the flames and determined to search the ruins at first light tomorrow.

The walk home along the darkened trail was more a dream than a reality. Ereben's thoughts wandered between Phaena and Chrysanthus. Both now seemed to be lost. Corban obviously was not about to discuss his daughter's future. He wondered how he would break the news of Grandpa's death to his parents. After Caris' death a year ago, this was too great a blow.

Descending the final slope through the darkness toward his home outside Rippleton, Ereben considered how his parents went about their business, content with the world, while he approached them through the blackness with such dark news. One moment they would be living a day like any other; the next, they would be plunged into mourning.

A candle illuminated the small house, throwing beams of yellow light through the open shutters. Ereben swallowed hard and entered. He would have to just come out and tell them. He knew no other way.

The common room was empty. A stool lay on its side. The house was quiet. Dread swept as a wave over Ereben. This was a different life than the one he had awakened to this morning. To the left was his chamber, the one he had shared with his brother

Caris until a year ago. He entered the chamber to his right, his parents' sleeping room.

In a way that Ereben could not understand, he felt no surprise at seeing the body of his father sprawled face up on the floor. Father was barefoot, wearing a linen tunic and partly laced, leather jerkin. Two blood-encrusted wounds pierced the front of the jerkin. His right forearm bore a yawning knife wound. He saw no sign of life. Blood no longer flowed. Ereben looked about the small chamber. His mother was not there. He passed through the doorway again and walked into his own chamber. His heart raced. Bile rose to his mouth.

His chamber was dark. Candle light from the common room cast his distorted silhouette across the floor and onto his brother's sleeping palette, reminding him of the creek by Grandpa's burning house. His world was coming apart. In the shadows of the far corner he made out the shape of his mother, slumped against a blood-splashed wattle wall. He approached slowly. She did not move. The left side of her neck gaped like that of a slaughtered animal. He moved close in the shadows. He saw no other wounds.

Kneeling before her, Ereben lifted her lifeless hand to his cheek and began to cry. *I should have been here, Mother. I should have been here.* He gently rested her hand on the floor.

Fleeing the horror of his home, Ereben ran toward Rippleton as fast as his aching legs would move him. He must tell the Protectors. He ran and cried and gasped for air. He entered the limits of Rippleton, running wildly up the shadowed road, past the first few houses. *Where do I go?*

Ereben's left foot caught on some unseen object. He crashed to the packed dirt of the road bed, striking his forehead. He could not breathe. He could not clear the confusion from his mind. Something held his hands. Cool steel pressed against his neck.

"Get up and be silent," a hoarse voice stated flatly.

He could not think. *I'm rushing somewhere. It's important.*

"Move," the voice said. He was lifted to his feet.

His assailant remained behind him, leading him into a house. *I should recognize this house. I should recognize that voice.* The door closed behind them. His attacker seated him on a three legged stool, then walked around to within Ereben's view. Yarnish

Blen stood before him, his eyes wild and frightening, or perhaps frightened.

"Listen to me, Ereben Leaf," Blen said. "Listen well and listen fast."

He's just killed my mother and my father and my grandfather. Ereben found that hard to believe even of Blen.

"The High Protector has put a warrant on your head. You have been accused of murdering your parents and your grandfather."

"How can they think..."

"Quiet!" he spat. "He intends to hang you by your neck."

Ereben felt a wave of nausea, his body suddenly cold to the core.

"Do not return to your house or to Chrysanthus' smithy," he continued. "They will search for you there, and along the trails you frequent. You must flee Rippleton if you intend to live past tonight."

Ereben considered his hatred of this gruff man. Why should he believe a man who would be the first in line to cause him grief?

"Now flee. If you go into town, you will be killed."

"Where do I go?"

"Seek out a Stump named Whittig Trench. He may be able to help you. He knew Chrysanthus."

"I don't understand."

"You will. Now run." Yarnish Blen shoved him out the door, into the shadows of the road.

Ereben froze. None of this should be happening. *And Blen! This makes no sense.* Surely Phaena would have warned him if her father had issued such a warrant. *Unless she's a part of all this.* But that made even less sense. *I should tell her what's happened. She might come with me.* The sound of approaching hoof beats spurred him into motion. He sprinted through the shadows away from the road and toward the blackness of the forested ridges east of Rippleton.

For three hours of blind stumbling, Ereben climbed, descended, flailed and crashed his way through darkness. At last, the half moon rose, allowing him to get his bearings. His first sight of the moon confirmed his suspicion that he had traveled farther south than he had intended. Exhausted and bruised, Ereben veered eastward, ascending to a ridge he knew well. Reaching the summit, he lay down on a boulder from which sprang stunted oak trees. To the southeast opened a panorama of moonlit mountains beneath a canopy of diamonds.

He looked about. It seemed as though days had passed since he had held Phaena in his arms, kissed her lips, and spoken of marriage. Now he didn't even know if Phaena might have played some role in all this horror. *She couldn't have known.* Tormented by his pain and his thoughts, Ereben drifted into fitful sleep.

A rustling in the nearby brush awakened Ereben. Without moving, he opened his eyes. Almost close enough to touch, a large buck stood motionless. After a moment, the buck bounded west down the slope. Ereben sat up. The sky was hinting at dawn to the East. He stood, brushed the twigs from his tunic, and walked briskly down the ridge, toward the now destroyed smithy.

Just before emerging from the trees, Ereben paused to study the open valley. Directly in front of him, wisps of smoke drifted from the charred ruins of the house and smithy. The valley appeared deserted in the pre-dawn twilight. He moved forward, hopped across the creek, and hurried to a position immediately behind the ruins. This spot offered a view of the valley while he inspected the ruins.

Within the smithy, the stones of the forge appeared to be surprisingly intact. Ereben walked slowly into the center of the dirt which had served as the floor of the smithy. He looked at the charred body. Its face was unrecognizable. There was no trace of clothing remaining. Ereben felt no emotion, only hollow exhaustion.

Ereben looked to either side of the burned body, searching for Chrysanthus' dagger, but it was not there. In the ashes of the workbench he found one of the knives he had planned to sell. The stone handle was cracked and separated from the tang. Its tin insignia was gone. *The tin must have melted.* He tucked the handleless blade into his belt. He saw no trace of the second knife among the workbench ashes. He spotted a dagger buried in ashes by the inside edge of the building. Its gold praying hands insignia remained perfectly intact. This dagger seemed to have suffered no damage from the fire. Ereben lifted it from the black debris and inspected the blade. At its base was the unmistakable notch he had created with the grinding wheel. It seemed to have been smoothed a bit with a polishing stone. In the center of the blade, the lamination lines appeared more contorted than he remembered. But this was definitely the dagger he had planned to present to his father yesterday. *He's dead. Mother is dead. Grandpa is dead.* More searching failed to turn up Grandpa's dagger.

Ereben looked up and down the valley. Nothing stirred. He moved into the remains of Grandpa's cabin. Its wooden floor was charred, but part of it solid enough to bear his weight. The walls were nothing but black rubble. No possessions remained. Movement on the floor caught his eye. It was Titus, Grandpa's mouse.

"Come here, Titus," he said. His voice seemed out of place in the silence and death of the ashes. "Titus."

The mouse scurried beneath a blackened floorboard. Ereben discovered that this particular board had not been pegged to the joists like the others. He lifted it. There sat Titus in a comfortable nest of shredded parchment. Alongside the nest he saw a parchment scroll, its end chewed away. It had apparently been the source of Titus' nesting materials.

The sound of riders echoed from the south end of the valley. Ereben folded the parchment and placed it and Titus into his leather pouch. Quickly walking east, in the direction of the privy, Ereben vanished into the forest.

ꕥ

Without family and without friends, living in solitude becomes a succession of immediate chores. One must search to find a context for the future.

Ereben Leaf: Chronicle of the Counterspell.

The linen wrap that Grandpa Chrysanthus had tied on Ereben's injured finger had vanished in the chaos of the previous night. Ereben sat in brush by the bank of the Iron River, inspecting the cut on his little finger. The tiny wound was red, slightly swollen, and a little painful to touch. That annoyed Ereben more than it worried him, since it caused him to be conscious of how he used his right hand. He leaned toward the river and thrashed his right hand in the sparkling water to wash away the dirt.

Ereben knew what he was running from. He had no idea where he was heading. All that he had ever cared about was lost. In his mind, he had turned over the past few days, the past few years. Nothing seemed to explain what had happened.

Using split twigs and green vine, Ereben covered and wrapped the edges of his daggers. The lacing from the neck of his tunic served to tie the two knives securely to his belt. Since his skill with daggers extended only to creating them, he knew he would need to practice using them sometime. He managed a hollow smile. Time seemed to be in plentiful supply.

Titus, the mouse, climbed onto Ereben's knee. This solitary survivor of his family had just returned from a foray of some sort. Probably finding food, he thought. Ereben's own hunger now surpassed his fatigue. He looked about him for anything that might be edible. Across the river, forty yards away, was a shallow filled with cattails. That was all the motivation he needed to cross the river.

When Ereben opened the top of his leather pouch, Titus scurried in without prompting. Ereben wrestled a log of driftwood, as big around as his thigh, to the edge of the water, then eased himself into the gentle flow. His right hand held his leather pouch out of the water, while his left held him close to the log. Using his legs to frog-kick, he moved out from the bank.

The current increased. The water became colder and less cooperative. Despite his efforts, he and his driftwood log were swirled about and swept further downstream. When he finally touched the bottom, about five yards from the eastern bank, Ereben had his back to the land, with the log turned toward the direction from which he had come.

"That was not fun," he said aloud. Still up to his chest in moving water, he struggled to gain his footing. His right arm ached from holding the leather pouch out of the water.

From the center of the current, a dark shape the size of a man moved rapidly toward him, beneath the surface. Ereben gasped and dashed backward, reaching for the bank. A long, narrow, fish-like head erupted from the surface of the water, clamped its well toothed jaws in the center of the driftwood log and snapped it in two. Ereben lost his balance, but dove to the safety of the land, still holding the leather pouch in the air. When he looked back at the water, he saw only two short driftwood logs heading south with the current.

The few times in the past that Ereben had visited the Iron River's western bank, he had seen some very large fish. Nothing in his memory approached what he had just witnessed. But the driftwood log was now two logs.

Shivering from the cold and the fear, Ereben looked about at his surroundings. To the East, up and down the bank, the land was open forest, with mountains rising in the distance. He looked back at the water again. It appeared as innocent as it had from the opposite bank.

After loosening the cord of his leather pouch to give Titus a bit more air to breathe, he checked the daggers tied to his waist. Both knives were secure. If the river was any indication of how friendly the world might be to him, the blades would be a comfort.

With no obvious food in sight, he decided to walk the half mile back up stream to the cattails. A narrow game trail paralleled the bank of the river. Ereben walked north along the trail through brush and a sparse canopy of swamp birch. Dappled midmorning sunlight shimmered on the path as a living thing, lifting his spirits. His lungs drew in moist river air, scented with bark and mud and moss. Birds in the distant trees maintained a constant chatter behind him and in front. As he passed, they fell silent, but only until he moved on. His passing was heralded also by a succession of frogs leaping from the river bank to the safety of the water. He shook his head at their questionable choice.

The path veered eastward at the verge of a swampy field of cattails. Ereben removed his boots and set them by a massive walnut tree, along with his leather pouch. Barefoot, he ventured into the shallows. Beside a stand of cattails, he palpated the mud with his toes, until he felt a cattail shoot emerging from the mud. He reached beneath the water with his hand and tore the shoot from its mother plant. After peeling the outer layer from the shoot, he devoured the flavorless pulp without hesitation. From a quarter hour of labor, Ereben filled his belly.

With his hunger satisfied, and his mind cleared, he leaned against the great walnut to consider his options. He knew he needed to put as much distance as he could between himself and the Protectors of Dragomin. Beyond that, his future was a blank slate. *Without Phaena.*

Titus darted into the leather pouch on the ground. Ereben became aware that the birds overhead had abruptly fallen silent. His muscles tensed. He cautiously turned his head from side to side, listening. There was no sound or movement. The sky darkened. Ereben fought his fear and looked up. A flight of several hundred ravens, black and silent, cruised just above the tree tops. They seemed to follow the river's course. The flight covered the entire width of the river, extending over the bank on either side. Their path showed no randomness. Their constant distance above the tree tops was unlike any flock of birds Ereben had ever seen. He thought he saw a darker, much larger shape flying high above the ravens, but his view was obscured by both the trees and the dense flight of ravens. He remained motionless until the resident birds resumed their conversations.

Ereben had seen ravens before, but no more than two or three together in one place. *And their size!* These ravens appeared to have bodies the size of dogs, and wingspans as wide as his own arms could reach. He thought of the dark shape flying above them. What ever it was, he knew it could not be good. Here among the stand of birch, he had been warned by the silence of the birds, and been hidden by the trees. What if these ravens returned when he was walking through an open meadow or across an exposed mountain ridge? Could they be looking for him? But what could they do? *What would they do?* He remembered Titus' darting into the leather pouch just before they appeared. Ereben reached into the pouch, lifted Titus from it and placed him on his left shoulder. The mouse circled the shoulder three times, then took up a perch near his collar.

"If you see those birds from Dragomin knows where, you let me know."

Titus did not respond.

With his few belongings gathered, Ereben circled east around the swampy area, then headed north along the river, keeping to the trees wherever possible. He had no idea where he was going, but at least the river was a direction to follow.

Mid-afternoon, he discovered a vast bramble of late-season raspberries, with fruit as yellow as autumn. He tasted one. It melted on his tongue sweet and tart. The next one he donated to Titus. Ereben then proceeded to eat with abandon. After much thought, he discarded half of his recently picked coltsfoot to make room for a supply of the golden raspberries in his leather pouch. As long as Titus doesn't spend too much time in the pouch, he thought, the berries should last a while.

Titus jumped into the neck of his tunic. Ereben instinctively fell to the ground and crawled beneath the brambles, ignoring the scratches and punctures of the thorns. The sky darkened. He lay immobile, unable to look up. When bright afternoon returned to the sky, he turned his head to the side in time to see the flight of ravens vanish to the South. Above them, a larger, indistinct shape glided on wings that, he guessed, spanned five or six yards.

"Thank you, Titus," he whispered, as the mouse returned to the shoulder perch. "But that was awfully close."

Ereben turned east, away from the Iron River and toward the nearby forested hills. It seemed safer. Up close, the trees here were older and more massive than the birch near the river. These were oaks and walnut, linden and gum. A path opened at the point where the forest met the raspberry bramble.

"Are you afraid of those birds?" asked a crisp, young voice from the trees.

Ereben halted. The trees were stately and graceful, but they did not seem to be capable of speech.

"Up here," the voice said, seeming to read his mind.

In the branch just above his head, Ereben made out a pair of eyes within the shadows. "Who's there?"

"Me!"

"Come out where I can see you," Ereben suggested.

"I can't come out."

"Why not?"

"Because there is no out," the voice explained. "I can only come down."

"Then come down," Ereben said. Feeling foolish, he realized that the voice was that of a child in the tree.

Feet covered with sandals extended from a low, robust limb. Then a small body appeared, dangling from the limb. With a thud and a grunt, the figure landed on the leafy ground, ending up on its backside.

"That wasn't too good," the child said, getting up and brushing off the leaves.

Ereben guessed that this energetic waif, in a well-worn and undersized tunic, was a boy of about ten years.

"I'm Jasper," the boy volunteered.

"I'm Ereben."

"Are you afraid of those birds, Ereben?"

"What a stupid question."

"Are you?"

"Why would I be afraid of a bunch of birds?" Ereben asked. This Jasper waif seemed a little pushy for a small boy.

"You looked like you were," Jasper persisted.

"How old are you, Jasper?"

"Almost eleven," he replied, seeming to expect Ereben to be impressed. "How old are you?"

"Sixteen. Do those birds always fly around here?" Ereben asked.

"No. I never saw them before today," Jasper explained, "but today they went by twice. They looked awfully spooky."

"Were you afraid of them?"

"Course not!" Jasper said. "They're just birds."

"Right. You live around here?"

"Yes, in Nilwid. It's a half-hour walk, that way." Jasper gestured at the path leading east into the forest. He looked at Ereben oddly.

"Do you think I can find a place to stay for the night?"

"That's really strange," Jasper said.

"Why is that strange?"

"There's a mouse sitting on your shoulder."

"Oh, I beg your pardon," Ereben stated with expansive formality. "Allow me to introduce my friend and traveling companion, Titus."

"He really stays with you?"

"Of his own choosing," Ereben replied.

"And rides on your shoulder?" Jasper's smile stretched across his dirt-smudged face.

"All the time. Except when he's frightened by something. Then he jumps down my neck."

Jasper convulsed with laughter. "You have to come with me back to Nilwid, so I can show Titus to everybody."

"Lead the way."

Ereben followed Jasper into the forest village of Nilwid. He counted twenty-three mud houses, all with thatch roofs. At the eastern end of the village stood a larger stone structure which he assumed was a temple of Dragomin, judging from the symbol of the sun etched above its doorway. At the first house, a short, well muscled man was occupied with dressing out a small, wild pig. The man waved a hand in greeting, then followed Ereben with a cautious eye. A woman tended an open fire while she prepared vegetables. By the time Ereben and Jasper had reached the third house, children of various ages had begun to congregate around them. By the fifth house, all forty-three children in the village knew Titus by name.

When they arrived at Jasper's home, near the center of the village, Jasper went inside and brought out a woman.

"Mother," Jasper said excitedly, "this is Ereben, and he has a mouse named Titus, who rides on his shoulder wherever he goes."

"I'm called Tira, Ereben," the woman said, lifting her cupped hands, palms up. "You look like one who has traveled far."

"Yes, Ma'am," Ereben replied. "Is there some work that I could do for food and a night's lodging?"

"No, there is not, young man. But you may eat and sleep here as our guest."

Her smile, a mother's smile, warmed his soul and pierced his heart. Ereben remembered his mother, a wound gaping in her neck. "Thank you." The words caught in his throat.

That evening, Ereben met Jasper's father, Javvic, a small man with massive forearms and two teeth missing in front. Javvic, he learned, was a woodcarver. This explained the dozens of intricate carvings of birds, animals and people that Ereben had observed decorating the walls and nooks of the common room. He also met Jasper's five year old brother, Willen, who spent the evening enraptured with Titus.

After a dinner of richly seasoned, boiled potatoes and syrup-drenched ham, Tira and Javvic sat with Ereben on decoratively carved wooden benches beside the outdoor cooking fire. Tira asked Ereben many questions about his journey. With her gentle encouragement, and the hypnotic flicker of the wood fire, he explained the tragedies that had so recently confused his life. When his story reached the point of his arrival in Nilwid, he fell silent.

"We should let you get some sleep," Javvic said.

"In the morning," Tira added, "we will see what things we can gather to make your journey more tolerable." She hugged Ereben and whispered, "You will be safe here tonight."

In that moment, Ereben recognized how precious had been the hugs of his mother. He recalled how ordinary they had seemed while she was alive.

As he settled down to sleep on the floor of the common room, Jasper crept in and lay down beside him. Ereben untied his daggers and placed them on the floor next to his opened leather pouch and his small smoking pouch.

"Does Titus sleep with you?" Jasper whispered.

"I think he runs off to look for food at night. He's probably raiding your larder now."

"Ereben..."

"What?"

"Where will you go, with your family...dead?"

"You listened?"

"I didn't mean to. Yes I did. I wanted to listen. And it made me feel terrible."

"I don't know where I'm going," Ereben said, mostly to himself.

"I could take care of Titus for you."

"We'll see."

Ereben awakened with cramps in his legs and back. The midmorning sun streamed through gaps in the shuttered windows. The house was quiet. Jasper was gone. Titus was not in the leather pouch. His dagger with the missing handle lay where he had placed it, but the good dagger, the special gift for his father, was missing. He stood and stretched his aching body. A quick peek in the two sleeping chambers confirmed that the house was empty. As he rushed out the door, he nearly collided with Tira.

"Did you sleep well?" she asked.

His fears subsided. "Yes Ma'am, I did. Where is everybody?"

"Everyone is getting little chores done before the service," she said, hanging small boy's clothing over a wooden rack to dry in the sun.

Of course, he remembered, it's prayer day. "When is the service?"

"Crotus, our priest, should ring the chime in about an hour. Oh, Javvic asked me to send you to the woodshop when you came out. It's just behind the house."

The entry to Javvic's woodshop was littered with planks and sticks of assorted wood, as well as various contraptions that appeared to be molds for bending wood into unusual shapes. The interior was illuminated by sunlight from three windows. Javvic sat hunched on a stool intently engaged in his work. On the workbench beside him lay Ereben's missing dagger.

"Ah, Ereben, I have something for you." Javvic dipped a wooden object into a basin of oily liquid. He removed it quickly, then rubbed it down with rags. "It's made of linden wood, so it will be light. I noticed last night that your knife had no sheath. What do you think?"

Ereben accepted the wooden sheath. It was indeed light as parchment. It was made in two pieces, bound together by crisscrossing leather thongs, which also provided a loop to tie it to his belt. The wood was stained a deep green by the oil. The center of the sheath bore a tiny engraving that matched the praying hands inlayed in the dagger's green stone handle.

"It's beautiful," Ereben replied, astonished by its intricate craftsmanship, and the apparent speed with which Javvic had completed it. He pressed his dagger into the sheath. It fit snugly, perfectly. The sheath was more beautiful than the sheath in which Grandpa Chrysanthus had carried his own ancient dagger. "My Grandpa would be pleased. I don't know how to thank you."

Inside the house, beside his few belongings, Ereben found a blanket roll, a backpack and a water skin stacked neatly.

"It's time for services," Jasper shouted, running in the door with Titus clinging tenaciously to his left shoulder.

Within the little temple, it seemed as though everyone in town had crowded in. Ereben was surprised at how similar the service was to those he had attended in Rippleton. The worshipers stood shoulder to shoulder, leaving space only around the altar. There, Crotus, the priest, sang praises to Dragomin in the same strange and unintelligible language used by the priests in Rippleton. At the climax of the invocation, Crotus moved his hands in the same manner, and a sphere of red light appeared within his hands, only to drift upward and out to the sky through the opening in the roof, just as it did in Rippleton. While the worshipers fixed their attention on the sphere of light, Crotus seemed to be more interested in Ereben.

After the service, Crotus approached him. "May your prayers be answered, young stranger," the priest intoned. "What might your name be?" Crotus was obese, his black robes reeking of incense. His eyes squinted, and his smooth, pig-face appeared greasy and repulsive.

Before Ereben could think of a false name, Tira introduced him, asking Crotus for his special prayers for Ereben's journey north.

When Ereben returned to Jasper's house, he strapped on his two daggers. Crotus had awakened a sense of danger. Ereben stepped outside in time to see a single raven flying off rapidly to the southwest.

Tira simply would not hear of Ereben resuming his journey so late in the day. Reluctantly, Ereben agreed to wait until morning to depart. Besides, Tira was baking bread for him. It wouldn't be ready for another hour. By then it would be late afternoon.

"Ereben," Jasper called out, "if you help me set some snares, then maybe you'll have rabbit for dinner tomorrow."

"Where do you set them?" Ereben asked. He didn't feel much like entertaining Jasper, but the prospect of roasted rabbit seemed sufficient grounds for indulgence.

"Come on," Jasper said with excitement, "and I'll show you."

"Can I come too?" Willen asked, bouncing up and down on his toes.

"No you can't come," Jasper answered contemptuously. "You're too little."

"Mother," Willen called, "can I go with Jasper...." He vanished into the house.

"Let's go, before my stupid brother scares away every rabbit for miles."

They set out east, behind Javvic's woodshop, and ascended a gentle slope of foothills. The first few snares were for rabbit. Jasper rubbed a loop of twine in the dirt, "so they don't smell me," then carefully laid it in a circle. In the center, the drawing end of the loop wrapped around a trigger made of two twigs kept in place by a piece of turnip. The twine then ran to the top of a sapling, bent toward the loop. Any animal disturbing the turnip, Ereben guessed, would release the trigger, be caught in the snare loop and hauled into the air by the sapling. Ereben was impressed by its clever simplicity.

For catching squirrels, Jasper leaned a fallen branch against the trunk of a tree which contained a telltale squirrel's nest at the top. He then piled brush around the trunk, leaving a convenient path only on the upper surface of the sloping branch. He dangled a twine loop from a branch higher in the tree, positioning the loop to a squirrel's "shoulder height" above the dead branch.

"They're really lazy," Jasper pointed out. "So they'll take the easiest way to get from the ground to the tree trunk. I've watched 'em get caught. When the squirrel feels the twine touch his shoulders, he tries to run away. That pulls the loop shut."

"Does that catch many squirrels?"

"If I put up three or four snares, I usually catch at least one squirrel."

"You're pretty good at this, Jasper."

"The best in Nilwid. Hey, Ereben. Do you want to see Nilwid from up there?" Jasper pointed to a ridge about sixty yards above them.

"That looks really steep," Ereben pointed out. "Have you ever climbed up there?"

"I climb up there all the time. It's the best spot there is."

For almost an hour Ereben followed Jasper. They walked a little and climbed a lot, but nowhere did it seem particularly dangerous. Ereben became more aware of the painful cut on his little finger. His left hand did most of the work of the climb. When they finally reached the overlook, Ereben had to agree with Jasper. This was the best spot there is.

Mountains rose steeply to the East. Below, to the West, forest swept unbroken to the Iron River. In the center of the forest was Jasper's tiny village of Nilwid. The flood plain of the river opened wider to the North and South, beyond the reach of the hardwood forest. West of the river, mountains rose again, undulating into distant blue haze. A breeze, carrying the scent of upland junipers, cooled Ereben's overheated muscles. The late afternoon sun cast the landscape in a deep relief of orange and green, dazzling his eyes, even with the lids closed. The rock beneath him radiated its accumulated warmth.

When Ereben opened his eyes to the West again, he had difficulty focusing on the mountains. It reminded him of exiting Grandpa Chrysanthus' smithy into the bright daylight. And of looking from the forge to a shadowed workbench, and back to the forge. As his eyes now reaccustomed themselves to the sunlit panorama, its reality stunned him.

From a smudge in the western sky materialized a great flock of birds. Without a word between them, Ereben and Jasper backed into the shadows of the rocks behind them. They watched the flight of ravens approach. Above the ravens, a giant vulture glided. Ereben could just make out what appeared to be a man riding the vulture, controlling the great bird like a horse, by reins about its head. Ereben knew that he was trapped. There was no way to climb up, and the descent was fully exposed for about thirty yards.

The path of the ravens dipped. They descended like hornets into Nilwid. He looked at Jasper. The boy stood staring, mouth open, eyes wide and wild. Muffled screams penetrated Ereben's awareness. The roofs of Nilwid disappeared beneath a dark blanket of ravens. The screams reached a crescendo.

Jasper bolted from the shadows of the rock and began the descent, abandoning all caution. Ereben followed. He knew that they could not possibly reach Nilwid in less than half an hour. What he would find when they arrived was too frightening to consider. His body followed Jasper's irresistible impulse to dash into harm's way.

Ereben reached the gentler slope below the rocks and broke into a sprint to catch up with Jasper. He dodged low branches, hurdled logs and glanced off trees, but could only match Jasper's pace. Screams from Nilwid grew louder. Ereben saw open sky through the trees ahead. That must be Nilwid, he thought.

Before Ereben and Jasper broke from the cover of the trees, they were halted by the roar of flapping wings and the calls of a thousand ravens. A black cloud of birds lifted into the air above Nilwid, transforming the fading blue expanse to a sickly, pocked spectacle. With a croaking caw that chilled Ereben's soul, a giant vulture rose to join the gathering ravens. Atop the vulture hunched a man dressed in the black leather armor and crimson cape of the Protectors of Dragomin. The terror of the sight held Ereben to the place where he stood. He sensed that Jasper remained beside him. The dreadful swarm circled once, gaining altitude, then streamed northward, splitting the sky in two.

The screaming from the village continued. Ereben broke free of his horror and began running again toward Nilwid. He passed Javvic's woodshop. Between the woodshop and the house, Ereben saw the first dead raven. Nearby, a bloody wooden pole lay on the ground. In the dirt along the side of the house, nearer the front, Ereben saw what appeared to be the skeletal arm of a child. A wave of nausea overtook him. He turned away and vomited. Jasper ran past him.

Ereben recovered to see one of the men of the village grab Jasper and hold him back, despite his protests. Ereben smelled death in the air. He ran toward Jasper, but was grappled by two men.

"He did this!" one of the men shouted.

"You brought this on our heads!" a woman screamed into his face.

The agonizing cries drowned any attempt by Ereben to answer his accusers. Men bound his hands behind him. In the road before him, Ereben counted the ravaged bodies of five adults and the partial remains of one child. Strewn about were several dozen dead ravens. Blood was everywhere.

"Where is my mother?" Jasper asked through his sobbing. "Where is my father?"

No one answered.

"Kill the stranger," a voice cried. "He's to blame!"

"Take him to Crotus," another insisted. "Crotus must judge him."

A blood-spattered woman ran up to Ereben, slapped him fiercely with the full swing of her arm, then collapsed to the ground, convulsed with sobbing. Rough hands shoved Ereben toward the Temple of Dragomin. He labored to remain on his feet. The villagers paid no heed to his pleas. He could not tell what had become of Jasper. Ereben's captors stopped him outside of the temple, their hysteria momentarily controlled, while one villager went inside. After a moment, the villager returned, his face ashen, and sat against the temple's outer wall. The mob fell silent.

Crotus slowly emerged from the temple door and stood trembling beneath the etched symbol of the sun. He held his stubby hands over his face. A smell of incense and death filled the air.

"The stranger is innocent," Crotus said. His voice was subdued and wavering.

"How can that be?" a woman asked, showing obvious deference to the priest.

"I have brought this death to Nilwid," he said to the astonished villagers, "and I have been punished by Dragomin for my ill deed." Crotus lowered his hands from his face.

The villagers gasped. Beneath Crotus' brow, Ereben saw only bleeding sockets where eyes had been.

"I have been punished," Crotus repeated, slowly turning and entering the temple. "I have been punished. I have been punished."

That evening Ereben stood alongside Jasper, holding his hand as the flames of the pyre lapped at the darkness, consuming the remains of the dead. All the surviving villagers chanted in mumbling, tormented tones, swaying gently from side to side. Children stood close to their parents, holding on to a hand or a sleeve. They appeared stunned.

From the short, well muscled man whom Ereben had first seen dressing a wild pig at the edge of the village, he learned what occurred when the ravens came. The Protector had gone directly to Jasper's house and demanded that Tira and Javvic turn Ereben over to him. When they refused, the Protector drew his sword, and with no further warning, slew Jasper's younger brother, Willen, then tossed his body to the giant vulture. The vulture devoured him, with ravens fighting over the pieces. Tira, Javvic and three other men of the village flew into a rage, grabbing whatever might serve as a weapon. These five villagers swung sticks and knives and axes at the ravens, but were quickly overwhelmed by the sea of birds, by the sword of the Protector, and by the claws and beak of the giant vulture. The slain villagers had barely struck the ground before their flesh was torn away by the ravens. Villagers who did not resist were left unmolested. The short man narrating these horrors to Ereben had also killed several ravens, but was able to escape. After a search of Jasper's house failed to turn up Ereben, the Protector and a small flight of ravens went to visit Crotus, before departing from Nilwid.

Jasper had been spared the details. But Ereben knew too well the pain in Jasper's heart. Like Ereben, Jasper had lost his family without warning, without recourse, and without the opportunity to try and save them. They had been a part of his life one moment, forever gone the next.

Still holding hands, they returned to Jasper's house. The boy went alone into his parent's chamber and returned to the common room with a second backpack, and a rolled blanket, which he placed near the neat stack of gear that his mother had set out for Ereben. Without speaking, Jasper curled up on the floor near Ereben and cried himself to sleep. As Ereben drifted into sleep, he wondered what would become of Jasper. The boy apparently had no relatives in Nilwid. Everyone in the village had abandoned him to his grief. *Maybe they blame Jasper for bringing me here.*

ꕥ

The Nilwid Massacre served as the common seed of divergent and momentous events. Looking back, the death of six people seems insufficient cause for what followed.

Ereben Leaf: Chronicle of the Counterspell

In the small hours of the morning, Ereben awakened. Among the nearby shadows of the common room, he could see the curled form of Jasper. The boy's soft breathing awakened a distant memory of sharing a sleeping chamber with his brother Caris. How long ago had it been? How much longer it seemed now. He had argued with Caris frequently, but would sleep near him when he was afraid. Now Jasper did the same with him. Ereben wondered what Jasper saw in him, a failed tinker and a consummate coward.

His former master, Yarnish Blen had taught him the tinker's trade, had dismissed him, humiliated him publicly, then saved his life. *It makes no sense.* "Seek out a Stump named Whittig Trench," Blen had said. *A Stump.* He had heard tales of Stumps, but had never believed them to be true. Stumps were supposed to be like people, but half their height and much stronger and much uglier. Tales told of them living in holes in the mountains, coming out only to chase disobedient children back to bed at night. These same tales located them only as not so far away.

Ereben put his feet loosely into his boots and went out into the crisp night air. The moon was not in the sky. He wondered where he should go. *And Jasper.* Was Jasper planning to go with him? The mountains to the East would be difficult to cross. Either north or south along the river would be easier walking, but the ravens seemed to know that as well. Traveling south would take him closer to Rippleton again. He decided to travel north, skirting the western edge of the mountains. That direction would at least be away from Rippleton.

He thought of Phaena. The immediate joy of the thought gave way to pain. "I love you, Phaena," he whispered to the western stars. "Are you thinking of me? I miss you." His eyes filled with tears. He was unable to ask the stars if she was somehow involved in all this death, but the possibility deepened his pain. He wished that there were some way to speak to her across the ether, some way to know her heart. If he knew that she needed help, he would risk anything to go to her. *But I told her about finishing the daggers. Then Grandpa was killed.* And two daggers were missing: one of his trade daggers, and Grandpa's personal dagger. But Phaena had longed to marry him. He had known her all his life. None of it made sense.

Ereben remembered that he had left the remaining trade dagger, the one without a handle, beneath the travel gear that Tira had placed on the floor. He had not thought of it in the chaos of the evening. He slipped back inside the house, straining to see in the deep shadows. Feeling with his hand beneath the backpack, he touched the cold metal of the dagger's tang. His sense of relief at finding the worthless dagger struck him as childish. He tried once more to get some sleep before resuming his confused journey.

"Wake up," someone said, shaking Ereben's shoulder.

"What?" he replied, not sure where he was or who was disturbing him. He had been dreaming of a great banquet where they served nothing but cattail shoots. One more cattail, and he would explode.

"Ereben, it's morning."

He squinted into the formless glare. Everything was too bright. As his eyes adjusted and his mind cleared, he recognized Jasper, wearing an oiled linen cape, which nearly touched the wood floor. Ereben sat up.

"I got some more things we might need," Jasper said. The boy's eyes were red, his face puffy and sober. "These were Father's," he said, holding out a brown striped cape made of wild pig skins with a white fur collar. "The collar is weasel fur. They turn white in the winter." In his other hand, he held a single silver coin. "We might need this."

"We?" It seemed to Ereben's foggy mind that Jasper was planning to go with him. "I don't even know where I'm going,"

Ereben continued. "And those ravens and that giant vulture thing will probably keep looking for me."

"Everybody blames me for bringing you here. I can see it in their eyes."

"It's my fault your family's...gone. Why would you want to go with me? It's all my fault. How can you even want to talk to me after all that's happened?" It was not clear to Ereben whether he was feeling guilt or just maneuvering to avoid the burden of taking Jasper with him.

"It's some your fault and some mine. Because it's my fault, I have to leave. I have to. Because it's your fault, you have to let me go with you. You just have to."

"Like a punishment?"

"Kind of. Don't you want me to come?"

Ereben hesitated. "I don't know, but I'm afraid it'll be really hard... and dangerous."

"You have to let me. I don't care about the rest. I want to go away from here."

Ereben accepted the cape and the coin. "Partners?" he asked, holding a hand out to Jasper. *What am I doing?*

"Partners," Jasper agreed, taking Ereben's hand and hoisting him to his feet.

Ereben watched as Jasper looked about the common room one last time. The boy's eyes lingered on his father's exquisite woodcarvings.

"I need to get something in the woodshop," Jasper said.

Ereben followed him out into the cool of dawn and around the house to the woodshop, passing the fly-covered remains of a raven along the way. Inside the woodshop, Jasper gathered some small tools, placed them into the pockets of a stitched square of canvas and rolled it into a bundle. This he put into his backpack. His gaze searched the woodshop, as if to imprint his mind with its memory.

"We should go now," Ereben suggested, "before anyone wakes up." He placed Titus onto Jasper's shoulder.

Together, they struck out north from Nilwid, aiming for the western slope of the mountains. Ereben hoped they could discover a course that would take them far enough east to escape the patrols of the ravens. Mile by mile, they gradually ascended the western foothills, following game trails that seemed to anticipate their direction through the mossy oak forest. At each rest break, Ereben drew his dagger to go through the motions of defending himself. This seemed to amuse Jasper, who spent the rests whittling the head of a walking stick with one of Javvic's carving tools. Titus would always wander off for a short time, then climb back aboard Jasper's shoulder before they resumed.

"You don't look very good at that," Jasper pointed out, after observing Ereben quickly draw his dagger from its wooden sheath, only to drop the dagger between his feet.

"Why do you think I'm practicing?" Ereben retorted.

"It just seems like you should draw it slowly."

"What do you know about fighting?"

Jasper continued to carve the walking stick. "Nothing. But father always said that it doesn't matter how sharp the knife is if you can't control it."

"My Grandpa used to say it doesn't matter how hot the forge gets if you can't control the hammer." He picked up the knife. "I guess they meant the same thing." He wiped the dirt from the blade and studied the wavy lines that were the hallmark of Grandpa Chrysanthus' forging technique. He had forgotten that the pattern seemed to have changed. When he found the knife after the fire, it had appeared untouched by the flames, but the patterns were not the way he remembered them. Since the lines, as permanent as the rings of a tree, were created by folding, then re-forging the steel, he couldn't imagine how they could change without enough heat to damage the blade and melt the gold from the praying hands symbol. But they were definitely different. He returned the dagger to its new sheath.

His right hand ached. The tiny cut on his little finger was taking on an angry red appearance. A thin streak of red seemed to be creeping toward his wrist. He remembered Grandpa's healing balm. He wished that he had looked for some at Grandpa's house.

"Jasper," Ereben said, as they continued walking, "do you know anything about what's north of here?"

"Not very much," the boy answered. "This is about as far as I've ever been from Nilwid."

Jasper looked silly with his dirty brown hair sticking out from one side of his head. Ereben licked his hand and plastered Jasper's hair back in place. "Do any people live up here?"

"Father said that the only thing up north was Shadows. He said they hide in the trees, and when children come by, they grab them and eat them."

"What are they?" Ereben laughed. The story reminded him of the tales about Stumps.

"They're tall and thin and dark," Jasper explained. "Father said he saw one once, but it ran away because he was holding a knife."

"Are they like people?"

"I guess they're something like people," Jasper continued, "but they live in trees and eat children that get too far from home."

Ereben laughed again. "That's so stupid."

"It won't be so stupid when they try to eat you."

Through the day, Ereben kept his attention divided between the trail before him and the sky above. There was no sign of the ravens. That evening, they camped in a clearing near a creek. Ereben kept the cooking fire small, to avoid searching eyes. Together they shared a small pot of soup made with a piece of potato and an onion. Into it they dipped chunks of parmak, a hard, dry travel bread that Tira had baked for Ereben.

Later, Ereben filled his applewood pipe with coltsfoot and stoked it to a satisfying warmth. After Ereben had made countless unsuccessful attempts to blow smoke rings, Jasper persuaded him to pass the pipe. Jasper drew one puff, then, in a fit of coughing, passed it back.

Jasper spread his oiled cape near the fire and curled up on it. A distant howl brought him upright again.

"What was that?" Jasper asked.

"It sounded like a wolf," Ereben replied, slowly drawing his dagger. "I think it was pretty far away."

Jasper put several sticks on the fire and fanned it to a brighter glow. Another howl sounded closer, but from the opposite direction. "I don't like this," Jasper said, moving closer to Ereben.

"Don't worry about it. They howl at night all the time outside of Rippleton. They don't like people, so they stay away from fires." Ereben replaced his dagger and casually took up a stout branch.

The sound of growling awakened Ereben. The fire had died down to glowing embers. In the darkness, he could see three pairs of glowing red eyes. He pressed back fear and rose abruptly to his feet. He realized that he still held the branch, nearly as long as a man. Instinctively, he raised the branch high above his head and shouted "Go away!" at the top of his voice. The eyes crept closer.

"What are they?" asked a high pitched whisper from behind.

"I don't know," Ereben answered. "Maybe wolves. I can't see them. It's too dark."

A pair of eyes moved to each side of them, staying beyond the reach of Ereben's branch. When the center pair of eyes dipped lower to the ground, the flash of teeth confirmed Ereben's fear. *Wolves!* From the teeth he could see, Ereben imagined a massive body he could not see. The center wolf lunged. Ereben brought the branch down with all the force he could muster. With a dull crack, the branch broke over the wolf's head. The wolf crashed to the ground, its legs fully extended, twitching. The wolf to his right made its move. With the yard long club that remained in his hand, Ereben spun to his right. Wood struck the leaping wolf squarely in the chest. The wolf fell onto its side, rolled once, then fled into the darkness. Ereben looked about expectantly, but saw no trace of the third wolf.

"Look," Jasper said, tugging at Ereben's arm.

A half yard from the embers of the fire, a great silver wolf lay in its death throes. Blood flowed in full pulsations from the roof of its skull. Ereben watched as the twitching slowly quieted and the bleeding ceased. With his own hands trembling, Ereben prodded the silver fur with the broken branch.

"It's dead," Ereben whispered.

"Look at how big it is," Jasper said. He knelt by the dead animal and ran his hand through its silver-haired coat. "It's so pretty."

"It tried to eat us," Ereben pointed out, still trembling from the confrontation.

"Can I take the skin when it's morning?" Jasper asked.

"What for?"

"It's a sin to just leave it," Jasper implored.

"I suppose we have to eat it too."

"I don't know about eating it, but we really ought to keep that silver pelt."

Ereben put several sticks on the embers, blew on them until they flared into dazzling light, then sat on the ground. "You'll have to skin it yourself. Then you have to treat it or something, to keep it from rotting and getting all smelly."

"I've done it with squirrels," Jasper said, "and with a small pig once."

"Let's decide in the morning," Ereben concluded. "One of us ought to stay awake to keep a watch. You go to sleep, and if I get too sleepy, I'll wake you up."

"You can sleep first," Jasper offered. "I can't sleep now anyway."

"Are you sure?"

"I'm sure," Jasper reassured him. "I'll wake you up if I get tired."

Ereben lay down. He pondered Jasper's fascination with the wolf pelt. Jasper sat between the fire and the dead wolf, stroking the silver hair, comparing the size of a wolf paw to his own hand.

The day was light and already warm when Ereben awoke. To his amazement, he found Jasper kneeling before a wolf pelt, smearing a thick, gray paste onto the underside of the skin with a stick. Nearby, the skinless carcass of the wolf swarmed with flies.

"By Dragomin," Ereben muttered, "you actually skinned it."

"It didn't take too long," Jasper said proudly. "The hard part was getting the brains out."

"The brains?"

"But you made it a little easier when you cracked his skull."

"Brains?"

"You mix the brains with ashes to cure the skin," Jasper explained, lifting the stick with a pasty mixture at its end.

Ereben twitched his nose. It all smelled pretty bad. The thought of preserving an animal's skin with its own brains made him feel slightly ill. His entire right arm ached. At first he assumed it was because of the fight the night before, but then he noted the red streak growing toward his elbow. Ereben remembered the tiny cut made by his dagger at his grandfather's smithy. His sheath was empty. He noticed his good dagger lying on the ground beside Jasper. "You used my dagger on that?"

"It made it a lot easier. It's so sharp. I cleaned it in the creek when I was done." Jasper looked up at Ereben. "I guess I should have asked, but you were asleep."

After Jasper had rolled the pelt, fur side out, and stuffed it into his pack, they crossed the creek and continued northeast, Ereben in the lead, Jasper behind, and Titus riding on Jasper's left shoulder. As they walked, they fell into the same pattern as the previous day, resting every hour, during which Ereben practiced with his dagger and Jasper whittled his walking stick. But by the third rest, Ereben's head throbbed. He felt episodically chilled. He could no longer grasp his dagger firmly with his right hand.

"You don't look like you feel too good."

"I don't," Ereben answered. "I think this cut on my hand is festered."

"Is that bad?" the boy asked.

"It feels bad. My Grandpa used to put a salve on cuts. I don't know what to do with it here."

"My grandmother used to have us eat a mushroom for things like that," Jasper said.

"Mushrooms are poison," Ereben pointed out. "You die if you eat them."

"Well, we ate them, and we didn't die."

"What did they look like?" Ereben asked.

"I don't know. She would just give us little dried-up, brown pieces."

"Great." Ereben had heard of people dying from festered wounds. But eating a mushroom seemed like quite a gamble.

After a rest at mid-afternoon, Ereben could not gather the energy to continue. His arm ached. A painful, swollen lump had appeared in his right armpit. He felt dizzy when he stood. Instead he convinced Jasper to let him take a short nap.

Ereben awakened once to see that it was nighttime. Jasper sat awake by a fire. Ereben's clothing was soaked with sweat. He drifted off again.

Horrible dreams plagued Ereben's sleep. One great beast after another attacked him. He fought them off with sticks and knives, but each time they attacked, they consumed more and more of his right arm, until only a bleeding stump remained at the shoulder. As he fought his dreamed adversaries, they choked him, pried his mouth open and forced him to eat things. In his dream he remembered the pungent, musty smell of Grandpa Chrysanthus' yellow healing salve. The beasts went away. He felt hope.

Ereben sputtered. He awakened to Jasper giving him water from the water skin. Daylight seemed to be the golden orange of sunset. His headache was gone, as was the pain in his arm.

"How long have I been asleep?" he asked.

Jasper hesitated. "Three days."

When Ereben sat up, he felt light headed. "Three days?"

Jasper wiped his eyes. "I thought you were going to die."

"What happened?" Ereben asked, trying to grasp the missing time.

"You had bad fevers, and you got crazy," Jasper explained. "You were asleep most of the time, but when you woke up, you said crazy things about bears and wolves, and you would swing your arms all around. And then you would fall back asleep. It got worse and worse, and I thought you were going to die, so I went out and found some mushrooms, lots of different mushrooms."

"You gave me mushrooms?"

"I didn't know which one to give you. If I gave you the wrong one, you would die. And if I didn't give you the right one, you would die."

"So?"

"Then I remembered your dagger." Jasper reached behind himself and lifted up an oddly shaped mushroom.

Ereben understood immediately. Jasper held a large, brown mushroom shaped like praying hands. Ereben took it and brought it up to his nose. The musty aroma filled him with the memory of Grandpa Chrysanthus. For the first time, Ereben realized that the symbol engraved on the daggers might not be that of praying hands, but the symbol of this mushroom. Ereben drew his dagger and studied the gold filled symbol. As the dagger neared the mushroom, its translucent green handle seemed to radiate warmth and a soft green glow. The red streaks on his right arm were gone. Ereben sensed a power within the mushroom, echoed by power within the dagger. Titus ran up Ereben's tunic and down his left arm. The mouse sniffed the mushroom, then scampered back up the tunic, down his right arm, and stood on Ereben's hand, touching his tiny paws to the symbol within the glowing handle.

ꕥ

It may be that the gulf which separates childhood from what we recognize as maturity is largely the awareness of one's own mortality.

Ereben Leaf: Chronicle of the Counterspell

In the weeks since Ereben had departed from Nilwid, he had learned to accept the rhythm of the forest. He came to anticipate the unique variety of creatures that defined each portion of the day and night. The predictable shifts of insects, birds and animals from sunrise to midday to dusk to midnight and on again to morning represented the only certainty in his life. That and the presence of Jasper, whose dependence and whose support had more than once rescued Ereben from despondency. He had not seen the flights of ravens in all this time. The days were occupied with obtaining food and with the effort to continue northeast toward their nameless destination.

Jasper had surprised Ereben with his ingenuity and creativity. The walking stick on which Jasper whittled at every pause had become a menagerie of animals, birds and fish spiraling in exquisite detail from one end of the staff to the other. On the head of the staff, Jasper had carved the praying hands mushroom, which had saved Ereben's life. The silver-haired wolf pelt had been transformed by the boy into a stunningly attractive cloak as well as a matching sheath for Jasper's small knife.

Ereben found himself moody at times, but discovered early in their journey that his mood spread easily to Jasper, who would then alternate between being impossibly stubborn, to sobbing over the death of his family. To make it easier on the boy and on himself, he now tended to hide his own sorrows and fears, allowing them to rise to the surface only during his turn at night watch.

The necessity of maintaining night watch grew from the wolf attack, but the wisdom of it was reinforced almost nightly by the nearby sounds of wolves, feral dogs and unrecognizable wild noises. On one occasion, Jasper reported the approach of two ring-tailed cats, the size of wild pigs. They stayed well clear of the campfire, attempting to steal food from the backpacks. Jasper had easily driven them off with his staff, but had to repeat the process three more times during that watch.

Tonight, Ereben tended the night watch during the first of four shifts, while Jasper slept. They had both learned to count the hours of night by the rotation of the stars. This night, the moon rose full and early, casting deep shadows across the meadow in which they had camped. Ereben preferred the illumination of moonlight to the closed darkness beneath a moonless sky. While most nights presented the forest in varying shades of gray, under the cloudless sky tonight he saw tints of greens and yellows among the tall grasses of the meadow. Titus entertained him with brief excursions into the surrounding grass, returning each time with a succulent grasshopper or beetle on which to dine.

Titus' latest treasure was a small lizard, which he carried up onto Ereben's knee. The mouse placed the dead lizard there, looked up at Ereben's face, bobbed his head three times, then ran off again into the grass. Ereben examined it. The lizard's iridescent green skin shimmered in the moonlight. He drew his dagger and prodded the dead lizard with its point, wondering how roasted lizard might taste. His diet had become more eclectic since leaving Rippleton.

A shadow swept across his knee. In the clear, black sky above, he saw the backlit silhouette of a large owl, wings outstretched, descending toward him. Instinctively, he tightened his grip on the dagger and pointed it in the direction of the bird. As it neared, wings still motionless in the cushion of air, it seemed to veer slightly to his right. *Titus!* Five yards away, Titus ran toward him in short zigzagging bursts of speed. The owl swooped silently toward the ground.

"No!" A deafening crack resounded in his ears. Searing cold rose through his right arm, as a bolt of dazzling green flashed from the dagger in his hand directly to the owl. The force threw him to his back. His vision collapsed to an undulating, pattern of yellow and black. An acrid scent of lightning filled the air. The chill of his arm crept upward, past his shoulder, groping for his heart. His mind pressed against the cold, slowing its progress. His heart heaved within his chest. In a last effort before lapsing into unconsciousness, Ereben drew the cold away from his heart, urging it into his mind. Yellow and black undulations yielded to utter black.

"Are you alright?"

Jasper. It's Jasper's voice.

"Ereben?"

Ereben opened his eyes. Jasper knelt over him. The blackness of the sky was stippled with tiny flecks of light moving about his vision. He blinked.

"Look, Ereben," Jasper said, pointing toward Ereben's feet.

Momentarily dizzy, Ereben raised himself onto his elbows. Near his feet stood a large gray owl, swallowing the last of an iridescent green lizard. On his shin stood Titus, ignoring the owl. Titus munched complacently on the hind quarters of a locust. Ereben slowly sat up. The owl turned its head, blinking one eye, then the other. It paid no attention to Titus.

"What happened?" Jasper asked.

"Something magical, I think." Ereben looked at the dagger lying in the shadow by his hip. It felt unremarkable as he lifted it and inserted it into its wooden sheath. He explained to Jasper what had happened, so far as he could remember. The gray owl seemed to listen to the brief narration, then spread its wings in the flickering fire light and lifted off into the darkness of the night.

Jasper cupped Titus in the palm of his hand. "Do you know what happened, Titus?" he asked, scratching the mouse's nose with his fingertip. "I'm glad that owl didn't eat you. Do you really think it was magical, Ereben?"

"I don't know," Ereben answered. He felt disquieted. It seemed as though he were on the brink of some great understanding, but it eluded him. "What I do know is that it was frightening and powerful. It seemed to draw something out of me. It..." He felt the center of his chest. "It's like it used my body the way those flames use the wood. For strength. And leave only ashes behind." Ereben trembled at the thought. He remembered fighting that force, unable to drive it back, barely able to direct its path within him.

"Did you make it happen," Jasper asked, "or did it just happen."

"It seemed like it just happened," Ereben said, "but I think it happened because of what I wanted. And this dagger made it work."

In the firelight, Jasper played quietly with Titus a while, then allowed him to run off again into the meadow grass. "Ereben," he said, sitting down to face him, "Crotus used to say that it was a sin to believe in magic."

"Who is Crotus?"

"You know, the Priest back in Nilwid." Jasper continued. "He said that true followers of Dragomin believed in his miracle, and that only sinners believed in magic."

"Do you think this was a miracle of Dragomin," Ereben asked, "like the ball of light that flies up to the sky from the temple?"

"It has to be," Jasper concluded.

"But owls are supposed to eat mice, and mice are supposed to get eaten. I don't believe in Dragomin anyway. I think its all children's stories."

"Don't say that, Ereben. Dragomin will punish you."

"Jasper," Ereben said with amazement, "it was the Protectors of Dragomin that killed your family. It was the Protectors of Dragomin that gouged out the eyes of their own priest!"

"But still..."

"No. This isn't almighty Dragomin working miracles. There's something else going on here. I don't understand it, but it's not miracles. Definitely not miracles."

As they continued northeast, the forest grew thinner each day. Now they walked in an open plain, broken only by forested creek valleys. Although they had not seen the flights of ravens for weeks, Ereben still felt uncomfortable about walking in the open so much of the time. The forest had offered countless hiding places. Here, there were none. The grass grew waist deep, so that one might hide easily from pursuers riding across the plain, but from the sky, Ereben knew, all would be visible.

A dry, chilling wind blew steadily from the North, bringing with it flocks of birds fleeing the coming winter. The trees of the creek valleys had already turned orange and brown, and were now beginning to shed their leaves. The grasses were yellowed and brittle. These signs told Ereben that they must decide soon on a place to hole up during the coldest months. Already, they were wearing their cloaks for warmth as they walked. They would surely be unable to travel once the snows fell. He guessed that several more weeks would pass before winter set in.

This morning, when a flock of birds appeared on the horizon, Ereben knew immediately that the ravens had at last returned. These birds erupted from the clouds south of them and flew north in perfect formation.

"Run for the trees!" Ereben shouted to Jasper. The nearest trees were hundreds of yards to the East. "They've found us." He ran toward the trees, Jasper five steps ahead of him. Each time he looked back over his shoulder the flight of ravens was closer. *We'll never make it.* With thirty yards separating him from the trees, Ereben drew his dagger, stopped and turned to face the onslaught of ravens. "Keep running!" he called over his shoulder. He saw through the darkening sky the massive shape of a giant vulture above the ravens.

Ereben's arms thrashed at the descending ravens. Each one that met his blade crashed to the ground flinging blood in all directions. His left arm guarded his face. As he fought for his life, all he thought of were the bleeding, empty eye sockets of the priest, Crotus. A raven's claw punctured his right forearm, opening his grip on the dagger. With a scream of pain, Ereben tore off his cloak and swung it over his head to hold back the uncountable birds. Many hundreds more swooped downward, while others pecked and clawed at his legs. Looming larger, the giant vulture continued to descend toward him.

To Ereben's amazement, ravens far beyond the reach of his cloak began to tumble from the air into flailing heaps on the ground. Ravens continued to attack him, but they seemed fewer in number, providing an opportunity to recover his dagger. As the giant vulture touched down in front of him, it collapsed, arrows appearing in its body and head. Its helmeted rider, dressed in the black leather armor and crimson cape of the Protectors, stood to his full height on the carcass of the vulture. In his left hand he held a round metal shield, in his right hand a long sword. He deflected arrows with the shield and approached Ereben with the sword held low before him. As he neared, the arrows ceased.

"Drop your weapon, Ereben Leaf!" he shouted. "Drop it or you will die."

The ravens cleared from around Ereben. A shout came from the trees behind. With a crackle of the air, green light flashed from the Protector's sword, exploding an approaching spear into a nest of smoldering splinters.

"Now you will die, Heretic!" the Protector shouted, his face flush with anger. With a full swing, he brought his sword down onto Ereben.

Instinctively, Ereben raised his dagger to meet the plunging sword. He knew in his heart that the massive sword would easily deflect his dagger and split him in half. As the two unequal blades met, Ereben felt no force against the dagger in his hand. Instead, green light flashed with a deafening crack and a now-familiar scent of lightning. The face of the Protector revealed first surprise, then horror. The two blades remained in motionless contact. With an agonizing scream, the Protector fell toward the ground. But the Protector's grip on the sword never released. His body hung from it like an emptying sack of grain. The sword, still floating at its contact point with Ereben's dagger, seemed to be sucking the Protector's flesh, drawing it into the sword's green pommel stone, which glowed increasingly brighter. Finally the Protector's clothes and armor fell empty to the ground, as the remnants of his flesh disappeared into the sword's pommel stone. The sword dropped harmlessly to the ground, its green pommel stone no longer radiating its unnatural light.

As Ereben's trembling hand sheathed his dagger, he realized that he had felt nothing in his arm. He sensed none of the gripping cold or pain that had accompanied the incident with the gray owl. Instead, his arm, in fact his whole body, felt refreshed, its fatigue completely gone. All that remained of his brush with death was trembling brought on by his now forgotten fear.

Many voices approached him from behind. Ereben looked up. The hundreds of uninjured ravens pounced upon the carcass of the giant vulture, and those ravens that had been wounded or killed. From beneath the trees, several dozen figures approached, led by Jasper, who jumped into Ereben's arms.

"That was incredible!" Jasper said, hugging him with enough force to reveal his own fear. Jasper released him to examine the empty clothing and armor of the vanished Protector.

Tall, brown skinned men, dressed in dark brown, neatly trimmed tunics surrounded him. Each carried a short bow and an empty quiver over one shoulder. Some carried spears nearly three yards long. Their hair was unlike any Ereben had ever seen, pitch black and tightly kinked against their scalps, revealing ears which came to a point on top. Their faces were narrow and sculpted, with thin, hooked noses. They were all much taller than the men of Rippleton. Taller than anyone he knew of in all Valand. The tallest among them came forward.

"Peace to you, great warrior," the brown man said, briefly bowing with both hands empty and outstretched before him. "I am called Otah Kadeef, Prince of Shouda. I pray tell us your name among your friends, that we may properly greet you."

"I'm Ereben Leaf," Ereben answered, "but there aren't many friends left to call me that."

"Now there are many," Otah said with a brilliant flash of white teeth. "Peace to you Ereben Leaf."

A great chaos fluttered about them as the ravens noisily rose into the air and flew off in every direction, each carrying portions of flesh in their beaks. The giant vulture remained as a foul, dripping heap of bones.

"You would honor us, Ereben Leaf, by staying to rest among us," Otah intoned in a friendly but formal voice.

"We would like that," Ereben answered.

"Look at this," Jasper said, holding the Protector's sword with two hands. "The blade looks like your dagger's blade, with all those wavy lines."

Ereben cautiously examined the sword, remembering what it had so recently done to its former wielder. Indeed, the enormous blade had been forged in layers, in the style of Chrysanthus' knives. He knew of no one with the skill and knowledge to forge such a large blade in this fashion. Beneath its curved brass guard, a handle of stacked leather disks ended in a brass claw which held a small round ball of translucent green stone, identical to the stone of his dagger's handle. Ereben retrieved its scabbard from the heap of clothing and armor on the ground.

"Come now, Ereben Leaf," Otah said. "We shall lead you to Shouda."

"Who are these people?" Ereben whispered to Jasper.

"They're Shadows."

ꝏ

An understanding of the importance of my role in the scheme of things came slowly, and only with my growing awareness of the magnitude of Corban's efforts to capture or kill me. During that same window of time, I began to recognize that the laws of nature were not as men believed them to be.

Ereben Leaf: Chronicle of the Counterspell

As Ereben followed Otah Kadeef and the other Shouda men toward their home, his curiosity grew. He wondered how the village of these tall and overly formal brown men would differ from the villages of ordinary people. For two hours they walked, across savannas demarcated by thickly forested creeks and over rounded ridges of scrub covered gravel. Ereben noticed that the men deferred to Otah in all decisions. Although Otah Kadeef was tall among these tall men, it was his bearing that seemed to set him apart.

"Do you think they'll have us for dinner?" Jasper asked with a wry smile.

Ereben considered the ambiguity of the question. When he noticed the impish expression on Jasper's face, they laughed together over their private humor. Jasper seemed to be quite pleased with himself for having discovered Shadows. He seemed equally pleased that they had not lived up to the legend.

The path climbed a slope into which had been laid white flagstone steps. The men ahead of him ascended the steps and passed out of sight over the rise. When Ereben reached the crest of the rise, the shock of what lay in the valley below caused him to stagger backwards. Having grown up in the town of Rippleton, his mind was completely unprepared for the startling beauty laid out before him. From the overlook he gazed down upon a broad forested valley. In its center, dozens of slender spires of white stone reached skyward, many times the height of the surrounding trees. The base of each spire sprouted from a square plaza of white stone. At the four corners of each plaza stood massive, squat pyramids, each larger than any house he had ever seen, and each made of the same white stone. The spires and their plazas formed a great square, nine plazas by nine. From the center of this great square rose a black pyramid, much larger than the rest. Its base covered nearly all of its plaza. Its height reached nearly two thirds the height of the spires.

"Ereben!" Jasper gasped. "Have you ever seen anything like that?"

"Of course," Ereben replied. "It's just a city."

They descended the remaining two miles of white flagstone stairs alternating with terrace traverses to the edge of Shouda. From the shade of trees closely surrounding the startling white structures, Ereben sensed a peculiarity about the place. Thatched roof houses clustered beneath the trees along the margin of the white stone plazas. The nearest line of squat, stone pyramids hid beneath an overgrowth of vines. The bustle of Shouda men, women and children seemed to avoid the vast array of white stone plazas, which extended at least a mile on each side. Though still beautiful, even breathtaking, the "city" of white spires, pyramids and plazas appeared to be deserted. The white pinnacles and pyramids, constructed of perfectly dressed, milky white stones, radiated an unmistakable antiquity that spoke of immeasurable centuries.

"Come with me, Ereben Leaf," Otah Kadeef said, motioning toward one of the larger thatched roof houses. "You must meet my father. Bring your Wolf Boy as well."

"My name is Jasper," the boy stated undiplomatically.

"Jasper?" Otah asked with a gesture which seemed to request the remainder of his name.

"Jasper of Nilwid," Jasper clarified.

With a momentary smile and a nod of acceptance, Otah rephrased his invitation. "Come with me, Jasper of Nilwid. Bring your warrior as well."

They entered a wattle building. Ereben was surprised to find himself standing in what appeared to be a meeting chamber ten yards long and half as wide. Its floor was hidden beneath deep wool carpets of multicolored patterns. Along each of two walls rested a half dozen straight-backed wooden chairs beneath carved wood panels depicting Shouda warriors engaged in combat with winged serpents of frightening size. In the background of the scenes, Ereben could identify the spires of Shouda. His attention was now drawn to a high-backed wooden chair, which seemed to dominate the chamber. Perched above the center of its back was a carved representation of the praying hands mushroom. Seated in this focal chair, and nearly the same color as its darkly stained wood, sat a slender, beardless, middle aged man dressed in a simple brown tunic trimmed with bright yellow piping. The man leaned over a small table to one side of the chair, writing with a quill onto a parchment scroll. Otah stood patiently until the man laid his quill onto the table and looked up, apparently not expecting to see strangers.

"Father," Otah stated formally, "I present to you a warrior who has defeated one of the Protectors of Dragomin: Ereben Leaf and his companion, Jasper of Nilwid. Friends," he said to Ereben and Jasper, "you are in the presence of Ibrah, Mufta Gebir of the Shouda."

Without hesitation, Jasper bowed, extending his hands, seeming to imitate the gesture of Otah at their first meeting. Ereben belatedly followed suit.

"I welcome you to Shouda," the Mufta said, rising and walking to them. "Come, sit." He motioned toward the chairs along the wall. When they were seated, the Mufta hefted one of the chairs to a position directly in front of them. "Tell me, Ereben Leaf, how you have come to fight the Protectors of Dragomin."

Ereben related his strange tale to Mufta Ibrah and his son, Otah. Both listened attentively, though the Mufta's eyes kept returning to the mouse on Jasper's shoulder. Jasper filled in details of the narration, including the discovery the healing power within the praying hands mushroom.

Ibrah pointed to the carved mushroom at the head of his throne. "Elloh placed it upon the earth to heal those who follow him. It is called munu, and grows in abundance here. You have surely pleased Elloh. He has rewarded you by revealing the munu in your time of need."

Ereben untied the long sword from his pack. "Mufta Ibrah," he said, handing the sword to the Mufta, "maybe your people can find some use for this. It was the Protector's. It's too heavy and way too long for me to use."

"I thank you, Ereben Leaf. You are both brave and generous." Mufta Ibrah hefted the sword.

"Father," a voice called from the doorway. A slender, strikingly beautiful Shouda maiden burst into the room. She halted abruptly, seeming to be embarrassed by the presence of Ereben and Jasper. "Excuse me, Father," she said, backing out of the chamber.

"What is it, Hanarah?" the Mufta asked in a kind, fatherly way.

"Mother asked me to call you for dinner."

"Thank you, Hanarah," he said. "We will be along shortly. Please tell Mother we will have two guests for dinner."

As they stood to leave, the Mufta said to Ereben, "I see that you are fascinated by the carved panels."

"Yes, Mufta Ibrah," Ereben responded. "What do they mean?"

"They are legends told to children," Otah said, smiling.

"Indeed," the Mufta said, scowling at his son. "The panels depict the War of Flames, which occurred many generations ago. The ancestors of the Shouda fought on the side of Elloh to save the world from evil."

At dinner, in a smaller building not far from the meeting chamber, Ereben was introduced to Otah's mother, Estheri, and his younger sister, Hanarah, whom he recognized as the girl who had interrupted their meeting with the Mufta. The meal, cooked by Hanarah and her mother, was a feast of roasted vegetables and baked fruit, served with sweetened goat's milk.

In the conversation that followed, Ereben learned that Protectors of Dragomin had attempted to invade the city of Shouda several times during the past two years. Each time, the Shouda archers drove them back. On none of these occasions had any weapon succeeded in wounding, or even touching, one of the Protectors. Only their ravens and occasionally one of the giant vultures had been wounded. Mufta Ibrah conjectured that the Protectors were surrounded by impenetrable evil, and thus could deflect the arrows and spears. He expressed his surprise that someone as young as Ereben could succeed where his warriors had failed.

"What do the Protectors want?" Jasper asked.

"They want only our shrine," Otah explained. "They say that they will leave us alone, if we allow them to inhabit the shrine."

Ereben was confused. "What is the shrine?"

"The great white stone structures that fill this valley," the Mufta interjected, "they comprise the shrine which our ancestors built to celebrate their victory over evil. It is the shrine which allows our city to thrive. The shrine protects us from the heat of summer and the cold of winter. It allows our crops to grow in great abundance."

"We do not know," Otah added, "why the Protectors should wish to have it."

Later, Ereben and Jasper were shown to a small wattle building, which Otah offered as their quarters "for as long as you choose to stay as our guests in Shouda." Jasper immediately identified a nook in the corner wall which he declared to be Titus' new sleeping chamber. The room was sparsely furnished, but the sleeping pallets were padded with deep wool carpets. That alone was sufficient to mark the place in Ereben's mind as definitely suitable for spending a night. Stout dowels protruding from the wall were perfect for hanging their gear. The only other furniture consisted of a pair of three legged stools.

When Jasper had finally wound down from the day's excitement and gone to sleep, Ereben took his smoking pouch outside. He filled his applewood pipe with coltsfoot, lit it, and strolled in the moonlight along the edge of the shrine. The rich smoke of coltsfoot sweetened his mood. He considered these friendly, pointy eared, brown people. He had not felt as hopeful or as safe since leaving Rippleton. The spires reached skyward, blue-white and mysterious in the moonlight. He wandered onto the nearest stone plaza, stepping carefully to avoid tangling his feet in the vines which had taken over the first yard of the plaza stones. At one of the squat pyramids, reaching many times his height, he leaned against the milky stone. He thought it curious that the stone was comfortably warm, even though the air was chill. The warmth of the stone complimented the warmth of his pipe.

He thought of Hanarah. She was truly beautiful, with her tightly kinked black hair puffed out into a halo. She was probably about the same age as Phaena. *Phaena!* Sadness choked him. Tears filled his eyes, causing the blue-white spires to dance under the stars. He missed her. An aching rose in the center of his chest. *How does she fit into what's happened?* Ereben walked about the stone plaza aimlessly, wondering how he had ended up so far from home. *I have no home.*

Ereben sensed a low pitched humming sound. He looked in its direction and discovered that he had wandered far from the pyramid, and was now standing a few yards from one of the spires. The cylindrical stone spire was five yards thick. He approached it. The humming sound grew louder, though still no louder than a hummingbird. He placed his hand on the stone of the spire. It felt as cold as the night.

Ereben took full advantage of the skills of the Shouda weapons master, Saikal Sahm. To Ereben, the white haired man with gnarled hands and brittle eyes appeared as harmless as a caterpillar. True, he was half again as tall as Ereben, but so thin that he seemed in danger of toppling with the first gust of wind. But with a short bow or a spear, Saikal had no equal among the Shouda. His uncanny accuracy with the bow and his effortless parries with a Shouda spear would be awesome in a man a third Saikal's age. For three weeks, Ereben had attended Saikal's lessons with Otah. Each day Ereben practiced for hours with the bow, the spear and his dagger. Jasper preferred spending his time practicing parries with his carved staff. Ereben had the impression that Jasper's proficiency with the staff advanced more rapidly than his own skills.

In return for his lessons, and the insistent hospitality of the Mufta, Ereben improved the forge that the Shouda used for making weapons, tools and kitchen implements. He taught the smith a technique for manufacturing steel arrowheads and spearheads to replace their traditional iron points. He showed him how to fold the hot metal in order to form stronger, thinner steel. The smith was amazed and delighted.

Today, Ereben brought a special spear to his lesson with Saikal Sahm. The master stood with his other pupils at the edge of the practice range, beneath an endless canopy of gray clouds. A leafless quiet inhabited the surrounding trees.

"What is this?" Saikal asked.

"I bound the blade of a dagger to the shaft," Ereben said, offering for Saikal's inspection a spear which carried his handleless trade dagger as its point.

"The point is much too long, Ereben Leaf," Saikal observed. "It will have too much weight at the end." An expression of curiosity crept over his weathered, brown face. He looked fifty yards down the practice range at a vine-filled leather bale, which served as their usual spear target. The bale was suspended by a rope from an overhanging tree branch. With a swift thrust of Saikal's arm, the spear soared in a graceful arc. As the spear disappeared downrange, the bale remained motionless. "The point is too long," Saikal repeated with a shake of his head. As they walked the fifty yards to the bale, Saikal explained to his students the importance of a properly sized spearhead.

"Saikal, look!" Jasper cried, as he reached the bale ahead of the group. Standing on his toes, Jasper peered into a hole in the center of the bale. "It goes clean through!"

Saikal inspected the hole through the bale. He rotated the bale and sighted through the hole to the spear shaft, which protruded from the ground fifteen yards away. "Young Jasper of Nilwid has seen the truth of it. It seems that your spear is able to penetrate the bale as though it were only a puff of smoke."

Otah smiled.

That afternoon, Otah Kadeef came to Ereben in his small quarters. He planted his lean body onto one of the three legged stools. His expression relayed a sense of concern to Ereben. Mufta Ibrah had already decided that Otah should accompany Ereben on his journey to locate Whittig Trench. "Father says that we must depart tomorrow, if we are to find this Whittig Trench before the Spring."

"Tomorrow?" Ereben gasped.

"The snows will soon block the passes through the Broken Mountains."

"Tomorrow," Ereben muttered to himself. Mufta Ibrah knew of a race of short people who lived beyond the mountains. Although the Mufta had never heard them called Stumps, he believed that it would be wise to pursue that solitary clue. The conflict with the Protectors of Dragomin seemed to be gaining momentum. Anything that might help the Shouda understand Corban's purpose was, in the Mufta's way of thinking, worth the arduous trek through the mountains.

"Can I bring Titus along?" Jasper asked excitedly.

Ereben didn't know how to break the news to Jasper. He turned to Otah for help.

Otah seemed to understand. "You must remain here, Jasper of Nilwid."

"But we're partners," Jasper retorted. He stared in disbelief at Ereben.

Ereben avoided his gaze. "It's just too dangerous," he said. When he looked up to see the tears in Jasper's eyes, he added, "And I think it's going to be an awful trip. We'll be back in the Spring. By then, you'll probably be so good with your staff I'll be afraid to practice with you."

Jasper, convulsed with sobs, jumped from his pallet and ran to the doorway. He spun around and shouted, "I hope you never come back." The boy turned and ran off.

ᘓᘐ

To those who accept life as the will of their god, no event requires explanation. It is therefore only in the acknowledgment of unexplained events that one is motivated to explore and learn and grow.

Ereben Leaf: Chronicle of the Counterspell

Ereben arose at the first light of morning. He had not slept well. His eyes remained heavy as he dressed for his journey across the Broken Mountains. He had decided, despite the Mufta's stern warnings, that he would allow Jasper to join him. But with morning came the realization that the boy had never returned to the quarters they shared. Ereben had not seen Jasper since he ran off, hurt. He laced his boots.

Otah entered unceremoniously. "I have something for you, Ereben Leaf." He held a glistening fabric over his arm.

Its weight surprised Ereben. He unfolded it and held it out with both hands. "It's a metal jerkin."

"I wear one beneath my tunic," Otah explained, "whenever we anticipate danger. The smith made that one for you. He tells me that he used a technique which you taught him. The metal of the chain was folded twice before drawing it into wire. I suppose that it is made much like your splendid dagger. He assembled mine five years ago, and tells me that your chain jerkin required considerably more labor."

"Have you seen Jasper?" Ereben asked.

"I am afraid that I have not seen him since our conversation yesterday evening."

"I think he should go with us," Ereben said.

"That would be unwise, Ereben Leaf," Otah reminded him. "We are likely to encounter severe hardship in crossing the Broken Mountains. Here, my family will look after him."

"I want him to come."

"As you wish, my friend."

Ereben pulled on the sleeveless chain jerkin and laced its top. "What if there is no one called Whittig Trench? What if there aren't any Stumps on the other side of the Broken Mountains?"

"Then we shall fail," Otah said with a sigh, "but at the least we shall have tried."

"How soon do we have to leave?" Ereben asked, assembling his gear.

"Father awaits a meeting with us now. We should depart as soon as possible."

"What about Jasper?"

"Against my better judgment, I accept his coming with us. But you must surely recognize, Ereben Leaf, that your young friend is ill prepared for such a trial."

"I'll take that chance."

They walked in silence to the meeting hall. In this final meeting with Ibrah, Mufta Gebir of the Shouda, the subject of Jasper was not discussed. The Mufta gave his son a map of the Broken Mountains.

"By whatever means," the Mufta warned, "you must avoid lingering on the Ledge of Leopards. The great cats there are said to be ferocious and stealthy. If you stay on the trail to Punishment Pass, you will risk only a brief crossing of the Ledge. You must cross the highest peaks before the heavy snows arrive."

"There is no trail marked on the southern slope," Otah observed.

"There are surely trails there," the Mufta conjectured, "but our map maker has no knowledge of them. Also, he tells me that the location of the city of Zink is not certain."

The Mufta offered two more items for their journey. The first was a pouch of dried Munu, the praying hands mushroom. The second was a jagged little stone, no larger than Ereben's thumb. To the stone was attached a half yard of fine, rawhide thong.

"This," the Mufta explained, "is a southstone. When suspended by the thong, the point of the stone will come to rest pointing to the South. In foul weather, it will assist you in finding your direction." Ibrah motioned to a man standing by the door. Three Shouda men entered the meeting chamber, all outfitted for travel. "Rifai, Minkar and Amal will accompany you."

After the meeting, Ereben checked his quarters once more for any sign of Jasper. The boy was not there.

"We must go now, Ereben Leaf," Otah said, placing a hand on his shoulder.

Ereben hefted his backpack over his pigskin cloak, shifting it until the chain jerkin felt comfortable. With his dagger at his side, and his new spear for a walking stick, he reluctantly headed south with the four Shouda men. The blue haze of the Broken Mountains dominated the distant horizon.

Aside from Otah, Minkar Jarad was the friendliest of the group. He earned his living, he explained to Ereben, by growing vegetables. With the harvest completed, he was free to go with them across the Broken Mountains. Minkar walked with Ereben, talking incessantly about Bahsa, his son, who, by Minkar's account, was a most talented four year old. While his stories never deviated from some adventure of Bahsa, Ereben found them entertaining. At times Ereben felt envious that any son should have a father so devoted to him. As Minkar Jarad walked and talked, he continually twirled his spear in one hand, never dropping it or striking the scrub growing alongside the trail.

Rifai Madin struck Ereben as a fairly slippery character. He was shorter than most Shouda men, though still considerably taller than Ereben. Although he had never crossed the Broken Mountains, he had once traveled east, he claimed, to a great sea. On his return to Shouda, he had earned a substantial profit on the strange and unique merchandise he brought back. At their rest breaks, Rifai's discussions tended to focus on commercial possibilities. He seemed discouraged to learn that Ereben had little interest in profit.

The least congenial of the group was Amal Hidad. Unlike the brown tunics of the other Shouda men, his tunic was of a deep green color, worn only by the Guard of the Mufta. His movements were rigid and precise. According to Otah, Amal possessed great physical strength. He seldom spoke, and always walked at the lead. His rapid pace tried Ereben's endurance. Otah explained that Amal, who had been a soldier all his life, presently held the title of the Mufta's Sergeant at Arms. He had replaced Saikal Sahm in that position, when the Weapons Master had grown too old for the post.

At midday, they paused to eat beside the first stand of fir trees in the high foothills. A narrow plateau afforded a convenient resting place with a spectacular view of the spires of Shouda far below.

"This looks like a bench," Ereben said, examining the white stone slab near the edge of the plateau.

"Father says the Shouda built this spot many years ago," Otah said between mouthfuls of nuts and water. "This and the small house beyond the fir trees."

"Where?"

"A trail leads above the stand of trees," Otah pointed out. "Just beyond it lies a stone house, like a guard station. I believe Father is mistaken."

Amal Hidad glanced at Otah. "You would do well to show more respect for the Mufta, my young Prince."

"I respect my father greatly, Sergeant Amal, but I believe that these stones, like those of the spires, are far too ancient to have been placed here by the Shouda."

"But, Prince Otah," Minkar said, "the Shrine was built by the Shouda to honor Elloh for our victory over evil. Everyone knows that."

"That is how we are taught," Otah replied, "but I suspect that a very ancient people built these things many generations before the Shouda came to this land."

"What ancient people?" Ereben asked.

Otah scratched his head. "I do not know. But there is no Shouda man alive today who possesses the skill with working stone to build such things. And no such stone as these milky white stones can be found anywhere in the Shouda lands, except those of the Shrine and little outpost houses like the one here. Where would the Shouda have obtained great blocks of the milky stone?"

"Perhaps," added Rifai Madin, "they bought them from traders of a far away land."

"Think, Rifai Madin," Otah scolded, "how many wagons would be needed to transport so many great stones. And how would wagons burdened with such weight cross the mountains?"

"With Elloh," Amal explained, "anything is possible."

Leaving the Shouda men to debate geography and theology, Ereben followed the path around the stand of fir trees. On the far eastern extent of the narrow plateau he found a house made of milky white stone. Its roof formed a pyramid. The entrance revealed no indication of ever having been mounted with a door. The width of the square house was barely twice that of the door. He entered it and stepped to the single window opening, opposite the door. It framed a perfect view of the spires of Shouda below. To his surprise, white light passed through the stones of the roof, giving the little house an airy quality. He reached his arm outside the window and placed it on the exterior stone. Through the milky stone wall, he could make out the shadow of his hand. He thought of sunlight shining through the roof of the snow houses he had built as a boy. The unmortared joints between the stones formed rectangular lines in the translucence.

As he turned to leave, he noticed that a single large slabstone in the floor rocked slightly as he stepped on its corner. Ereben studied the pattern of the stone floor. It was laid in small, rectangular stones around the sides, with a single square stone, one yard wide, in the center. He noticed one curious variation in that pattern. One of the side stones, near the window, was twice the width of the others, and beside it was a gap, partly filled with sand and dust. Ereben brushed away the debris from this gap, revealing a groove at its floor parallel to the edge of the center stone. The larger side stone bore a slight indentation. He drew his dagger, cleaned the stone groove with its point, then replaced the dagger in its sheath. With a modest pressure on the indented side stone, he was able to slide it along the groove. Its displacement exposed a horizontal ledge along the margin of the square center stone. His heart beat faster, as the excitement of discovery took hold of him.

Ereben placed his fingers under the ledge of the center stone and lifted. With a grating noise, the center stone tipped smoothly upward. Counterbalanced, he thought. Beneath him, a white stone stairway plunged downward in a tight helix. The unknown below beckoned with a milky white glow.

A noise stirred in the nearby scrub outside the house. He looked around, but saw nothing.

"Ereben Leaf!" a voice called from the direction of the stone bench at their resting place. "We must continue now."

Ereben felt the joy of knowing a secret that others did not know. Surely Otah would have mentioned the stairway, if he knew of it. He closed the center stone and slid the stone latch back to its original position. With his boot, he kicked sand back into the groove. *What's down there?*

He left the sentry house and started for the trail around the stand of fir trees when he heard a noise from the brush again. Again he saw nothing. Uneasy, he continued. Along the sloping trail above the trees, Ereben noticed scuff marks in the rocky dirt, scuff marks that suggested to him that someone besides himself had recently passed this way. He returned to the others at the stone bench.

"Did you see it?" Otah asked.

"The house? Yes," Ereben answered. "Did one of you walk back along that trail?"

"We have walked enough," Rifai said, "without adding more steps to our journey."

"Nobody followed me?"

"We have all been here, Ereben Leaf," Minkar assured him.

"Then I think somebody's following us," Ereben concluded. "I heard something moving by the house, and I saw boot marks beside the trail."

Without comment, the Sergeant at Arms took up his spear and walked toward the stand of fir trees. Ereben followed with the others.

"These," Ereben pointed out, indicating the boot marks.

They continued to the stone house. Amal located more boot marks in the scrub near the house.

Amal returned to where the others stood and said in a low voice, "It appears that we have been followed, but I find no one in this area. I see tracks of only one person, but they are indistinct on the rocky ground." Then looking at Otah, "I would suggest, Prince Otah, that we continue our journey, but with more attention to what, or who, may be behind us."

In the late afternoon, the sky thickened with gray clouds. Ereben found the climbing easier with the sun blocked, but as they climbed farther, approaching a stopping place for the night, the clouds let loose with a torrent of rain. The wind whipped raindrops horizontally into Ereben's face, and chilled him through his cape.

Otah pointed to a relatively level area within a drainage. The slope swept viciously above them, reaching for the high plateau. "Pitch the tents here," he shouted through the howl of wind and rain.

Ereben extracted an oiled linen tent from his pack. As he unfolded the earth colored fabric and set out short segments of curved wood sticks, rain seeped around the hood of his cloak and through the front ties. By the time he had figured out the arcane arrangement of the pole segments and finally pitched the tent, he was drenched. He crawled into the low dome, secured the flap with its thongs and finished tying the curving poles. He spread his pigskin cloak on the wet ground. Sitting in the center, Ereben removed his wet clothes and the chain jerkin, draping his bedroll around his shoulders for warmth. A fire would feel wonderful.

"How do we cook dinner?" Ereben called through the tent wall.

"We can not cook tonight," answered Amal's voice.

Ereben drank from his waterskin, knowing that his stomach would resume its growling soon. He curled himself in the bedroll, being careful to avoid the wet ground beyond the edges of the cape.

When he awakened, shivering in total darkness, the sound of the rain had changed. It sounded more like sand striking pottery. The interior surface of the tent fabric felt cold and rigid. A brief look outside revealed a world of crystal encased trees and shrubs. Tiny bits of wet ice fell from the darkness, freezing in place as they struck. Ereben peeled the frozen edges of his cloak from the ground. Curling up even smaller than before, he wrapped the cloak over the top of the bedroll and went back to sleep. He awakened frequently, cold and cramped. Each time, he shifted a bit, then fled again into the oblivion of fatigue.

Morning came as a merciful end to the night's torment. His frozen clothing required massaging before it became flexible enough to put on. Everything was painfully cold. After the ordeal of dressing, Ereben stepped out of the tent. The cold was temporarily eclipsed by refracted beauty all about him. Light echoed from every leaf and branch of every shrub, every tree.

Even the mud-brown ugliness of the tents was transformed into a fantasy of ice.

The high range of the Broken Mountains was hidden by the plateau overhead, but as far above him as he could see, the world was ice. Sagegrass drooped and swirled in a motionless image of a windswept sea. Trees groaned and crackled in the breeze, their branches burdened with crystal. Though the cold was scarcely bearable, Ereben's mind flooded with the excitement of beauty and power flaunted in the capricious boldness of this mountain. *The strength. Are you greeting us or warning us?*

Through the day, Ereben struggled behind the four Shouda men clawing their way up the ice covered switchbacks of the trail. They held their spears inverted, using the point to gain traction on the treacherous surface. As evening approached, they settled on a rocky outcrop beneath a steeply pitched slope. Stunted fir trees reached no taller than Ereben's knee. Minkar and Rifai constructed a stone bed on which to build a fire for drying their wet clothing and for preparing a steaming pot of marmot stew.

"Tomorrow," Amal Hidad said, "we will climb past the Ledge of Leopards. It is said that a rare antelope lives only upon the Ledge, which stretches many miles to the East. The great leopards kill the antelope for food. Since the antelope never climb above or below the Ledge, the leopards also confine themselves to the Ledge."

"Must we cross over this Ledge?" Rifai asked.

"Yes," the Sergeant at Arms replied. "The trail climbs steeply to the Ledge, then crosses it for only a quarter mile. If we remain alert, and move quickly across it, then we should encounter little difficulty."

"Do these leopards hunt alone," Otah asked Amal, "or in groups?"

"That, I do not know." Amal seated himself near the fire. From a small pocket in his dark green tunic, he extracted a circular sharpening stone and began to restore the dulled point of his spear. Ereben and the others followed his example.

The rocky location of their campsite precluded their pressing stakes into the soil to anchor their tents. Instead, they tethered the tent margins to small stones, held to the ground by larger stones. To Ereben, it seemed woefully insecure for such a windy place. But he saw no alternative. The prospect of shivering his way through another night like the previous one caused Ereben to question his ability to complete this journey. After dinner, he curled up in his squat dome of oiled linen and immediately fell asleep.

In his dream, Ereben is held captive by a family of great leopards. The leopards are made of sparkling ice. They argue over who among them is entitled to eat which part of their prisoner. They agree to take turns choosing body parts, the largest leopard first, then progressing to the smallest. The chief of the leopard family strides slowly to where Ereben is lying on the ground. This greatest of leopards looks him over from head to toe, considering each part for a few moments. After his careful study, the chief leopard's gaze meets Ereben's. "The head," it growls, placing its enormous ice paw on Ereben's cheek.

Ereben opened his eyes. Against his face, the frigid, oiled linen of the tent pressed its sagging surface. He pushed it away, feeling the weight of what he knew must be an accumulation of snow. The entire tent sagged inward, straining against its thin wood supports. Ereben stepped out into the blue-white darkness of the snow and brushed the heavy layer off of his tent. The wind tore at his face. He hurried back into the tent and into his bedroll. His fitful sleep was disturbed again by the fearsome flapping of the tent as it stood against the gusting wind.

With a grating of rocks, and a sudden silence, followed immediately by the shocking cold of snow dumped onto his face, Ereben awakened to find himself lying on the ground beneath a star-filled sky. Swirls of blowing snow danced about him.

ഇര

The compulsion of youth to explore new places and experience new sensations absolves them of violating the laws of nature. They are immortal.

Crotus: Wisdom of the True Faith

Jasper of Nilwid smiled at the mouse riding calmly on his shoulder. Titus had lounged there all morning, not seeming to care that his change of scenery had been at the expense of a considerable exertion on Jasper's part. Although Jasper accepted the challenge of following Ereben and the four Shouda men without being seen, he would much rather have been a member of their party, instead of an uninvited sneak. He stopped to rest in a stand of fir trees not far from Ereben and his companions.

They sat about a bench constructed of milky white stone, much like the stone of Shouda city. To Jasper's dismay, Ereben turned from his resting companions and headed toward him. Determined to remain hidden, Jasper circled the upper edge of the fir trees and crouched among the scrubby sage. Below him stood a small building made of what appeared to be the same white stone. He looked back. Ereben was moving closer along the pocked dirt trail toward the little house. Jasper crept nearer, struggling against the temptation to confront Ereben.

Ereben entered the tiny house. From his vantage, Jasper watched as he knelt on the floor and moved a small stone. The floor opened upward. Ereben's face assumed a ghostly appearance, as though light were shining from below.

"Ereben Leaf!" It was a voice in the distance. "We must continue now." Jasper recognized it as the voice of Otah Kadeef, Prince of the Shouda.

Jasper watched as Ereben closed the floor and retraced his steps to the waiting Shouda party. Jasper followed. As he approached the far side of the fir trees, as close to the others as he could be without walking out into the open, he heard Ereben speak of someone following them. Jasper realized, in the span of one muffled gasp that he would be in big trouble if they discovered him. He scurried back through the fir trees to the white hut. The only path beyond it would allow him to be seen. He dodged into the hut and studied the area of the floor that Ereben had opened. Jasper sat on the stone floor, his back resting against the wall beneath the window. With his fingertips in the gap where a floor stone seemed to be missing, he attempted to lift the center stone. It would not budge.

Voices approached. "Come on," Jasper whispered through clenched teeth. He paused for a moment of urgent observation. *It goes sideways*. After a brief glance of apology to the mouse on his shoulder, he slid the latch stone sideways, hoping the soft grating sound had not reached the others. He grasped the exposed lip of the center stone and, as hard as he could, jerked himself upward. The great stone pivoted near its center and clanked against the floor. Jasper winced.

"Holy Dragomin!", he whispered to himself, "This is light as a loaf of bread."

He peeked around the doorway. Still about fifty yards off, Ereben and the Shouda walked toward the house with no sign of having heard the noise.

Jasper looked down into the opening in the floor. Instead of darkness, a tight helical stairway radiated a milky glow. The light seemed to emanate from the white stone of the steps themselves. Quickly, he jumped into the stairway and pulled the door closed. A tug at his waist reminded him of Ereben's leather pouch, the one that served as Titus' travel home. The pouch was trapped above the door. He took a deep breath, lifted the door enough to free the empty pouch, then closed the hinged rock and slid the latch that was visible beneath it.

Within the lighted stairway, Jasper recognized it was sunlight that filtered through the milky white stone. It offered adequate light with which to see his way down the steps. After a descent of about thirty yards, the stairway ended at the start of a downward sloping tunnel. Though the tunnel was not as brightly illuminated as the stairway, Jasper could see light ahead. He sat on the bottom step, wrapped his arms about his knees and cried.

He had no particular idea why he was crying. Yes, he missed his mother. He missed his brother. He pressed the carved head of his staff against his cheek. *Father will never see this.*

He considered Ereben abandoning him. *Partners.* The trip could not be more dangerous or difficult than what they had already been through. *I saved your life.*

Titus jumped from Jasper's shoulder and sprinted down the corridor.

"Titus! Titus! Come back here, you stupid mouse! By Dragomin, you're going to end up being some critter's lunch."

Jasper sprinted after the mouse, waving his carved wooden staff before him to tear away the spider webs that seemed to fill every open area. Tiny spiders which inhabited the webs clambered and jumped out of the path of Jasper and his staff. He found his footing less sure where the slope of the floor increased. From the layer of dry grit and dust, he guessed that nobody had walked here for a very long time.

Titus managed to stay ahead of him by tracing a zigzag of fits and stops down the corridor. After running what seemed like hundreds of yards of the spider web gauntlet, Jasper watched as Titus disappeared ahead to the right. He reached the point of Titus' right turn, finding it to be the intersection of two corridors. To the left was darkness. Ahead the corridor assumed an eerie green glow. To the right, the passage into which Titus had vanished, there seemed to be a room off in the distance. He turned right. Titus was nowhere in sight.

He approached the room. A milky light, like that of the corridor, illuminated it. Rich, earthy smells filled has senses. He entered an alcove to the right and was startled by a bulky spider web spanning the width of the alcove. At its center rested a brown, fuzzy spider twice the size of Jasper's fist. He backed up a step. The spider seemed to ignore his presence. Behind the spider was a stone box-like bench mounted to the wall. Its upper surface was perforated by five large, round holes. A latrine, he thought, for a lot of people. He reasoned that the odor of the latrine had vanished with time, like pig manure left for a long time. He inspected the corners behind the spider web, but saw no sign of Titus.

The tiny screech of a mouse sounded from behind him. He turned and entered the opposite alcove. There he found Titus attempting to break free from the sticky strands of a heavy spider web like the first. The resident spider deftly scurried over the web toward the disturbance created by the thrashing of the mouse. Jasper swung his staff. It struck the web one strand shy of the spider, which was launched by the impact into the far wall. The spider struck the stone with the sound of a pine cone thrown against a tree trunk. It dropped to the floor, righted itself, and ran directly toward Jasper. The end of his staff was stuck fast in the web. As the spider neared Jasper's foot, he kicked as hard as he could. This sent the spider sailing back to the wall, but caused Jasper to lose his footing on the dusty floor. He crashed to the stone, breaking his fall somewhat by the still-suspended staff. The spider raced toward his head. With a tremendous tug, Jasper stretched the web enough to allow the head of the staff to reach the floor, striking the spider, breaking two of its legs.

As the injured spider attempted to crawl away, Jasper reached his small whittling knife and forced it into the spider's back. Instead of dying immediately, the spider surged toward Jasper, pulling the knife from his hand. The spider lunged, with the knife protruding from its back. He evaded it by rolling away onto all fours. A slap of his hand against the knife handle flung the spider into the air, where the knife handle made contact with the spider web. There it held fast, with the impaled spider thrashing helplessly on the end of its blade. After a few moments, the spider's movements ceased and its legs curled inward.

Jasper carefully freed Titus from the web and placed him in the leather pouch. He pried his knife from the web. The dead spider would not shake off the blade, so he wedged the spider against the bottom of his foot to extract the knife. As an afterthought of retribution, Jasper picked up the dead spider by the tip of one leg, walked to the other alcove and tossed it onto the web. The second spider raced to the new prey, but after a moment simply cut it free from the web, allowing it to fall to the stone floor. *I guess he's dead enough.*

His staff required more effort to liberate from the web strands. Using his whittling knife, he scraped it free, strand by strand. "Hit the spider, not the web," he said aloud.

At the intersection of the corridors, he looked left, in the direction from which he had entered, then to the right, to the glowing green light. The dark passage straight ahead did not look like fun. He turned right, again clearing the webs of the tiny spiders with his staff.

Near the end of the corridor, it became obvious to Jasper that it opened into another room. The eerie green light seemed to emanate from the surface of the walls themselves. Glowing green appeared to have dripped onto the walls from the ceiling, reminding him of his mother's pea soup spilling over the brim of a pot. It left the milky white stone of the lower wall untouched.

He entered the room cautiously, on the lookout for large spiders. There were none. There were not even tiny spider webs. The entire ceiling was uniformly covered with glowing green. Along the walls were empty indentations, each about the size of a tall man's bed, sixteen in all, eight just above the floor and eight more a yard above the others. Between each pair of "beds", he decided to call them, were two stone hatches, which on first sight had appeared to be blank wall. But Jasper recognized the sliding stone latches, similar to the entry at the top of the steps.

Within each bed indentation, the walls bore hundreds of words, written in different styles at different angles—some sideways, some upside down. The letters did not resemble the writing in the books of Crotus, the now-blinded priest in Nilwid.

Jasper unlatched one of the sixteen wall hatches. A stone swung downward gently, coming to rest in a horizontal position, like a workbench. It appeared to be a storage compartment. It was empty except for a yellow metal spoon, bent in the middle of the handle. The spoon straightened with little effort. He placed it into his backpack. With growing curiosity he proceeded to open each of the other compartments. Most were empty. One, however, held a thin steel tool, which bore a small ring at one end and several intricately bent tines at the other. This also he placed in his pack.

On the one uninterrupted expanse of wall, he noticed a faded drawing. At the bottom was a sketch of a winged serpent. Just above it a tiny square was labeled with glyphs. A line extended upward from the square, where it intersected a horizontal line. To the right of the horizontal line was another square divided into halves with a row of five dots along the side of each half. *The latrine! This is a map!* The vertical line beyond the intersection disappeared beneath the glowing green that had "spilled" from the ceiling. Jasper touched the green. It felt brittle, like birch bark. He peeled it upward, revealing a square on the map depicting the room in which he now stood. His excitement increased. He looked at the line to the left of the intersection. It would be the dark corridor that he had avoided. It too was hidden beneath the brittle green material that illuminated the room. He dug at its edge with his fingernails, but it was more firmly attached than the piece he had peeled away. Using the tip of his knife he scraped the edge free, then grasped it and tugged. A dry, tearing sound startled him. A yard-wide segment of the green material tore free, all the way to the top of the wall.

Revealed on the wall was a complex of intersecting lines and boxes, labeled with glyphs. Near the top of the map, the lines connected with a huge square, within which were drawn rows of tiny circles and squares. His feeling of amazement grew. Nine rows of nine circles, with a larger square in the center, all within the huge square. *The Pinnacles of Shouda! These tunnels connect to Shouda City! Underneath the Shrine!* The familiarity of the white stones of the corridors now made sense to him. It was all part of the same construction. *And the size of it!*

He decided to explore one more room, then return up the tunnel from which he had entered. He would tell Mufta Ibrah about what he had discovered. He was sure that the Mufta did not know that passages existed beneath the Shrine. Besides, he was getting hungry.

Jasper studied the map. The glyphs beside the tiny entrance square at the bottom of the map were identical to the labels on two other tiny squares, which also bore nearby sketches of winged serpents. He wondered if these also opened to the surface. But, judging from the dimensions of the city square, he assumed these possible exits were separated by miles of intersecting tunnels. He wished he could read the lettering. If one tiny square is a latrine, and one is a bedchamber, then one might be a larder. He didn't know how long ago this place was abandoned, but he bit his lip at the prospect finding something to eat.

He stared at the map a moment longer, then turned to leave the bedchamber. His foot kicked the sheet of green material that he had peeled from the wall. He examined it closely. While the chalky green surface glowed with a soft light, the back side was an opaque gray. He decided to keep it. After rolling it into a tube, Jasper noticed that the green interior of the tube glowed. He opened it then rolled the sheet with the green to the outside. Carrying it out of the bedchamber and into the dimly lit corridor, he was satisfied at its ability to function as a lantern. "Ha!"

At the intersection of the corridors, Jasper turned right, into the dark tunnel he had avoided earlier. With his new "bark lantern" held high, he walked boldly into the tunnel. After ten paces, he realized why it had seemed so dark. The floor of the tunnel inclined steeply upward for about ten yards, obscuring all but its floor when viewed from the intersection. When he reached the base of the incline, he looked back once at the intersection, then stepped onto the incline. Three paces up the slope, Jasper was startled by a loud metallic clack. The floor dropped from beneath him.

When Jasper awakened, he was aware of only two things: his head throbbing and the sensation of many tiny things crawling over his skin. He opened his eyes and sat up. His surroundings were illuminated green by his bark lantern, which lay on the floor. Walking over his legs were dozens of spiders, all with very tiny bodies and legs as long as his own fingers. He brushed them away. He was sitting on a mat within a small stone room. A doorway stood across from him. He remembered the fall. Looking up, Jasper determined that this was not the same place. "I've been moved!" he said aloud. His backpack leaned against the nearby wall, beside his carved wooden staff. Titus' leather pouch rested upon the backpack, its tiestring opened.

Jasper attempted to stand, but discovered that he ached all over. He chose to remain seated. If I have been moved, he reasoned, then someone or something moved me. If it was something, he continued, then I would probably be dead. His exercise in logic was interrupted by an appetizing aroma wafting in from the corridor. He forced himself to stand, despite the discomfort. *Pain is one thing, but hunger is another all together.*

In the corridor, he proceeded to an intersection. A small fire burned in the center of the corridor ten yards ahead. Another burned twenty yards down the right corridor. To the left, the corridor was dark. Movement by the fire in the right corridor attracted his attention. A man seemed to be squatting on the far side of the fire.

"Hey," Jasper called.

The man stood. He was tall and dark skinned with pointed ears, appearing to be Shouda. He spoke something which Jasper could not understand. The man repeated it, gesturing with his hand for Jasper to come.

Jasper considered returning to the room for his wooden staff, but realized immediately how silly that was. He approached the small fire, which burned from pieces of black rock. A breeze carried most of the dense smoke away. Two small bodies, the size of squirrels, roasted upon a metal grating propped over the fire. Pale greens cooked in an earthen pot. The meat smelled wonderful, so he decided not to think about its resemblance to rat.

"Menash," the man said. After a pause, he slapped Jasper's shoulder, pointed to himself and repeated, "Menash." He then pointed to Jasper, waiting for some response.

"You're Menash?" Jasper asked, pointing back at the man.

The man smiled and pointed at himself again. "Menash."

"Oh!," Jasper blurted, "I'm Jasper." He pointed to himself.

"Owimjasper," Menash repeated.

Jasper slapped himself in the forehead, shaking his head. "No, no, no." He pressed a finger to his chest. "Jasper."

"Jasper," Menash repeated.

"Yes, Jasper."

Menash brought his palms together beneath his chin, then spread his arms as he bowed. "Silim."

Jasper imitated the bow, that seemed to be a variant of the Shouda bow.

Following their introductions, Menash shared the meal with Jasper. Conversation was a continual struggle, but Menash seemed friendly enough. He appeared to be remarkably resourceful with the simple materials available within the tunnels.

During the succeeding hours, Jasper surmised that the faint light illuminating most of the corridors was sunlight, transmitted through the milky stones from stone structures above the ground. The tunnels became black at night, and light again in the morning. Menash showed him other rooms: a smithy with a collapsed forge, through which the smoke of Menash's fires exited; a room full of rust near the chamber in which Jasper had awakened; a jumbled stone barrier in the tunnel extending beyond Menash's room, caused by the ceiling's collapse. Near the blocked corridor, an earth tunnel, barely large enough for a man to crawl through, opened from a crack in the wall. A steady gust emanated from the opening, bringing with it the distinctive smell of an animal's nest. When Jasper looked into it, Menash drew him back, making a gesture of clawed hands and gnashing teeth. Jasper understood clearly.

Around a corner in a different corridor, a massive wooden door blocked the path. When Jasper went to open it, Menash shook his head and pointed to an odd shaped opening beneath the handle. Menash then clasped one hand over a clenched fist. Jasper motioned for Menash to remain there. He sprinted back to Menash's room and retrieved the peculiar metal tool with the bent tines. When Menash saw him returning with it, he laughed aloud and danced with Jasper in a circle toward the door. Whatever Menash was saying seemed to accentuate the man's excitement.

Menash inserted the object into the odd shaped hole beneath the handle and turned it with pomp. The door opened inward. The interior was illuminated by a green glow from the ceiling. Both of them gasped. Row after row of weapon racks, filled to capacity, crowded the room. Along one wall were at least fifty longswords, identical to the sword carried by the slain Protector. There were hundreds of long spears, all arranged in orderly fashion on wooden racks. Center racks bore short bows and thousands of arrows which, like the new Shouda arrows, were tipped with points of steel. Against another wall were dozens of spear-like weapons with ax blades near their spear heads. On the far wall were myriad types and shapes of armor, some made of steel plates, some of steel chain, some of a combination. Helmets hung from pegs above. Shields were supported on a rack near the floor.

Jasper and Menash wandered through the green glow of the room, hefting and fitting various items of weaponry and armor. A shirt made of tiny steel chain links attracted Jasper's attention. It was much lighter than Jasper had guessed. He pulled it over his head. The half-sleeves reached almost to his wrists, and the body seemed more like a long tunic, just touching the tops of his knees. Jasper ran once around the room, swinging his arms to dodge the corners of the weapon racks. He decided that it fit him perfectly. Among the weapons, he found a knife somewhat longer than Ereben's dagger. Its handle was carved of a translucent, milky red stone, which fit his grip comfortably. The guard and pommel glistened yellow. Its double edged blade, Jasper noticed, bore wavy lines like Ereben's dagger. He lifted the chain of its sheath over his head and one arm. With several adjustments of the catches, it hung neatly at his hip. *It's more like a sword.* A thrill surged within his breast as he sheathed his new sword.

Menash seemed to focus his excitement on the rack of spears. He balanced one in his open palm, then returned it to the rack. One by one, each spear was evaluated, until Menash appeared satisfied. He twirled the chosen spear expertly in the fingers of one hand. A small knife, shorter than Jasper's, caught his interest. He examined its blade, then strapped its sheath about his waist.

All of the shields were too large for Jasper, but the steel helmets were of various sizes. After trying on several, he chose one which was only slightly too large. This one had no visor to cover his face, only a curled nose guard and hinged steel flaps to cover his ears. When he thought about its appearance, it seemed to be an upside down stew pot with three dirty spoons stuck to it. But it would have to do for now.

When they left the weapon room, Menash locked the massive door and offered the tool which had unlocked it to Jasper.

"You keep it," Jasper said, with overdone gesticulations.

They retraced their steps past an intersection and past the cooking fire. Before turning into Menash's room, Jasper noticed that the small fire in the opposite corridor had gone out. Menash, also seeing the fire out, returned to the cooking fire, where he extracted a glowing coal using a rusted fragment of a metal bucket. He gathered some pieces of the black rocks, then turned up the corridor to restore the neglected fire.

From the darkened room adjacent to Menash's sleeping room, the room of rust, Jasper heard a scratching noise. He looked in, but could see nothing in the darkness. The room carried the strong odor of rusted metal. He turned back into Menash's room and retrieved his bark lantern. With the comforting green glow illuminating the way, he stepped cautiously into the next room. Hanging by hooks on the ceiling were dozens of metal utensils: pots, scoops, dips, spoons. A workbench, much like the one in his father's woodshop, stood along one wall. On its surface were no utensils, only puddles of dark liquid. Similar puddles seemed to drip down the legs of the workbench to join an enormous dark puddle on the floor, extending from the rear wall to the center of the room.

Motion to his left caused Jasper to reach for his new sword as he turned. His helmet flew from his head onto the floor. In the corner by the door crouched a rat the size of a small pig. It bared its teeth, then attacked. With a single swipe of his blade, Jasper split the rat in half.

"Holy Dragomin!" he muttered, poking the rats clawed feet with the tip of his now blooded sword. He turned to recover his helmet. Near the center of the room, he saw the unmistakable curl of the metal nose guard, but the rest of the helmet had merged into the puddle of dark liquid. He watched as brown liquid rose slightly to envelope the nose guard as well. Jasper stepped back. As an after thought, he wiped the blood of his sword onto the fur of the cleaved rat.

"Rat Slayer," he said aloud, lifting the sword above his head. "I name you Rat Slayer." Jasper sheathed his newly dubbed sword and turned, colliding with Menash, who was standing with his arms folded across his chest.

"Radsleer," Menash intoned, pointing to Jasper's sword.

Jasper stood with Menash above the sloping corridor into which Jasper had fallen the day of his arrival. He guessed that he had been with Menash for about two or three days now. To Jasper's disappointment, no amount of cajoling and gestures could prompt Menash to return with him to the surface. Menash appeared to be saddened at his imminent departure.

Menash showed him the sliding latch in the rock of the wall, which would prevent the floor from tipping under a passer's weight. After firmly sliding the latch, Menash gestured to Jasper that it was now safe to proceed. Menash hugged him. "Jasper," he said. And with a pat of his hand on the sheath of Jasper's sword, he added, "Radsleer."

"Good-bye, Menash," Jasper said tenderly. "And thank you." He stepped down the slope.

"Goodba, Jasper," echoed from behind. "Silim."

Jasper turned right at the intersection. He stopped, extracted his rolled bark lantern from his backpack, then ran back up the slope toward Menash. With his sword, he sliced the lantern in half, handed half to Menash, then ran back down the slope. From the intersection, he ran up the long corridor toward the stairway. From the bright light passing through the milky stone, he decided that it must be morning. His excitement grew. He climbed the helical stairway two steps at a time. On reaching the hatch at the top, he unlatched it, swung it open, and leapt into the fresh morning air.

"Clouds! I forgot about clouds," he said to the mouse riding on his left shoulder. Jasper closed and latched the entry and stepped out into the sunlight. He drew his sword, held it above his head toward the azure expanse and spun around until he laughed aloud. Looking back to the window of the tiny stone house, a movement in the sky caught his attention. He walked across the entry hatch and looked out. Streaming from the West, a smudge of black descended toward the gleaming white pinnacles of Shouda. Above the smudge, a cloud of great birds followed the descent.

ꕥ

Our interpretation of the struggle to survive is predictably tainted by our relationship to the creature struggling for its survival. The struggle of man to survive is noble. The struggle of a rat to survive is infestation. The struggle of a leopard to survive is depredation.

Ereben Leaf: Chronicle of the Counterspell

Ereben shoveled into the drifted snow with bare hands. His tent had been so cramped that even a modest snow cave would seem luxuriously large by comparison. Against the bank of snow, Ereben already enjoyed shelter from the wind that rasped its way across the narrow ledge of their campsite. When the cave was deep enough for Ereben to crawl completely inside, he sealed the door opening with a pile of snow. Using his dagger, he punctured two air holes high in the outer wall. He was delighted with how much warmer the snow cave felt than his draughty Shouda tent. With his cloak keeping the bedroll mostly off the snow, he curled up in the darkness. He would find the remainder of his gear in the morning.

Two spots of white light drilled through his closed eyelids. He brought his hand over his eyes to make them go away. *Morning!* His attempt to sit up abruptly reminded him of where he was. He cleared a portion of the snow from the doorway. Outside, in the blinding white of morning snow, the four Shouda men knelt over Ereben's backpack.

"It makes little sense to continue," Minkar said softly.

Otah's shoulders heaved with a long sigh. "We may yet locate this Whittig Trench and perhaps learn why the Protectors have become so hostile toward the Shouda."

"I believe that may be important," Amal concurred.

"But in this snow," Rifai said, "we might all be lost."

"If we go ahead to the Ledge of Leopards," Minkar continued, "we may find ourselves preferring to end up where young Ereben Leaf has gone."

"It is warmer than the tent," Ereben said through the small opening in the snow.

Four brown faces spun around to look in his direction. The men looked back at one another, then broke into fits of laughter. They rose to their feet, slapped each other's shoulders and walked in little circles, laughing at the cloudless sky. Even Amal Hidad, Sergeant at Arms, laughed until he could hardly breathe. When Ereben had scrambled out of the snow cave with his cloak and bedroll, Minkar Jarad threw his arms about him and danced once around the campsite.

"We thought you had been blown off the mountain," Minkar said through his laughter. "We looked for you below. We found only an empty tent. We thought you were in the arms of Elloh. Instead, you were sleeping three yards away!"

"We welcome you back among the living, Ereben Leaf," Otah proclaimed, with a formal bow, arms extended in the Shouda way. "You must tell us of your midnight adventures."

Ereben recounted the night's events to a jovial audience, timing the ending to coincide with the last of the hot porridge breakfast. Since the Shouda men were not familiar with snow caves, Ereben elaborated on the technique of their construction. As he talked, the warmth of the sun merged with their growing friendship to drive away the fatigue and hardships of the previous days. The joy of the moment remained with Ereben as they resumed their journey.

Up the ever steepening switchbacks of the snow covered trail, Ereben and his four Shouda companions moved toward the high pass of the summit. On Otah's map, the crossing of the summit ridge was labeled, "Punishment Pass." This name alone was sufficient to breed discouragement, but separating them from the pass was the Ledge of Leopards. Ereben knew they would cross its eastern extent this afternoon.

"Why do they call these the Broken Mountains," Ereben asked Minkar. "They don't really look broken."

"It is not the mountains which are said to be broken," Minkar explained, "but rather the men who cross them."

"Sorry I asked."

The trail presented Ereben with more difficulty than on the previous day. The ice now lay hidden beneath a blanket of new snow as deep as his knees. He noticed that Amal, in the lead, paused more frequently to locate the path. Near midday, they found themselves standing at the base of a massive cliff, with no trail other than the one they had come from. They backtracked for nearly an hour, until Amal identified the point at which he had strayed off the main trail. By then, a lowering sky was promising more snow. Flurries began as they climbed the final approach to the Ledge of Leopards. At Amal's suggestion, they once again sharpened the worn points of their spears.

Otah opened his map. "There is too little detail here to follow any landmark across the Ledge," he said. "The trail appears to exit the ledge somewhat left of this entry."

"It looks like the clouds are almost touching the Ledge," Ereben observed. Fine flakes of snow swirled about them in an ever thickening haze. "How are we going to follow the trail?"

"We will move quickly across," Amal instructed, "in a straight line. When we reach the rising ground on the opposite side of the Ledge, we will travel along it to the left, until we come upon the continuation of the trail."

It sounded simple enough to Ereben. They would rush across the Ledge, then find the trail on the other side. He looked north into the distant valley of Shouda. All he saw was white. The nearby terrain was accentuated only by the dark stone exposed on vertical rock. Everything else bore a featureless, dull white. He saw no shadows, no depth, no boundary between earth and cloud and abyss.

"Stay close," Amal said, as he ascended the break leading to the Ledge of Leopards. His footing seemed precarious, but with the aid of his spear, he mounted the plateau and moved quickly out of sight.

Otah followed. At the verge of the plateau, he lost his balance, dropped his spear and slid back toward Rifai. Rifai managed to halt Otah's slide. The spear, however, did not stop until it had pierced the side of Minkar's boot.

"Agh!" Minkar uttered, as he fell, sliding several yards.

Ereben caught him. "Are you hurt?" Ereben asked the wounded Shouda. Blood seeped slowly from Minkar's right boot. The spear lay nearby.

"Not badly," he answered. "No worse than tripping over a plow."

They regrouped and climbed onto the plateau. Ereben could see only the three Shouda men in front of him. In the featureless terrain, his eyes could not separate the land from the sky. Everything was white. Blowing snow caused him to squint his eyes as he attempted to make out any sign of Amal.

"Amal Hidad!" Rifai called out.

"Keep quiet!" Otah rasped. "You will attract the leopards."

Rifai bolted from the group. "He is just ahead," he said as he ran past Otah.

"Rifai Madin!" Otah called softly. Rifai vanished into the whiteness. "The man is such a fool," Otah mumbled.

Minkar limped more with each step. Ereben looked behind. All that was visible was a ribbon of bright red dots, like a foot trail marked on a parchment map. The snow-filled air merged with the snow covered ground.

"Let me help you, Minkar," Ereben said, bracing Minkar against his shoulder.

"Ereben Leaf," Otah's voice called softly.

Ereben looked up. He saw no trace of Otah ahead of him. "We're right behind you," Ereben said. "Keep on going." With those words, he and Minkar tripped over each other's feet. They rolled into the snow.

"We must look ridiculous," Minkar said with a strained chuckle. "Bahsa will never stop laughing when I tell him about this."

"How is your foot?"

"It is painful. The bleeding does not want to stop."

Ereben leaned close to Minkar's boot. The blood was slow, but continued to ooze. The mark in the snow beside Minkar caused Ereben to gasp.

"Look!" he whispered. Deeply pressed into the snow was an unmistakable footprint of a cat. Its width was greater than the span of his fingers. It appeared as fresh as if the animal who made it were sitting next to them. "A leopard!" Ereben spun his head in a full circle, but saw only white. They both stood.

"Which way do we go?" Minkar asked.

"I don't know," was all that Ereben could whisper in reply. His heart sank. He dropped to his knees to find the shadowless footprints left by the others. "The footprints go this way," he said, "but the snow is filling them quickly."

Arm in arm, Ereben and Minkar Jarad followed the vanishing footprints, able to see only two or three yards ahead. Ereben's eyes ached from their continuous squint. The snow had been blowing from the South, directly into his face. As he followed the footprints, which now seemed to be those of one man, the wind was striking him from the right instead. Either the wind had changed, he thought, or they were veering toward the East.

"Whoever made these tracks," Ereben said, "might be just as lost as we are."

"If we continue to follow them," Minkar said jovially, "at the least, we can be lost together."

Ereben stopped. A second set of footprints joined the first.

"A leopard's tracks mark over the boot prints," Ereben said.

"This is not good," Minkar observed, as he turned his spear so that the point was up.

They continued to follow the footprints. Ereben's muscles grew tighter at the realization that the leopard's prints were spaced farther apart than when he had first seen them. *It's moving faster.* Ten yards ahead, he saw movement. He paused and pointed. Something was there in the snow, but it did not move. They approached cautiously, spears at the ready. As the distance closed, the bright red staining of the snow became apparent. When they reached the bloodied area, the sight sickened Ereben. In its center, lying in the red snow, a torn pile of intestines reeked its foul odor. A Shouda spear lay in the snow nearby, its point unbloodied. Beside it, a quiver lay partly crushed, its arrows scattered about. The only other remains of the victim were a few shreds of bloody, brown linen. Ereben saw no body and no backpack or bow. Leading away from this site of unspeakable horror, a trail of leopard tracks mingled with a bloody gouge of something that had been dragged away in the snow.

Minkar gathered the spear and unbroken arrows. Ereben looked about, unable to see any texture or contour to the land.

Everything was white. Everything except the imprint of freezing blood.

"May your spirit rest in the arms of Elloh," Minkar said, pressing his hands together before his face, then spreading them toward the sky.

"Can you tell who it was?" he asked Minkar.

"No," he said, examining the bloody fragment of brown linen. "But it is not Amal's color."

"Which way should we go?"

"Any way is as reasonable as any other," the Shouda farmer answered. He looked about with an expression of complete bewilderment. "I think that I will spare Bahsa this part of the story."

The mention of Minkar's son, Bahsa, reminded Ereben of his own insistence that Japer come along on this journey. He wondered what Jasper might be doing now. Whatever it is, he thought, it's better than being here.

Ereben took out the southstone and held it by its thong. The wind kept the stone spinning and swaying. He put it away. "Let's head into the wind again," Ereben suggested, "and hope that it hasn't changed direction."

"A perfect solution," Minkar agreed.

They trudged side by side through the snow, faces to the wind. Both of them looked back and to the sides frequently. The pall of death hovered over Ereben's thoughts. With no footprints to follow, no landmarks for bearings, and no way of knowing who had died, each step seemed to hold them immobile, as though they were suspended within a cloud. Ereben recalled Otah's map. If its distances were correct, they should have reached the opposite side of the Ledge by now. They should find the trail through the cliffs into the upper reaches of the mountains. They should be safe from the leopards by now. But the snow-covered plateau seemed to go on endlessly.

Through a brief window in the snowfall, Ereben saw cliffs to the right.

"Over there!" he shouted. By the time the words had died in the hissing snow, he could no longer see the cliffs, but he knew they were there.

Still helping Minkar to walk on his injured foot, Ereben turned toward the vision of the cliff and picked up his pace. The distance was much farther than he had assumed from his brief glimpse. His error, he realized as they approached the cliffs, was in his estimate of the height of the cliffs. They were at least three times as tall as he had guessed. The jagged, gray wall towered upward, vanishing into the falling snow. As far as he could see in either direction, there was no break in the nearly vertical rock. Assuming that they had been traveling east while they were lost, he chose to move west along the base of the escarpment.

With the rock wall as a marker of their movement, a sense of progress drove the dark thoughts from Ereben's mind. For a quarter hour, they walked west. The exit from the Ledge of Leopards was marked not only by a break in the wall, but also by a dramatic increase in the velocity of the wind. The sting of the blown snow was now joined by the howling of wind, gusting with enough force to cause Ereben and Minkar to stagger backwards.

"This must lead to Punishment Pass!" he shouted. He could not hear Minkar's reply.

They forced their way against the wind and snow, climbing slowly up the broken slope of the gap. A natural staircase of waist-high stone ledges offered the only passage. After surmounting the second ledge, Ereben looked up to find the easiest route up the next. Through the lashing snow, he saw two blue eyes fixed upon him. He blinked. The eyes gathered a ghost of a body about them. Crouched on the ledge before him, an Ice Leopard maintained its gaze. Ereben pressed his fingers into Minkar's shoulder. The leopard's breath steamed from its nostrils. Its deep white fur, faintly mottled with hazy gray spots, so closely resembled the snow covered rock that Ereben could not clearly see the size of the cat. The distance between its eyes would suffice for an animal three or four times the weight of a man. It rose slightly from its crouch. Ereben knelt, planting the butt of his spear against the rock behind his right foot. Minkar drew an arrow from his quiver.

The Ice Leopard lifted from the rock ledge with graceful power. *It's so beautiful.* Ereben slammed to the ground. The leopard struck the spear and continued with its momentum over the edge of the rock step. Ereben rolled to his hands and knees. Two yards away, on the ledge below him, Ereben saw Minkar scrambling to his feet. Beside Minkar, the Ice Leopard trembled, its legs rigid. From the top of the leopard's skull sprouted the entire blade of Ereben's spear. Its shaft protruded from below the leopard's jaw.

"Behind you!" Minkar shouted through the howl of wind, again knocking an arrow to his bow.

Ereben, still on all fours, turned his head. A second Ice Leopard stood, full height, on the same ledge from which the first had sprung. It jumped down to Ereben's ledge and paced slowly toward him. The resonance of its growl dulled Ereben's mind. He crawled slowly to the rock wall opposite the leopard. A high pitched whine issued from the leopard as it spun about in a tight circle. An arrow shaft stood out from the skin above its shoulders. Rather than injure the leopard, it had only enraged it.

The cat pounced to within one half yard of Ereben. A spear sailed over the leopard's head, clanking on the rock ledge. With glistening white claws extended from its paw, the leopard swiped across Ereben's back. He spun to the ground, unable to breathe. *The dagger!* Ereben drew his dagger. The leopard lunged for Ereben's neck, but pulled away at the last moment, a second arrow now protruding from its shoulder. Ereben raised his dagger and plunged it into the leopard's back. In response, the leopard spread its massive jaws and clamped them onto Ereben's chest. In that twinkling of a moment, Ereben remembered how the Protector of Dragomin had been made to vanish. With all his mind, he willed the leopard to do so.

Agonizing cold crept from the dagger into Ereben's arm. Time seemed suspended, as he fought the empty cold.

"The leopard!" he screamed.

A flash of light and deafening boom were accompanied by an expanding wave of heat that knocked Ereben off the ledge. His hand throbbed where the dagger had been. His ears rang. For a few moments, he could see nothing.

"What happened?" asked the voice of Minkar above the noise of the wind. "Are you injured, Ereben Leaf?"

Ereben's vision returned. Despite the violent wind, he smelled burnt hair. The leopard had gone. Where he and the leopard had been entangled in mortal combat, there remained only a broad area of bare rock. A half foot of snow had melted in an area five yards across, leaving dry, steaming rock. In the center lay his dagger, its green stone handle radiating an aura of green light.

"How did the fire appear?" Minkar asked over the howl of wind.

"Fire?"

"Look at your cloak, Ereben Leaf."

Ereben looked at his pigskin cloak. Smoke drifted from it. His cloak was the source of the smell of burning hair. The subtle stripes of brown hair from the wild pigs had been singed away completely. The white weasel fur of the collar was partly singed, where it extended beyond the cape. He felt his face. His eyebrows were gone.

"Did you see where the leopard went, Minkar?"

"I saw only a great flash of fire. The leopard vanished. This, I will tell to Bahsa. I remember when you defeated the Protector. This was very different, Ereben Leaf. You do strange, fearsome things."

Ereben climbed back to the dagger. Its handle still glowed. He touched it lightly, but felt only a soft warmth, so he lifted it from the dry rock. The dagger seemed somehow different. The blade showed no trace of blood. Its wavy patterns of fine lines had changed. Ereben doubted his own observation. He studied the pattern carefully. Indeed, it had again changed somehow. When he returned the dagger to its carved wooden sheath, the glow of the shaft, though diminishing, still cast a green light against his hip.

Ereben jumped down to the dead body of the first leopard and removed his spear from its skull by pulling the blade end, drawing the handle completely through the skull.

"This would make a warm replacement for your smelly cloak," Minkar suggested.

"I don't know, Minkar."

"For a man who has just killed two Ice Leopards, you are surprisingly squeamish. Give me your dagger."

"It's too dangerous here."

"How many leopards can there be?"

"Already more than I expected."

"Give me your dagger, Ereben Leaf."

Within a half hour, Minkar had completely skinned the leopard and carved off one haunch for food. Meanwhile, Ereben looked at his own skin beneath the chain Jerkin. He was bruised, but the claws and teeth had not penetrated the links of the jerkin, links of layered steel. When Minkar returned the dagger to Ereben, the handle's glow had ceased.

Ereben and Minkar proceeded up the break in the escarpment, struggling against the wind and increasing snow. He was worried that they had not yet met up with the remaining Shouda men. He wondered who had escaped and who had died. After another half hour of climbing, he halted his daydreaming at the sight of more leopard prints.

"I thought these leopards never left the Ledge," he said.

"I suppose," Minkar replied, "that anyone who might have argued to the contrary was unable to do so."

The leopard tracks were partly filled with new snow, but they seemed to represent the prints of a group of leopards. They entered a long and narrow cul-de-sac. The walls reached twice Ereben's height, softening the ferocity of the wind. When he realized that it was a blind trail, they turned to retrace their steps through the drifting snow. Standing in the exit from the cul-de-sac stood a large leopard. Three leopards paced along the top of the left wall, four on the right.

ꕥ

Repetitive effort may improve a skill to competence. The same repetition transforms talent to perfection.

Ereben Leaf: Chronicle of the Counterspell

"Elloh, spare us," Minkar gasped.

Ereben's mind raced. Fighting a single leopard had nearly cost him his life. Only the chain jerkin had prevented the leopard's teeth from puncturing his chest. Now, eight leopards at once. The enormous cats seemed to wait for Ereben and Minkar to make the first move.

"Perhaps we could distract them with pieces of the leopard meat," Minkar said, reaching slowly into his backpack.

"Yes," Ereben agreed. "We can throw a piece onto either wall, and maybe the big one there will go after the bone. But will they ignore us long enough?"

Minkar pulled the skinned leopard haunch from his pack and held it for Ereben to cut with his dagger. "I am afraid that, if we can leave, they will simply follow us."

"Maybe they aren't hungry," Ereben said, hoping to convince himself. He slid his dagger into the chunk of leopard flesh. Two leopards crouched, ready to leap. *Don't look at us like that!*

The stone handle of the dagger glowed green between his fingers. The slab of flesh he was attempting to carve seemed to shrivel away, leaving the remainder in Minkar's hands.

"Dear Elloh," Minkar whispered, dropping the diminished haunch, "this is not right."

Ereben looked up at the leopards on the wall. Their intense gaze had faded into vacant eyes. The large leopard at the entrance yawned and lay down in the snow.

"This is unholy, Ereben Leaf," Minkar said with derision. "I do not like this. Only a demon can work such unnatural things."

"Let's get out of here," Ereben suggested, heading for the entrance to the cul-de-sac, "and talk about it somewhere else."

They walked at a cautious, deliberate pace toward the leopard lounging at the entrance. Neither it nor the other leopards seemed to notice them. Even as they passed within a half yard of the leopard, it rested its head on one paw and closed its eyes. Ereben accelerated his pace to a jog and, seeing no other path up the ravine, headed back down toward the Ledge with the gusting snow at his back.

The body of the skinned leopard was not where they had left it. Something had dragged it away to the East through the deep snow of thc Ledge. Ereben turned west and continued to follow the wall, hoping to find another break that might be the trail to Punishment Pass.

A quarter hour later, they turned up a narrow gorge with a trail of fading footprints in the snow. Since leaving the cul-de-sac, Minkar had remained uncharacteristically silent.

"I see that you have decided to join us," Otah remarked. He stood in a cleft, beyond reach of the blowing snow.

"Is Rifai with you?" asked Amal, who was seated farther into the cleft.

Now Ereben knew who had died on the Ledge. He had never liked Rifai Madin. But, with the fear and urgency of the Ledge behind him, the horror of Rifai's death pierced him with sorrow. Ereben wept.

Minkar answered Amal's question by presenting him with Rifai's spear. "Rifai Madin rests in the arms of Elloh."

Otah took thc spear from Amal. He studied the spear, then looked at Ereben and Minkar. "How did he meet his end?" he asked softly.

Minkar sighed. "A leopard. From behind."

Amal Hidad stood. He raised his arms in unison with Otah and Minkar. "May he rest in the arms of Elloh," the Sergeant at Arms intoned.

Ereben raised his arms to join them in remembrance. Rifai had died for his willingness to accompany Ereben on this dubious quest. Ereben felt he had no right to dislike a man who would have been alive today, had he remained in the safety of the white spires and pyramids.

"We found no sign of leopards," Amal commented. "I had decided that the great cats must have sought shelter from the storm."

"They don't seem to notice the storm," Ereben said. "The wind and the snow and the leopards are all part of the storm."

Otah looked at him curiously. "You saw the leopards, Ereben Leaf?"

"We have confronted ten leopards," Minkar explained. He spoke as though describing the details of a crime. "Two on the first occasion and eight on the second." Otah attempted to interrupt, but Minkar silenced his prince with a raised hand. "The first leopard was slain by Ereben Leaf in a manner befitting a great warrior. With a single thrust of his spear, he cast the leopard dead upon the ground. The second leopard he slew also, but by powers found only among demons."

"That's not...," Ereben interrupted.

"Let Minkar Jarad speak his mind," Otah snapped. The prince seemed to be disturbed by Minkar's words.

"He called up flames from the Pit of Pain," Minkar continued, "which consumed the leopard, until there was no trace remaining of the animal. I did not understand what had occurred. Later, when we were surrounded by eight leopards, and surely about to be killed, Ereben Leaf called upon demons by his hidden words. This cast an enchantment upon the leopards, which allowed us to depart as though we were not there. Then I understood. No mortal man is able to do these things unless he has joined hands with a demon."

"Are these words true, Ereben Leaf," Otah asked sternly.

"Well, yes. No!" Ereben's mind reeled at the sudden animosity from his only friends. *Except Jasper*. Jasper could explain all this. "It's true about what happened. But it's not true about demons." Ereben tried to explain what little he understood of the unusual events that he had witnessed since fleeing from Rippleton. The three Shouda men listened quietly, not seeming to care that the wind and snow howled unabated just beyond the entrance. When Ereben had completed his story, the Shouda men appeared to be no less convinced of his complicity with demons.

"Elloh would not smile upon us," Otah said, "if we abandoned you, Ereben Leaf, to die high in the mountains. But we would likewise imperil our spirits if we approve of your dark actions. Since you are not of our people, we are not obliged to sit in judgment of your faithfulness to Elloh. We shall continue to accompany you as warriors, as the Mufta has ordered us, but let that not be mistaken for friendship."

Ereben felt the hollow loneliness that had taken hold of his life in Rippleton, when everyone whom he cared about had been swept out of his life. With his head lowered, he turned into the blowing snow to continue his ascent to Punishment Pass. As he climbed, he wondered if Minkar might be right. Maybe the source of this strange power was a demon. But he doubted that demons even existed. He longed for Jasper's companionship. *Even Jasper gave up on me.*

That night, while the Shouda men slept in their tents, Ereben lay alone in the utter silence of a snow cave. The deeper snow had allowed him to create a more spacious room than the previous night. At least he could turn over without kicking the wall. His life now seemed to have pruned itself to the single task of discovering a Stump named Whittig Trench. If such a person existed at all, Ereben might be unable to find him. If he found him.... *What then? What next?*

His thoughts turned to his father. He remembered situations, but could not conjure his father's face. It all seemed so far away—a distant world. And so long ago. It stunned Ereben to acknowledge that only months, rather than years, had passed since he had lived at home, sharing ordinary days with this now faceless man. Ereben knew that he loved his father and missed his presence, if not his advice. This faceless inhabitant of his recollections, however, offered nothing to which Ereben could bind himself. He wanted a shroud of mourning to enfold his thoughts, preferring that pain to his present emptiness. But the faceless man would not oblige. He drifted into dreamless sleep.

Ereben awakened with a start. A sense of danger caused him to sit up and clarify his thoughts. *I must escape. I must escape.* He hurriedly gathered his gear in the faint green light of the snow cave and scrambled out into the black of the bitter cold night. Ten yards from him, barely visible beneath a rocky overhang, clustered the tents of the Shouda men. He turned away, but was halted by an inexplicable urgency to join the Shouda. *I must escape.* Confused, he ran toward their tents. A muffled concussion filled the night. Like distant thunder, the mountain rumbled. He pressed his body against the rock of the overhang, unsure of the source of the sound. The rumbling stopped. Heads popped out of the Shouda tents.

"What is this noise?" Otah asked, his voice coarse with sleep.

"I don't know," Ereben answered.

The Shouda heads turned in all directions, still protruding from the tents. In the darkness, they appeared to Ereben as hunchback beasts mired in the snow. He stood waiting for the noise to recur. When the night remained silent, he decided to return to his snow cave. *It couldn't have been a dream.* Five steps later, his feet encountered chunks of ice strewn about the path to his snow cave. He squatted to see the path more clearly in the darkness. Where the path had been, he now found a slope of broken snow, its surface as hard as stone. His snow cave was gone. *A green light.* Ereben looked down at the dagger strapped to his hip. It appeared to be only a black silhouette in the night. Somehow, this dagger had warned him. *But how? How can a dagger know there's danger?* He returned to the rock overhang and curled up in a nook to sleep for the remainder of the night.

Ereben awakened with first light. A few yards beyond his feet, the mountain dropped away in a tumultuous sculpture of ragged rocks in a sea of white. No clouds blemished the expanse of pristine blue overhead. Although the cold stung his nostrils, the still air brought with it the clean smells of winter morning. The Shouda tents had lost their beastly character in the early light. They were now simply tents.

He stood and walked beyond the rock overhang. In place of his snow cave, a frightening slope of broken snow extended from thirty yards above him to the brink of the narrow platform on which they had camped for the night. The slope gave the appearance of tumbled snow, but its surface was frozen and impenetrable. Even his spear, which seemed to pierce anything in its path, could only scratch the shell of ice.

Closing his eyes, Ereben analyzed the events of the previous night, moment by moment. *Yes. The dagger.* His dagger had played some part in this. He drew it from its carved, wooden sheath. He examined it, recalling each step in the lengthy process of forging it—the heat of the forge, the acrid steam that billowed from the quenching trough, the ringing in his ears after the hammer blows had stopped. He had made this knife, yet it had become something other than what he had made it. He had drilled the translucent green stone and fitted it to the tang. But the stone had become alive in a way that he did not understand. The other dagger, now the head of his spear, had been made in the same way, only with fewer foldings of the steel. True, it made an admirable spear, but it never behaved in ways that caused others to accuse him of working in league with demons. The spear head demonstrated only the attributes of a fine piece of steel. *The dagger. The dagger is different.*

"I wish I understood your secrets," he whispered to the dagger.

Cold seared the fingers holding the dagger. Its stone handle glowed green for an instant. Fear flooded his awareness. Ereben released the dagger, allowing it to fall to the snow beside his foot. The Shouda men began to stir in their tents. Ereben cautiously retrieved the dagger and returned it to its sheath.

That morning they climbed the ever steepening trail through the snow to Punishment Pass. The Shouda men occasionally spoke in muffled tones to one another, but no conversation was directed to Ereben. He walked alone, in an isolation more painful than forced solitude. This seemed to him more punishing than any hardship nature could throw at him. He wondered what greater punishment the Pass could present.

His arrival at Punishment Pass appeared without prelude. Ragged granite pillars soared above him on either side. In front of him, and far below, stretched an undulating forest. At the far horizon, plains merged with puffy clouds. A warm breeze, like the wake of a hummingbird, rose from the South into the Pass. He turned to the North for one last look at the jagged, snowswept terrain, then followed the silent Shouda men through the pass.

Near midday, after descending the most strenuous switchbacks of the trail, they came upon a deteriorating, wooden shack perched at the edge of a magnificent vista. As they approached the shack, a woman emerged from its doorway. She seemed as frail as the tattered brown robes thrown about her. Thin tangles of white hair escaped from a black shawl covering her head and rested against a hump in her back. Her halting gait worried Ereben. She appeared as though she might fall with each step. She supported herself with a twisted cane held in the gnarled grip of both hands.

"We greet you," Otah said, extending both arms in the traditional Shouda bow.

"The Shouda wander far," she crackled, raising her weathered face toward them. From the depths of almost skeletal eye sockets glistened opaque eyes, as milky white as the Pinnacles of Shouda.

"We journey in search of a Stump," Otah continued, his voice not as certain as before.

The old woman aimed her frightening face directly at Otah, as though she could see from her marble eyes. "There be no Stumps here," she said, and turned back toward the broken door.

"A Stump called Whittig Trench," Otah called after her.

The old woman stopped. When she turned around to face them again, her deeply shadowed eyes moved about in their sockets. The opaque globes fell on Ereben, probing him from his scalp to his boots. For a moment they seemed fixed on Ereben's spear. "I have heard of a Whittig Trench dwelling in the city of Zink," she said directly to Ereben. "That be down below, at the base of the mountain."

"How can I find him?" Ereben asked. He immediately felt a pang of embarrassment at asking a blind woman to give directions.

She hesitated, then nodded to herself. "The Baillie. The Baillie may send you to him. The Baillie harbors ill feelings for the Shouda. Go alone to the Baillie." She teetered her way back into the shack.

Just after noon of the following day, they descended into gently rolling hills. The first indication of nearby inhabitants was the globular appearance of the trees, a shape which Ereben had learned years ago was the result of domestic animals grazing on the lower branches of the trees. Soon the hills were sprinkled with flocks of sheep and small herds of cattle. In one clearing thirty yards from the mountain trail, a hog lay in a mud hole. From either side of its neck, the ends of a yard long crossbar hung beneath a wooden yoke. The yoke seemed to be designed to prevent the hog from wandering through the hedgerow surrounding the wallow on three sides. Enclosing the area on the fourth side, a neatly cut stone wall merged into a broad earthen mound. Ereben guessed, from the trails which converged on the mound, that it might be a barn or dwelling, but its height seemed insufficient. His impulse was to ask the Shouda men if they thought it might be a farm house, but they had not spoken with him since the previous day. He walked past in silence, seeing no sign of its inhabitant. The mixed woodlands and pasture changed gradually to predominant pasture land, dotted with increasing numbers of the strange mound houses. Aside from the grazing animals and an occasional hog, Ereben saw no indication that these dwellings, if that was what they were, contained people.

The trail led them toward the summit of the most prominent hill in the vicinity. As they came within a half mile of the hill, Ereben recognized the man-made contour of its flattened top. A mounded wall surrounded the entire summit, obscuring the view of whatever structures might stand within. Nearing the wall, Ereben was heartened to hear the sounds of mingled voices, hundreds of voices, coming from the summit. Within twenty yards of the wall, the true nature of the structure became apparent. The trail led them to the lip of a broad, dry moat, ten yards deep. The moat seemed to wrap completely around the outside of the wall. Their trail led to a narrow wood platform, wide enough for two men abreast, that extended half way across the moat. The remainder of the distance was spanned by a moveable bridge that could be raised by ropes from the top of the wall, which reached twice the height of the outer rim of the moat. At the wall, the path over the bridge entered a tunnel, which seemed to be the only way into what Ereben guessed was the city of Zink.

With a gesture of his arm, Otah signaled to Ereben to take the lead in crossing the bridge. Ereben did not appreciate the questionable stability of the outer half of the bridge until he reached the wobbling inner half. He checked frequently on the progress of the Shouda men behind him, mostly to be sure that they had not abandoned him. His discomfort grew as he made out the shapes of two armed guards standing within the shadow of the entry tunnel. Though these guards held their well worn battle axes with arms thicker than Ereben's thigh, and though their chests seemed like the trunks of trees, their arms and legs were half the length of Ereben's. The tops of their helmeted heads reached just above Ereben's waist. *Stumps!*

One guard pointed his stubby arm at Ereben's spear. "Ye can not tak that intae Zink," he growled in a guttural speech.

Ereben instinctively touched the dagger hidden by his cloak. He immediately recognized his slip.

"Nor can ye tak that, stranger," the second guard added with a smug grin. He twirled his stubby fingers through a dusty beard.

Ereben reluctantly handed his spear and dagger to Amal, who then gathered the weapons of Minkar and Otah. The guards whispered to each other, making obscure gestures in the direction of the Shouda men. The ensuing laughter of the guards seemed to carry a derisive quality that caused Ereben to deeply regret divulging his dagger.

Their weapons now in the care of Amal, who was retracing his steps toward the outer rim of the moat, Ereben entered the tunnel with Minkar and Otah.

He turned back to the guards. "Where can I find the Baillie?" he asked.

"He wad be in the hall with the gray banner," one of them answered. Neither had bothered to turn toward Ereben. Their attention seemed to be fixed on Amal, with his collection of weapons.

"I don't like this," Ereben said softly.

"Amal can certainly care for himself," Otah replied.

They proceeded into the tunnel. Ereben soon discovered that its ceiling was of a height more suitable for the Stumps than for normal people. He dipped his head as he walked in the guttering torchlight. Otah and Minkar, on the other hand, needed to bend at their waist. For forty yards they followed the slight incline of the tunnel, heading for the daylight of the distant opening.

Ereben expected to emerge into a collection of mound dwellings like those he had seen earlier. What he saw at the tunnel exit was a city of a hundred carefully masoned stone buildings, most the height of two houses, some the height of three. A central square was packed with people, all with a stature similar to that of the guards outside the tunnel. They jostled about dozens of market stalls. In the center of the square, on a raised platform of stone, the figure of a man in a black robe hung by his neck from a wooden frame. They worked their way through the noise and exotic aromas of the crowded square. Some of the diminutive people stared at them, but most were too busy haggling over sacks of millet or cages of chickens to notice. All of them ignored the black-robed man dangling from the gallows.

As Ereben neared the center of the square, he recognized the robe of the hanged man as that of a priest of Dragomin. "Excuse me," he said to a stall keeper who was stacking potatoes. "Excuse me," he said louder, "what happened to him?" He pointed at the corpse.

"A waywart preacher, he wes," the balding Stump said, shaking his head. "Part o' that cult o' the True Faith, or so he said afore they stretched his neck the day. This is not the sort o' place tae be preachin' strange words. Not the sort o' place." He returned to his vegetables.

At the far end of the square stood the tallest of the stone buildings. Mounted above its doorway, a gray banner hung limp in the still air. Beneath it, on either side of the door, stood two Stump guards, wearing the same helmets and holding the same worn battle axes as the guards outside the tunnel.

"You must go in alone, Ereben Leaf," Otah said.

Ereben gave Otah his pack. He watched as Otah and Minkar turned back into the throng of the market. "I need to see the Baillie," Ereben said to the guards.

Without words, one guard opened the massive oak door, then closed it after him. Inside, a dozen Stump guards lounged about in several groups, all talking loudly. Ereben approached the nearest group.

"Where can I find the Baillie?" he asked.

One of the guards indicated a member of an adjacent group, which burst into laughter over some unheard joke. Ereben stepped over to the group of laughing Stumps.

"I'm looking for the Baillie," Ereben said.

"Who might ye be, my red haired young man?" the Baillie asked in a casual voice.

"I'm Ereben Leaf, Sir," he replied. "I was told you might know how to find Whittig Trench."

The Baillie placed his chubby hands across his rotund belly. With a broad smile that ignited obvious delight in his eyes, he said,

"Indeed I do." To the guards he said with equal joviality, "Please escort young Ereben Leaf tae the quarters o' Whittig Trench."

Ereben almost jumped for joy. After frustrations at every turn, he could hardly believe his present luck. One of the guards motioned Ereben toward the door. When he turned, both his arms were seized. Glancing over his shoulder, Ereben saw the unchanging smile on the Baillie's face. The corpulent Stump turned to an assistant.

"Send word tae Lord Corban that his young heretic is our guest," he said, smiling more broadly than before.

ꟗꟗ

As a mighty hammer blow, the hand of Dragomin sent forth Corban the Wicked to smite the brown skin heathen upon the anvil of justice.

Crotus: Wisdom of the True Faith

"The Shadow scum are gone, Lord," stated one of the nearby Protectors. A crimson cape spread to the milky white stone of the plaza on which the man knelt. "We have flyers searching farther from the pinnacles," he continued, "but they seem to have vanished." There was a long pause. "We're certain to locate them soon, Lord Corban."

With a wave of one hand, Lord Corban, High Protector of Dragomin indicated that the kneeling protector should stand. "Yes," he said. "Yes. I know that you've done your best, Kirin." Even from his hiding place near the central black pyramid, Jasper could sense the venom in Corban's voice. Corban patted the trembling Protector on the cheek. "I have a special message for you to deliver. Wait there by my mount." Corban pointed toward the giant goshawk that had landed him in the center of the Shouda Shrine. The High Protector waited for Kirin to walk the twenty paces to the restive goshawk. "Gentlemen," Corban said to the dozens of Protectors standing about him, "you really must try harder." With that, Corban turned toward his goshawk and flashed a rapid hand signal.

Standing a yard taller than the hundreds of giant vultures in the Shrine, the regal gray and white goshawk spread its enormous wings, exposing their white underfeathers. In a single pounce, the goshawk impaled Kirin with the talons of one foot. Kirin's agonized scream withered to a muffled gurgle as the goshawk tore away the flesh of his throat with its beak. Several vultures stepped toward the thrashing body, but were sent back to their places by the goshawk's penetrating stare. Returning its attention to the now still body of Kirin, the goshawk meticulously tore away strips of black leather armor, before devouring him piece by piece.

"Do I make myself understood?" Corban asked softly.

Two dozen Protectors slapped their right arms to their chests in salute, then hurried to mount their waiting vultures. Great black wings thrust swirls of dust across the milky white stone as they lifted into the air to join those already searching.

Jasper had been able to sneak into the city from the East without difficulty, but the flyers now searching close in made escape impossible. He knew that the Shouda would never turn over their Shrine without a fight. But here was Corban, standing at its center, with hundreds of vulture mounted Protectors, and uncountable ravens. Jasper watched as Corban and a small group of guards dressed in hooded crimson robes walked to the northern face of the black pyramid. They gathered before a pattern on the face of the stone. It appeared to be a triangle with one point toward the ground. Jasper could see, above the horizontal top line, a finger sized slot in the stone. A similar slot was located on each side of the triangle. Corban caressed the black stone.

"We should find what you have come for, Lord Corban," said one of the crimson robed guards, "and avoid battle, thereby saving your forces for other matters."

"What I have come for," Corban said, still facing the black pyramid, "is here. But there are two small matters that presently keep us from it." Corban drew two daggers from his belt, each dagger identical to Ereben's dagger. "Thanks to Kirin's blunder in Rippleton, I have only two daggers. The portal," he explained, pointing to one of the slots beside the triangle, "requires three daggers. And all the fools I have sent to find Chrysanthus' sorry excuse for a grandson have not measured up to the task." He glanced in the direction of the feeding goshawk. "The boy must have the dagger, but I doubt he has the slightest inkling of its power."

"And the other?" an aid asked.

"The other?" Corban said, clearly irritated at the interruption.

"You mentioned that there were two small matters, Lord. The missing dagger is one that should be resolved shortly."

"Yes?" Corban's eyebrows rose with expectation.

"We have just received word from the Baillie of Zink that the boy is in his safe keeping. I have sent three Protectors to see to it." The crimson robed aid dipped his head.

"We shall see," Corban said. "The second matter is one of timing. The portal will open only at the winter solstice. So even though we may retrieve the boy's dagger, we must maintain control of this valley for six more weeks. At that time, with the true power of Dragomin, all our concerns will take on a different complexion."

Jasper evaluated his possible escape routes. The nearest cover beyond the Shrine seemed to be the sparsely forested hills to the West, beyond the Shouda village. But he would have to run half the length of the Shrine to reach it. Dozens of vultures and hundreds of giant ravens stood in that path. A voice sounded from above. Jasper looked up. From one of the vultures circling above, a Protector pointed toward him, shouting. Jasper jumped from his hiding place and sprinted toward the village.

He rounded the far side of the black pyramid. The voice of Corban shouted orders. With Rat Slayer in his right hand and his carved wooden staff in the other, Jasper plunged into the gauntlet of predatory birds. Human footsteps clattered on the stones behind him. The first vulture opened its yard-long beak, emitting a fearsome cackling. Jasper's staff fell across it with an awful crack. His sword slashed into the bird's neck. He continued to run. Diving ravens swooped toward his face. His staff drove them aside. He felt the impact of ravens on his shoulders and back, but his steel chain tunic turned their beaks and claws. He looked at the distant trees. He was halfway there. The sound of the footsteps behind him seemed to be gaining on him, but he was afraid to turn and look. The gaping beak of another giant vulture descended toward him. Jasper thrust his staff with all his strength into the open mouth. The bird dropped to the stone. From side to side, his flailing staff and sword drove him through the onslaught of confused beasts. Twenty yards from the edge of the Shrine, Jasper's feet slipped on the milky white stone. He tumbled and skidded.

Running toward him were two Protectors, their swords above their heads. From above, a vulture descended with claws extended. First one Protector, then the other staggered backwards with spears protruding from the center of each forehead. Jasper rolled, swinging his sword as he went. The descending vulture's claws spurted a shower of blood. Then the great bird collapsed with spears penetrating the heads of both the bird and its rider. Hands grasped Jasper's clothing and dragged him toward the trees.

Shouts echoed as thousands of resting ravens lifted from the Shrine. Jasper was helped to his feet by two Shouda warriors. They ran to the line of trees, where Saikal Sahm, the gray haired Weapons Master of the Shouda continued to cast spears with deadly precision into the unprepared Protectors. When Jasper and the two warriors reached Saikal, the old man gathered his remaining spears and joined them in their flight up the hill.

The zing of bow strings, hundreds of them, resounded from the tree covered slope. Jasper turned to watch a wall of arrows sweep into the rising flock of ravens. Thrashing black shapes fell lifeless to the ground, staining the milky white stone of the Shrine with coalescing pools of blood. Another fusillade of Shouda arrows filled the air. Jasper stared in amazement as the oversized ravens aligned themselves into perfect rows streaming toward the hills, some moving toward him and others directed at the hills south of the Shrine. Although many ravens fell as the arrows struck, most of the arrows sailed harmlessly between the rows of birds. Thousands of ravens neared the trees.

From the leafless tops of the trees, Shouda men rose precariously to their feet. With near synchrony, they cast spears straight up. Jasper could see fine netting spanning the space between the soaring spears. As the ravens impacted the wall of netting, great swarms of them became entangled and fell to the ground like a huge caterpillar, writhing and screeching, but unable to free themselves. The remaining ravens turned back toward the Shrine, climbing as a chaotic flock in migration. Cheers rose up from the hills above the Shrine, but rapidly faded.

"Jasper of Nilwid," Saikal Sahm shouted to him, "climb to the ridge. The Mufta awaits you there." Saikal then turned back to directing the Shouda warriors along his slope of the hill.

Jasper climbed the steep embankment, using shrubs as handholds. The battle continued behind him and in the air above him. A raven struck his back, just below his pack. Jasper twirled his staff, allowing the shaft to trap the raven against the pack. It tumbled down the slope, dangling one wing as it fell. He continued to the ridge. There, on the white stone path that Jasper recognized from his first arrival among the Shouda, the Mufta stood among his green-clad, personal guards. All but the Mufta were firing arrows in rapid succession. Ibrah, Mufta Gebir of the Shouda, observed the battle, giving frequent orders to Shouda boys who then sprinted to various parts of the battle front. The Mufta motioned for Jasper to join him.

Seven great vultures appeared above them, shielded by a swirling mass of ravens.

"Use the fire!" the Mufta shouted.

Each of the Shouda archers knocked an arrow batted with pitch covered fabric. Runners with lighted torches passed among them. Within moments of the Mufta's order, dozens of arrows carrying flaming pitch rose toward the attack of Corban's Protectors. Most of the flaming arrows were stopped by the shielding ravens, but four of the attacking vultures were struck. Their convulsive response threw their riders, who plummeted to their death. Protectors on the three uninjured vultures dumped baskets of small objects onto the Shouda below. Jasper grasped the Mufta by his arm and tugged him off the paved path, causing both of them to fall into the brush beside the paving. Ibrah opened his mouth to speak, but was interrupted by the screams of his personal guards. Many of them lay dead on the stone pavement. Darts the size of daggers protruded from their heads and shoulders.

The Mufta looked up at the increasing number of airborne vultures. Some of their riders appeared to be carrying a burning substance within large containers. "Only by the hand of Elloh can we possibly defeat this enemy. Go, Jasper of Nilwid, and wait with the women and children among the trees on the western slope of this ridge." The Mufta turned to rejoin his surviving guards. "You have the courage," he said over his shoulder, "of a Shouda warrior."

Jasper climbed to the crest of the ridge. He looked back. From vultures too high for the reach of the Shouda arrows, Protectors poured flaming liquid onto the trees from which the fiercest volleys of arrows originated. Jasper turned away from the screams swelling from the valley of the Shouda.

He saw below him, among the sparse vegetation of the west facing slope, clusters of Shouda women and children. Below them spread the valley in which Ereben and the Shouda had defeated the first Protector. Grassy plains beyond seemed to shimmer peacefully in the wind. Tears blurred his vision. So many horrible things were happening. He wanted it to end. The wrenching noise of battle would not release his thoughts. In the western plains, even the waving grass began to appear ominous. He rubbed away the tears and concentrated his attention on the grass. *It's moving!* A sick tightness rose within his chest. Hundreds of animals were moving in ordered ranks across the plain toward him. Jasper shook his head, rubbed his eyes once more, then looked again. A legion of silver wolves advanced across the valley.

Waving his staff and shouting, Jasper bounded down the slope toward the startled Shouda women and children. He recognized the Mufta's wife, Estheri and her daughter Hanarah. "You have to get away from here!" Jasper shouted. "Wolves are coming from the valley."

"Of what are you speaking?" Estheri said sharply to him, grasping his shoulders. "You will panic all the women and their children. They must remain safe from the battle."

"You have to believe me," Jasper pleaded, freeing himself from her grasp. "There are hundreds of wolves running this way, like an army, like the ravens."

Estheri looked down the slope, but could not see them from their position. She frowned, apparently unable to decide if she should believe him. "How do the warriors fare in battle?" she asked.

Jasper hesitated. "Not good. But the wolves will kill us for sure."

"All of you must follow me," Estheri commanded. "Hanarah, come!"

"But mother...," Hanarah protested.

Estheri's glare was sufficient to set her daughter in motion. Most of the others reluctantly began the steep climb toward the crest of ridge—toward the slaughter of their men. Some, however, would not move from their place of hiding. Instead, these few women, with their children, pressed their hands over their eyes and began to pray.

Jasper reached the top with Estheri. From there it was plain to see that the battle was lost. A broad phalanx of Protectors marched slowly into the retreating Shouda warriors. These Protectors wielded short bows mounted sideways on thick handles, firing small arrows with a greater range than the arrows and spears of the Shouda. They aimed and fired into the trees and shrubs as they advanced. Mufta Ibrah, standing on the paved path just below Jasper, had now taken up a bow. Only three of his personal guards remained alive. The white stone path was littered with dead Shouda warriors and ravens, some dead and some engaged in eating the dead and wounded. Blood pooled in the worn center of the stone pavement and flowed slowly down the gentle slope of the path to the left.

With consuming grief, Jasper surveyed the horror. He looked back to the West. The wolves had already reached the bottom edge of the slope. Soon they would reach those women and children who had refused to climb back to the ridge. He looked back to the river of blood wending its way down the milky white paving stones. *We're all going to die.* He stared at the flowing blood. It reached a point just before the steps descended the slope, but the blood did not flow to the steps. It simply stopped abruptly there, without accumulating.

The pinnacles of Shouda spread out in the valley before him. Jasper remembered the map on the wall of the sleeping chamber, the map that had been hidden by the bark-like material that glowed green. *An entrance!*

Screams echoed from behind. Jasper knew that the wolves had reached the women and children still hiding down the slope. Nothing could save those poor people now. Jasper slid down the eastern slope on his backside, stopping on the white stone pavement. He ran to the left, to the head of the steps. There, at the point where the river of blood vanished, he saw a square of dirt and sand, as though a stone were missing. The perimeter of this end of the paving showed signs of a square foundation of what might have been another stone house. He frantically dug at the dirt with his hands, then with the point of his sword. When the slot was cleared of dirt, he attempted to slide one adjacent stone, then another. The second moved part way into the opening.

The women and children above him began to scream and run in all directions, some falling to their death, others colliding with ravens and arrows. Jasper forced the sliding stone the remainder of the way. With a heave, he swung open a stone hatch. Beneath it opened a helical stairway, which glowed milky white, spattered with dark blood.

"Here!" Jasper shouted. "Mufta Ibrah, we can get away through here!"

The Mufta looked in surprise at the opening. "Take the others and go," the Mufta shouted, gesturing to the few women and children now cowering on the stone pavement.

Saikal Sahm climbed up to stand beside the Mufta. He carried a single spear. His quiver was empty. When the weapons master saw the opening, he looked about him, then turned to his Mufta. "You must escape and survive, Ibrah. I will give you some time, my friend." He clasped arms with the Mufta, then returned to swiping ravens from the air with his spear.

Jasper reached into his backpack and extracted the silver wolf cape. He drew it about him and fastened it. With his staff for support and his sword held high he climbed the slope above the paved path. Before him, he saw a wreckage of mangled bodies. Estheri was dead, with three silver wolves fighting over her. He found Hanarah holding the hand of a small boy, while she fought off a single wolf with one of the darts that had fallen from the baskets of the Protectors. Jasper raised up his staff and his sword, like a wolf armed and upright. His shouts and his appearance caused the wolf attacking Hanarah to momentarily cower. In that moment, Jasper brought Rat Slayer down into the wolf's head, splitting it in two. He grabbed Hanarah's sleeve and ran with her and the small boy toward the spiral stairway.

The Mufta took the two children and, with a final glance toward Saikal Sahm, entered the secret entrance. Jasper followed. With the hatch almost closed above him, Jasper saw the great gray and white goshawk of Corban light on the ridge near the spot where the old weapons master stood his ground. High Protector Corban, in his black leather armor and crimson cape, slid down from the bird's shoulders. Corban's sword remained in its sheath as he strode over the carcasses of ravens, toward Saikal Sahm, who stood poised with his spear ready.

In a flash of motion, Saikal Sahm cast his last spear into Corban, striking him in the center of the forehead. It passed through him to the pavement beyond. Corban remained standing, as his body began to shimmer. The gaping wound in his head widened. The High Protector's face seemed to melt as his entire body fragmented into a pulsing swarm of hornets, each black with a crimson stripe. Hornets streamed as a bolt of lightning into the gaping mouth of the astonished weapons master. He snapped his mouth shut, but too late. A convulsive gag dropped him to his knees, among his dead and dying warriors. Eyes wide with panic, Saikal Sahm gazed to the tree tops as he sank to the blood stained pavement. At once, his dark brown skin assumed the silky white texture of his hair. Facial features vanished beneath a spreading mat of hazy filaments.

Jasper realized that he had been holding his breath. He swallowed past a dry throat, then exhaled. After one more breath, Jasper observed specks of black emerging from beneath the ghastly white husk of what moments before had been Saikal Sahm. A black moth, bearing a large crimson spot on each wing, tore free from the surface of Saikal's right cheek. Another moth climbed from the back of Saikal's right hand. White shreds fell away as hundreds of black and crimson moths, each the size of Japser's palm, erupted from the exposed flesh of the weapons master. The cloud of moths circled randomly skyward to the tree tops that had been Saikal's last view of life, then spilled downward into a tumultuous heap beside the giant goshawk. One by one, then two by two, four by four, the wings of the growing pillar of moths coalesced into the form of Corban, High Protector of Dragomin. Where Saikal Sahm had fallen, there remained only a skeletal heap of shredded flesh, clothed in a tattered, dark green tunic. Beside it lay a bow and empty quiver.

Jasper gently closed the hatch above him and latched it. He slumped his exhausted body against the cool, white stone, stained with blood, and wished that today had never happened. Saikal Sahm had saved his life today as he ran from the Protectors. Now, Saikal Sahm was no more than dark bones and a memory. With a start, he remembered his fall through the floor trap at the other entrance. "Wait for me!" he shouted down the helical stairway, as he descended.

At the bottom, Jasper saw how complete the defeat of the Shouda had been. Seated against the wall of the corridor Mufta Ibrah allowed his daughter Hanarah to tend to his small wounds. Beside him sat two Shouda warriors and a small boy, who stared blankly at the opposite wall.

The Mufta looked up at Jasper. "I commend your courage, Jasper of Nilwid," the Mufta said sadly, "but I am not certain that you have favored us by helping us to live. All is lost. The forces of Corban have seized the holy Shrine. And we now sit trapped in a place that I never knew existed, hidden even from Elloh." Ibrah paused, staring expectantly at Jasper. "How did Saikal Sahm meet his end?"

Jasper swallowed the bile that rose in his throat. "He died bravely." He could only look away from the Mufta—only look down the corridor. Beyond countless webs of tiny spiders, a soft green glow seemed to radiate. "Wait here, Mufta Ibrah," Jasper said. "I'll be right back." He hurried down the corridor, swinging his staff to clear the webs. Past one corridor entering from the right, his present path led to a room glowing green. As he expected, the green lighted room appeared to be another sleeping room. He entered cautiously, finding it, like the first sleeping room, entirely free of insects and any sign of animal habitation. In this sleeping room, the glowing material seemed also to have crept from the ceiling onto the upper walls. To his delight, the wall beside the doorway bore a map similar to the map in the southern tunnel. He sprinted back to the resting Mufta.

As they walked, Jasper explained to Ibrah his discovery of the entrance in the foothills south of the city, and of his adventure within the labyrinth. The Mufta seemed to find the story difficult to believe until he saw the map on the wall. Then Ibrah walked about the sleeping room touching the walls with reverence. The bed shelves, like those Jasper had seen before, bore written words inscribed at various angles. Ibrah examined the inscriptions, tilting his head at different angles as he moved from one to the next.

"These are names," he said, "inscribed in the ancient script, the script of the Tor, the Great Book. Each appears to be written by a different hand. Each name has a date measured by an unfamiliar reckoning. Perhaps these were the people who slept here in some ancient day." The Mufta looked into the eyes of the survivors. "It is written that they shall be led by a child, and shall find the truth. This is surely a sign from Elloh."

"You can read that?" Jasper asked with excitement.

"Some of it," the Mufta answered.

"Can you read these words?" Jasper asked, pointing to the labels on the map. With the Mufta's affirmative answer, the two of them, with the two warriors watching, pointed to each item on the map and named its label.

That evening, the six of them shared the small rations carried by the two warriors. Jasper learned that one of the warriors was called Neebah, the other, Oor. The small boy was Bahsa, whose father, Jasper was told, had accompanied Ereben across the mountains. The Mufta wanted to locate one of the other entrances and escape toward the mountains, but Jasper related the conversation he had overheard at the black pyramid. It seemed clear that Corban's forces would remain for at least six weeks.

After some hours of restless sleep, Jasper was awakened by Neebah Dir. The Mufta had decided that they would look further in the corridors. Jasper gathered his things and led the way. When they reached a steep upward slope in the floor of the corridor, Jasper explained the floor trap and its latch on the far side.

Oor Shakur devised a plan to allow Jasper to cross the trap and then lock it for the others. The Mufta and the two warriors would insert their spears into the crack of the floor where it would tip downward. With a running start, Jasper would sprint up the ramp while the spears prevented the floor from moving. When the spear tips were planted, Jasper stepped back a few yards, then raced forward. The spears held the trap floor until Jasper was within two yards of the top of the ramp. Then, with a grating of stone against steel, the floor behind him fell as the floor in front of him tilted upward. He lunged for the upper edge of the rising floor, grasping it with both hands. As he pulled himself upward, the balance of the stone rapidly reversed its motion. He saw in an instant that his fingers would be crushed as the floor returned to its resting position. With a supreme effort, he vaulted himself up the edge of falling stone and onto the solid floor beyond. The stone trap slammed back into place with a thunderous crash.

Jasper searched the wall further down the corridor until he recognized the lock for the trap. At his signal, the others ascended the ramp and joined him. Just as the map had indicated, the corridors in this area were far shorter and less complex than those of the southern portion of the labyrinth. They walked directly into the great square beneath the pinnacles.

Jasper was shocked to discover a steady breeze within the great square. This was accompanied by a low pitched whistle, almost a hum. The area was not the open space that Jasper had imagined it would be. Instead, at the location of each of the small corner pyramids of each small plaza, a milky white wall extended in a square from ceiling to floor. The cylinders of the pinnacles likewise seemed to penetrate through the great square to some region below. Although the great square was lit by morning sunshine passing through the translucent stone, the silhouettes of Corban's great birds cast shadows where they rested. Jasper guessed that the thickness of the stone ceiling must be great enough that the Protectors walking about were not visible.

Hanarah screamed. To Jasper's left, a millipede of enormous size marched toward them. The beast towered three times Jasper's height, moving on rippling waves of legs. At its head, jaws large enough to snap a man in two were held open. When Jasper looked back at the Shouda warriors, Neebah Dir pointed to their right. Twenty yards away stood a man armored from head to toe in gleaming plates of steel, capped by a closed, visored helmet. He wielded a massive two-handed sword.

ഇ

We search for certainty. On close inspection, the product of that search dwindles to a single certainty: events never transpire according to our expectations. Expectations, all derived from the past, are no longer applicable the moment they are conceived.

Ereben Leaf: Chronicle of the Counterspell

Ereben's eyes strained to see ahead of his stumbling steps in the dim light of the corridor. Acrid smells, immediately familiar and sickening, unnerved him. The two Stump guards who roughly forced him forward had not spoken since leaving the company of the Baillie. They had climbed a brightly lit, helical stone stairway, always turning to the right. By Ereben's count of the doorway landings, the present darkened corridor, no taller than the tunnel beneath the city wall, was the fourth and top level of the building. With his head slightly bowed, to avoid striking the stone ceiling, he moved past massive wooden doors on either side. Their bulky hinges and latches appeared to be crudely wrought iron. Opening in the center of each door, a tiny, waist-high, rectangular slot illuminated the corridor with the feeble light reflected from dark stone walls within. At several of the door slots, eyes silently followed Ereben's course.

A door opened. Unyielding hands tossed him into a foul chamber. Like the blow of a smith's hammer, the iron clank of the door latch smote his spirit. Memories of wandering through oak and meadow, of clouds caressing distant horizons, of curling up warm and tired within his Shouda tent against the blowing snows, all of these things rushed in upon his mind. And the mystery of his dagger. He had not yet discovered its secret. But all of it, the wandering, the searching and the fighting had led him only to the inescapable stench and confinement of this cell. The stone cubicle, three yards on a side, and not quite tall enough for Ereben to stand upright, glowed a dull gray from light entering a fist-size opening in the upper edge of the far wall. Moving to the hole, he savored fresh air while he looked out to a path surmounting the earthen wall of the city. The small bore of the opening, combined with the half-yard thick stone of the cell wall provided only that unchanging view.

A snorting sound startled him from behind. Ereben spun around, but saw nothing until he stepped to the side of the only source of light. In the corner beside the door, like a heap of dung in a stable, a filthy mound of a man slept, his bearded cheek pressed against the stone wall, which glistened beneath with a trail of saliva. Ereben stepped closer, but was repulsed by the reek of rotted barley. He returned to the clear air of the tiny, round window for a few breaths, then turned and slumped to the floor. He found himself wishing they would take him soon to his execution, so that he would not have to endure the walls and the smells any longer. He began to cry. *Why is this happening to me?*

For minutes or hours, Ereben wasn't sure how long, he stared at the bare stone walls. Though their outer surface was only roughly dressed, the seams between the blocks of stone were perfect. With no mortar, the junctions would not admit even his fingernail. The stones of the floor were no smoother than the walls, and their joins made with equal precision. The floor seemed to tilt at a barely noticeable angle toward one outer corner of the cell. In that corner, Ereben discovered another fist-sized opening that angled downward through the outer wall. A drain. Peering through the drain, he could see the flat roof of a nearby building.

He had no idea if Otah Kadeef or the other Shouda men would attempt to find him, or if they might even be pleased at his imprisonment. But since they represented his only hope of rescue, he decided to put aside his doubts about their allegiance. Using his teeth, Ereben tore the edge of his tunic, then carefully split the fabric to form a yard long strip about the width of his finger. To its end he tied a fragment of the singed, white weasel fur from the collar of his cloak. *It's so small.* The other end he tied to his applewood pipe, at the center of the stem. He pitched the fur end into the drain hole, then blew down the hole until he was so dizzy that he forgot what he was doing. The pipe stem clicked against the opening. He regained his bearings and positioned the pipe to hold securely. *Maybe Otah will see it. Maybe he'll recognize the fur.*

The heap in the corner stirred with a loud grunt. Late afternoon sun shining through the vent hole created a disk of bright orange light on the opposite wall, reminding Ereben of the sphere of light in the temple of Dragomin. It drew a poignant contrast with the wasted soul slumbering beneath it. One eye opened slowly above the tangled nest of filthy gray beard. It closed briefly, then opened with clearer focus. Now both eyes examined Ereben from the far side of the cell.

"What brings sech ...," the man cleared the sleep from his voice and continued, "sech a fine tall lad tae visit?"

"I was looking for somebody," Ereben said, "but I was tricked by an old blind woman."

"That maks everythin' clear," the man said, seeming perfectly satisfied with the answer to his question. "What might yer name be?"

"Ereben."

"Well, Ereben redhair, yer luck has landed. I know every person in Zink, who he married and who he swindlt."

"I'm looking for a Stump called Whittig Trench."

"A Stump indeed!"

"I didn't mean to... I don't know what to call... I didn't even think they existed until I came to..."

"Dwarf! Polite folk say, Dwarf."

"Dwarf. Then I'm looking for a... dwarf called Whittig Trench."

"Why ye would look for that wastrel I can not imagine."

"I'm not really sure. Things happened, terrible things. The one person who helped me said I should look for a Stump... Dwarf called Whittig Trench. I don't even know why. I just know that Corban is trying to catch me."

"The High Protector o' Dragomin? That Corban?"

"That's the one. They've been chasing me. Tried to kill me once."

"All o' this oot o' the clear blue?"

"It all started after my grandpa died. He was a bladesmith. Something happened, a fire I guess. Then I found my family...." Ereben choked on the words. "They were killed."

"Who was the man who sent ye tae find Whittig Trench?"

"A tinker named Yarnish Blen." Ereben looked about the darkening cell. "I guess it's all been for nothing now."

"Perhaps. Perhaps."

The latch of the cell door creaked. Ereben watched as the door opened wide enough to allow two bowls to be placed on the floor. The door slammed shut. Ereben at once recognized the source of at least one of the cell's odors. The bowls contained a gruel reeking of rotted barley.

"Turn up yer nose if ye like," the man grumbled, "but all those rascals serve here is the likes of that. They soak it in Zink lager. If ye're hungry, ye eat it. If ye eat it, ye give 'em nae trouble. It'll keep ye befuddlt 'till sunrise."

"I'll pass," Ereben said, noticing the growls of hunger growing in his belly. In his despair, he had completely forgotten about food.

"Now listen tae my words, Ereben redhair. Unless ye have hope o' powerful friends tae beg yer release from oot o' this stye, ye hed better accustom yersel tae the vittles settin' afore ye. With nae nourishment in ye, sober or not, they'll be draggin' yer corpse away inside o' the week." He scratched his whiskers, releasing a small cloud of gnats. When the scratching ceased, the gnats vanished again into their refuge. "Now I would not wish for ye tae misunderstand. If ye conjure some way o' breakin' oot tae the sunbeams, ye may certainly count auld Barrow amongst yer friends. This auld carcass has seen a fight or two. An' perhaps we could locate the... Stump... ye been lookin' for."

For two days, Ereben forced himself to eat the rotted barley gruel, after squeezing it with his fingers to remove the Zink lager. Water was provided daily in a mildewed waterskin. Several times each day, Ereben crouched by the drain hole to make certain that his tiny "flag" was still attached to the stem of his applewood pipe. By the end of the second day, Barrow had managed to extract most of Ereben's story: the events in Rippleton, his flight from Corban, the massacre at Nilwid, and his trials with the Shouda. Ereben carefully avoided any details that related to the strange powers of his dagger. After his experience with the Shouda's accusations, he preferred to take no chances with his new ally. The only reason for Barrow's imprisonment seemed to be that he owed the Baillie a sum of money.

That night, Ereben was awakened by a grating sound near the floor. He fumbled in the dark toward the drain corner. A wooden shaft protruded from the drain into the room. It rested against the side wall, held up from the floor at an angle which matched the slope of the drain.

"Who is there?" he whispered through the drain. There was no reply. He went to the upper vent hole and repeated the question. Still no answer.

He sparkled with hope, returning to the wooden shaft. As Ereben touched the wood, it immediately slipped further out the drain. He slammed his body into the drain corner, trapping the end of the shaft against the wall. With more care, he firmly grasped the wood. Because of the thickness of the stone through which the drain passed, the shaft would slide into the room only when pulled at exactly the angle of the drain. Ereben stood as he moved toward the door end of the room, drawing the shaft inward. When his hand bumped the far wall, he heard the scrape of metal against stone. *A spear!* With its far end clear of the drain hole, he was able to lower the shaft safely to the floor. Feeling his way along the shaft to the other end, Ereben confirmed his suspicion that this was his own spear, with its specially forged blade. Near the blade, he found his applewood pipe, which he returned to its tiny pouch.

With this blade, he thought, he could carve his way through the massive wooden door. He tried to remember the location of the doorlatch from when he first entered the cell. But his plan of escape vanished as quickly as it had come. The shaft of the spear was so long that he could not turn it around to point toward the door. He felt stupid for not remembering that the point had barely cleared the drain when the shaft touched the far wall. The blunt end of the shaft would be his only weapon unless he could get the spear into the corridor outside the door.

He left the spear on the floor and squatted near Barrow. "Barrow," he whispered, prodding his reeking companion. "Barrow."

"Let me be, lad."

"Barrow, you have to wake up."

"Indeed." Barrow cleared his throat. "It hed better be a pardon from the quean o' dwarfs, wakin' me oot o' a dream so fine."

"My friends have slipped a spear into the drain."

"Here?"

"It's on the floor, but the point is toward the window and the shaft is too long to turn it around."

"Do I understan' that your fine friends have delivert ye a spear that ye can only use for a stick?"

Ereben remained silent.

"Well, young Ereben redhair," Barrow whispered, "ye're in sore need o' some sort o' plan. When the guard brings the vittles, he always looks in the peep slot afore unlatchin' the door. Only one chance will we get tae spring free."

After planning their escape, Ereben stooped by the upper vent hole to enjoy its clean air. Soon he would be free of the stone walls and the stench, free to stand up straight, to dance about. He looked out to the moon setting over the earthen city wall. That one of the Shouda would take any risk to help him seemed a mystery. Ereben's hope now was that his Shouda companions would be nearby when he made his break from the prison. He recalled the priest hanging from the gallows in the square. These Stumps...dwarfs might be awfully unhappy with the two of them if the attempt failed. If he were caught, he might end up on the gallows himself. *It's not a whole lot worse than being in here.*

The sky began to lighten. It would be another hour before the guard came with food. He rehearsed his plan in his mind. *Block the light. Hold the spear above me. Door opens. I hit him with the shaft.* Ereben shook his head. The guard usually opened the door barely enough to pick up the empty bowls and slide in the filled ones. *The water!* In the morning he always brought in a filled waterskin. Maybe he would reach in far enough today to make the plan work.

The noise of a doorlatch echoed from the central corridor. *He's starting early!* "Barrow!" he whispered. Ereben prodded the dwarf with the spear shaft. "Barrow, get ready!" Barrow grunted, nodding his head slightly. Ereben brought the spear up to the stone ceiling. One quick look out the vent hole almost caused him to drop the spear. Clearing the horizon of the earthen wall, three giant vultures descended into the city. Each carried a man wearing the black armor and crimson cape of the Protectors of Dragomin. Ereben forced himself to think only of his immediate plan of escape. He wondered how many of the Baillie's guards would be assembled within this building to meet the Protectors.

The clang of his cell door unlatching startled Ereben. His involuntary shrug allowed the spear to slip away from his shoulders. The dwarf guard responded to Ereben's sudden movements by tossing the waterskin at Barrow, who appeared to be asleep. The spear fell to the floor as the guard moved to slam the door shut. Barrow exploded from his corner by the door, grasped the shaft of the spear and jammed it through the vanishing gap in the doorway. With a resonant thud, the massive wooden door bounced open. Barrow took hold of the full waterskin with his free hand and stepped into the doorway. A full swing of his stubby arm heaved the waterskin into the guard's head, which struck the stone wall with a sickening, hollow sound. With the impact, the waterskin burst, sending a shower in all directions. The guard slumped to the floor, tipping a bucket of gruel across the stones. Barrow motioned for Ereben to follow.

In the corridor, Ereben found enough room to back the spear shaft toward the blind end, leaving him with its point toward the stairway. Other than the unconscious guard lying in a spreading puddle of gruel, the corridor was empty. Ereben saw no eyes at any of the other cell doors. He followed Barrow to the steps, which twisted downward, turning to the left. Barrow had told Ereben that the stairs were designed so that someone climbing the steps would have no room to swing his right arm, while a defender above could use his weapon with full advantage against an attacker. For Ereben, however, the greatest challenge was to carry his Shouda spear without it scraping at either end.

They descended past two deserted doorways, then into the main entry hall. At the front door, a guard stood gazing through the partly opened door at something in the plaza. Barrow directed Ereben to a corridor in the opposite direction. Sleeping against the doorpost of the back door, a guard sat with his legs blocking the rear door. Barrow casually lifted the guard's legs by their leggings, moved them out of the way and opened the door. Ereben passed through quickly with the spear. The guard's eyes opened in surprise, but were promptly returned to their slumber by a single blow from Barrow's massive fist.

"Which way do we go?" Ereben whispered. They stood in an alley that reeked of rotting vegetables.

"Under the wall...a secret passage," he replied, pointing to the West. "Come alang."

As they crossed a side alley, Ereben caught a glimpse of three giant vultures tethered in the plaza near the gallows. The Protectors were not in sight.

"They'll know we're gone pretty soon," Ereben said.

"Hush lad. Just follow me."

Through a warren of cobbled side streets and dirt alleys, Ereben followed Barrow's lead. Barrow knocked on the side shutter of a small building twenty yards from the western edge of the city. The earthen wall loomed overhead. After a whispered conversation at the window, Barrow took Ereben around to the door. There, they were met by a disheveled dwarf, a young man, wearing a glossy white sleeping gown. He admitted them silently.

"Ye'er carryin' quite the smell, Maister Trench," the sleepy dwarf commented.

"Compliments o' the Baillie's hospitality," Barrow replied.

"Trench?" Ereben asked, incredulous.

"Aye," Barrow said with a small shrug, "Whittig Trench at yer service."

Ereben considered his conversations with Barrow over the past few days. The dwarf had seemed more interested in the details of Ereben's story than a stranger might be. But Ereben had attributed that to the dwarf's isolation. Ereben did not understand why Barrow would choose to hide his identity from him.

"My nephew," Barrow indicated the young dwarf, "will fare best afore the Baillie by remainin' ignorant o' yer name for now. And we would be wise tae lift our steps a bit."

Barrow's nephew pushed the base of a brazier to reveal a trapdoor in the wooden floor. Barrow opened the entrance to an unlit tunnel. He stepped into it.

"Light a fire in the brazier," Barrow reminded his nephew, "the moment we have gone."

"That I shall do, Uncle Barrow."

Ereben followed Barrow into the hole, deeply gouging its dirt floor while forcing his Shouda spear to make the turn. The hatch closed above, leaving them in total darkness. Crawling on hands and knees, Ereben kept close to Barrow as they proceeded. He thought how fortunate he was that dwarfs are not as thin as they are short, otherwise he would never have fit into the tunnel. The air was stale and moist. For a quarter hour they continued along a gradually descending course, then abruptly climbed a short, steep incline.

"The passage opens here in a rig o' heather," Barrow said at last. "This is one route from Zink that the Baillie hes never discovert."

Daylight shot in as Barrow opened the wooden disc at the end of the tunnel. Barrow climbed out.

"How far are we from the city wall?" Ereben called out. He could not see Barrow. There was no reply. Ereben's spear was caught in the final angle of the tunnel. He left it and vaulted through the opening. "How far..."

There among the yard-high heather stood Barrow, flanked on either side by a Protector of Dragomin twice his height. Each held a longsword to Barrow's sides. Ereben turned. Behind him stood a third Protector, sword drawn.

"Give me your weapon," the third Protector demanded.

"I don't have any weapon," Ereben answered.

"Tell me where you have hidden it."

Ereben detected a definite expression of concern creeping onto the face of the Protector. If they had wanted to kill him and his companion, Ereben surmised, they could easily have dispatched them as he and Barrow climbed from the tunnel. He forced himself to avoid looking in the direction of the tunnel opening, where his spear lay wedged below the entry. "They don't allow any weapons in the..." His words were cut off by a fearsome blow from the Protectors sword hand. Ereben sprawled face down in the heather, his lip tasting of blood mingled with dirt.

"Check the tunnel," one of the other Protectors said.

A frightening screech sounded nearby. Ereben looked up, but could not see above the heather. Other horrid screeches followed.

"Stop them!" shouted one Protector.

As the three protectors turned away from Ereben, he watched a giant vulture lift into the sky, flames sprouting from its neck and wings. Two other vultures, also alight with patches of flame, rose from the surrounding heather. The gyrations of their agony seemed to fan the flames. Higher they struggled into the misty blue sky of dawn, flapping and flailing wings and legs. As hated and as hideous as these creatures were, Ereben could only feel horror and pity as the relentless flames consumed them. One by one, their screams fell silent as they dropped from the sky. Sounds of battle filled the air.

"Back in the tunnel!" Barrow shouted, as he dove past Ereben.

Ereben crawled toward the tunnel opening. Unable to resist the urge to know what was happening, he raised his head above the heather. Before him, in the heather-choked valley west of the city moat, the three crimson and black clad Protectors battled dozens of figures dressed in cowled black robes. A crackling of light and fire danced back and forth between the two sides. The Protectors deflected each assault. Some of the robed assailants lay on the ground as smoldering heaps of burning rubble. One of the robed figures, of its own accord, burst into flames and collapsed. An acrid smell of burning flesh brought home the reality of what his mind could not accept.

A stubby hand with a grip of iron pulled Ereben into the tunnel. The lid slammed shut. In complete darkness he still saw flames.

ꝏ

The struggle to reach a goal is often of greater value than achieving it.

Ereben Leaf: Chronicle of the Counterspell

As Ereben waited with Barrow in the dark tunnel entrance for the sounds of battle to fade, Ereben explained what little he had seen of the strange combat. He again avoided any reference to his own experiences that might explain the powers wielded by the Protectors and their opponents.

A grunting sound approached from within the tunnel. "Owf..."

"Mither o' the gods!" Barrow exclaimed.

"Uncle Barrow?" asked a voice from the darkness of the tunnel.

"What in the name o' the starns are ye doin' here, Vestal Pit?" Barrow grumbled.

"The Baillie hes learnt o' the tunnel," the voice replied. "His maid warned me that they were comin' tae tak me. So I thought I hed better mak for it. What are ye doin' still in the tunnel, uncle?"

"It appears that we all are waitin' tae be carried off tae the gallows. Three o' Corban's butchers nearly finished us, but they were distractit by a group o' unhappy folk from the upland."

Sudden light seared Ereben's eyes. Someone had opened the tunnel hatch from above.

"Elloh be praised," spoke a familiar voice from above. "There is little time for us to escape. Come now."

Ereben's eyes gradually discerned an unmistakable silhouette against the sky. "Otah Kadeef, am I glad to see you. What happened out there?"

"Later," Otah replied. "We must go now."

"My spear is trapped at the turn here," Ereben pointed out. "We need to gouge the opening just a little, right here."

Two other heads peered into the opening of the tunnel, then three spears began to loosen the dirt where Ereben's spear would pass. His spear cleared the opening. Ereben hopped out, followed by Barrow and his nephew.

"We must go now, my Prince," insisted Amal Hidad, starting off toward the North.

"Nae, not that way, my brown friend," Barrow said. "This way." He pointed a stubby finger toward the open plain.

"There is more cover toward the hills," Amal pointed out, apparently irritated by the intrusion of the dwarf.

"Indeed the hills mak safer travel," Barrow continued, "but young Maister Ereben will be needin' to speak with someone who bides across the desert t' the sou'weslan."

The eyes of the Shouda men fell on Ereben. He could only shrug.

"This way," Barrow said to the Shouda. "Ye may want t' consider makin' yersels a bit shorter. The heather can hide only so much of a man's height."

The Shouda men were clearly annoyed by Barrow's lack of diplomacy, not to mention his aroma. Ereben could see the bickering continuing until they were all arrested. "Otah," Ereben interceded, "allow me to introduce Whittig Trench."

Otah Kadeef, Prince of Shouda, raised his eyebrows in surprise, then bowed in the Shouda fashion, introducing himself and his companions. Barrow grasped their extended hands, one by one, nodding his head to each. Since Barrow ignored his nephew, Ereben introduced Vestal. Vestal simply stared with wide eyes at the tall, brown men.

After reclaiming his belongings from the Shouda, Ereben departed from the city of Zink, crouching through the stands of heather, following Barrow's lead. Ereben was amused that, even under the open sky, the dwarfs could walk upright, while he and his Shouda companions were obliged to stoop.

An hour of walking carried them far enough from Zink to permit a slower pace. Otah Kadeef and Minkar Jarad explained what had transpired during Ereben's escape. The Shouda men had taken up hiding places along the earthen wall in locations which provided a vantage of the Baillie's building.

Shortly after dawn, three giant vultures, ridden by Protectors of Dragomin, landed in the central plaza. While the Protectors went to the Baillie's hall, dozens of black-robed priests entered the city through the main tunnel. They marched to the gallows and claimed the body of the hanged priest. The returning Protectors were accosted by the angry priests, but managed to escape on their vultures.

The Protectors flew over the city wall, directly to the opening of the tunnel. There they waited for Ereben and Barrow. Meanwhile, the robed men ran out of the city entrance and surrounded the giant vultures. Praying together, the priests conjured balls of flame, which they cast onto the vultures. Only with the screams of their vultures did the Protectors realize that the priests had followed them out of the city.

Minkar described the battle that followed in terms that sounded too familiar to Ereben. From their swords, the Protectors called up demons of fire which caused priests to burst into flames. The priests chanted together and cast balls of flame back at the Protectors. The flames sent by the priests had no effect on the Protectors, but when one of the flames struck a Protector's sword, the Protector wielding it exploded into cinders. In this manner, the priests defeated the Protectors. When the battle was over, two dozen priests lay dead. Nothing remained of the Protectors but their longswords and shredded armor. The surviving priests refused to touch the Protector's swords, proclaiming that they were unclean.

The Shouda men waited until the priests had gone, then descended the wall. They decided that, since the swords seemed to carry a special power, they should be collected and carried back to Ibrah, Mufta Gebir of the Shouda. Each of the Shouda men now carried one of the longswords lashed to his pack.

"Yonder priests are fortunate that those butchers didna bring their flock o' corbies along with the great bizzards." Barrow spoke over his shoulder as he continued to walk in the lead.

"What are corbies?" Ereben asked.

"A corbie is a ill-theif, mirky bird what reaves yer crops and chickies. But, once afore, nirly two month past, I saw one o' Corban's butchers ridin' a great, black bizzard. Flyin' close aneath, came a whole flock o' corbies, every blastit one as big as a highlan' kerr. They swoopt across the wes'lan brae, castin' a blood cold shadow that covert the grass like a swerlie plague."

"The ravens?" Ereben asked, excited. "You saw the ravens?"

"Aye, lad, ravens is what they call them in the wes'lan parts."

For another half hour, the six of them, Ereben, three Shouda men and two dwarfs, trudged silently to the southwest, following no path that Ereben could discern. He ached to ask Barrow what he knew of his grandfather, Chrysanthus, or of the horrors that had swept into his life so suddenly. *Like a flock o' corbies.* But he feared the reaction of Otah, Minkar and Amal. So much of what he presently understood would be seen by the Shouda men as the work of demons. "Why do they call you 'Barrow'?", he asked absently.

"My brithers have called me by that name ever since I was a weenie."

"I was telt," Vestal said from behind Ereben, "that they called ye 'Barrow' on account o' ye bein' larger than both yer elder brithers pit thegither. Nae disrespect intended, Uncle."

"Vestal, lad," Barrow responded, "I must tell ye how glad I am that ye'er here tae clarify such mysteries."

"Barrow..." Ereben said.

"Yes, Maister Ereben?"

"Where are we heading?"

"Many day away, across the barrens, there bides a man called Hobart. He was a dear friend o' yer grandfather, Chrysanthus. And I trust Hobart can answer some o' yer questions about the doin's o' the High Protector o' Dragomin. The night, though, we stop at the home o' Liddie Burn, a bonnie, and I must say, sonsy lady."

"Sonsy?" Ereben inquired.

"Aye, better endowed than most, up where it counts, if ye know what I mean. She hes a coo farm in the suthron strath, aside the Clootie River. I have been dreamin' o' bathin' in the river and swoomin' in her arms every night in the Baillie's cell. Naturally, her farm stands right along our path."

Toward sunset, the party descended a long and gradual slope to the banks of a crystal river coursing over its rocky bed. Ereben could see cattle grazing on the far bank. Beyond them stood a farm similar to the mound buildings in the foothills above Zink. When Barrow was within fifty yards of the river, he began to remove his filthy clothing, dropping it as he walked. By the time he reached the water, he was walking completely naked.

Vestal, still walking behind Ereben, laughed aloud. "Uncle Barrow has finally revealt the better side o' his character."

"He has no shame," Minkar commented.

"What I have," Barrow shouted over his shoulder as he plunged into a deeper spot in the river, "is a stench that is better left behind."

Ereben waded across the rushing water. When he reached the southern bank, he removed his pack, tossed it onto the dry land, then spread his arms and fell backward into the water. His companions exchanged glances, then followed suit. There they lay for a quarter hour.

"What is all this goin's on?" called a robust feminine voice. A handsome dwarf woman appeared at the southern bank. She wore dusty leather trousers, a leather vest and a broad brimmed leather hat. Her hands rested upon solid hips, emphasizing her breasts. The expression on her face reminded Ereben of the many times his mother had discovered him and his brother getting into mischief.

Ereben sat up, chest deep in the water. He turned to see how Barrow, still bathing bare-skin, would react.

"Ahah!" Barrow shouted with a gaping grin. "Liddie Burn, this is yer lucky day. Auld Barrow has come t' save ye from the boredoms o' the farmin' life." That said, he stood up naked and strutted to the water's edge.

With no sign of embarrassment, the dwarf woman pursed her lips in concentration and surveyed Barrow from top to bottom. "Aye, I can see as how there could be truth amongst yer braggin', Maister Trench. Come in the house and dress yersel afore the kelpies nibble away yer treasures."

Liddie Burn extended one hand to assist Barrow up the rocky bank. Arm in arm, they walked toward the house, both chuckling as their hips collided. Ereben searched the water surrounding him. He did not know what kelpies were, but felt safer seeing nothing but water moving about him. He noticed Minkar Jarad also looking about him. When their eyes met, they exchanged a smile of understanding. Vestal laughed aloud as he climbed from the water and vanished in the direction of the house.

Ereben and the Shouda men climbed the bank. Doffing as much of their clothing as modesty would allow, they spread clothing and metal jerkins to dry in the waning sunlight.

"Thank you for helping us to escape," Ereben said to Otah.

Otah stood, staring pensively at Ereben. "Your strange powers have concerned us greatly, Ereben Leaf. But each day we see yet stranger events. We have discussed this among ourselves, and reached the conclusion that there is much that we do not understand—can not understand. The Tor, the Great Book, teaches us that which is right and that which is wrong. It speaks of the powers of evil, which when embraced, drag one irretrievably into the pit of pain." Otah came and sat beside Ereben. "We have come to know you and to worry for you. Because you have wielded strange powers to work good rather than evil, we must acknowledge that there exist powers not mentioned within the holy confines of the Tor. While we do not condone your use of these powers, we likewise can not condemn you." He stood again, placing a hand on Ereben's shoulder. "And you are our friend."

Ereben forced back tears. He nodded his head once, then stood and bowed, both hands extended, in the Shouda fashion. Otah solemnly returned the bow. Minkar and Amal stood and bowed as well. Warmth rose within Ereben's breast. The emptiness he had felt since their confrontation above the Ledge of Leopards filled with a sense of belonging.

From a distance, the neighing of a horse dissolved their silent bond. Near the river bank, fifty yards east, a horse struggled to free itself. Ereben and the Shouda men ran toward the distressed animal. It was mired in the shallows, apparently unable to find firm enough footing to extricate itself from the mud. The white mare wore no halter by which they might assist her. Ereben looked for wood or flat stones to place over the mud, but with few trees in the area, and only small round stones nearby, he saw no easy way to assist.

"Be still," Minkar said gently to the mare, as he stepped into the mud, holding his hand toward the mare's nostrils. When he reached her, he simply rubbed her behind the ears and mumbled soft words.

Otah began to spread small stones into the mud between the mare and solid ground. Ereben joined him.

"I'm afraid her hooves will slip around them," Ereben pointed out.

"Amal has the answer," Otah replied.

Amal, who had gone back to their clothing, returned with four steel jerkins draped over his arm. When the bed of small stones reached to solid ground, he spread the chain jerkins over them. With one hand grasping her mane and the other under her mouth, Minkar led the mare up onto stones and free of the mud. Amal tied a halter of twine, and with it led the mare to the side of a cattle pen near the mound house. There he tied it to a post.

"She is a strong and handsome mare," Amal observed.

"The finest I have ever seen," Minkar added.

The four of them walked to the darkening river to wash mud from themselves and their steel jerkins. When they returned to the house, the mare was gone. Ereben looked within the pen and about the broad expanse of valley, but saw only cattle.

Barrow appeared at the entry slope of the house wearing leather trousers and a baggy brown shirt. "Come and dry yersels at the hearthfire. Liddie, bless her, is warmin' up a cauldron o' stew."

Ereben stooped through the entryway. He was relieved to see that the floor of the house was sunken below ground level. From the outside, the house had appeared to be barely high enough for a dwarf's head to clear the roof. Inside, however, he could just stand upright without touching the slabs of the roofstones. The Shouda men were not as fortunate, although once seated in the hearth chamber, they seemed as comfortable as the rest. The internal walls of the house were constructed with vertical slabs of stone, with nooks here and there for food and household items. Even the dwarf-size beds were stone, covered with cushions and hide blankets. The hearth was recessed into a central wall, its stones radiating warmth throughout the chamber. From an iron hook, a crusted, black kettle hung low over the fire, bubbling and filling the chamber with aromas of beef and onions.

"I am called Otah Kadeef," Otah said formally to Liddie Burn. His bow vaguely resembled a Shouda greeting, since he remained seated beneath the low ceiling. As he introduced Minkar Jarad, Minkar stood in a bowed position, arms awkwardly extended. When Minkar rose from the bow, his head banged the roofstone. Everyone, including Minkar, broke into laughter. "And," Otah continued through his laughter, "my Sergeant at Arms, who will remain seated, is called Amal Hidad."

"Well, laddies," Liddie responded with a broad smile, "my name is Liddie Burn. Anyone whats can put up with this randie bastard, with his hair all tousie and his bum showin' for all the world t' see, is a welcome guest in my house."

Into the evening, they exchanged stories. Ereben learned from Liddie of a new religious sect, called the True Faith, that had been preaching against the High Protector of Dragomin, and that Corban's Protectors had been hanging these priests as heretics. She thought this might explain the battle witnessed outside the walls of Zink.

"I'll wager that Corban's butchers keep a better watch over thir mounts in the future," Barrow said, as he moved about the hearth chamber, offering them cups of yellow liquid.

"Speaking of mounts," said Ereben, "we pulled.... What is this stuff?" The odor from the cup of liquid vaguely reminded him of the stench of the Baillie's prison.

"My very own barley-brie," Liddie answered proudly, "stored a hundert day."

"It's very... full flavored," Ereben added, forcing himself to swallow a sip without gagging. "We found your mare stuck in the mud of the shallows." He noticed that Liddie appeared puzzled, so he continued. "We got her out and tied her to a post by the pen, but somehow she ran away again."

Liddie looked to Barrow, who only shrugged. "Yer manner o' speakin' is a wee bit hard to follow, Ereben," she said.

"We discovered your mare," Minkar attempted to clarify, "caught within the deep mud beside the river."

"But I have nae ponies, Maister Jarad," she stated.

"This was no pony," Minkar went on, "but a fine and tall horse."

Liddie paused to look at each of the Shouda men, then at Ereben. "There are nae horses in all Knurlan. We have only ponies. Dwarfs are not tall enough t' mount a horse... excep' from a ladder." She paused again. "Ye must have seen a kelpie."

With those words, Barrow and Vestal exchanged worried glances.

"Is a kelpie like a horse?" Ereben asked. He wasn't certain that he wanted to hear the answer.

Barrow cleared his throat, emptied his cup of barley-brie, and said, "A kelpie is a water demon. They tak pleasure seein' people drown. I have heared it telt that they sometimes cause people to drown. They can alter thir shape, lookin' like a horse one time, like a winged fish the next."

"The mare," Minkar protested, "was a well bred animal, showing fear while trapped in the mud, and showing gratitude when comforted and assisted."

Liddie replied in a deliberate staccato, "There are nae horses in Knurlan."

"We seem to be surrounded by demons," Amal said with obvious sarcasm.

From outside came the neighs of many animals, accompanied by hoof beats and the splashing of water. The Shouda men grabbed their bows and quivers as they ran, stooping, toward the entry. Ereben drew his dagger and followed them. When he stepped into the chill night air, he found that he was standing before seven dwarfs, armed with battle axes and mounted on ponies half the size of the mare they had freed earlier. The dwarfs carried torches, which enabled Ereben to recognize the lead dwarf as the Baillie of Zink.

"Throw doon yer weapons," the Baillie demanded.

"There," a voice from the rear said, "he's got it in his hand."

Ereben saw, beyond the glare of the torches, a wagon drawn by four ponies. On the seat of the wagon were two full size men, dressed in black armor and crimson capes. Though fear settled over Ereben like a smothering blanket, he attempted to understand what he now saw. *They can't fly the vultures in the dark. And they're too tall for the dwarf's ponies.* By now, Barrow, Liddie and Vestal had come out of the house. Ereben remembered that he had once defeated a lone Protector, but two, accompanied by armed dwarfs seemed hopeless.

"Give me your dagger, Ereben Leaf," one of the Protectors said, as he stood in the front of the wagon, his sword drawn. "Give me the dagger, and we will leave you all unharmed."

So that's it! They don't care about me. Only my dagger. Grandpa's dagger was missing. They killed him! They killed my family! Blind with anger, Ereben reached behind and grasped his spear, which had been left outside the entryway. He took one step toward the dwarfs. "They murdered my family!" he shouted at the dwarfs. They murdered my family!" He stepped closer.

The mounted guards hopped from their ponies, battle-axes held high. Three Shouda men knocked arrows in their bows. Barrow, wielding a massive cudgel, advanced to stand beside Ereben. Liddie came with him, holding an iron flail. The Baillie, still mounted, sidestepped his pony away from Ereben and closer to the wagon bearing the Protectors of Dragomin.

"If it is death that you wish," the Protector shouted, "then it will be death." He and the second Protector jumped down from the wagon and walked slowly toward Ereben, their longswords held ominously before them.

All the ponies reared and bolted without warning. The Baillie was thrown to the ground. Each of the ponies ran in a different direction. One of the four hitched to the wagon tore away from its harness. The other three sent the wagon careening into the river. The guards looked about in confusion. The two Protectors of Dragomin continued to approach Ereben.

From the darkness of the river, three full size horses cantered to a position between Ereben's party and their attackers. While the dwarf guards stared in amazement at the horses, the Protectors continued their advance, their longswords now held high. Two of the horses, stallions, reared up to face the Protectors, flailing their hooves. Without hesitation, one Protector brought his longsword full swing into the neck of a stallion. It sliced cleanly through. The horse seemed uninjured. He swung again into the stallion's neck. Again it passed through, and again the horse seemed uninjured, though angrier. The second Protector advanced on the second rearing stallion. With his sword held in both hands, he drove the yard-long blade into the stallion's heart. With the blow of a single hoof, the Protector was thrown onto his back. He scrambled to his feet.

The two Protectors then stood side by side. Flashes of light leapt from their swords into the bodies of the stallions. Both horses staggered backwards. A terrifying groan filled the air. Ereben watched in disbelief as the stallions began to melt. The third horse, a white mare, did not move. The melting stallions shrank to the shape and size of wolves, as the deafening groan continued. They rose up on their hind legs, their bodies swirling rainbows of changing colors. As their shapes continued to change, their size began to increase. The Protectors sent searing tongues of flame again into the shapes before them. Instead of staggering or showing any sign of injury, the shapes grew more rapidly, with the sickening crunch of torn joints.

Between Ereben and the Protectors, there now stood two great, horrid creatures, three times the height of a man. Each stood upright on two cloven hooves. Their backs were deformed, with a hump at one shoulder. The spidery, clawed hands of these beasts continued to lengthen as they dangled beside backward knees. Perched upon equine necks, their heads resembled that of a horse with a wolf's muzzle. Goat-like eyes glowed sickly red.

One beast swallowed the flame of a Protector's sword, then stooped and decapitated him with a single bite. The Protector's body toppled like a felled tree, pumping appalling spurts of dark blood over the dry ground. The second Protector turned to flee, but was grasped in the claws of the other beast. The Protector screamed and thrashed as the beast devoured one leg, then the second. The screams began to fade as the beast bit off the left arm, then the right, allowing the sword to drop to the ground. After eating the armored torso in two bites, the beast placed the head on the severed neck of the first Protector.

All of the dwarf guards turned and fled unpersued. With a sizzling noise, the two demon beasts shrank once again to the forms of stallions, then cantered into the river, where they vanished beneath the gurgling surface.

The remaining horse, the mare, turned to face the Shouda men, who stood motionless. She reared up with a deafening neigh. Otah, Amal, Minkar and Ereben bowed, arms extended in the Shouda fashion. The mare turned a full circle, then followed the stallions into the dark waters of the Clootie River.

ഋരദ

It shall be well with those who seek the will of Dragomin, for they shall eat the fruit of his bounty. But woe unto those who seek him not, for they shall be cast headlong from the edges of the earth into the pit of everlasting destruction, and shall be no more.

Crotus: Wisdom of the True Faith

The pounding in Jasper's chest resounded in counterpoint to the tiny footsteps on his shoulder. Titus ran from Jasper's left shoulder to his right, then dove into the silver wolfskin hood, which drooped onto his backpack.

Steel plates clanked with each step, as the armored man approached Jasper and his companions. From the opposite direction, endless waves of legs propelled the giant millipede toward them with surprising speed. The Shouda men assumed defensive positions, their spears held ready. Hanarah stood behind her father. Bahsa clung trembling to Jasper's left leg. Jasper was frozen with indecision. Either of them, the millipede or the armored man, could easily overwhelm the six of them. Jasper drew Rat Slayer from its sheath as the group stepped slowly back toward the corridor from which they had entered the great square.

The millipede turned to follow Jasper and the others. The armored man stepped directly toward the flank of the millipede. Swinging the two handed sword back and over his head, he struck the millipede. Nearly two yards of steel blade glanced from the equally armored skin of the millipede, severing three of its countless legs. The millipede convulsed. Green liquid oozed from the severed stumps. Tipping its head to the side of the injury, the millipede slammed into the armored man, throwing him to the floor. Its massive jaws instantly grasped the man's torso.

Jasper freed himself from Bahsa's grip. Two Shouda spears bounced from the millipede's glistening black armor. With Rat

Slayer held before him, Jasper lunged at the base of one of the millipede's two antennae. Only the tip of the blade penetrated between the joints of armor, but the creature jerked back, dropping the armored man, and turned once again toward Jasper. From his supine position, the mysterious armored man rolled and stood just behind the creature's head. Carefully placing the tip of his great sword at the joint of the millipede's armor, he plunged it to the hilt. The writhing of the millipede lifted the man to the ceiling. Still he clung to the sword with both hands, his momentum sweeping the blade within the creature's body. Again the millipede lurched, rolling away from Jasper. The great sword slipped out as the creature curled against the stone cylinder of a pinnacle. There it remained, as pungent, green liquid poured from its wound and spread across the floor.

The armored man staggered to his feet. With the sword held high, he approached Jasper. "Rodsleer," echoed from within the steel helmet. The man shook the great sword three times.

"Menash?" Jasper exclaimed. He was aware of Titus resting once again on his left shoulder.

The man struggled briefly with the visor, then raised it to reveal a victorious smile on the dark brown face of Menash. He sheathed his sword, then pressed his palms together before his face, spreading them into a Shouda-like bow. Menash watched curiously as the Shouda men bowed in response. Bahsa joined them. Menash spoke to them in his unintelligible language. To Jasper's surprise, Mufta Ibrah answered haltingly.

"He speaks the ancient tongue, Shadae" the Mufta said, "the language of the Tor."

With Mufta Ibrah as interpreter, each member of the party was introduced. In keeping with Shouda custom, Hanarah was introduced after all the males, including Bahsa. When the Mufta realized with apparent embarrassment that he had omitted himself, he said simply, "Ibrah Kadeef."

"Ibrah, Mufta Gebir," Oor Shakur added.

Menash dropped immediately to one knee and bowed his head. Ibrah touched the steel plate covering Menash's shoulder and spoke soft words to him in Shadae, the ancient language. Menash rose with a mournful face, drew his great sword and presented it to the Mufta. He removed his steel helmet and again knelt respectfully before the Mufta with Shadae words that even Jasper understood to be solemn. Ibrah, Mufta Gebir of the Shouda, bid him rise and returned the sword to Menash.

"What does all that mean?" Jasper asked.

"Ssss!" Oor Shakur signaled, shaking his head.

"It is well that he should ask," Ibrah said to Oor. "Menash tells me," he said to them all, "that he was cast out by his people for his refusal to believe their prophecy that some day the Mufta would come to deliver them into freedom. I do not understand the meaning of this. Nevertheless, Menash has asked for my forgiveness and pledged his service."

For three days, they lived within the relative safety of the labyrinth of tunnels, away from the larger creatures which, according to Menash, inhabited only the Great Square. Mufta Ibrah spent much of his time speaking with Menash in the ancient language, Shadae. Despite Jasper's endless questions, the Mufta revealed little of what he learned from Menash. So Jasper passed the time exploring with Bahsa, who still refused to speak, though he eagerly awaited his turn at having Titus ride on his shoulder. On their excursions, they were sometimes accompanied by the Mufta's daughter, Hanarah, and always guarded by Neebah Dir, whose patience seemed endless. Oor Shakur went daily to the southern sleeping room, where he meticulously traced the map of the labyrinth onto the dark brown skin of his abdomen and chest using an ink made from the soot of the cooking fire. On completing each section of the map, he traced over it once more with the point of a small knife, drawing blood as he went. This done, he spread a paste of munu mushroom over the injured skin to prevent it from festering.

As the milky white stone of the labyrinth darkened with evening on the third day, Ibrah led them together to the armory. Neebah Dir drew in his breath at his first sight of the weapons mounted in dazzling ranks over the walls and across the racks. Bahsa and Hanarah simply stood and stared.

"Menash and Oor Shakur," the Mufta said, "have traveled to each of the three entrances from the surface. The Protectors and their great vultures keep vigil, preventing our escape."

"Can we never leave, Father?" Hanarah asked.

"Those entrances are closed to us now," he answered flatly. With a gesture toward Menash, the Mufta continued. "I have learned that there exists a waterway which delivers water from Shardas Lake into...the rooms which lie beneath the great square."

"It goes down farther than this?" Jasper blurted out.

"Menash has traveled there," the Mufta said, ignoring Jasper's question, "and tells me that it is inhabited by terrible beasts. He believes that we may be able to pass through the waterway, which is too small for the beasts to follow. I have decided that we should use the shadow of night to aid our stealth in slipping past the beasts undetected. Each of you must look about this room of weapons and armor. Choose whatever may be useful to you. We shall undertake this dangerous course when we have finished here."

"Is Menash coming with us?" Jasper asked.

"Yes, Jasper," the Mufta answered.

"Menash," Menash said haltingly, "no goodba."

While the Shouda men replenished their quivers and inspected various pieces of armor, Jasper led Hanarah and Bahsa through the armory, helping them to find something that suited them. Bahsa gazed covetously at the bows, but all were too long for his tiny stature. The spears, likewise, were much too long and heavy for the boy. Hanarah located a small knife, which she hitched to Bahsa's waist.

"This is very sharp," she said to him in a maternal tone, "so you be very careful with it."

Bahsa pouted over the diminutive size of the weapon until he noticed that the glistening yellow guard and pommel, and the red stone handle of his new knife matched Jasper's Rat Slayer. Now apparently pleased with his weapon, Bahsa took up a thin steel greave, which he carried on his left arm like a shield, holding it by its chain clasps.

A snap of wood sounded. Menash approached Hanarah with a spear that he had shortened to match her height. He had whittled through most of the shaft, then snapped the thin core of heartwood. "Hanarah take," he said to her.

Hanarah gratefully accepted the spear from the armored man. She then dressed herself in a chain shirt with an attached hood also of chain. Her final selection was a round metal shield, less than a half-yard across.

The Mufta looked at his daughter and Bahsa. "We have come to this," he said, shaking his head. "Now Shouda children dress for battle." Ibrah accepted a new bowstring from Neebah Dir to string on the bow he had selected. He climbed into a steel chain shirt and added a simple steel helmet. He lifted one of the peculiar weapons which mounted an axe-like blade beneath the spear point. Ibrah held the weapon before Menash and spoke in Shadae.

"Halbart," Menash answered.

"I choose the halbart as my weapon," Ibrah said softly, to no one in particular.

Oor Shakur and Neebah Dir fitted themselves with steel chain shirts and plain helmets, which, like the Mufta's, appeared to Jasper to be nothing more than metal bowls. Each of them selected two well balanced spears.

"When we go below," Neebah Dir said to Jasper, "you and Hanarah and Bahsa must stay behind me. It is your particular duty, Jasper of Nilwid, to guard the safety of Bahsa. Keep him always within your reach. Hanarah," he said directly to the girl, "you are to remain near me. Oor Shakur will have enough to do without worrying for you." He turned to Bahsa. "Bahsa Jarad, you must guard Jasper. Do not allow him to become lost. Do you understand?"

Bahsa silently nodded his head, then shook a scolding finger at Jasper. When Jasper looked to Neebah for an explanation of his strange instructions, the tall Shouda man surreptitiously winked.

They left the security of the armory with Menash in the lead, holding his portion of the bark lantern that Jasper had given him when they had parted before the battle. Neebah followed, with Jasper, Bahsa and Hanarah close behind. Titus rode securely within his leather pouch, tethered to Jasper's hip. Oor Shakur walked in the rear, holding Jasper's half of the bark lantern, with the Mufta directly in front of him. Within a quarter hour, Menash had led them into the breezy southern end of the great square, which continued its ceaseless, low-pitched whistle. In the darkness, illuminated now only by the eerie green glow of the bark lanterns, they passed a patch of debris in which Menash had planted edible weeds. Menash plucked a white flower from a gangly stem, offered what appeared to be a salute to the garden, then ceremoniously ate the flower. As they walked on, Jasper looked for the body of the giant millipede that Menash had slain in the center of the Great Square several days earlier, but the darkness was impenetrable beyond the green glow.

On reaching the southwest corner of the Great Square, they were greeted by two huge moles, the size of pigs, circling nervously in the shadows of a descending stairway. They snorted and clawed the stone floor threateningly. Bahsa took hold of the carved staff in Jasper's left hand. Menash dispatched them both with a single sweep of his two handed sword. He spoke in Shadae.

"Menash says that we must go down here," the Mufta said.

"Yes," Menash added, "doan heer."

"Hold on to my cloak here," Jasper instructed Bahsa, in order to free his staff.

They descended into the stone stairway against an updraft of warm, moist air, reminding Jasper of rat's nests and fox holes. He strained to see the edges of the steps profiled in the glow of Menash's bark lantern, but he moved mostly by the feel of the staff on the steps. The constant pressure of Bahsa's hand holding tight to the wolf fur behind his thigh kept him mindful of watching out for the small boy. He wondered why Bahsa would not speak. Beyond the sounds of their own footsteps, and the constant whistling hum of the Great Square, Jasper thought he could hear a gentle rasping, like winter branches against the wall outside his sleeping chamber in Nilwid. He remembered his younger brother, Willen, killed by the Protector. Willen had been only a little older than Bahsa. Jasper sheathed Rat Slayer, switched his carved staff to his right hand, and took Bahsa's trembling hand into his own. Bahsa squeezed tightly. Jasper returned the squeeze.

At the bottom of the stairway Menash held up the bark lantern, their agreed signal to halt. Mufta Ibrah worked his way to the front of the group to confer in whispers with Menash. Jasper sensed a caution or nervousness about them, something that he had not seen from either of them in battle. He wondered what could be more terrible than the giant vultures or the great millipede. What could be worse than witnessing Lord Corban crumble from one hateful human to a countless swarm of hornets, or whatever they were. He looked about in the darkness. The little that Jasper could see of this lower level of the Great Square seemed the same as the upper, except for an abundance of dust and animal litter scattered about the floor. *And the smell.*

A shadow darker than the surrounding darkness swept past Jasper's face. Only the wind of its passing seemed real. "There's something flying in here," he whispered. It passed again. He swung his staff over his head. It struck a soft object, which emitted a shrill squeak. Soon everyone was swinging either a weapon or their hands, thrashing at a cloud of shadows that seemed to have engulfed them. As quickly as the shadows had appeared, they vanished. Something twitched and rustled at his feet. Jasper looked down to see Bahsa plunging his new knife into the body of what appeared to be a large rat with wings of skin. When the creature moved again, Bahsa stabbed it again.

"It is a bat," Neebah Dir whispered, "a very large bat."

"Can they hurt you?" Jasper asked.

"It is said that they come at night and drink the blood of animals," Neebah replied.

"Now your knife has a name," Jasper whispered to Bahsa. Bahsa looked up from the dead bat, but Jasper could not see his face clearly in the darkness. "You have to name it after the first thing you kill with it. I killed a big rat with my sword, so I had to name it Rat Slayer. Since you killed a bat, your sword has to be called 'Bat Slayer'." Even in the darkness, Jasper could see a smile spread across Bahsa's face. The small boy ceremoniously returned Bat Slayer to its sheath, adjusted the greave he carried on his left arm, and for a moment, posed with unmistakable pride beside his conquered quarry.

The group moved on, now more quickly than before. Jasper guessed that they were walking along the western wall of the Great Square. They proceeded hurriedly to the far corner. Jasper heard the single clink of a sword against the stone floor ahead. The pace of the march did not slow. A few steps later, he was startled by the writhing shape of a serpent. Its severed head lay still on the bloody stone beside its dying body, which appeared to be as big around as Jasper's thigh. Bahsa grasped Jasper's hand once again, as they reached another stairway and descended into its updraft of foul air.

At the bottom of the stairs lay the contorted skeleton of a man, its blackened bones unbroken and clean. A humid stench of rotting flesh wafted from the darkness of this third tier of the Great Square. Menash looked about nervously, then signaled for them to move quickly to another nearby stair, from which issued the sound of rushing water. As Jasper was about to follow Menash, Neebah Dir and Hanarah into the waterway, he turned to look again at the skeleton. Instead, he saw in the eerie green glow of the bark lantern an eye the size of a shield slip from behind a stone pillar. In the darkness, he could not imagine the size or shape of the creature to which it belonged.

"Behind you!" Jasper shouted to Oor Shakur and the Mufta.

Ibrah and Oor looked once over their shoulders, then shoved Jasper and Bahsa down the stairway and into chilling, waist deep water. Bahsa scrambled onto Hanarah. Jasper looked up the steps in time to see the Mufta slip on the damp stone. His fall caused Oor Shakur to trip over him, sending Oor head first down the stairs. Neebah Dir pushed past Jasper and the dazed Oor Shakur and climbed back up the stairs to the aid of his Mufta. Ibrah returned to his feet and swung his halbart in a great arc. A terrifying growl filled the air. When Neebah Dir reached the top of the steps, he hesitated for a moment, then grasped the Mufta from behind with both his hands and threw him down the stairs, into the water. The Mufta's halbart slid down after him, handle first. Blinding light dazzled Jasper's eyes. He heard no scream, only a deafening roar of flame.

"Al Dragoma!" Menash shouted.

Jasper remembered the death of Saikal Sam, and could not stand by and allow Neebah Dir to be killed. He drew Rat Slayer and bounded up the stairs. The Mufta, with a stricken expression on his face, exaggerated by the light of the fading flames, grasped Jasper's right arm and took away the sword. Jasper pulled free and climbed the steps, holding only his carved staff. Three steps from the top, he stopped. He saw no beast, only the smoldering remains of Neebah Dir, his flesh completely burned away. Neebah's steel chain shirt lay partly melted. Of Neebah's spears, all that remained were the steel points glowing dull red against the blackened stone floor. Jasper's nostrils stung with the smell of burnt flesh and burnt fabric. A sound of claws against stone receded into the darkness.

A hand from behind gently led Jasper back down the stairs and into the cold water. "He gave himself to save his Mufta," Oor Shakur whispered, as they waded through the deepening water of the tunnel. "He dwells now in the arms of Elloh. Menash will now guard the Mufta's daughter. You, Jasper of Nilwid, must alone guard Bahsa Jarad until we are free from danger. We will be close by."

When the flowing chill of the water reached Jasper's chest, he took Bahsa from Hanarah and held him in his left arm, propped against his hip. That simple act brought with it a flood of memories of his brother Willen, whom he had carried like this so many times. Jasper began to cry as he trudged against the steady flow of water. He wished there had been some way to save the people he cared about, but he was too young, too small, and always too late to do anything but feel the pain. He hugged Bahsa and kissed him once on the cheek. Bahsa rested his head against Jasper's shoulder.

The roof of the waterway gradually lowered, so that only their heads extended above the water. Jasper gave Bahsa Titus' pouch to hold high. Menash had removed his steel helmet. After half an hour of fighting the water, they stopped. The roof ended at a wall, beneath which the water flowed toward them. Menash spoke with the Mufta.

"Menash has never gone beyond this point," Ibrah said. "He does not know how far we must go under water before we will find air to breathe."

"I will swim through," Oor Shakur volunteered. "If I do not return, then you must go back to the labyrinth."

"Go no greater distance than will allow you to return safely, Oor," the Mufta instructed him. "I do not wish to lose you."

Oor gave his weapons and gear to Menash, then disappeared beneath the dark surface of the water. No one spoke. Bahsa held more tightly to Jasper. With a sudden splash of water, Oor surfaced.

"The distance is short," Oor said, somewhat out of breath. "It is perhaps three or four yards."

"What about Bahsa?" Jasper asked.

"I will take him," Oor Shakur stated. He reached for Bahsa, but Bahsa clung tenaciously to Jasper's neck.

"Can you hold your breath?" Jasper asked him. The boy nodded. "I guess I'll take ..." Something grasped Jasper's right ankle and immediately pulled him under the water. He was unprepared, and needed to breathe. Bahsa came with him, still holding Jasper's neck. Jasper released his staff, drew Rat Slayer and passed it beside his right leg. The blade struck. The grip about his ankle tightened. He plunged the blade into the dense tissue that held him. He was free. Jasper erupted from the surface of the water, banging his head on the roof of the waterway. He looked at Bahsa, who simply smiled, as though this had been a test of his ability to hold his breath. Bahsa's left hand sealed the opening of Titus' pouch in its tiny grip.

"Your staff," said Oor Shakur, also seeming to be unaware of the attack.

"I think we should go now," Jasper suggested, with some urgency. "We have company in the water. Are you ready?" he asked Bahsa. The boy nodded. With a deep breath, Jasper dipped again beneath the surface and swam with Bahsa into the submerged portion of the waterway. After only a few strokes, they surfaced into total darkness. The air was rich with the smells of autumn. The floor of the waterway bore the irregularities of a natural cave.

"That was pretty easy, wasn't it?" Jasper said to the boy clinging to his side. He reached to his right, but felt no wall. The cave seemed to be much wider than the stone tunnel. From behind came the slosh of someone else surfacing. A bark lantern cast a green glow, illuminating the spacious, brown walls of a cavern curving into the distance. Water streamed through the center, with a sandy shelf along either side. A muskrat fled out of sight around the curve. "Did you see that, Bahsa?" Jasper asked. "That muskrat means there's a way out." Bahsa handed Jasper the leather pouch in which Titus had made the underwater journey.

Hanarah climbed out of the water and approached Jasper. "Tell me what happened to Neebah," she insisted in a whisper. "Father will not say."

Jasper closed his eyes for a moment, bringing back the horror of Neebah's smoldering body. "He was killed by a beast."

"Was he eaten?" Her eyes fixed expectantly onto Jasper's.

This seemed to Jasper to be her true question. "No."

Hanarah nodded once, then returned to stand beside Menash, who spoke in Shadae with her father.

"I believe this cave leads to the bluffs near the exit of Shardas Lake," the Mufta said. "I know nothing of a cave there, but such was also true of the labyrinth beneath the Shrine. We should go while the night still hides us."

"Two boats were tied by the shore," Oor Shakur said. "We could cross to the far side of the lake."

"No," the Mufta replied. "There may be Shouda warriors who escaped from the southern hills. If any survived, we must find them. The boats will allow us to pass the city safely, on our way to the south-eastern shore. From there, we will climb into the foothills and search for our people."

"A wise decision, Mufta Ibrah," Oor Shakur stated with little conviction.

Ibrah motioned with his hand for Jasper to lead. He accepted the bark lantern from Menash and, setting Bahsa to the ground, gave it to him to hold as they walked along the edge of the water. For nearly an hour they wound their way through the cavern, sometimes having to stoop to clear the low ceiling, but usually walking upright and as comfortably as their wet clothing and armor allowed. The soft sound of rushing water could be heard ahead. As Jasper walked farther, the sound grew louder and the air filled with mist. When the roof of the cavern lifted away, he found himself standing on a stone outcropping behind an enormous waterfall. A small sidestream fed water into the cavern. From the overhanging stone above, a curtain of water roared past the ledge on which he stood and crashed into the darkness below.

"I see now," Oor Shakur shouted above the thunderous noise of the water, "why we were not aware of this cave."

"I see no path leading upward," the Mufta said.

"Heer," Menash shouted, pointing to a steep descent through the side spray of the waterfall.

"It appears that we must climb down," the Mufta decided, "but it is far too dangerous to undertake in the dark. We will rest in the cave until dawn."

Ibrah shouted to Menash in Shadae, then led the group back into the cavern, where they slept under the watch of Menash. When Jasper was awakened by Bahsa, he gathered his belongings and followed the group down huge blocks of water-slicked, brown stone which buttressed the side of the waterfall. At each step, Bahsa was handed down to someone below. A half-hour later, they stood at the base of the waterfall. Jasper looked up in amazement at the great height from which they had climbed. Water cascaded from the cliff above, as though it were pouring directly from the dawn sky.

After removing their armor and setting it out to dry, the men went about constructing a raft of logs and split vine. Jasper took a portion of the split vine and looked for a good spot to place a snare. With Bahsa observing, he looped a snare over the entrance of what appeared to be a rabbit burrow on the side of a dirt bank. He and Bahsa then hid above the hole and waited. When a rabbit finally appeared, Jasper yanked the snare. A deft blow of his staff to the back of the rabbit's neck killed it instantly. He skinned and cleaned the rabbit, then carried it and a bundle of twigs back to the others. Hanarah had gathered wild carrots and onions. At Hanarah's insistence, her father and Oor Shakur loaned her their steel helmets, which she filled with water and placed onto the small fire that Menash had started.

Titus was finally set free from his leather pouch. In a flash, he was off into the underbrush. Bahsa attempted to follow the mouse, but gave up in frustration. Instead, he waded into the edge of the river and collected mussels clinging to the rocky bottom.

Jasper quickly whittled crude wooden spoons. By the time the fifth spoon was carved, rabbit stew and roasted river mussels were waiting to be consumed. Rather than stave his hunger while he carved another spoon, Jasper handed out the five he had carved, then rummaged through his wet backpack until he located the yellow metal spoon he had found during his first trip into the labyrinth. With this, he dove into the pot of stew. He had sucked down three spoonfuls of stew when he noticed that Hanarah, Oor Shakur and the Mufta were staring at him.

"What?" he asked through a mouth filled with stew.

"May I examine your spoon?" the Mufta asked quietly.

Jasper hastily licked the spoon clean, then passed it to the Mufta.

"From where did this come?" Ibrah continued, as he passed the spoon to Oor Shakur.

"I found it in the sleeping room when I first went down into the tunnels."

"I believe," Oor Shakur said, "that it is solid gold."

"I've never seen gold before," Jasper said. "Crotus, our priest back in Nilwid, used to talk about the kingdom of Dragomin that had streets paved in gold. I always thought it was like rocks."

The Mufta showed the spoon to Menash and spoke in Shadae. Menash's reply caused the Mufta's eyebrows to briefly raise before his usually placid facial expression returned.

"What did he say?" Hanarah asked.

"He says that... he has seen this before. He did not know that it was valuable."

Something in the Mufta's manner suggested to Jasper that the Mufta's answer had not left him with a clear conscience. So much of the Mufta's conversations with Menash seemed to leave surprise on the Mufta's face, but his explanations of what he had learned were suspiciously boring.

The log raft drifted lazily down the Iron River, steered only by a long oar at the stern, controlled by Oor Shakur. Menash, who apparently was afraid of sinking with the weight of his plate armor, situated himself in the exact center of the raft. Jasper had often seen the river on his frequent excursions from Nilwid, but had never actually ridden on the water. He found the ride exciting and wonderful. Bahsa as well, was transfixed by the sloshing and swirls of the current, and the occasional spray of water leaping from the bow in the rougher stretches.

Three hours of travel called for a break on solid ground. Oor Shakur maneuvered the clumsy craft through a field of lily pads to the western bank, where they pulled one corner of the raft onto the ground. While everyone walked and stooped to stretch their legs, Titus found bountiful hunting of fat insects on the field of lily pads. He jumped from one to the next, catching a cricket here, a mantis there.

Jasper's attention was drawn to a large swirl which suddenly appeared in the water several yards from the lily pad on which Titus was consuming his latest catch. The swirl was replaced by a wave in the water beneath the lily pads. The wave seemed to head directly toward Titus.

"Titus!" Jasper shouted. "He's a goner this time." Jasper looked out over the river at a large bird that seemed to have also spotted the mouse. The bird swept silently above the water, aiming for Titus. If whatever is under the water doesn't get him, he thought, that bird will.

The water beneath Titus' lily pad erupted with a flash of silver. Titus was quicker. Leaping from pad to pad, the mouse stayed one jump ahead of the fish. But with each jump, Titus was forced farther from the bank, toward the open water. The bird, a large gray owl, circled once, then dove in again. When the mouse reached the edge of the field of lily pads, the fish and the owl converged upon him. Water splashed. Titus was gone. As the owl circled, Jasper could see the squirming mouse within the owl's talons. Jasper's chin quivered as he watched the owl rise into the cloudless blue of mid-day. He saw the owl's flight scribe a great circle in the air, then descend toward him. It flared its wings as it touched the sandy bank two yards from where Jasper sat. From its talons, Titus bolted across the sand and into his leather pouch. The gray owl faced Jasper, blinked one eye then the other.

"Thank you," Jasper whispered. He wondered if this could be the same gray owl that he had met with Ereben. The owl spread its wings and disappeared across the water. Jasper wondered where Ereben was at this moment. He realized for the first time in many days that he missed him

Bahsa, who alone of Jasper's companions had witnessed the rescue of Titus by the gray owl, extracted Titus from the leather pouch and scratched the fur of his back with one finger. Bahsa behaved as though the rescuing of a mouse by an owl was a perfectly ordinary occurrence. When they all resumed their journey down the river, Bahsa took charge of Titus and his leather home.

The river moved their raft swiftly southward. After riding a long and tiring series of modestly steep rapids, their progress slowed where the Iron River widened. Oor Shakur expressed concern at the sighting of a group of five garfish, each the size of a man. Their speed through the water enabled the garfish not only to keep pace with the raft, but to circle it as well. The Mufta followed the movements of the garfish, his halbart in hand.

As the afternoon sun rapidly gave up its warmth, and the shadows grew longer, the Mufta spoke of stopping for the night. Since the river banks had become rocky and steep, they decided to continue a little farther, in hope of spotting a more hospitable place to haul out the raft.

The raft jarred suddenly, as though they had struck a submerged boulder.

"May Elloh protect us," Oor Shakur uttered. "A garfish has broken the oar."

Jasper looked to the stern. Oor Shakur held the remaining half of his oar, which nested uselessly in its crudely lashed yoke.

"We must use our hands to paddle to the bank," Oor said. "I can no longer steer the raft."

Everyone moved to the edges of the raft and began to stroke the water. The Mufta was able to effectively use his halbart as a paddle. Jasper, like everyone else, was forced to use his hands. The dipping of hands into the water of the Iron River seemed to draw the garfish into a tighter circle around the raft. Without a word of suggestion, all hands snapped back from the water. Except for the continuing strokes of the halbart, which the garfish avoided, they abandoned the raft to the will of the river. Southward it glided, slowly rotating in the flows and eddies.

As twilight approached, the noise of the river increased. Fifty yards ahead, the river seemed to drop through yet another series of rapids.

"We will overturn in the rapids," Oor Shakur said to the Mufta.

"Such a fate," the Mufta answered, "is surely better than jumping into the company of the garfish."

Jasper watched the shadows of the garfish beneath the darkening water. They seemed also to sense the approaching rapids. Their circles became tighter and more frantic. Ten yards from the head of the rapids, it happened. The yard long jaws of a garfish rose up from the surface of the river and latched onto the log beside Jasper. Hanarah screamed. From his kneeling position, Ibrah brought a mighty swing of his halbart to rest on the garfish's head. At the same time, two other garfish attacked from the opposite side of the raft. The split twine lashings began to unravel. The raft neared the verge of the rapids. In the fading light and growing desperation, the rapids appeared to Jasper to be steeper and much longer than any they had traversed.

With the first turbulence of the rapids, the raft disintegrated into individual logs. Jasper was heaved into the powerful tumult of current, but not before grasping the arm of Bahsa. Together, they tumbled, swam and ricocheted their way through fountains and boulders and drains. Jasper had strapped on his pack so that he would not lose it. Now he was unable to jettison the deadly weight from his back. Between rare gasps of air, his lungs ached to breath. Each time he surfaced, he struggled to lift Bahsa's head above the heaving surface. The combined weight of his pack and steel chain shirt, and the effort to save Bahsa quickly exhausted him. Only the random upwelling of the current as it passed over the bouldered river bed offered any opportunity to breath. When the violence of the rapids finally ended, Jasper tried to swim, but found himself sinking relentlessly to the river bottom.

As Jasper's mind began to blur from the cold, exhaustion and lack of air, he sensed something solid beneath him. It seemed to lift him through the water. Within moments his head broke the surface. He gasped. Bahsa gasped behind him. Jasper had forgotten Bahsa. He had only been aware of the importance of holding whatever was in his left hand. In the dark twilight he saw that his right hand was grasping the mane of a horse, only the head and neck visible above the water. Bahsa sat behind him and wrapped his arms about Jasper's waist. The horse swam toward the eastern bank. Jasper could not imagine where the horse had come from, to find them at the bottom of a river. As they neared the bank, he was able to retrieve his carved wooden staff when it floated within reach. This he inserted between his back and the pack straps, freeing both his hands to hold tight to the horse's mane.

Jasper expected the horse to stop after climbing the bank, but to his surprise, the horse broke into a gallop, skillfully dodging overhangs and smoothly jumping ditches and obstacles. Southward it galloped for a quarter hour. In the light of the half moon, Jasper could see they were gaining on another galloping horse and rider ahead. The nearer they came, the more certain Jasper became that the rider was Menash, in his steel plate armor, complete with helmet. Like Jasper, Menash held tightly to his horse's mane with both hands. When they came up to a position just behind Menash, the two horses matched their gait.

"Menash!" Jasper yelled.

Menash turned his head in surprise. "Jasper!"

Jasper suspected that Menash had no more idea where the horses had come from or where they were going than he did. He looked behind. Bahsa had buried his head against the side of Jasper's pack. To Jasper's distress, there was no sign of the others. The three of them had been rescued, and were being carried to Dragomin knows where. The others, he guessed, were either rescued as well, or had drowned, or had been eaten by the garfish. He looked back again. No one followed.

On through the night they galloped, farther and farther south. They veered eastward, away from the river and into grassy plains. Jasper found his mind drifting. In the night shadows he saw the empty eye sockets of Crotus, the priest. These merged into the empty eye sockets left by the moths as they departed from the dead Saikal Sahm. He shook his head to clear it. Menash now galloped beside him. Whenever he noticed Bahsa's grip loosening, he slapped the boy's thigh to awaken him. Some time past midnight, they sloshed across a shallow, gravel bottom river. It was there that Jasper thought he saw other horses in the distance, but he wasn't sure.

Their clothes had long since dried out in the wind, but the night air was chill. He was grateful for the warmth of Bahsa's body pressed against him. With this thought, Jasper realized that the body of the horse gave no warmth, despite its galloping for hours on end. There was something clearly unnatural about the horse's appearing from beneath the water. And its endurance as well. What seemed more frightening than both the lack of body warmth and the complete abandon with which it and its partner careened southward, was the definite, gradual increase in their speed. After galloping all night without rest, their pace was accelerating.

Jasper pulled back on the horse's mane, in an attempt to slow the animal, or whatever it was. The horse ignored every attempt to slow its pace or change its direction. Jasper looked at Menash, who only shrugged his armored shoulders and shook his head. If the wild ride continued any longer, Jasper was certain he would no longer be capable of holding on.

The sky began to lighten with dawn. Jasper realized that they were galloping through a barren wasteland at a terrifying pace. All he could do was hold tight to the mane. Any horse's mane would have been torn out by the roots by now, he thought.

They approached a darkness spreading across the horizon, perhaps another river or ravine. Jasper could not see well enough in the early light to make sense of the dark gap. The distances were deceptive, with no shrubs or trees to judge the size of things. Their approach to the dark gap took much longer than he had expected. He guessed that it must have been very far away when he had first seen it. With a surge of power, the horse accelerated even more. A terror filled Jasper's heart. As they sped nearer the gap, it seemed to grow wider and deeper. He blinked his eyes to make them understand. The cold certainty of death swept over him as the earth in front of them fell away. Thirty yards ahead yawned a gaping canyon of shear cliffs, thousands of yards deep and many miles across. The horses sped directly toward the verge of the precipice. Without the slightest hesitation, both horses leapt into the emptiness. Jasper looked down from the unspeakable height to tiny puffs of fog so far below. He knew he and Bahsa and Menash would soon be dead.

Jasper's feet were pushed forward from behind. He looked down again, but could no longer see the puffs of fog or the canyon floor. His view was obscured. With the sudden understanding that comes not in a series of steps, but as a flash of knowing, he saw wings, great wings spanning fifteen yards. *My horse has wings!*

ꝏ

Sometimes we risk our lives searching for what we have always possessed.

Ereben Leaf: Chronicle of the Counterspell

"Those little wee blasties sleep aneath the sand," Vestal Pit complained, as he twisted himself to examine a boil on his bare, right buttock, "prayin' tae their little wee hornie gods for a taste o' flesh tae come along for dinner."

"That looks pretty bad," Ereben commented. "Maybe you should treat it so it doesn't fester."

"With that foul smellin' fungus paste the Shadows put on their every wee scratch? No, thank ye".

"My grandfather used the same stuff for cuts. It really works."

"That is nae cut." Vestal pointed out in as dignified a manner as was possible while pulling his trousers up from his knees.

"I've put some on my ankle, and the bite looks like it's healing."

Barrow returned with Otah Kadeef and Amal Hidad from their climb down to a spring for water. For two days, the six of them had worked their way into the barren canyons of the Burnt Desert. The only trail followed a narrow shelf of scree just below the northern rim of the great canyon. With each westward mile, the canyon grew deeper and the shelf farther above the river. Where they camped this evening, the only source of water was three hundred yards below them, down the precipitous black granite of a side ravine. According to Barrow, the only point for crossing Death River, which tore viciously at its stony entrapment at the bottom of the great canyon, was a solitary footbridge nearly two days away.

"Mither o' the gods!" Barrow gasped, dropping two large water skins beside Minkar Jarad's pitiful twig fire. "The climbin' doon hurts the feet enough withoot turnin' around and climbin' right back up tae the topmost rig o' the canyon."

Vestal turned to his uncle with mock disgust. "I didna hear Maister Kadeef nor Maister Hidad complainin' about bein' so ramfeezl'd over a little walk tae the water."

"We have not breath with which to complain," Otah said dryly.

Barrow noticed the bite on Ereben's ankle. "Where did ye acquire that bite?"

"I don't know. Somewhere yesterday."

"If ye would allow me tae tak a closer look," Barrow said, seating himself with his back toward Ereben and Ereben's foot in his lap. Ereben felt some pressure over the sore on his ankle, then a sharp pain.

"Ow!" He tried to pull his foot away, but Barrow's grip held his leg firmly. "What are you doing?"

"Ye've managed tae get a sand worm. The desert people call it loa loa."

"Aawh!" Ereben cried out. "That hurts."

"That wee worm aneath yer skin needs tae come oot, afore it grows and multiplies. Once that happens, ye're in a terrible fix."

"Did you get it?" Ereben asked. He saw Vestal signaling that he should keep quiet about his boil.

"Nae," Barrow said with a smile of satisfaction, "but I've tied his tail ontae this little twiggie. Four time a day, turn the twig a quarter turn, and it'll wind him oot in three day."

"Can't you just take it all out now?"

"If ye try to pull him all oot at one time, he'll break off, and I'll have tae dig his tail oot again."

Ereben looked at his ankle. The end of a tiny worm was wound onto a twig, held in place with a strip of cloth. Ereben added a touch of munu paste to the wound.

"You may wish," Minkar said, "to wipe away the munu. It may serve to heal the worm as thoroughly as it heals your injury."

Ereben hastily wiped away the munu paste. The tiny twig caused little discomfort when he inserted his foot into his boot. Vestal stooped beside him.

"I'd rather leap off this cliff than let my uncle get near my backside with that knife!"

"But he said it's got to come out."

"I'll tak care o' that mysel. Ye see'd how tender and delicate he can be with the blade."

Low in the western sky, the sun flattened to an orange mound against the edge of earth. Shafts of gold sprang out from its ruptured sphere, leaping across the unimaginable distance, only to spill their richness over the highest elevations of the distant cliffs south of the now darkened canyon. Valleys and tables in between were barren shadows. The unbroken cap of the highest table seemed to reveal the distinctive unevenness of a forest seen from a great distance. The sun seeped away, leaving darkness beneath a starless canopy, stained blue with twilight.

Ereben thought of Phaena's golden hair, alive with echoes of the late day sun, shifting in the summer updrafts of the mountains above Rippleton. Where her face should be, he could only remember tenderness and love. He concentrated on her eyes, her lips, but could not compose a face. Not years, but months, he told himself. So many things had changed over so short a time. *I miss her so much.* He pressed his hand into the center of his chest to blunt the aching. He looked up into the western sky. *Do you still care about me? Did you ever care about me? If there was a way. If I could know your thoughts right now. If I could know that you were safe... that you missed me. This would all be easier. If I could only know.*

A thought snapped him from his reverie. In the darkness, Ereben drew his dagger from its wooden sheath. *Can you glow?* A gentle chill crept slowly from his right hand toward his elbow. The translucent green stone of the handle glowed barely bright enough to convince Ereben that it was not just his imagination. He focused on the chill, encouraging it back toward his hand. The glow dimmed. He released the chill, allowing it to ascend to his upper arm. The glow intensified. A sense of exhilaration filled him as he moved the cold up and down his arm, each time causing a corresponding change in the glow. His whole body shivered. Somehow, he reasoned, the dagger was drawing heat from him. The longer the glow continued, the colder he felt, even though he confined the odd, moveable chill to his right arm. Ereben forced away the chill. The glow extinguished itself.

Ereben sensed that he was on the verge of a significant understanding, but the details would not come together in his mind. He thought about each of the times the dagger had come alive. Each time seemed completely different. The circumstances were different, the sensations he experienced were different, and the outcomes were different. Sometimes he felt nothing. Other times he felt as if he were about to be consumed.

The worm. Ereben removed his boot and loosened the tie over the twig holding the loa loa. In the darkness, he gave it a tiny rotation, then tightened it again. He remembered the mushroom. It might heal the worm as well as the injury. *Munu—praying hands. The praying hands!* Ereben considered the relationship between the praying hands symbol on the knife and the strange power of the knife. Perhaps it was more than mere coincidence that the praying hands symbol which decorated the knives of his grandfather Chrysanthus, and the knives that Chrysanthus had guided him in making, was not only a representation of the munu mushroom, which heals wounds and sickness, but it was also a symbol of the munu revered by the Shouda as a gift to them, given directly by Elloh. The presence of the symbol on his dagger, and at the head of Jasper's staff had certainly encouraged the Shouda to assist him in his search for Whittig Trench—Barrow.

From his leather pouch, Ereben extracted a piece of dried munu. Touching it to the handle, he focused his awareness on bringing light from the stone. Nothing happened. "Great idea," he whispered facetiously. When he turned to place the munu fragment back in the pouch, he was unable to locate the pouch in the dark. Now I need the light, he thought, finding some humor in the irony. The handle glowed. Ereben was startled by a sensation of warmth being drawn from his left hand holding the mushroom, toward his right hand holding the dagger. He discovered that by relaxing and focusing on the passage of warmth through his body, he could slow the flow to dim the light, or release the flow to make it brighter. He knew there was some difference in the way he desired the light, compared to his first attempt with the munu. The two desires came from different aspects of his being. At first, his mind decided on making light. Now, it was something deeper within him that brought the dagger to life. When he finally extinguished the light, the fragment of munu felt smaller, but he was not certain of that.

"You frighten me, Ereben Leaf," a voice said from behind. It was the voice of Minkar Jarad. "You appear to play with demons."

"It's the dagger," Ereben replied. "It acts like a fire. It takes the warmth out of my body to make light. And if I hold the munu, the dagger takes the warmth from it instead of my body. It's like I put a stick in the fire to make it brighter or take it away to make it go out."

"How can it be that a dagger can do such things without the aid of demons?"

"I don't know, but there's something in the munu, and in me, that... turns into light. But it never happens without the dagger. This particular dagger."

"Can your dagger be of such great importance that Corban wishes to have you killed in order to obtain it? Perhaps the dagger is cursed."

"My grandfather had a dagger just like this one, and they killed him for it. And he was just a kind old man."

"Surely a dagger which gives off light is not of so great a value. But the slaying of the Protector near our home, and the slaying and enchantment of the leopards bespeaks a far greater power than the giving off of light."

"I haven't figured that out exactly."

"You appeared to control the light just now. Did you control these other happenings as well?"

"I don't.... No. I didn't control them. But I think those things happened because I wanted them to. All except the Protector. That was really strange. I don't remember thinking anything except how to keep his sword from hitting me. It was like the dagger had a mind of its own."

"The things we speak now would be a sufficient transgression against the laws of Elloh for me to be cast out from the Shouda tribe. The Mufta would declare me haram, accursed, and no Shouda man, woman or child, including my own precious Bahsa, would be permitted to speak with me again for the remainder of my life."

"I'm.... I didn't know.... That's stupid. Why would they do that just for discovering something different... and wonderful?"

"The strength of our people lies in our observance of the laws written in the Tor. If we allow one man to step beyond those laws without consequence, then that which is our strength would be forgotten, and the Shouda people, chosen of Elloh, would be dispersed among other peoples and be no more."

"But this isn't evil. It's just hard to understand. And if you don't understand, then maybe Corban will."

"Such matters are not so easily..."

"And if this dagger gets into Corban's hands, there may not be any Shouda tribe to get thrown out of."

"There may be truth in what you say, Ereben Leaf. It is for that reason that I place my soul in jeopardy to understand these mysteries. But as I grant you my encouragement to explore the nature of these powers, you must understand the very great danger in which I place myself."

"That still seems wrong."

"Whether our laws are right or wrong, they are the laws of the Tor, and they are real, and they may be used to bless or to condemn us both."

Ereben awakened to the dry morning chill of the barrens. He had spent the night in the open, some distance from the others. His pigskin cloak, with its fur singed away in front, had been almost warm enough through the night. It was voices, not the chill, which had awakened him. He gathered his belongings and walked the twenty yards to the camp perched on the high shelf of the great canyon. Vestal and his uncle seemed to be embroiled in another of their frequent and inconsequential disagreements.

"It is only a wee touch o' the grip," Vestal insisted as he backed away from Barrow in short, dwarf steps.

"Ye look as pale as a puff o' steam," Barrow said, "and the grip wouldna' cause ye tae be limpin' like a lame pony." Barrow trapped Vestal against the rising wall of stone. "Now, oot with it. What have ye done to yer leg?"

"It ain't the leg."

"It ain't the leg," Barrow echoed. "Then what in the name o' the starns is it, ye stubborn fool?"

"A spider bite or somethin' has blistered up a boil. It swelt up durin' the night."

"Let's have a look at it."

"It's a wee bit awkwart."

"Vestal," Barrow said impatiently, "I'm growin' mighty tired o' all this argy-bargy. Show me the damn boil!"

"It's on my bum."

"Then turn yersel arselins and show me yer bum!"

Vestal hesitated, looking vainly to Ereben for help, then slowly turned himself around and dropped his trousers. The boil that Ereben had seen the previous evening had healed over. In its place rose a livid mound as big around as a man's hand.

"Mither o' the gods!" Barrow whispered.

Ereben and the three Shouda men crept closer to examine the strange swelling on Vestal's right buttock. A separate living thing seemed to move beneath the taut surface of the skin. Barrow lightly touched the swelling with his fingertips, then wrung his hands together.

"Vestal, my young and foolish nephew," Barrow said in an suddenly kind voice, "It appears that ye didna hear me yestereen speakin' about the sand worm, the loa loa."

"I didna want ye to cut me with yer knife, Uncle."

"I fear that cuttin' with my knife will nae longer provide us with a cure. But I havna any ither way t' get rid o' the blastie." Barrow strode somberly to his pack and returned with a clay bottle, wrapped in wicker and capped with a wooden stopper. He twisted out the stopper and lovingly inhaled the aroma that issued forth. "Drink it all," he said to Vestal, handing him the bottle after one final caress of its wicker cover.

Vestal winced as he took a sip. Barrow indicated to him with the wave of a hand to continue. When the bottle was nearly empty, Barrow took it from his nephew and drained the last drop into his own mouth.

"That was the last o' Liddie's barley-brie." Barrow said regretfully. "Now, lay yersel doon on the ground." As Vestal placed himself prone, Barrow signaled to the others to move in close enough to assist.

While they instinctively knelt at each of Vestal's extremities, Ereben and the Shouda men looked at one another, their faces reflecting an ill ease at what might need to be done. Vestal turned his head to see what his uncle was about to do. Otah Kadeef, who knelt by Vestal's right arm, placed a knee above Vestal's shoulder, blocking the view. Barrow poured a small amount of water onto the blade of his knife, then wiped it across his trousers.

"Our friends are goin' tae help ye remain still, while we tak care o' this," Barrow said as he nodded to the others.

Using the razor point of his knife, with the blade edge turned away from Vestal's skin, Barrow flayed the red swelling in a single motion. Vestal screamed and struggled, but could not move. Blood welled up from the cut. Barrow reached into the gathering pool of blood with his left hand and slowly pulled something out. Trapped within his bloody fingers was the end of a writhing worm, as thick as one of Barrow's stubby fingers. Barrow pulled slowly and firmly. The blood-covered worm slipped through his fingers and vanished into the blood of the wound.

"Blast!" Barrow muttered, plunging his fingers once again into the wound. Despite Vestal's screams, Barrow moved his fingers about the interior of the wound, seeming to locate a deeper hole that admitted one finger. Barrow withdrew his hand and washed it with water. "Dress that with some o' yer fungus medicine, and bind it so it won't be bleedin'." He walked away a short distance.

"You can't get it out?" Ereben asked.

"The worm hes gone deep intae the flesh. There is naught that we can do."

"What will this worm do?" Amal Hidad asked.

"Aye, what will it do," Barrow repeated, throwing his empty bottle of barley-brie into the depths of the canyon. "It will kill the poor fool if we cannot get him tae Hobart in time."

"Have you seen such a thing happen before?" Otah asked, as he cleaned and dressed the wound.

Barrow walked away without answering. He only shook his head. Ereben understood that to mean that he had, and that it wasn't something he wished to recall. Vestal had mercifully passed into sleep.

Ereben removed his boot and gave a twist to the twig Barrow had attached to the worm in his ankle. Looking at the tiny, pale worm, Ereben found it difficult to believe that it could so rapidly grow into the creature that now infested Vestal's body. This tiny worm showed no sign of having grown at all.

Using Shouda spears, they created a litter on which they placed Vestal Pit. The five of them took turns bearing the litter as they walked to the West along the narrow trail of the high shelf. Where the trail offered enough width to safely stand two abreast, four of them would carry Vestal. But where the shelf narrowed, two of them would bear Vestal's entire weight, which was greater than his small stature would have suggested.

By evening, Ereben stood at the head of a trail that would carry them, tomorrow, to the floor of the great canyon, now nearly a mile below. Through the day, they had been unable to find water except at two seep springs near the trail. From here to the bottom, there would be no more water. Ereben could see that the descent would be difficult enough without carrying Vestal on his makeshift litter. With him, it would be dangerous. Already, the five of them were exhausted from the additional burden, and that after carrying him only along the relatively flat terrain of the high shelf.

Vestal had spent most of the day's journey asleep, but when he had awakened he had not known where he was. His pallor had become more noticeable through the day. Now only his breathing and occasional, brief periods of delirium endowed him with any recognizable hint of being alive. Ereben doubted that the young dwarf man would survive the night.

After a dinner of dried beef and bread, the five of them sat quietly watching the sun set. A forlorn sense of growing futility blanketed their spirits. Ereben wondered if this Hobart would be of any real help. The Shouda had been kind to help him, but they were really no closer to finding an explanation for Corban's vicious dealings than when he had fled Rippleton in the night.

"Barrow," Ereben said.

"Aye, lad,"

"What do you know about my grandfather?"

"He was a good man."

"Why was he living in Rippleton?"

"That was his home."

"Only after my father was born. He always seemed kind of out of place there. He sold knives, but he never made very many, only enough to buy food. He always seemed like he should have been doing something more important, like teaching at the academy or sitting as a judge in the court."

"Chrysanthus spent his life doin' only important things. Ye were just not auld enough tae be telt about it. I suppose that since ye're runnin' for yer life, and carryin' the newest o' the daggers, maybe the last o' the daggers, ye have a right tae know what it all means."

"What do you know about the dagger?" Ereben asked with excitement.

The three Shouda men moved closer. In the growing darkness, Ereben could see different purposes on the face of each. Minkar Jarad seemed openly interested in learning more about the dagger. Otah Kadeef gave the appearance of a man gathering evidence for an impending condemnation. Amal Hidad, Sergeant at Arms of the Mufta Gebir, seemed to want cold facts, tactical information.

"The tale is a long one," Barrow began, "and great pieces o' it are missin'. I'll tell ye what I know." He cleared his throat. "Long ago, many hundert year, maybe longer, all people were the same race. That was afore there were the little races, like dwarfs and sech. The people discovered the mirky mysteries, what gave powers tae mak things and change things. They called it magic. Now some o' those folk got more clever than the ithers, and did terrible deeds with their magic. Some created beasts tae build great armies and defeat their enemies. Efterin' a mighty stretch o' wars and destruction, their magic got oot o' control. It changed some people intae the little races we see the day."

"You mean dwarfs were made by magic?" Ereben asked.

"Nae, they were the result o' people gettin' exposed tae the wild magic. Their weenies, their babies all came oot little, like dwarfs. An' the dwarfs only gave birth tae more dwarfs. That is how the race o' dwarfs began. And not only dwarfs. Their were ither races that came oot o' the magic wars."

"You speak of other races. What are these other races?" Minkar asked.

"Elfs and gnomes and goblins and trolls and giants. That was long ago. Over the centuries, most o' them have died oot." The old dwarf gazed into the distance, scratching his beard. "Well, the magic got so powerful that those ancient people destroyed each ither. Among the survivors, a group o' twelve families bandet thegither for one purpose, tae mak sure nae one learnt magic ever again. They called their group the Guardians o' the Ruins, and they set oot tae hide every wee bit o' magic from the rest o' the people."

"While I do not wish to doubt your sincerity," Otah said, "your words sound much like the tales told to children. Do you believe, Whittig Trench, that this story is a true accounting of events?"

"The truth about ages ago," Barrow said, "is not somethin' tae which I am privy. But listen well tae my words, Maister Kadeef. Yer life, and perhaps the lifes o' yer whole tribe may be in great peril. Ye seed ample reason tae believe about magic when the kelpies saved our hides back at Liddie's farm."

"Are you one of the Guardians?" Ereben asked. It seemed clear to Ereben that Barrow played some important role in the story he was telling.

Barrow looked at each of his listeners, then scratched his whiskers again. "Will ye swear tae the gods an oath o' secrecy?"

"Sure," Ereben answered eagerly.

"To the gods," Amal said, "I will swear nothing. But I will say before Elloh that your secrets shall be mine."

"That is certainly good enough," Barrow replied. He looked at Minkar and Otah. "Will ye say afore Elloh that ye will keep my secrets?" When all had agreed, Barrow continued. "For many a year, the Guardians studied the places where the knowledge o' magic was kept, and wrought tae hide them forever. But a few folk learnt o' the existence o' the magic anyhow, and plotted tae break intae the ruins and get their hands on the magic. Well, the Guardians was good at studyin' auld things and makin' wise decisions, but they we nae good at fightin'. Tae mak a long story short, they got help from ither people, what came tae be known as the Society o' Watchers. The job o' the Watchers was tae offer help tae the Guardians and tae fight tae defend their work. Over the many year since then, the Watchers have broken intae two groups, those what still follows their duty tae the Guardians, and those what wants tae find the magic for their own evil purposes. That second group o' folk are now called the Protectors o' Dragomin. Those that still follows their duty are, tae this day, still called the Watchers, but it is a secret society, on account o' the Protectors' ardent desire tae find and kill every last one."

"Then you're a Watcher?" Ereben asked, somewhat confused by the twists and turns in the story.

"Aye, that I am."

"And Hobart?" Ereben continued.

"Hobart must reveal his own secrets," Barrow said, "But I feel I can tell ye that yer grandfather, Chrysanthus, was one o' the last o' the Guardians. That responsibility would have been passed on tae yer father, and then on tae yersel, but they was kilt afore it all got done."

"What?" Ereben's thoughts swam in excitement and confusion. *Magic. Grandfather was a Guardian. Passed on to myself. The dagger. Magic. The dagger was for father. The Protectors are traitors. Magic. They're trying to get the magic of the dagger. The dagger. If I could only understand. Magic!*

"Ye've gone limp, lad," Barrow was saying, "It's a heavy burden tae have plopped in yer lap."

"What was Grandfather doing in Rippleton?"

"His purpose was tae be close tae Corban, tae keep track o' his efforts tae get a hold o' the magic."

"Had he not the protection of the Watchers?" Amal asked.

"Aye, he did. I have not heard o' the details o' what went wrong, but the presence here o' young Ereben is a hint o' their handiwork. He certainly would'a been kilt otherwise."

"Yarnish Blen!" Ereben exclaimed.

"I cannot spill anither man's secrets. The rest o' this tale, I'll leave for Hobart's tellin'."

When morning came, Ereben felt as though he had walked all night. Tangled knots of ancient societies and bloody intrigues prevented him from finding any restful sleep. The title 'Guardian' loomed over his thoughts as a tormenting specter. He had set out to learn the answers to painful questions. Now, he had more answers than he could grasp, and even more unanswered questions than when he began. Before dressing, he attended to his ankle. With the fate of Vestal still in the balance, he took no chances with this tiny worm. He gave the twig a quarter twist. The worm slipped free from the wound in his ankle and began to writhe its way off the twig. Ereben threw it to the stony ground and crushed it with a rock until nothing remained of it but a dusty paste.

Vestal Pit appeared to be no worse than the previous night, but he was certainly no better, remaining unconscious most of the time. For the difficult descent to Death River, at the bottom of the great canyon, they lashed Vestal to the litter with twine. All of them agreed that Vestal could never survive long enough to reach Hobart, who lived across the canyon, on its high, southern rim.

They descended the punishing incline of the trail to the river. With each step, the temperature grew hotter. By midday, they had reached a massive formation of dark purple stone, which pounded them with heat from all directions. Ereben's feet burned within his boots. With little breeze, only their forward and downward motion helped to cool the sweat from their tortured bodies. So, through the two hours of descent over the purple stone, they did not stop to rest, for fear of succumbing to the heat. When at last they halted to rest, it was a mere hundred yards above the river, less than an hour away.

"The bridge across the river appears to be intact," Otah said, as he stood on a promontory, surveying the remainder of the trail. "Judging from the force of the river, we would not be able to cross it otherwise."

"This is the last of my water," Amal pointed out. "We will come to the river in time to drink from it. I would not wish to climb this trail from the bottom, although that appears to be the only path home"

They gathered their gear, hefted Vestal's litter, and, in less than a half-hour, were standing on the trail ten yards above the raging water, separated from it by a shear cliff. As they approached the near end of the footbridge, the path on which they were walking seemed to stop dead at the base of a massive boulder, six yards high. It completely blocked the entrance to the bridge, and presented no apparent route to the footbridge.

Two people appeared on the other side of the river, approaching deftly on the fully exposed, yard-wide footbridge. These were the first people Ereben had seen since they had left Liddie Burn's farm. As these two neared, it became apparent to Ereben that they were quite small, perhaps half the height of Barrow, but all their features were tiny and in proportion. One was a man, in a dark brown robe. The other seemed to be a woman, dressed in flowing purple. Tucked into a rope about the woman's waist was a small sickle, its point toward her feet.

"Don't see too many travelers," the woman said.

"No, no," the man said, "not many travelers at all."

"Sorry to be so slow," the woman continued. She walked directly up to the boulder and waved her arms. "Out of the way."

To Ereben's utter amazement, the enormous boulder appeared to shrink until its surface merged with that of the trail. Only a slight difference in color distinguished it from the rest of the trail.

"It gives us a bit of time to see who's coming," the woman said. "Come on, folks, it won't bite or anything."

The Shouda men proceeded onto the footbridge, keeping a close watch on the former boulder. Two of them carried Vestal. Barrow and Ereben followed. Ereben concentrated on the dried planks of the bridge, so as not to notice the roiling of the water beneath. When they reached the opposite side, the two tiny people led them to a small shack sheltered beneath a stone overhang.

"Do you and your wife live here?" Ereben asked.

"No, no, no," the man answered. "We aren't married. We're fellow workers in the holy orders. I'm Brother Eretz Mor, and she's Sister Zaratha. We're assigned to take care of the bridge. We're not married. Not married at all. Just fellow workers."

"What's the matter with him?" Sister Zaratha asked.

"A sand worm has got intae his flesh," Barrow answered. "A loa loa."

Sister Zaratha and Brother Eretz Mor looked at each other fleetingly. "Bring him out over here," the Sister said, indicating a flat, sandy area twenty yards from their shack. "Do you want us to say words over him now, or after we're done?"

"Efterin yer done doin' what?" Barrow asked.

"You dwarfs are always so hard to understand," she replied. "He's got to be burned. You want us say some words then burn him, or burn him then say some words?"

"He remains alive," Otah said with obvious contempt for the tiny woman.

"Not for long," she said. "And you don't want him to die before we burn him, do you?"

"There will be nae burnin' while he lives!" Barrow shouted in a fury of indignation.

"Sister Zaratha's right, you know," Eretz Mor said. "It's a cruel thing to let him die of the worms."

Amal and Minkar set the litter down in the sandy area.

"Perhaps we could obtain some water?" Amal asked coldly.

"Sure," Zaratha answered. "In the barrel by the shack."

Vestal screamed, struggling to free himself from the twine which anchored him to the litter. Ereben realized that it had been many hours since the dying dwarf had regained consciousness. Barrow untied him.

"Now rest yersel, lad," Barrow urged his nephew. Vestal clawed at his chest and abdomen, apparently unaware of his uncle's presence. "Are ye feelin' pain there?" Barrow opened Vestal's shirt. The appearance of Vestal's torso seemed to throw Barrow off balance. The old dwarf stumbled, caught himself, then approached Vestal with caution.

Ereben understood Barrow's response when he and the Shouda men were close enough to see. The skin of Vestal's chest and belly pulsated with vermicular movements. Vestal let out one more scream of agony, gagged, then vomited a nest of tiny worms, each as thin as a cat's whisker. The young dwarf stopped breathing and became completely flaccid. No sooner had the worms spilled themselves onto the sand than they burrowed beneath the surface, completely disappearing before Ereben realized what was happening. Movement beneath Vestal's skin intensified. Worms began to emerge from every orifice, writhing their way by the most direct route to the sand, then disappearing like the others. Ereben felt a wave of nausea gathering, but it was stifled by the horror unfolding before him. Holes began to appear in Vestal's skin, on his face, on his belly, everywhere. From the holes, thousands of tiny worms cascaded into the sand. When the gruesome exodus of worms had expended itself, the holes in Vestal's motionless body oozed dark, lifeless blood.

While the five of them stood in shock, staring at the remnants of what had so recently been Vestal Pit, Sister Zaratha intruded into their circle and began pouring a thin oil over the body and the sand surrounding it. "I don't mean to be unkind or disrespectful," she said, avoiding their gaze, "but this has to be done for our own safety. There's nothing more that anybody can do for the poor soul now."

Brother Eretz Mor offered Zaratha a burning twig. She held it up and looked to Barrow for his approval. Barrow nodded once. "May the fire of your life and the fire of your death follow the upward path and the downward path. From dust to fire. From fire to dust. May your living moments remain always in the hearts of those who knew you." With that said, Sister Zaratha ignited the oil into a sudden conflagration, which drove the witnesses away from its heat. She looked up into the sadness of Barrows eyes and said softly, "I know that dwarfs never burn their dead, but it's only you who has to understand the necessity."

"Aye," was all that Barrow said in response. He watched the flames die down, then walked off to the bank of Death River alone.

Brother Eretz Mor took Ereben to the shadows of his shack, where the heat of the fire and the heat of the sun could not penetrate. "Have some water, Ereben Leaf," he said, handing Ereben a clay cup of cold water.

"How do you know my name?" Ereben asked in surprise.

"We know your name and the names of your friends," Eretz Mor said with a cheery smile. "And we know that you're looking for Hobart."

For all the secrecy, their identities and their destination seemed to be fairly public. Ereben studied the wrinkles of age in the Brother's kind face. With the stature and tiny features of a small boy, the wisdom painted in the lines of his face appeared peculiar. "How do you know these things?"

"We know," he said simply. "It's important that you keep Corban from getting any more powerful."

"Now wait. I don't understand who you are or why you think you know so much."

"Some things are not too good to talk about. Please believe that me and Sister Zaratha are friends. I'll draw you a map of the trail out of the canyon. Otherwise you won't be able to find the springs, and all of you'll die before you reach the top."

This strange little man raised many questions in Ereben's mind, and answered none of them. "You must be one of the little races that Barrow talked about."

"Yes, yes, yes," Eretz Mor said impatiently. "Sleep here for the night, then start before the sun rises. That way you'll make it to the first spring by mid-day." He extracted a piece of parchment from a small compartment built onto the outside of the shack and rapidly drew a map. "Right here," he marked the map, "is the only path up the final cliff."

That evening, the two strange, little people managed to avoid answering any direct questions about themselves or their source of knowledge about Ereben and his party. Exhausted by fatigue and sorrow, Ereben slept soundly until awakened before dawn by Brother Eretz Mor. They said an unfeeling thank you and good-bye, then departed for the southern rim of the canyon, leaving the ashes of Vestal Pit to the care of Sister Zaratha and the Brother.

With the aid of Eretz Mor's map, Ereben, Barrow and the three Shouda men reached the rim of the canyon a little before sunset. Ereben's mind wavered in a haze of heat and thirst and staggering fatigue. As he ascended the final switchback and cleared the rim, he was startled by the presence of two people sitting casually on a flat boulder beneath a gnarled juniper. He was surprised to see anyone at all, but was confused by who he thought he saw. Ereben stared, rubbing the dripping sweat from his eyes with the heel of his hand. One of the figures wore armor made from plates of steel. The other, smaller figure, bore a strong resemblance to Jasper, whom Ereben knew could not possibly be sitting before him at the southern rim of the great canyon of the Burnt Desert.

ꝏ

If truth is locked away for fear of its power, then only thieves may wield it. If truth is judged a heresy, then only heretics may find it.

Ereben Leaf: Chronicle of the Counterspell

"The yellow one is Kehlibar," Jasper explained, pointing to a huge stallion. "He belongs to Menash. And the white one is Dantel. She's mine." Perched on Jasper's shoulder, Titus seemed to follow the conversation with his tiny mouse eyes.

Ereben watched as Minkar Jarad approached the white mare on which his son sat, and stroked her mane. Nothing about the appearance of either of these horses suggested to Ereben that they were anything other than the beautiful animals they appeared to be. However, Jasper's story of his rescue and incredible journey to Hobart's home at the canyon rim left little doubt in Ereben's mind that these were kelpies, river demons. Kelpies had inexplicably saved Ereben when the Protectors had surprised them at the cow farm of Liddie Burn. But in light of Barrow's accounts of how capricious kelpies could be, Ereben still kept a wary eye on them.

Since their arrival at Hobart's house on the previous evening, Ereben had heard tragedies and adventures, and told some of his own, but had been far too exhausted to delve into the mysteries that had brought them to pass. He had learned from Jasper of the fall of Shouda City and the slaughter of its people. He had met the armored Shouda man, Menash, who spoke a language only Hobart understood.

Hobart seemed an odd little man, stoop shouldered and thin, unable to fill out his flowing gray robe. His squinty brown eyes nested too close together above a generous, hooked nose. A wisp of gray hair sprouting from the tip of his chin was all the beard he seemed capable of growing. Constant shifting and sudden glances endowed Hobart with a deceptive, mercantile quality, one which

Ereben would never have associated with great learning and wisdom. During the conversations last evening, Hobart had contented himself with listening. Despite Hobart's passivity, Ereben had noticed concern on the old man's face growing with each new bit of information revealed. The one definite thing that Hobart had said was that they would talk of serious matters tonight.

Ereben looked out to the North. The lush greenery of the plateau withered abruptly into the canyons of the barrens which reached northward almost to the misty, blue mountains above Knurlan. Somewhere up there, he thought, is Punishment Pass. It seemed ages since he and the Shouda men had descended from the mountains to the city of Zink. To the Northwest, the horizon was disturbed only by the slightest undulation. This, he knew, was Valand, the range of mountains surrounding Rippleton, where he had been born, and where his family had been killed by Corban's Protectors. *Do you know my thoughts, Phaena? Can you tell that I'm thinking about you? I miss you.* His chest tightened. *I love you. I wish I could know if you loved me, or if you even remember me. Or if you plotted to have me killed.* He looked away. Hobart's gray, stone house rested in a kind of border zone between the grasses of the plateau and the dense forest farther south. Hobart had told him this morning that almost no one else lived on the entire plateau, only a few shepherds tending scraggly flocks.

"Ereben?" Jasper asked.

"Yeah?" he answered absently.

"Are you alright?"

"What?"

"You don't look so good," Jasper said.

"I was just thinking about everything that's happened."

"Oh." Jasper paused. "I try not to think about it. It's all pretty awful. It seems like it just gets worse."

"It's not all bad. You're alive."

"But look at Bahsa," Jasper said. "It was so bad that he won't even talk anymore. He watched his mother get eaten by wolves."

"I guess that's pretty bad."

"I saw it too. And I saw stuff that was a lot worse than that." Jasper squatted to the ground and sat with his legs crossed, burying his face in his hands. Titus climbed down to Jasper's lap and circled until Jasper took notice and scratched the mouse's nose with his little finger.

Ereben seated himself beside Jasper. "Are you sorry you came with me?"

"Sometimes." He wiped his eyes with the backs of his thumbs.

"I'm sorry you had to go through all this." Ereben sat silently alongside Jasper and watched two white and black swifts perform acrobatics in the updraft from the canyon.

The room of Hobart's hearth was smoky enough to sting Ereben's eyes. A smell of burning logs mingled with the aroma of tea made from roasted barley and sumac. Hobart had been recounting the story of the ancient people who learned to use magic.

"Two thousand years?" Minkar asked.

"Yes," Hobart replied. "Two thousand years has passed since they destroyed themselves with magic. And for two thousand years the Guardians have succeeded in keeping the locations of their ancient ruins secret."

"What's so important about the ruins?" asked Jasper.

"The ruined cities contain libraries and tools and weapons of magic," Hobart continued. "Their rediscovery might allow anyone of evil intent to learn the skills which destroyed the ancient ones. Over the last fifteen years, Lord Corban, High Protector of Dragomin, has succeeded in locating and looting two of these ancient ruins. From them he has learned powerful magic and has obtained hundreds of the magic swords which you have described, and which our Shouda friends have brought with them. Sadly, the time has now come in which we must end our effort of the past two millennia to hide knowledge of the existence of magic. It is no longer a secret. It is only with magic that we will be able to turn aside Corban's aims."

"What exactly are the aims o' that butcher," Barrow asked, "aside from tryin' tae kill everybody what doesn't please him?"

"Judging from young Jasper's report," Hobart explained, "he is attempting to release Dragomin."

"Dragomin is the false god he and his priests worship," Otah Kadeef interrupted. "What is there to release?"

"The meaning of Dragomin has long been forgotten. The ancient people were finally destroyed by the magic of a rival to their king. He succeeded in locating the bones of seven great beasts from eons past, winged serpents. Using his magic, he resurrected them to destroy the king's armies. It was these seven beasts which finally destroyed all of the people. In the ancient language of Shadae, Dragomin means simply 'the dragons'."

"Al dragoma," Menash said, holding up one finger. "Settah dragomin," he then said, holding up seven fingers.

"You mean that's what killed Neebah Dir in the tunnels?" Jasper asked, his attention suddenly fixed on the discussion.

"Neebah Dir," Menash said, "yes, al dragoma." He made a hand motion of something coming from his mouth. "Al dragoma."

"Stories told to children," Amal Hidad said smugly to Otah. "There is truth in them."

Hobart continued. "The legend has come down through the Guardians that the ancient king somehow imprisoned the seven dragons, but died in the endeavor. If this is true, where that might have been has continued to be a mystery until Jasper's account of Corban's plans. In my conversations with Menash, if such a poorly understood dialog can be considered a conversation, I have become convinced that the legend is true, and that the dragons have been held captive for two thousand years beneath the pinnacles of Shouda. Corban plans to use the daggers to release them and control them."

"If, as you have said, the swords of the Protectors are magical, then I do not understand the importance of the daggers," Minkar said.

Hobart drew the dagger at his side. It appeared almost identical to Ereben's. "Each Guardian has carried a dagger which has been endowed with powerful magical wards. Their purpose was to protect the Guardians from many forms of attack. But their magic is of a magnitude much greater than that of the Protector's swords. When any three of these daggers are gathered together, in a specified arrangement, a field of protection and power is created far out of proportion to the power of each individual dagger. Apparently the portal of the black pyramid was designed to use three such devices. Corban obtained the first by killing Ereben's elder brother, Caris."

"He died by an accident!" Ereben protested.

"He died at the hands of the Protectors," Hobart said conclusively. "The second was taken from Chrysanthus, Ereben's grandfather."

Ereben's thoughts wandered from Hobart's words. *He killed my brother too. He killed them all.*

"...were it not for his daughter's warning. When Corban learned of her betrayal, he cast her into prison. Such is Corban's craving for power. Now he has pursued..."

"Wait!" Ereben interjected. "What did you say about his daughter?"

"Yarnish Blen sent word to me that he was warned of Corban's plan to arrest you and charge you with the deaths of your parents. This warning was provided by the High Lord's own daughter. When Corban learned of this, he cursed her and sentenced her to death at the gallows, but by the following morning had mitigated this to imprisonment in the stone tower of his palace in Rippleton. Do you know the girl?"

"Yes," was all he replied. His heart overflowed. He clenched his teeth to avoid the foolish smile that wanted to sweep over his whole body. Phaena was alive and cared about him. Phaena had saved his life. *Oh, Phaena.*

"May I go on?" Hobart asked, not waiting for the answer. "We must prevent Corban from releasing the Dragons. He must believe that, once released, the beasts would be under his control. But whether he controls them or not, it would be a calamity for all people. Since the portal seems to be attuned to the winter solstice, we must prevent Corban from obtaining a third dagger during the next month. That would allow us a year to find some more permanent way to stop him."

"How many other such daggers exist?" Amal asked.

"One dagger is worn by each surviving Guardian. I carry one. Ereben, who is not a Guardian, carries another. The third, and last, is carried by Ailantha, who is old and blind and near death."

"The old woman below Punishment Pass?" Ereben asked.

"Yes. We are all that are left of the original families of Guardians."

"Could not the Watchers be gathered," Amal suggested, "to protect the three daggers?"

"Aye," Barrow answered, "there are many Watchers, but they are scattered over a dozen lands, watchin' and reportin' the actions o' the Protectors o' Dragomin. The organizin' would tak time."

"Rather than directing our efforts at preventing Corban from carrying out his plan," Otah stated flatly, "we should find a way to kill him."

"I don't think you can," Jasper said. "Saikal Sahm sent a spear right through Corban's head. It just came out the other side. Corban broke apart into a million hornets, and after they killed Saikal, he went back together again."

"I believe Jasper is correct," Hobart said. "Corban's magic would be difficult to surmount. Recently, a splinter group of the Priests of Dragomin have been preaching that magic is unclean. They have been trying, obviously without notable success, to kill Corban and his Protectors. Many of these priests have been hanged throughout the cities and towns. The leader of this renegade sect is a blind priest named Crotus."

"Crotus?" Jasper said. "The same Crotus that was in Nilwid?"

"I am not certain. His origin is obscure. But his followers are fanatical. I'm afraid that they would find my own belief in magic just as heretical as Corban's. These priests, who call their belief the True Faith, are as much a threat to the Guardians as they are to Corban."

"They can not be so great a threat as Corban," Amal Hidad said.

Hobart shifted his close-set eyes across the group. "Corban seeks power. He will do whatever is in his best interest, even if that would mean curbing his cruel inclinations. A zealot, however, will sacrifice anything, even himself, to remain in accord with his prejudices. That can be very dangerous."

"On the issue o' dangerous," Barrow interrupted, "what about yon kelpies struttin' around the pasture?"

"I have wondered about their intentions," Hobart replied. "Since they are purely magical beings, they must sense the threat to themselves, should Corban succeed in controlling the dragons. So far, they have acted with honor, and seem willing to continue their assistance." Hobart stood. "It is late now. Tomorrow, we will go to the ruin of Ephesia, the ancient capital, and remove as much of the library as possible. Good night."

As they filed out of Hobart's house, Hobart took Ereben aside. "Come to me at dawn," he said. "We have an important matter to discuss."

Ereben arose before dawn. The canyon lay to the North as an enormous trough of porridge. Fog filled it from rim to rim, healing the wound that time had torn into the face of the desert. The billowing bridge of vapor invited him to run across and rescue Phaena from her father's cruelty.

"We greet the day early," Minkar said softly from behind him.

"Yes," Ereben replied.

"Across that sea of cloud, is the life to which I had expected to return by now. Instead, all that is left for me to cherish is here now, on this island of rest and safety."

"I'm sorry about your wife... and your home."

"Each of us carries his own loss as well as the losses of his friends. Come, I will walk with you to Hobart's house."

"I think he wanted to talk with me alone."

"You and I both know what it is that he plans to discuss. I wish to stand with you."

At Hobart's door, the old man squinted at the two of them. Dark bags beneath his eyes told of a night with little sleep. "I need to speak privately with Ereben."

"I wish to stand with him," Minkar explained, "when he takes on the burden of Guardian of the Ruins."

Both Hobart and Ereben looked up with some surprise into the dark brown face of the Shouda farmer. Hobart sniffed twice, and said, "Do come in." He escorted them to a rickety, wood bench beside the hearth.

This morning, Hobart's eyes fixed directly upon Ereben, with no sign of their usual shifting glances. "The oath of the Guardians, for two thousand years, has been to guard the secrets of magic in order to save all living things from the consequences of our own ambitions. Perhaps, now that the practice of magic has once again become a threat to all, it may be fitting for the Guardians to be relegated to the dusty tomes of history. Ailantha will die soon. I am quite old. Both of us have suffered the pain of surviving all our own children. If there is yet a role for the Guardians to fill, it must be to teach others the wisdom they will need to live in a new world, a world aware of magic. Will you take this weight upon yourself, Ereben Leaf?"

"It seems I already have," Ereben answered softly.

"It is a gift from Elloh," Minkar added, "that a man should acknowledge the responsibilities which are his alone."

"Indeed," Hobart said to Minkar, "you have taken up the duties of the Watchers without awaiting a solemn induction. I will inform the Grand Master to prepare the ceremony."

"What ceremony do I have to do?" Ereben asked.

"It is an arduous one. You must spend long months learning the secret of folding steel, until your skill is so finely attuned to the nature of steel that you are able to forge a dagger of five hundred twelve layers. This dagger is to belong to your father. You then must study the nature of magic, its role in the laws of all nature, and the paths by which it is manifest. On the death of your father, you assume his responsibilities as Guardian of the Ruins, wearing a dagger forged by your own son." Hobart's gaze remained on Ereben. "Your knowledge of magic is limited. So like every Guardian, you must spend the remainder of your life endeavoring to increase your understanding of it, and your control of it. Since you are the youngest Guardian in two thousand years, we will have to overlook the protocol of carrying a dagger forged by your son."

Hobart stood and motioned for Ereben to stand. "Give me your dagger."

Ereben hesitated, remembering how costly it had been for him to possesses it. He handed it to Hobart, who grasped its translucent green, stone handle. Immediately the handle began to glow. Ereben detected a fleeting expression of surprise on the old man's face.

"Grasp the blade," Hobart instructed.

Ereben looked at the razor sharp edges. A twinge in his little finger reminded him of the tiny cut that had nearly cost him his life. He reached out and clamped his grip onto the two edges. A surge of power jolted his posture. His image of the room faded. All was white. Hobart stood before him as a radiance, brighter than white. He looked at Minkar Jarad. He too embodied radiance. The dagger in his hand, its handle and its blade, appeared as sculpted crystal, echoing light in points of brilliance. *It is a conduit.* Within the sparkling purity of the crystal dagger, there seemed to be a shadow that immediately separated into two shadows, then merged again to a single shadow, continually repeating its cycle of division and coalescence. He released his grip. The room returned. Without looking at his hands, he knew they had not been cut. He also knew, without asking, that there was something about the dagger that was not as it should be.

"There is something else that you should see," Hobart said. He unrolled a tattered scroll. It appeared to have been stitched together from hundreds of shreds of parchment. Some of its edges were burned. There were obvious gaps where portions of it were missing. "Young Jasper discovered this within the leather pouch which served as home for his mouse. He tells me that he does not know where it came from."

Ereben's jaw dropped as he slapped his forehead. "It was Grandfather's." For the first time since fleeing from Chrysanthus' burned smithy, he remembered retrieving a parchment from beneath the floorboard of the burned house.

"Jasper noticed that one of the fragments bore markings similar to those beneath the Shouda Shrine. Last night I pieced them together." Hobart turned the ragged parchment so that Ereben and Minkar could see.

"It is a drawing of an ax," Minkar said.

"A remarkable and very strange ax," Hobart pointed out. "The crescent of the blade is curved into a barbed point which is directed away from the edge, and another barbed point extends in the same direction from the mounting ring of the head, as though it is intended to be used backwards."

"What do these words say?" Ereben asked, pointing to the rust-brown glyphs scattered over the page.

"Most of the text which is still readable describes how the blade is to be forged of steel in one thousand twenty four layers. This part explains that the handle is to be made of blood locust, a tree which is not familiar to me. The purpose of the ax seems to be explained here, where much of the text is missing. And the unburned portion of the name at the bottom appears to be the signature of Chrysanthus."

"Why would he have hidden it?" Ereben wondered aloud.

Hobart stooped his shoulders a little more than usual and rolled up the patched scroll. "If I understood the intended use of the ax, perhaps I could answer that question." He sighed. "We must depart soon for the ruins of Ephesia."

Outside Hobart's house, Minkar said, "Come to my tent, Ereben Leaf. I have something to commemorate this important day." At his tent, Minkar opened his pack and brought out a bundle, handing it to Ereben.

When Ereben unrolled it, he immediately recognized it as the pelt of the Ice Leopard he had slain with his spear. He had forgotten how beautiful it was, with its ghostly spots. Minkar had sewn it into a hooded cape as regal as any Ereben could imagine. He put it on. "Thank you, Minkar. It is beautiful."

"It befits a friend and a Guardian of the Ruins," Minkar said, offering a formal bow, in the Shouda fashion.

Ereben returned the bow.

For two hours, the nine of them trudged along an overgrown path into the forest south of Hobart's house. Hobart had described it as jungle. Ereben had never seen such lush growth of plants and trees. Everywhere the sun struck, deep greenery abounded. The trees, some over fifty yards tall, formed a dense canopy far above, leaving them to walk among the steamy shadows. Swarms of tiny insects hovered across the trail, seeming to wait for Ereben's passage, at which they would flurry about his face, occasionally biting his exposed skin. He was certain that they preferred him to the other members of his party.

"This is Ephesia," Hobart said abruptly.

Ereben looked about him. In the jungle shadows, he saw nothing but vegetation gone wild—vines choking trees, trees strangling other trees, each fighting to capture the scarce patches of sunlight missed by the high canopy. Gullies were filled with thick, succulent leaves. Hillocks were overgrown in webs of roots and vines. Nowhere did he see even the suggestion of a man-made structure. The others looked about with the same bewilderment. Hobart approached a steep hill, nearly thirty yards high. By simply separating two huge leaves near its base, he revealed the square angle of a dressed white stone.

"The land here," Hobart said, "is flat. All the hills and depressions you see are the houses and temples of Ephesia. Although the jungle has had two thousand years to reclaim its property, this temple, which I entered seven years ago, appears no less a part of the jungle's domain."

"Do you even know what's under most of this stuff?" Jasper asked.

"Many centuries ago, the Guardians mapped the ruins," Hobart explained. "Since their interest was only in protecting the knowledge of magic, the other buildings have been largely unexplored since then. This temple housed the library, in which many books and scrolls of all subject matter were stored."

"The temple seems best hidden if left undisturbed," Amal observed.

"Quite true," Hobart replied. "But we have reason to believe that Corban has obtained a map which would enable him to locate Ephesia. It will only be a matter of time before his Protectors are busy uncovering every structure in the city. We must retrieve the most revealing materials and hide them elsewhere, in a location unmarked on any map."

"Hobart!" Menash cried out. The armored man drew his mighty, two-handed sword and stepped toward the old Guardian. "Bad!" he shouted, as he swung the great blade behind his back and up over his head. Amal spun the shaft of his spear into Menash's torso, where it glanced away from the steel breastplate. Menash ignored Amal and brought down the blade, missing Hobart's shoulder by the slightest distance. Otah and Minkar, by now, had reacted to the danger, ready to drive their spears into the unprotected gaps in the back of the armor.

"No!" Hobart said, holding up both hands to halt the Shouda warriors' attack on Menash.

"Mither o' the gods!" Barrow gasped. He pointed to the tangle of massive roots behind Hobart. "That fine, wee root was about tae swallow Hobart, robe and all."

Ereben's gaze followed a river of blood through the maze of vegetation to a moving mass of flesh. A serpent, indeed large enough to swallow Hobart, slowly writhed among trunk-like roots. Its head had been cleanly split down the middle, leaving the grotesque halves attached to its body.

"There is something not right about this man," Amal said quietly to Otah.

"He is no less worrisome than the demon kelpies," Otah replied.

It struck Ereben as odd that these Shouda men should so distrust a man who seemed to be one of their own tribe. True, Jasper's story left curious questions about his origin. And Menash spoke a language that only Hobart could barely understand. *But he seems so... Shouda.*

Hobart said incomprehensible words to Menash. Menash nodded and replied. "Now stand back a little ways, while I put this poor serpent to use." Hobart drew his dagger and touched its point to the cleavage in the dead serpent's head. With a sizzling noise, the head fused itself back together. Bahsa hid behind his father's leg.

The serpent immediately began to consume the massive roots and vegetation covering the doorway of the temple. Roots splintered and runny sap flew in all directions. The thick, sleek body of the serpent bulged and disfigured with the shapes and volumes of what it consumed, but it continued until the doorway was cleared. It then lumbered, as a great heap of rubble, to a spot ten yards from the doorway, where it began the process of regurgitating all that it had swallowed. Rather than a mass of destroyed vegetation, what emerged from its throat were whole plants and vines, which immediately took root and, as soon as they were completely free of the serpent's mouth, leapt skyward to gain the paltry offerings of sunlight. In a groaning slurp, which ended in a tiny hiss, the serpent turned itself inside out, regurgitating its tail and body, and even its own mouth, and merged as a fertilizing shred of detritus into the tangled roots of the newly transported vegetation.

"It is a transgression against Elloh," Otah said solemnly, "to manipulate the order of things in such an unnatural way."

"I recognize the source of your concerns, Otah Kadeef," Hobart replied, "but you must understand that for two thousand years the Guardians have attempted to hide the very fact that magic is a part of the natural order of things. It is a part of nature, and accessible to anyone willing to explore its hidden connections to all that exists. The accessibility of magic caused us to fear its power. We did what we could to mislead. It was the Guardians who asserted most convincingly the impossibility of magic. The time has come for us to learn to manage the truth."

"The great book speaks clearly of those who practice such deeds as this," Otah continued. "I am deeply disturbed by all of this."

Hobart led the way into the darkened entrance of the temple, causing a soft glow from his dagger's handle to illuminate the way. Ereben, with his clearer insight into the function of the dagger, noticed that Hobart's other hand reached into the contents of a pouch tied about his waist. Something in the pouch was the source of power for the light. *The dagger is only a conduit.* Jasper brought out a roll of bark-like material from his pack. Ereben was puzzled by its ability to emit a similar green light. Jasper's bark seemed to use no power from another source.

"Before we go to the library," Hobart said, "we may find some useful things in here." He turned into a side chamber. "As well as I can determine, this room was the office of the Chamberlain. On my last excursion, I found within a hidden compartment the items you see now on the table." Ereben saw on the stone table pieces of armor and a great ax. Each piece glistened yellow. Into each was mounted at least one translucent green stone.

"Bein' as how we are among friends," Barrow said, "and bein' as how we are puttin' aside the secrecy, I'll tak a moment tae put a question tae Maister Jarad." Barrow lifted a massive battle-ax from the table and held it out toward Minkar. "Grasp the handle." Minkar did so. "Do ye, Minkar Jarad o' the Shouda say in the presence o' Elloh and yer friends here that ye will protect the life o' Hobart and Ereben and Ailantha and their successors as long as the power is in ye tae lift a weapon?"

Minkar answered, "Yes."

"As Grand Maister o' the Society o' Watchers, I declare ye worthy o' the duty. Ye can release the ax." Barrow placed the battle-ax onto the floor beside the table. From the collection of armor, he lifted a golden girdle of metal plates, which he clasped around Minkar's waist. "Look about the table and find somethin' that might suit one o' yer friends."

Minkar surveyed the armor. He took up a golden breastplate, with a green stone at each nipple, and presented it to Ereben. Ereben chose golden epaulettes, which he gave to Otah. From the table, Otah chose a pair of golden gauntlets for Amal. Amal, in turn, presented Jasper with a golden helmet. Jasper placed a golden chain hood over Bahsa's head. On Bahsa's behalf, Hobart instructed the boy to offer a golden shield to Menash. Menash saw that there was nothing left to give to Hobart, so he reached beneath his steel armor and brought out a small pouch, which he handed to Hobart. Hobart opened the pouch and poured five translucent red stones into his hand. To Ereben, they seemed to be the same stone as the handle of Jasper's sword and Bahsa's dagger.

Hobart led them out of the Chamberlain's office and down a stairway, into a large room which glowed green from its green ceiling. The room contained racks of books and scrolls. Hobart explained that only those items that dealt with the subject of magic would need to be taken, and he set about the task of identifying them and placing them into a pile on the floor.

Ereben looked through the growing collection to be hauled away and saw a wooden box, less than a half-yard on a side and about one finger length deep. He opened its hinged lid to reveal a flat, circular, metal device, shaped like four ax heads attached at the center. The face of each blade had been inscribed with glyphs, each blade bearing four rows of different glyphs. "What is this?" he asked Hobart.

"That is the Glaive of Brenden," Hobart answered, still sorting through the library. "I believe the design represents the ordering of the schools of magic, as well as the path by which each may be approached. No one has fully explained why the ancients inscribed it onto metal rather than parchment."

When Hobart had completed his sorting, each member of the party packed out his share. Within two hours they had returned to Hobart's stone house on the plateau above the canyon.

"Are you going to hide all this stuff in your house?" Jasper asked.

"I have a special place where no one will ever look," he answered. "But first we need some transportation." Hobart knelt beside a low stone wall, drew his dagger and held it upright, with its point touching the stone. After a moment, he stood and instructed Jasper and Ereben to bring two sacks of grain from his small granary. "Place them in the clearing," he said.

"What are you going to do?" Jasper asked.

"We are going to recruit some volunteers." Hobart looked overhead, then nodded with satisfaction as two white doves descended to the sacks of grain. Pointing his dagger at the doves, Hobart mouthed words which Ereben could not hear. Light crackled from the dagger, striking the doves. A groaning rumbled through the ground. Both of the doves began to enlarge. As they did so, the sacks of grain grew emptier, until two giant white doves stood side by side upon empty jute bags. "Otah Kadeef, Prince of the Shouda, and Amal Hidad, Sergeant at Arms, these great birds will allow you to accompany Menash, as he rides Kehlibar back to learn the fate of Mufta Ibrah. Now, bring out two more sacks of grain." The giant doves walked to the edge of the pasture where Kehlibar and Dantel grazed, stretched their great wings, then the two white birds nuzzled their heads against each other.

When two more sacks of grain had been placed, a gray mole crawled its way up onto one sack. "Oh my," Hobart mumbled. "That wasn't what I had in mind." He shook his head, pointed the dagger, then squinted his eyes in concentration. Light flashed from the dagger. This time, Ereben noticed that Hobart held a large piece of munu mushroom in his other hand. The mole grew. As it grew, its appearance became indistinct. When its form resolved more clearly, Ereben saw a giant peregrine falcon standing in the mole's place. The great bird looked about as though it were seeing the world for the first time. "Whittig Trench, Grand Master of the Watchers, this refurbished creature will be your mount."

"Flyin' around on a great bird what was a weenie mole is not a source o' comfort."

"Would you prefer to cross the canyon on foot again?" Hobart asked.

"A mole couldna be worse than that blastit canyon."

One sack of grain remained. Hobart scratched his wispy beard, then instructed Barrow to drag an oak log into the clearing beside the grain. "Place your mouse onto the grain,' he said to Jasper.

"But he's my friend as a mouse," Jasper protested.

"We need him now," Hobart added.

Jasper reluctantly placed Titus onto the sack of grain. A dark silhouette in the sky dove directly toward the mouse.

"The owl!" Jasper shouted. "Remember the gray owl, Ereben?"

The owl flared its wings and settled on the sack beside Titus. Titus jumped onto the log and sat up. When Hobart leveled his dagger at them, only the owl was affected. It grew to a size as large as the giant peregrine falcon, lifted into the air, then circled them once before lighting beside the doves. "Minkar Jarad, Watcher, this owl will serve your bidding."

"What's going to happen to Titus," Jasper asked.

"Here," Hobart said, holding out a fist size munu mushroom to Jasper. "Give this to the mouse. Titus, you see, was not born as a mouse. He became a mouse with the help of Chrysanthus, who found him in the frozen nether reaches to the North. With the mushroom, he will be able to return to his proper form."

Jasper placed the mushroom on the log, beside Titus. The mouse began to eat. With surprising speed he consumed the entire mushroom. After a moment, his color and form began to blur. When Ereben could see Titus clearly again, he saw, not a mouse, but a white gyre falcon standing nearly a yard tall. His white wings were subtly stippled with ghostly suggestions of gray. Titus spread his wings, then bounded onto Jasper's shoulder, where he had ridden for so great a distance.

"You're a gyre falcon?" Jasper asked the bird with amazement. Titus turned his beaked head in acknowledgment.

"Titus," Hobart said, "if you would be so kind as to return to the log, I will adjust your size a bit." When Titus jumped down to the log, Jasper stepped back. "We need you to be a bit bigger than the others, since you will be carrying both me and Ereben." He brought his dagger to life again. A deafening crack heralded the transformation. When Titus stopped growing, he was half again as tall as the other giant birds. In his talons he now held a tiny twig that, moments before, had been an oak log. Titus dipped his regal, white head and nudged Jasper. Jasper scratched him above the beak, using his entire hand, instead of the tip of one finger. Ereben considered Hobart's comment about Titus' origin. He could not remember a time when his grandfather had not had Titus. He felt foolish for having never thought about Titus' age, which was far too great for any ordinary mouse.

That evening, Minkar instructed everyone in the art of making a harness. Menash, who seemed to understand very little of the discussion, finally caught on to the purpose of the project and joined in as well. By midmorning of the following day, all of the magical tomes and scrolls had been loaded onto the great birds and the kelpies, who had apparently chosen to maintain their equine forms. With Hobart and Ereben riding Titus in the lead, the improbable fleet of giant birds and winged horses lifted off from the green pastures of Hobart's home and headed north, toward the great canyon of the Burnt Desert. In less than a quarter hour, they settled on the sandy flat beside the shack of Brother Eretz Mor and Sister Zaratha, at the bottom of the canyon.

"Oh, how wonderful!" shouted Sister Zaratha. "Kehlibar and Dantel. And Titus, you're looking more like yourself." She looked at the great peregrine falcon, upon which Barrow rode. "Hmmm. You look much less like yourself, Pelegri. Greetings, Krey," she said to the gray owl of Minkar and Bahsa. "I don't think I know you." She stood before the doves of Amal and Otah. "Yes, good to know you Fantas and Pneuma."

"How do you know their names?" Jasper asked.

"Oh, that's easy, Jasper. At least with animals it's easy. The kelpies are harder, because they don't want us to know their real names."

"If you could stop talking long enough to breathe," Brother Eretz Mor interjected, "these folks could get about their business. Sister Zaratha gets... enthusiastic, what with only me and those dumb rocks to talk to."

"Dumb rocks?" she said, "They usually have more to say than you do, Brother."

"Well, that's true. But that's because they don't have much else to do with their time, do they."

"Sister," Hobart interrupted, "where should we take these things?"

"Come, come, come," Eretz Mor said, with rapid jestures of his hands. "Sister Zaratha's got a place all fixed up." He led them to the base of a boulder ten yards high. In the face of the boulder were four deep compartments. "Here, over here," he said excitedly. "Just put it all in here."

They placed their collection of books and scrolls, and the wooden box containing the Glaive of Brenden into the four compartments. Eretz Mor arranged them and pushed them back from the opening. When he was satisfied with their positioning, he turned, folded his arms and tapped his foot until Sister Zaratha noticed that he was ready.

"Okay!" she shouted. "Close 'er up!"

Ereben felt a rumble beneath his feet. The boulder took on a softer appearance. A thick, stone arm erupted from the side of the boulder, reached across the openings of the storage compartments, and smeared what appeared to be the surface of its belly across the openings. The hand patted its belly once, then merged back into the body of the boulder. Ereben touched the sealed surface with his hand, then tapped it with the shaft of his spear. It seemed like an ordinary boulder.

"That's pretty good," Jasper said with a smile.

Otah took on his usual expression of discomfort when presented with an act of magic. "You are quite correct, Hobart. Corban will never look for these things here."

"Let us return to my house," Hobart said, "and discuss what needs to be done now."

"If you will forgive our apparent lack of appreciation for your hospitality," Otah said to Hobart, "Amal and I would like to depart now to search for my father and my sister."

"And Menash?" Hobart asked.

"Yes," Otah replied, "Menash should accompany us, since, according to your understanding of his intentions, he wishes to serve my father."

"May your travel be safe," Hobart said. "We must do anything necessary to prevent Corban from completing his plan."

They all said their good-byes, then the white doves, Fantas and Pneuma, bearing Otah and Amal, lifted into the updraft of the canyon. Menash, with his new shield tied to the harness, urged his kelpie, Kehlibar into the air. The three of them circled their way along the rising air toward the northern rim of the canyon, then vanished from view. After engaging in some private words with Sister Zaratha, Hobart joined Ereben on the back of Titus, and they lifted into the air toward the southern rim. Minkar and his son followed next, on Krey, the gray owl. Pelegri, the peregrine falcon, carried Barrow. And finally, Jasper cantered his kelpie, Dantel until wings sprouted and lifted him toward his companions.

By late afternoon, the great birds became restless in their pacing about the pasture beside Hobart's house. Hobart suggested to the kelpie, Dantel, that she show the birds where they might find food large enough to satisfy their newly enlarged appetites. So Dantel and the birds flew off south, over the jungle in search of food.

Hobart took Ereben aside. "You must have noticed, when we both held your dagger, that something about it is not right," Hobart said. "There is something which alters its function in conducting power."

"Yes," Ereben answered. "I did notice something like a shadow inside it. What is it?"

"I could not see through the interference caused by the power of my own dagger." Hobart drew his dagger and handed it to Ereben. "Take this back to my house. That should be far enough away to allow a clear viewing of your dagger's aura."

Ereben handed his own dagger to Hobart, then carried Hobart's dagger to the house. On his return, he found Hobart in deep contemplation. "What did you find?"

"The lines of the steel layers seem to form glyphs, but I am not certain that I understand its meaning. Are the lines different from when you first forged the blade?"

"Yes. It was different after grandfather died."

"Are you sure he died?"

"Well... I saw a body, but it was all burned."

"I believe that Chrysanthus is the shadow within the dagger."

"How can that be?" Ereben's mind raced. *Grandfather within the dagger? Can he be alive?* "Is that possible?"

"It is possible," Hobart said, "but the path for such a transformation would likely release an enormous quantity of power as the matter of the body is extinguished."

"There was a loud noise. I heard it miles away. When I got there, everything except this dagger was burned. The walls were torn away and burning."

"If anyone possessed the magical knowledge to bring about such an event, that person would be your grandfather. His facility with magic was greater than my own."

"If Grandfather is in there, is there a way to get him out?"

Hobart set the dagger on a stone and stared at it. His index finger pressed against his hooked nose while he thought. "Perhaps. I believe that Ailantha studied a tome of releasing spells many..."

A dark shadow passed over them. Ereben assumed that the great birds were returning from their hunt. He turned and looked up in time to see a bolt of light flash from a dark silhouette in the sky. A gushing, sizzling noise sounded beside him. He was thrown to the ground by a sudden concussion. Where Hobart had been seated, there remained only a mass of torn, steaming flesh within the shreds of a bloodstained gray robe. Horror swept over him. He looked about. Five giant vultures flared their wings and landed all around him. One Protector, in black armor and crimson cape, hopped down from his mount and lifted Ereben's dagger from the stone where it lay. Two other Protectors seized Ereben's arms.

"His people are coming." the first Protector said. "Let the vulture take care of him."

Ereben looked back toward the house. In the distance, Barrow and Minkar ran toward him. Something grasped his torso painfully. At his waist he saw the grotesque claw of a giant vulture holding him fast. With a colossal flutter of wings, the Protector's vultures lifted from the ground and headed north. Ereben found himself being carried beneath one of the great vultures. The grip of the claw was so tight he could hardly breathe. Shortly, they cleared the southern rim of the canyon. The earth yawned below him, its gaping maw nearly a mile deep. As the grip about him eased, Ereben took a deep breath. The breath merged into a gasp as the vulture's grip released him.

ꝏ

The love we imagine within the heart of another has its measure only in the actions of love.

Ereben Leaf: Chronicle of the Counterspell

Ereben tumbled through the warm, dry air of the great canyon. *It can't end here! It was too hard to get here. Phaena! I'll never see you again. Fly! I've got to fly. Magic! There's got to be...* Ereben extended his arms and legs. *It works!* His tumbling stopped as the buoyancy of the air pressed against his body. He looked to the right. The elation that had thrilled his spirit vanished as he watched the cliff wall speeding past. The roar of the wind in his ears confirmed that he was still falling. When he moved his arms, his body followed, but no matter how hard he tried to slow his descent, no matter how much he wished to fly—needed to fly, the wall of the canyon cliff continued to reveal the truth. He could not fly. He could only steer himself toward which ever spot on the floor of the canyon he chose for his rapidly approaching death.

The fall seemed to take so long, yet it was so short a time in which to live the remainder of his life. He saw the shack of Brother Eretz Mor and Sister Zaratha far below. *They aren't dwarfs. They're too little to be dwarfs.* He realized that he would strike the stone of the canyon floor not far from where Vestal Pit had died and his body burned. One particular boulder below him resembled a huge pillow—a bed for his final sleep. He steered himself toward the center of the "pillow". The stones rushed toward him at an increasing speed.

It can't possibly hurt. It must just... Everything turned pink. *So this is what it's like to be dead. Everything is pink. And I'm not breathing. I can't feel my body. But I really want to breathe. I need to get up. I need to turn over.* Ereben's arms and legs began to tingle. *I've got to breathe.* With a jerk, he lifted his head.

Air rushed into his lungs. The pink changed to countless tiny sparkles swirling about. He extended his arms. His body rolled over, but he felt no surface to support him. His vision was filled with eddies of brightness. The smell of desert vegetation came to his awareness. And the smell of the river.

As his vision began to clear, he saw the world divided into a dark half and a light half. With frustrating sluggishness, his mind assembled the notion that he was looking up at a wall to the left, and sky to the right. A rushing sound crept into his awareness. *A river is nearby.* He held a hand before his face. Its image was blurred, but it moved in response to his intention. *I'm not dead. I'm just at the bottom... of something.* He remembered the fall. *I landed on a pillow. I landed on a big pillow.* He sat up, but was too dizzy. He lay back down. *It feels like a pillow. It can't be a pillow. It's a rock. I landed on a rock. I fell into the canyon. I should be dead, but I don't think I'm dead.*

Ereben's armpits and waist began to throb where his golden breastplate made contact. As he lay on his back, the pressure from the clasps of the breastplate dug between his shoulder blades. He slowly sat up. In the surface behind him, an imprint of his body remained, like a footprint in the sand. He touched it. To his fingertips, the unyielding surface was nothing but the warm, dusty sandstone of the canyon. But there it was, a sculpted impression of the back of his body. *I landed face down.*

"That was a close thing." The balding head of Brother Eretz Mor rose above the edge of the boulder. "I didn't think you'd do it in time. When I didn't see your brains dripping over the sides of the rock, I knew you were fine. Here," Eretz Mor said, offering a hand to Ereben.

"What happened?" Ereben asked, still shaken.

The tiny man brushed dirt from the front of his brown robe. "What happened? You fall a mile into the canyon, land on a rock, then ask me what happened."

"I should be dead."

"I guess you're not."

"Look," Ereben said, pointing to the impression where he had lain on his back. "I landed face down, but that's the shape of my back."

"Well, that's easy. You turned on your back before you decided it should be like a rock."

"Decided."

"You're a little strange," the Brother said. He scrambled down the side of the boulder to the path below.

"They killed Hobart," Ereben said.

Brother Eretz Mor turned and looked up at Ereben. The usually flippant expression faded from the little man's face. "We saw those overgrown vultures come through the canyon and go up over the rim. I always thought Hobart could take anything the Protectors served up and throw it back in a double dose. Come, come. Lets go back to the house, so Sister Zaratha can hear."

Within the shack that Brother Eretz Mor and Sister Zaratha called a house, Ereben sipped at a cup of hot, brown liquid. Despite its slightly bitter taste, it seemed to clear his head. He recounted to his hosts the events surrounding Hobart's death. Saying the words seemed to bring home a finality that left him with a sense of hopelessness. "I barely know anything about magic."

"You sure passed the test when you landed down here," Zaratha said. "It takes just the right touch, right here," she thumped the center of her chest, "to get those rocks to listen. They're just plain slow sometimes."

"But we hadn't even come up with a plan to stop Corban. Now Hobart's dead and Corban's got my dagger. I don't know what to do."

"The hardest part," Eretz Mor said, "is just deciding to make a decision. It isn't what you decide, so much as just getting up and deciding."

"But how do I decide? I don't know enough about any of this stuff."

"When you're older and wiser," Zaratha said, "you'll figure out that knowing things is only a tiny part of deciding. Nobody can know enough to have what he knows make the decisions for him. You have to decide what the direction needs to be. Knowing comes in when you work out the details. So your details will be a bit rough."

"It's in your hands," Eretz Mor added, "and there's nobody else that knows any better about what to do than you. If you don't decide, there's nobody else that's going to fill in for you."

The crush of responsibility seemed unbearable. "This is so hard," he said.

"Would you rather have hard choices to make," Zaratha asked, "or be splattered on that boulder out there?"

"Okay," Ereben decided, aware of an immediate sense of relief mingled with apprehension. "Where do I start?"

"Well," Zaratha began, "you've got a natural touch with magic, but you really don't know doodly about it. And we can't teach you the kinds of things you need to know. So we'll just look over all that stuff you brought from Ephesia this morning, and pick a few things for you to take with you."

At the boulder that hid the tomes and scrolls of magic, Zaratha said, "Open up."

The great stone into which they had placed the magical knowledge of ancient Ephesia opened its four compartments. This time, though, instead of appearing to be within the belly of the rock, the same compartments opened as four toothless mouths, stacked one on top of the other. Ereben thought that the top mouth betrayed a subtle smirk of satisfaction at its own cleverness.

"I don't know what's what," Zaratha said, looking though the materials. "It's all written in some funny language. Oh! Look at this one." She lifted a small, leather bound volume and handed it to Ereben.

"This looks a lot newer than the others," Ereben said. Its cover bore no title, but on the first page, written in uniform, black strokes, was the title "Treasury of Shadae". Beneath the title, written in a more fluid script, was the name, "Hobart of the Eighty-seventh generation." Ereben looked through the pages. Each was divided into two columns. Each column contained words written in unrecognizable glyphs, followed by words that Ereben could understand. "Hobart wrote this. I think it tells the meaning of the stuff we can't read."

"Here's another one by Hobart," Eretz Mor said. "The Ephesiac Fragments," he read from the title page. "I think this would be good to take."

Ereben opened the wooden box containing the Glaive of Brenden. "I think what this says is important, but it's awfully heavy."

"Bring it in the house," Eretz Mor said. "I've got an idea."

Ereben grabbed another book and a scroll, both chosen at random, since he could not read them. "I guess that's it for now," he said to Zaratha.

"We're done," she said to the boulder.

Each mouth in the face of the rock, starting with the bottom one, closed and vanished.

In the deepening shadows of dusk, Sister Zaratha accompanied Ereben and Brother Eretz Mor back into the shack.

Eretz Mor brought out a blank sheet of parchment and placed it over the glyphs engraved into the steel surface of the Glaive of Brenden. He then rummaged among his cooking utensils until he found a rusted iron cooking pan. By rubbing the rusted surface over the parchment, he created a copy of the Glaive's engraving on the parchment. "This'll be easier to carry. And it won't smear if it gets wet."

Ereben now understood how the brown glyphs on his Grandfather's ax drawing had survived, despite getting wet on many occasions. He accepted the new scroll from Eretz More. "I guess I'll climb back to Hobart's house in the morning."

"Morning is good," Zaratha said.

After a dinner of baked river fish and fried plantain, which he was told came from the jungle of the south rim, Ereben walked alone to the bank of Death River. Below him, dark water surged and roiled over the boulder-strewn riverbed. *Death River. Vestal died here. But I'm alive. How many more times can I cheat death?* He looked up to the slice of stars visible above the canyon walls. *Phaena. Do you know that I'm coming for you? Tomorrow!* His chest felt as though it would burst if he felt even the slightest bit more exultant. *Tomorrow I'll see you. And you'll fly away with me. And we'll always be together. And then we'll find a way to kill Cor...* Ereben's exultation soured to nausea. It was Phaena's father that he planned to kill. *Do you understand, Phaena, that it has to be done? Or will you hate me for it.* He gazed into the tumultuous shadows beneath him. *I wish I could just flow wherever the riverbed carried me, instead of having to figure out which way to go. Maybe that's all I'm doing anyway. Maybe my choices aren't really choices.*

The following morning, Ereben arose early to begin the long climb to the south rim. He found Sister Zaratha outside, engaged in an animated discussion with a massive boulder at the foot of the trail out of the canyon.

"Here he is now," Zaratha said to the boulder. "Good morning. Did you sleep alright?"

"It was very comfortable," he replied.

"I know it was comfortable, but were you comfortable awake or comfortable asleep?"

"Mostly asleep."

"Well, I've had a little conversation with our hosts," she said, gesturing toward the boulder, "and they've decided, since you seem to get along pretty well with rocks, that you can take the short way up."

"What way is that?" Ereben asked.

"Straight up."

"I don't understand."

"It's a little hard to explain. You sort of become rock. Well, not exactly rock. You go over to their view of the world, as if you were part of them. It's hard to explain. You see, the way the world is to them is different from the way we look at it. And if you approach it, so to speak, the way they do, then you can travel in their world."

"You mean like going inside the rock?" Ereben asked, fighting off the urge to laugh at the tiny lady.

"Well, that's it. The way we look at rocks is, you know, solid. But you saw for yourself, yesterday, that how solid a rock is depends on your point of view. Anyway, they've agreed that you'd be good at seeing things their way. They seem to know quite a bit about you. Strange."

"You can hear the rocks talk to you?"

"Not exactly, but that's a long story. My biggest worry is that once you see things their way, you might just decide to stay with the rocks. Not come out again."

"Oh, I'll come out. I've got something very special planned for when I get to the top." A vision of Phaena filled his senses.

"You had better have something special, because a rock's point of view is mighty seductive. You see, time rushes past us like a moth circling a fire. For rocks, it's different. And all the little things that seem so important to us, so urgent, all look silly when you see it through the eyes of a rock, so to speak."

"How do I know which way I'm going?"

"Whatever way you have in your mind when you go in is the way you'll go."

"How long does it take?"

"Now that's a hard one to answer." Sister Zaratha inserted her little finger into one ear and scratched while she thought. "To somebody on the outside, it might seem like no time at all. But when you're inside, time is... well, it isn't, if you know what I mean. That's why you have to have the will to come out again. Otherwise..." She shrugged.

"So, how do I do this?"

"You just do it. Get your things and go in. Right here is as good a place to go in as any."

"Here," Brother Eretz Mor said, approaching from the shack. "Put this piece of Nagel radish in your mouth. If you get confused, just bite it to clear your head."

"That's such nonsense," Zaratha commented. "If you get confused in there, you won't remember to bite the radish."

"Phhh! It's helped me lots of times," Eretz Mor replied. "Brother Thomas recommended it."

"He's never been comfortable with their point of view."

Ereben ended the discussion by placing the dark brown slice of Nagel radish in his mouth. Bitterness ached in the corners of his jaw. "Thith ith awful," he said around the radish.

"Now, go!" Zaratha insisted.

With his books and scrolls rolled into a strip of jute sacking tied about his shoulder, Ereben stepped toward the boulder, then hesitated.

"Just go in," Zaratha said with a flutter of her tiny hands.

Ereben sensed, in some unreachable part of his being, that the boulder was inviting him to enter its world. He stepped effortlessly through the surface of the stone.

There was nowhere to be. The universe was compressed and contorted, yet uniformly so. He saw nothing, but sensed blackness... and familiarity. He knew no notion of change. He felt loss. *I am the root of a mountain, yet I am not. There is no mountain. There is no remnant of my birth. I am complete within myself. I am.*

Color! But I can not see. Flat. I am the deepest indigo, through which a million million tiny things have sifted, only to be stilled. Never to move. The antiquity of my being, revealed only in the crumbling of my frayed exposures. So momentous a secret I bear. In me it has arisen. I am content to share my moment.

I am Ereben Leaf. Nothing acknowledged his distinct existence. *I am nothing save the broken remnants of what has surged past and scurried to and fro, only to cease to be. The waters of eternity seep through my body. If this trick of matter is to trap the light of eons past within the greeness of my existence, then it must succeed now, or settle into the layers of oblivion.*

I nearly died yesterday, but a rock by the river... The threads of his consciousness began to unravel. *...the river. A river has died. It has died upon me, leaving the fragile bones of evanescent creatures embedded within my yellow flesh. I offer no sorrow for your insignificance. Your fleeting gyrations are but a sliver of an instant. Your futile struggles but a cosmic joke. To be alive is to be doomed.* Ereben knew the truth of it. *A flutter of time, and you are nothing.* Ereben understood how petty were his dangers and his urgencies. From a view of permanence, he saw the irrelevance of his worries and desires. He savored the peace of being outside their reach. *Layer upon layer, the fragmented bones attested to their meaninglessness. All life is fleeting. All treasure is but stone. Fleeting. Stone. I am stone.*

Red stain upon gray. Red, but not red. And how large these immobilized remnants. Great fish to rule. Great in death. Great in killing. To live and explore and offer up yourself in sacrifice to those greater.

True red. Of silty smothering. Red of blood. Ultimate predation. No safety in life. Ereben's mind reached out to catch the dissipating fragments of himself. *I am... Ereben... Phaena... journey... Corban.... No shrub broad enough to hide the bounty of your flesh. And that enormity which consumes your being, yet will I turn the play about and, in the end, consume it too. I am the greatest of predators. All shall find their end within my bowels, while your magnitude and terror has been erased. Only I will remember... Phaena.*

So dark a desolation dances white upon the cresting dunes of lifeless desert mound. And only doomed survivors wander hopelessly for life preserving water never found. No chance of life's experiment avoiding its demise when I its final pulse impound.

Endless the amber granulations. Countless the centuries of accumulated detritus. I have no being other than the dismembered echoes of reef and shell. I am their memorial. I am Ereben... I am no more than the sea of their transience. I am no less than the child of their end.

Locked within the jasper columns and broken shards of my memory, the explosion of exuberant forest now rests undisturbed by wind or rain. Rather by massive movement of rivers solid and cold, your visage is cleaved. Left exposed. Torn asunder. Now quiet. Phaena....

Ereben felt himself swallowed within the timeless, painless jaws of permanence. All questions were inapplicable. All goals trivial. The futility of life's gestures left only the slightest twinge of bitterness. *Bitterness. Bitter!*

"Bite the radish, Ereben," Hobart's voice whispered into his being.

He clamped his teeth into the Nagel radish. *I have teeth! I have myself!* Warmth and light flooded his mind. He saw everything, but could understand none of it. Green, blue, white, wind, sun, grass. He spit out the radish. As his senses cleared, he recognized the plateau on which he stood. *A face. I see a face. I should know the face.*

"Ereben?"

Yes. I am Ereben. Ereben Leaf. I am myself. "Jasper?" he said. The image of Jasper stood immobile, ten paces from him.

"Are you... like a ghost?" Jasper asked cautiously. The boy's face bore stains of sorrow and exhaustion.

"I... No. I'm not a ghost. More like a rock. I know what it is like to be a rock." Both Jasper and the sod on which the boy stood seemed so frail, so transient.

"But I saw you fall," Jasper said weakly. His chin began to quiver. He looked away, staring fearfully into the yawning depths of the canyon.

"Yes. I fell all the way to the bottom. But the stone turned soft, like a pillow. Like a pillow, it caught me."

"I thought you were dead," Jasper sobbed, "like Hobart. And then you just pop up out of the rock. You just popped up from nowhere. You just pop up!"

Ereben reached out to Jasper, but the boy backed away. "I'm afraid too," Ereben said.

Jasper threw his arms around Ereben. The tightness of his grip and the convulsive sobbing brought tears to Ereben's eyes as well. Minkar Jarad ran toward them and, without hesitation, reached his arms around both of them.

"I feared that you were lost, that all was lost," Minkar said. "But you are more resourceful than any of us could have imagined. Come and take some water and rest. You must be tired."

"I am," Ereben answered. "I am."

On their silent walk back to the house, Ereben saw a fresh mound of dirt. Beside it, a simple wooden marker displayed the name, "HOBART", carved in the unmistakable style of Jasper's skillful hand. Beyond the house, the heads of the three giant birds turned to watch them approach.

Hobart! Ereben now understood that even though Hobart's body had been destroyed, his being had somehow passed into the rock of the great canyon. *He spoke to me.* There he would remain, beyond time.

"I can not agree, Maister Ereben," Barrow insisted. They had been discussing what to do for over an hour. "If Hobart had lived, he would have travelt tae see Ailantha. Bein' able tae bring Chrysanthus from oot o' yon dagger may be our only hope o' stoppin' Corban. Unless ye have anither way o' stoppin' the bastard."

"But Corban's got my dagger now," Ereben explained again. "I have Hobart's dagger, but it's...it's not the same. How am I supposed to figure out how to release Grandfather, if he's really there, if I don't even have the dagger?"

"That is exactly why ye need tae talk with Ailantha."

"I still think I should go to Rippleton first."

"That is for ye tae decide. But I was surprised tae learn that Ailantha was still alive. She may already have died since ye talked with her. She may not wait for ye tae dallie."

"Perhaps," Minkar said, "we should travel directly to Ailantha, learn what she may offer, then go immediately to Rippleton for the girl."

Ereben looked at the faces of his friends. He had little doubt that they all felt the urgency of finding Ailantha. Excepting, perhaps, Bahsa, who had captured two small beetles, which seemed more interesting to him than their discussion of plans. "Okay. We will go to Ailantha and see if she can help." The words carried with them a resignation. He had to acknowledge that the prospect of seeing Phaena had driven his concerns about Corban far into the background. Phaena would have to wait.

While the others gathered belongings and lashed them onto the great birds and the kelpie, Ereben went into Hobart's house. He sensed a sadness about the place. With Hobart gone forever into the rock, so many of the things scattered about no longer seemed to have importance. Cooking pots and trinkets, items of clothing and battered furniture, all were of no use to anyone. He collected a writing quill and ink, along with several blank sheets of parchment. From the mantle, he took the leather pouch of translucent, red stones that Menash had given Hobart in the ruins of Ephesia. Among the few remaining books, he found a small dictionary of Knurlish, written by Yarnish Blen. He kept it. Looking about, he ached with the magnitude of his loss. He had hoped to learn so much from Hobart—to learn magic. Now it seemed as though the knowledge of magic would forever be locked within the rocks of the great canyon. He picked up the patchwork parchment bearing the design of the mysterious ax that his grandfather had drawn. In a web of dust beside the hearth, he found a thin alderwood staff only a yard long. Near its angled head, it bore three glyphs burned into the wood. It seemed about the right weight and length for Bahsa. He took it. "Good-bye, Hobart," he whispered, placing his hand to the base of the hearth, the only portion of the floor exposing bare canyon rock. The tips of his fingers entered the rock. *Yes, Hobart is there.*

Outside, he lashed his spear and remaining baggage to the harness on Titus, now a great Gyre Falcon instead of the mouse he had known. He looked at his companions. Barrow, Whittig Trench, Grand Master of the Watchers, sat upon Pelegri, with the golden ax of the Chamberlain lashed at his side. Minkar Jarad, wearing the Chamberlain's golden plate girdle, sat high on the shoulders of Krey, the gray owl. The smallest mount of them all, Dantel, carried Jasper, in his wolf cape and Chamberlain's golden helm, with Bahsa riding behind, proud in his golden chain hood and steel greave shield. Ereben handed the alderwood staff to Jasper. "This was Hobart's. I thought Bahsa might like to have it." They appeared ready for battle. *We may find it.* He looked down at himself, in his golden breastplate and ice leopard cape, which seemed to match the white and ghostly stippled feathers of Titus. He realized how different he must appear from the boy who fled from Rippleton—how much they all had changed. *And these giant birds. And a flying horse!* "Okay, Titus, let's go back to the mountains."

The great gyre falcon glanced back at Ereben with an eye larger than Ereben's entire head. White wings spread their power against the wind and lifted Ereben from the plateau. The others rose to join him—the kelpie, with Jasper and Bahsa behind to his right and the gray owl and peregrine falcon behind to his left. Whenever Titus veered or rose or descended, the others followed in close formation, as one mighty organism, soaring aloft with skill and purpose. Ereben glanced once into the depths of the great canyon, thinking how wonderful it would be to actually fly as Titus could now fly. The canyon vanished behind them as they headed north toward Punishment Pass, high in the Broken Mountains.

In mid-afternoon, at Jasper's urging, they landed in the grassy plains of western Knurlan, then continued northeast toward the distant notch in the high reaches of the mountains. Ereben found that Titus needed little guidance—an occasional touch of the reins. He thrilled at the rush of wind and the boundless horizon. With the rise of the land, the great birds pumped steadily to gain altitude, while Ereben tried to identify the location of Ailantha's ramshackle house. When it came into view, Ereben urged Titus downward, but to his annoyance, the gyre falcon continued to climb. Of the others, Minkar alone seemed to notice their error, but signaled that Krey seemed to be following Titus. Up they climbed, into the raw cold of the high currents, leveling off into a wide circle above Punishment Pass.

"What are you doing?" Ereben shouted at Titus. "We need to go down." It was then that Ereben recognized what had prompted Titus to climb.

To the North and well below them, tiny specks flew southward in a straight line for the pass. Ereben could not count them, but they seemed to number less than a dozen. From his altitude, Ereben guessed that the intruders were some of Corban's giant vultures. The vultures' path would carry them directly through the pass, and beneath Titus' high circle of flight. Ereben found it difficult to imagine how Titus could have seen them long before his own eyes could distinguish anything from the distant haze.

By the time the vultures began to stream out of the southern opening of the pass, Ereben had clearly counted eight. Each seemed to carry a rider. Titus abruptly drew in his massive wings and dove toward the flight of vultures. Krey, Pelegri and Dantel followed. Ereben pressed his body close to Titus' shoulders. They seemed to be falling much faster than Ereben had fallen in the canyon. As they dropped into the rear of the unsuspecting flight of vultures, Titus flared his wings and extended his deadly talons. Ereben hardly felt the contact. Titus' leg threw the vulture's rider from his seat, while the talons deftly punctured, then released, the body of the vulture. Krey and Pelegri felled two other vultures in the same manner. Dantel, kicked a rider from his seat, then, with a single blow of one front hoof, crushed the skull of the vulture. Four vultures and their riders tumbled from the sky.

The Protectors on the remaining four vultures were now aware of their attackers. Two vultures broke to the left, two to the right, circling back to confront Ereben and his companions. The great predatory birds and the magical kelpie were able to gain altitude more rapidly than the lumbering carrion fowl. To Ereben, it appeared as though the Protectors were able to keep the vultures in the confrontation only with fearsome tension on their reins. Finally one of the Protectors drew his sword and pointed it at Jasper and Bahsa on their flying horse. A crack of lightning issued from the sword.

Dantel opened her mouth and swallowed the bolt. The kelpie groaned, as swirls of color swept through her body. Her head elongated to the shape of an eagle's head, with a yard long beak. From her front hoofs sprouted great eagle talons. She fell upon the vulture bearing the Protector that had attacked her. Dantel's talons sank into the body of the vulture. The Protector scrambled over the leading edge of Dantel's wing. Bahsa pulled Hobart's alderwood staff from Jasper's pack and struck the Protector across the forehead. Frost crystallized on the Protector's immobile face. Bahsa struck him again. The man's head shattered into hundreds of fragments. Pelegri swooped to another vulture. His talons missed, but Barrow's golden ax swung across the rider's shoulders. The Protector's body sat headless for a brief moment, then toppled backwards, allowing his vulture to flee to the North. The two remaining Protectors banked their vultures steeply toward the pass, but Krey and Titus fell upon them before they could escape. Only one riderless vulture cleared the pass and disappeared to the North.

Ereben wondered how Titus, Krey, Pelegri and Dantel performed so effectively in combat with so little direction from their riders. Their initial tactic of climbing to great altitude had been carried out despite his own urging to descend. What puzzled Ereben most was that if Titus understood his needs by reading his mind, then how would that lead the gyre falcon to disobey instructions on account of a danger that Ereben had not even considered until after Titus' actions. *There is so much I don't understand. You could have explained it all, Hobart.*

With the vultures dispatched, Dantel resumed her less fearsome incarnation as a horse with wings. Titus banked into a gently descending circle toward the tiny house perched on a level area in the upper slopes of the mountain. Here the snow of the higher elevations had dwindled to scattered patches in the shady areas. A small garden extended over a terrace to the downward side of the house. At the approach of the great predatory birds, a shaggy, white goat tugged fiercely against its tether, but was unable to free itself. Several chickens dove into a wooden shed nearby. The mounts of Ereben and his companions settled among gusts of flapping wings into the clearing in which Ereben and the

Shouda men had first met the aging, blind woman. Dantel once again appeared to be only a fine white mare.

Dismounting, they approached the door of the house. No one came out to meet them. Barrow knocked. "Hallo!" he called. "Ailantha, it's Barrow."

"I be not deaf, you old fool," a voice crackled from within the house. "Unless you and your friends want that your dinner be burned, you'll have to open the door yourself."

Barrow opened the door, releasing the fabulous aroma of Ailantha's oven. Bahsa ran to the side of the house to investigate the goat. Jasper went after Bahsa, while Ereben and Minkar followed Barrow into Ailantha's house.

Inside, Ereben stepped onto deep, stunningly colored wool carpet, which reached nearly from wall to wall. It vaguely resembled the carpets of the Shouda, though the patterns were different. Beautifully carved chairs were neatly arranged about a carved table, set with glistening white dishes, crystal drinking glasses and silver eating utensils. The walls were hung with woven tapestries, some depicting great cities of towers and pyramids, others the combat of men with beasts of every imaginable sort. One tapestry which caught Ereben's attention showed a man in golden armor engaged in mortal combat with a golden dragon of enormous size. Flames issued from the dragon's mouth. The man stood in mid-swing with an ax held back over his head, the ax's blade facing backwards. Two barbed prongs of the ax aimed at the dragon's throat.

"Yes," the broken voice of the old woman said, "that be the ax your grandfather wished to re-create."

Startled, Ereben looked at Ailantha. She faced away from him, stooping over the door of her oven. When she lifted a steaming pie and turned toward him, her sunken eyes were as opaque and marble-like as he had remembered. She placed the pie on the counter and retrieved a second from the oven, then closed the oven door.

"Ye look as though ye were expectin' us," Barrow commented.

"How else could I have food ready for your dinner?" she said. "Now all three of you go out to the spring and wash your hands. And bring the boys with you when you return."

Somehow she can see. Ereben looked more carefully about the room. Everything was spotlessly clean and meticulously arranged. Only Ailantha herself seemed disheveled, her stiff, white hair going off in several directions, carrying scattered twigs and brown leaves.

"Your hands be no cleaner than the others, Ereben Leaf," she said, still going about her preparations.

"Yes ma'am," he said sheepishly. Something about her manner suddenly reminded Ereben of his own mother. A pang of loss smote his heart.

As he turned to exit, Ailantha whispered softly, "I know. I'm sorry."

Ereben looked back at the old woman. She was busy slicing pies.

Soon, they were all seated around the table, gorging themselves with Ailantha's spectacular pies, made from vegetables, hen's eggs and goat cheese. Embedded within them were huge chunks of onion and mushroom fried in oil. Ereben recognized immediately that the mushroom was munu, not from its appearance, sliced and fried, but from the gentle wave of rejuvenation that seeped from the center of his belly to every part of his body. The fatigue of the journey and the stress of the aerial confrontation melted away.

Their conversation settled on seemingly trivial matters, such as the view from aloft, or the diet of the great birds. Any mention of past or impending events elicited the same, "I know," from Ailantha. She was already aware of Hobart's passage into the rock, and the sequestration of the magic library of Ephesia. She knew of the fall of Shouda City and the massacre of its people. When pressed for details, Ailantha stated that the Mufta, his daughter, and his guard Oor Shakur were alive in the hills above the city, and that Amal, Otah and Menash had not yet located them.

"Do you know what will happen?" Minkar asked.

"One seldom understands the attunements of such matters until they come to pass," she said, nibbling at her food.

"But do you know?" he persisted.

She lifted her marble eyes to Minkar. "Of this be certain, Minkar Jarad, you must follow a path fraught with sorrow and suffering, yet you have no other path upon which you may tread."

Minkar glanced at Bahsa, who ate his dinner, oblivious to the conversation.

After dinner, Ereben finally approached the question for which they had made their journey. "Hobart said that my grandfather was inside my dagger. Is that possible?"

"Hobart told you that it was possible," she said. "You wish to know if there be a path whereby he may be released."

"Yes."

"Many years ago, Chrysanthus caused a hen's egg to vanish into the trunk of an oak tree. Two years later, he finally devised a spell by which to release it again."

"What happened?" Jasper asked.

"When he cast the releasing spell, a fully grown hen emerged from the oak tree."

"Wow," Jasper said.

"But the hen never laid eggs." Ailantha tracked her opaque eyes across the faces in the room. "For the rest of its life, the hen laid only acorns. And if these acorns be planted in the ground, a sprout would eventually break through the surface, but could produce only feathers in the place of leaves. So, each of these would soon die."

Grim possibilities flashed through Ereben's mind. *Grandfather may be different, or dead, if he comes out. How could an old man share anything about the dagger?* "Do you know the spell, Ailantha?"

"I know it."

"Well, I was able to go into the stone of the canyon and come out the same. Maybe Grandfather can do the same thing."

"The stone invited you. You emerged similar, but changed. The stone bore the consequences of the counterspell."

"Changed?" Ereben asked. "How have I... What counterspell?"

"Hobart passed into the rock before he could teach you the great trap of using magic. Many wondrous things may be carried out with the use of magic. But it be called magic, because it changes the common paths of matter and power. In order for any spell to bring about an effect, it must also bring about a counter-effect. This be the first law, the law of the attunement of nature. When you cast a spell, it be the paths of the counterspell which maintain that attunement."

"I don't understand."

"When a shield deflects the blow of a sword, the path of the sword be altered. But for this to occur, the path of the shield must also be altered. Power be passed between them. If you deflect the path of the sword with a pot of boiling water, it may indeed deflect the sword, but you pay the price by being scalded. Wisdom in the practice of magic requires that you never cast a spell without first understanding the counterspell which will also be cast. Spell and counterspell be always cast by the same words. Such an oversight cost me my eyes."

Ereben thought of the way in which his dagger consumed the munu mushroom in order to cast light.

"A spell has no power of its own. It simply redirects the paths of the horizon as they engage the events which unfold before us."

"I suppose," said Barrow, as he stood up, "that all those paths and powers fit thegither somehow. For me, it's like tryin' tae mak a log whole again efterin ye just chopt it tae flinders."

"What does that mean?" Jasper asked.

"Mither o' the gods, boy! It maks nae sense." Barrow stepped outside, shaking his head.

Later, when everyone else had found a warm spot on the carpeted floor to spend the night, Ailantha took Ereben into her small sleeping room. She sat on a three-leg stool and, by candle light, began to explain the nature of the releasing spell that Ereben was determined to use as soon as he regained possession of his own dagger. The old woman's patient explanations again reminded Ereben of his own mother, who would sit in the evening teaching Ereben and his brother. He and Caris would argue over who got to comb Mother's hair. Ereben's eyes strayed to a partly toothless comb resting on a stand beside Ailantha's bed. Without asking, he took the comb and began to gently remove the twigs and leaves from Ailantha's brittle, white hair. She continued her explanations while Ereben combed her hair. When he was done, he sat on the foot of the bed and faced the old woman. Although her words continued uninterrupted, tears flowed from the sunken sockets of her marble eyes. She stopped.

"Ereben Leaf, you bring a joy that you can not understand. Nearly eighty years have passed since one of my sons last combed my hair. You have a depth to you that no one else has ever seen. I wish there be some way to spare you from what lies ahead, but you be the only hope this world has for a future. There will be others, as time passes, but today you stand alone in that responsibility."

"Can't you come with us to confront Corban?"

"I am barely able to walk about this tiny house. The power that I once wielded has gone the way of all things."

"Won't the munu mushroom give you the strength?"

"Without it, I would have died years ago. Only by its power am I able to be as you see me now."

"How old are you?"

"I have truly lost count, but I will guess 115 years."

"Do you use magic to read my thoughts?"

"That be only magical to someone who has no understanding of intent. Thoughts and intentions be there for all to read, if we put aside our resistance to them. That be why it makes no difference whether you cast a spell from within yourself, or speak the words aloud. The spell...and its counterspell...are cast as you will it."

Long after the others had gone to sleep, Ereben left Ailantha's room and quietly stepped outside. His breath left trails in the crisp winter air. From the ridge of mountain above, a sparkling blanket of the night sky arched overhead and on to the farthest reaches of the South. To the West, mountains blocked his view of Valand's undulating horizon, but the exact location of Rippleton seemed as clear as when he stood on the ridge above the town so many months ago. He tilted his head to the sky, as if to bounce his words against the stars and on to Phaena. "Nothing will stop me tomorrow." *I will see you tomorrow. I will touch you tomorrow.* Thirty yards away, the ghostly silhouette of Titus seemed to turn toward him and nod its head in affirmation.

When morning came, and all the gear had been lashed to their mounts, they offered their thanks and farewells to Ailantha. Bahsa ran up to her and put his arms up around her neck. The old woman hugged him with one arm, while steadying herself with her cane.

"Yes, yes, I know," she whispered to Bahsa. "She will always be in your heart."

Finally, Ereben placed his arms around Ailantha. "Thank you." He was distressed to discover how little flesh padded her skeleton.

"You see how useless I would be on your journey," she said. "You have all the strength within you, Ereben Leaf." As Ereben released her, she grasped his shoulder in her bony hand. "Do not let your love for Phaena blind you to danger."

"It won't," he said halfheartedly. He mounted Titus and gave the signal. The birds and the kelpie lifted them from the clearing by Ailantha's house and steered southwest. The plan was to fly far south of Rippleton, then turn northeast into one of the valleys that converged on the town. The Protectors would be least likely to watch for intruders there. As a further precaution, they would land several miles outside of the town and wait there until nightfall. Ereben's intention was to fly alone, under cover of darkness, and to land on the top of the palace tower. He knew from Hobart that Phaena was being kept in the tower. With luck, he might land undetected, rescue her, and escape without having to draw blood.

The flight proved to be beautiful and uneventful. When they had flown low in the valley and landed near Rippleton, Krey and Pelegri were hidden at the foot of an overhanging cliff. Dantel, of course, appeared to be an ordinary horse, and did not need to be hidden. As twilight merged into the darkness of night, Ereben settled himself on the shoulders of Titus and lifted from the valley, circling to gain altitude. The faint lights of Rippleton appeared as jewels against the blackness of the intersecting valleys.

Hundreds of yards above the palace of Corban, High Protector of Dragomin, Ereben glided in lazy circles, watching for any sign of alert. When all seemed quiet, he took Titus into a tight spiral directly to the top of the stone tower. It was only at the last moment that he saw the lone guard casually leaning over the parapet. As Titus touched down, the gust of his wings and clatter of talons alerted the guard. Ereben swung the handle of his spear full force into the guard's head, knocking him senseless to the deck of the tower.

"Don't let him go anywhere," Ereben said to Titus, as he slid down from the gyre falcon's shoulders. He dashed down the open stairway to the top floor of rooms. Two doors opened onto the landing. Both were locked from Ereben's side. Readying his spear, he picked one door at random and unlatched it. When the door opened, he gazed into the bruised face of Yarnish Blen, the old tinker from his past life.

"Wonders never cease," Blen said.

Ereben was stunned. He immediately dismissed a twinge of guilt over his initial glee to see that Blen had been beaten. He had always hated the man. But since Ereben's flight from Rippleton, he had learned surprising things about Yarnish Blen, not the least of which was that Blen was probably a Watcher for the Guardians. He ached to see Phaena, but knew he should not abandon Blen in the prison. "I didn't expect to find you," he said limply.

"They threw me in here a week ago. If it's your sweetheart you've come for, you better be cautious. She knows you didn't kill your family, but she believes you want to overthrow her father. Since I'm sure you do, you should watch your words until you're well clear of here. How in the willows did you ever get past all the guards?"

Ereben pointed a finger to the roof. "Came in from the top. Let me get Phaena, then the three of us can get out of here." Ereben exited the cell, looked up and down the stairs, then, after a slow, deep breath, opened the other cell. There, in the candle light, sat the most beautiful sight he had seen since before his life came apart. He had forgotten how petite she was, how perfect every feature. Phaena looked up with only puzzlement on her lovely face. Her golden hair danced across tiny shoulders.

"You look different, Ereben."

"I know. But you look as wonderful as ever. I've come to take you out of here." His heart pounded within his chest. A subtle scent of almond mingled with strawberry intoxicated him in a way that Liddie Burn's barley-brie could never approach. He could feel his ears turning red.

"How did you get in here?"

"That doesn't matter. We need to go quickly."

Phaena closed a book and aligned it carefully on the corner of the small table beside her chair. "I can't go with you." She drew a thick, gray cloak of boiled wool about herself and held it closed by its green brocaded border.

"What?" His mind became hazy. "You're in a prison. I've come to take you away."

"But you're a wanted criminal, and I'm the daughter of the High Protector. I can't go with you. Why did you come back?" Anger flared in her face.

"But Phaena, I thought..."

"Go away. If they catch you this time, it's your fault."

Ereben was near tears. He approached her and took her hand. "I love you." She withdrew her hand. "Phaena, we have to go now. Now!" He gently grasped her forearm.

"Help!" she screamed. "Guards, help!"

Footsteps echoed in the stairway.

ꙮ

Although the weapons of man may defend civilization, it is the daily struggles of woman that sustain civilization and make it worth defending.

Ereben Leaf: Chronicle of the Counterspell

Ereben could hardly believe that Phaena, the one person he loved more than anyone else in the world, had screamed for the guards rather than escape with him. He knew he must leave immediately or risk capture, but he was paralyzed by the thought of leaving without her.

Yarnish Blen rushed into Phaena's cell. "Son, we have to go now. Guards are coming!" When Ereben failed to move, he added, "Leave her if she won't come. We have to go."

Two guards entered, short swords drawn and ready. They were followed by a guard lieutenant, whom Ereben vaguely recognized.

"If it isn't our own local fugitive," the lieutenant said.

Phaena drew her cloak about her and stood behind the guards. "He tried to take me away," she said tentatively.

"I don't know how you got in here, Ereben Leaf," the lieutenant said, "but you'll be leaving feet first. There is already a warrant of death on you. Kidnapping the High Protector's daughter certainly can't make the penalty any worse." He looked at Yarnish Blen. "I'm not surprised that the two of you are in league. Kill them both."

"Here?" one of the guards asked.

"Kill them both. Now!"

Ereben took one step away from the guard and slowly lowered his spear. He lunged, but the guard parried with his sword. From behind the guard, Phaena swept her cloak from her shoulders and over the head of the guard. The second guard turned from Blen, apparently unsure of what action to take against Corban's daughter. In that instant, Yarnish Blen tipped his shoulder and planted one boot solidly into the side of the guard's head, slamming him against the stone wall. The guard dropped to the floor. The instant that the first guard pulled Phaena's cloak from his head, Ereben's spear drove into his belly. When Blen took up the sword of the second guard, the lieutenant fled from the cell and down the stairs, calling for help.

For a moment, Ereben looked with puzzlement into Phaena's expressionless face.

"Let's go," she said, retrieving her heavy cloak from the stone floor.

"That way." Ereben pointed up the steps.

On the roof of the tower, the watchman still lay unconscious. Yarnish Blen and Phaena were both clearly frightened at the sight of the huge gyre falcon.

"He's on our side," Ereben said, immediately regretting his choice of words. He wondered if Phaena considered herself to be on his side, or on any side, for that matter.

As Phaena fastened the elaborate frog at the collar of her cloak, she returned Ereben's gaze with a distant, dispassionate expression, as though she were seeing him for the first time. Her eyes slowly moved from his face to his ice leopard cloak, then to his golden cuirass, the dagger strapped to his waist, and finally to the Shouda spear, its blade still wet with blood. She drew her cloak more tightly, took a deep breath and, with a disconcerting formality, allowed Ereben to assist her in mounting. Blen looked about, shrugged his shoulders and followed Phaena.

Ereben climbed onto the broad back of Titus, in front of his reluctant passengers. A guard emerged from the stairs with an arrow knocked in his bow. He leveled it at Titus' breast, but instead of releasing the arrow, he stood erect and tipped backwards over the parapet, vanishing into the darkness. Three more guards reached the top level as Titus spread his wings and lifted into the night sky. Each of the guards, in rapid succession, crumpled to the deck with a long, Shouda arrow protruding from his chest. The silhouette of a great owl swept past.

"Oh, Bahsa," Phaena scolded, "you're soaking wet." The boy had just come into the cabin from playing in the snow. Phaena removed his padded cape and hung it near the fire.

Ereben sat across the small cabin at the table. He watched Phaena while Minkar, who sat with him, droned something about the difficulty of keeping the birds fed.

"Now wait," Phaena continued. "Just look at your tunic. Lift up your arms." Bahsa hesitated. "Up." Phaena pulled the wet tunic over his head. "Honestly, Bahsa, where are your underclothes?"

The naked boy sheepishly rolled his eyes toward his father, who had not been following the events. Ereben kicked Minkar's foot beneath the table. Minkar looked from Bahsa to Phaena, and then shrugged. Phaena draped a blanket over Bahsa's shoulders, then ushered him to a stool beside the fire. As she arranged a spot for his wet tunic to dry, she spoke, not quite making eye contact with either Ereben or Minkar.

"All of you should be ashamed. If you choose to dress like wild animals and live like wild animals and be hunted like wild animals, and probably die like wild animals, well that's your business. But it's certainly no way to raise two children." Phaena snatched up her gray, boiled wool cloak, swept it over her shoulders and fastened the frog.

The door opened. Jasper, wrapped in the pelt of the great silver wolf, sauntered in from the snow and said, "Oh, it's good in here!"

Phaena abruptly walked around him and exited, slamming the door behind her. Jasper looked to Ereben.

"Do you think you could come up with a sewing needle?" Ereben asked him.

"Sure. Why?"

"I think we need to make some underclothes for Bahsa before dinner.

Nearly two weeks had passed since their escape from the tower. The first storm of winter had blanketed the land with a half-yard of heavy snow. During this time, they hid in a deserted cabin south of Rippleton, near the town of Brookton, watching the daily flights of vultures heading to the south and far west reaches of Valand, apparently in search of Ereben and his fellow outlaws. Now that the patrols became less frequent, they fled in a long, arching path, first to the South, then swinging up to the eastern bank of the Iron River.

Yarnish Blen brought with him information about the growing power of the True Faith cult. Crotus, known to his followers as The Redeemer, had succeeded in rallying the support of most of the priests of Dragomin for a religious war against the "heretic" Corban and his practice of magic. Blen had learned that priests of the True Faith were moving through the countryside levying "donations" from peasants in order to supply their crusade against the Protectors.

Phaena remained aloof, though cooperative. She hardly spoke to anyone but Bahsa. When Ereben would approach her, she would draw her cloak about her and grow silent. He decided not to force the question of their relationship, even though he wanted nothing more than to hold her in his arms. However, something deep within him saw the passing weeks as a mere flicker of time. *I can wait. Like a rock. I can wait as long as I need to wait.* Meanwhile, he endured the continuous frustration of her unbreachable isolation.

"I think we ought to go into Nilwid," Jasper suggested one morning.

"Those priests o' the Cult are likely tae be there," Barrow pointed out. The dwarf had managed to purchase a heavy red and brown blanket in a small village. He now wore it as a cape against the bitter cold.

"That's the whole idea," Jasper replied. "The people there aren't really fighters, so they probably have just a few priests who won't expect a fight."

"Ye want tae fight them?"

"Well, just kind of capture them. Then we can make them tell us what's going on with the rest of the priests."

Minkar elbowed Ereben. "Young Jasper offers a reasonable suggestion. We might be able to learn of Crotus' plans. Since we must stop Corban before the solstice, it would be well to know what the priests are intending."

Ereben immediately considered dozens of things that could go wrong if they entered Nilwid. "Let's do it. We could be there in a quarter hour, land outside the town and sneak in to have a look."

Half an hour later, they were standing knee deep in snow within the oak forest surrounding Nilwid, Jasper's former home. Phaena remained with Bahsa and Blen with the protection of the kelpie, Dantel, while the others crept into the village. Ereben had explained to Titus that he should come at the sound of a whistle, but he was not at all certain that the gyre falcon understood.

The four of them approached Nilwid from the forest southeast of the town. This seemed to provide the densest underbrush, enabling them to move undetected within ten yards of the snow-covered plaza at the entrance to the temple of Dragomin. A crowd of townspeople had gathered into a line which ended at a wooden table by the temple door. Each person in line carried a sack of grain or thrashing chickens or a squealing pig. At the table, one black-robed priest recorded names and quantities, while two other priests stacked grain and penned the animals.

"Two chickens is not enough," said the priest at the table. "Surely your faith is in need of strengthening."

"We gave more the last time," the peasant pleaded. "We will go hungry as it is. If we give more..."

"Enough of this," the seated priest said softly. "Go and wait over there." He pointed to a bench where two frightened women and a senile old man sat shivering.

"But I have no more..."

"Go and wait quietly, or things will be much worse."

Jasper stepped out from behind an oak, drew Rat Slayer with his right hand, adjusted his golden helmet and walked toward the table, his carved wooden staff at his left. Ereben was about to follow him, but was stopped by Barrow's hand.

Those standing in line turned to watch Jasper's approach. "Jasper." "It's Jasper," murmured through the crowd.

"I don't know who you people think you are," Jasper said to the amazed priests, "but you're not going to steal any more food from my town."

Gasps were heard within the crowd. "He's not one of us," a voice called from the line. Heads turned in panic toward one another.

"Put down your knife, boy," said one of the standing priests. "Don't force us to do you harm."

"Do as he says," a voice said from the crowd.

"I'll put it right into your belly," Jasper replied, "if you don't just leave all that food right where it is and go away."

Ereben could see that the situation was about to get ugly, but Barrow signaled for him to wait in hiding a moment longer. He reluctantly nodded.

The priest at the table offered a fatuous smile, then rubbed his hands together. The other two priests moved slowly away from the table, toward Jasper's side. A ball of light flashed toward Jasper from the hands of the seated priest. Jasper jumped in surprise. Even though it struck Jasper squarely on his golden helmet, he appeared uninjured. The ball of fire only succeeded in melting a ring of snow a half-yard from Jasper's feet, and causing a cloud of steam to rise up around him.

Ereben could wait no longer. When he stepped into the open, Barrow and Minkar followed. The sight of the three of them stunned the crowd to silence. The priests, now apparently unsure of the efficacy of their "miracle" balls of fire, and confronted by the young man, the dwarf and the tall, brown Shouda warrior, all armed and armored, turned and fled. Ereben put his fingers to his lips and whistled as loudly as he could. Three great birds flew over the village so fast and so low that by the time the people of the town looked up, they were gone. Moments later, two priests ran back into the village.

"Stop them! Call them off!" one of the priests shouted.

Titus swooped into the plaza and dropped the third priest from his talons. The people of the town scattered in every direction. Pelelgri and Krey lighted at the exits to the plaza. Barrow, Minkar, Jasper and Ereben rounded up the terrified priests and took them into the temple.

"Your weapons do not frighten us," one of the priests said, hurrying just beyond the point of Minkar's spear.

"We are not afraid to die for our faith," another blustered.

"I wouldna think o' killin' a holy priest," Barrow said, "but yon hungry birds might mistak ye for their dinner."

"What do you want?"

"I want you to leave these people alone," Jasper said.

"That would be a good start," Barrow commented. "But we need a tiny wee bit o' information."

"We will never betray our faith," one priest insisted. "And heathens who reject the message of The Redeemer will suffer pain and damnation."

Barrow stroked his beard, smiled and nodded at the contentious priest, then turned to Minkar. "Tak this one oot tae the birds," Barrow ordered.

"Wait! Wait! What do you want to know?"

ഇഗ

The power within each of us is sufficient to move the multitude. The balance of that movement, whether it favors nurturance or conflagration, is swayed in proportion to one's understanding of what it is to be a part of that multitude.

Ereben Leaf: Chronicle of the Counterspell

Ereben leaned his head beyond the leading edge of Titus' massive wing. The battle raging far below him seemed more like distant shrubs waving in a breeze than the mortal struggle of two great armies. The blink of fireflies, he knew, must be the searing flashes of magical fire and lightning cast between the Protectors and the priests of Crotus. Thousands of dark-robed priests comprising Crotus' left flank poured southward around the snowy eastern shore of Lake Shardas to reinforce their center, which now drove into the northern edge of the Shouda Shrine. The white of the snow covered plain merged into the milky white stone of the Shrine, where no snow accumulated. Corban held his foot guard, thousands strong, in a firm line against the priests, while vulture mounted Protectors harried Crotus' left flank, to the East, and orderly ranks of wild beasts spilled over the western hills into the priests' right. Dog-size ravens swarmed like gnats over the black-robed army.

Barrow, flying Pelegri close to Ereben's left, signaled that they should remain at their current height above the battle. Minkar, riding Krey to Ereben's right, nodded his understanding. Ereben knew that today was the winter solstice, the day that Corban must attempt to open the portal in the black pyramid. Barrow's plan was to allow the two armies to dissipate themselves against one another for as long as possible. When Corban and his crimson-hooded assistants turned their attention from the battle front to the black pyramid, that would be the time to intervene.

A dollop of Crotus' reinforcements formed themselves into an empty triangle of perhaps a thousand priests on the north shore of the lake, opposite the Shrine. Points of light appeared above each priest in the triangle, then rose and coalesced above them to form a dazzling triangle of flame. The flaming triangle moved slowly south, over the waters of Lake Shardas, then suddenly shot beneath the surface. Even from the great height at which Ereben circled, he could hear the vicious hiss of flame forcing water into steam, though the sound reaching Ereben was delayed by a count of five after the appearance of the steam. The blast of steam launched southward, just over the heads of Crotus' main body, instantly erasing a swath of ravens from the scene.

Another body of priests, on Crotus' right flank, to the West, transformed every tree and bush of the western hills into a wall of fire, leaving the ordered ranks of wild beasts cut off from the battle. Crotus' army appeared to be gaining the upper hand, as the center drove toward the black pyramid. Again a triangle of flame appeared north of the lake, and again it plunged into the water, sending its ferocious cloud of steam over the heads of the priests.

A flight of fifty vultures lifted from the Shrine in a spiral, then broke directly for the north of the lake. Circling above the triangle of priests, yet still a thousand yards below Ereben and his companions, the Protectors emptied baskets of small objects onto the heads of the priests. The triangle disintegrated into chaos, as the priests either fell where they had stood, or ran for their lives. At the northern edge of the Shrine, along the center of both opponents, columns of Protectors launched coordinated volleys of lightning from their longswords into the ranks of priests, blasting them down dozens at a time.

As the tide of battle surged in Corban's favor, a small circle of crimson-hooded men pulled away from the front and headed for the black pyramid at the middle of the Shrine. Within the moving circle walked one man.

Barrow pointed his hand down three times, the signal to descend. Ereben glanced at Minkar. Minkar was frantically trying to wave them off. He motioned for Ereben to look to the south of the Shrine. There, it appeared that a reserve of Corban's ground troops was sweeping from the southern edge of the Shrine toward the black pyramid. Ereben realized that he and his friends would be trapped between the two bodies of Protectors. He looked back to warn Barrow, but Pelegri was already carrying the dwarf down in a tight spiral above the black pyramid. Ereben and Minkar followed him down toward the towering stone pinnacles.

Within a hundred yards of the ground, Ereben saw a dozen Protectors urge their vultures into the air to meet them. Barrow and Minkar broke to either side. The First vulture to reach Ereben was immediately eviscerated by Titus' expertly aimed talons. A second swooped above and dove toward him, its beak opened to catch Ereben. With the point of his spear, Ereben slashed across the vulture's throat, sending a shower of blood in every direction. Two more vultures moved to attack, one on either side. The Protector riding the vulture to the right aimed his sword and released a blinding flash. The impact of the bolt struck Ereben squarely in his golden breastplate, throwing him free of his harness. Ereben grabbed at Titus' feathers, but slipped over the edge of his wing. Titus banked and dove. Ten yards from the milky white deck of the Shrine, Titus caught Ereben with the talons of one foot. Before the great gyre falcon could set him to the ground, three more vultures approached, but they never reached him. Each of them crashed to the stone of the Shrine, arrows bristling from their bodies and wings.

Ereben looked to the South. The force of nearly a hundred, which had surged toward the black pyramid, was led by a man in full steel armor, wielding a two handed sword and riding a magnificent, amber stallion. *Menash!*

Titus set Ereben to the ground. As Ereben attempted to climb back onto Titus, the great bird pulled away from him and bounded into the air. From the direction of the black pyramid, a gray and white goshawk, nearly the size of Titus, flew straight toward Ereben. Titus tipped into its path and parried the attack, then rose nearly straight up, leveling then pumping his mighty wings. The goshawk followed. Three, four, five times the enormous predatory birds dove at each other, and each time the attack was parried. So high were they above the pinnacles that Ereben lost sight of them.

Ereben looked to the black pyramid. The circle of crimson-hooded guards had reached its northern face. Ereben raced through the chaos of combat toward the black center of the Shrine. Something struck him in the back, knocking him to the white stone pavement. He rolled over to find an arrow nearby, apparently turned by his steel jerkin. Ignoring the pain between his shoulder blades, he jumped to his feet and started again for the black pyramid. Ten yards away, he crouched, set down his spear, and with Hobart's dagger in one hand, and the other hand pressed firmly into a pouch of munu mushroom, he watched for Corban to expose the dagger that held Chrysanthus.

Titus! Ereben looked overhead. Now within his view, goshawk and gyre falcon locked talons, neither yielding to the other, despite their acceleration toward the stone below. Four wings thrashed uselessly as they tumbled through the cold air. One wing of the goshawk struck the top of a pinnacle, just north of where Ereben crouched. The locked birds twirled downward, like a maple seed, from the full height of the pinnacle. They struck a small white pyramid and slid to the pavement.

For a moment, Ereben watched to see some sign of life, but neither of the birds moved. His mind clouded. He forced his attention back to the black pyramid, but his view was blocked by a curtain of red. He raised his eyes. Standing before him, a crimson-robed Protector lifted a longsword overhead. Before the sword could fall, the guard's head and left arm sailed away in a flash of steel. The mutilated body crumpled to the white pavement and spilled its blood. Above Ereben stood the armored figure of Menash, who touched one hand to his helmet, then walked on toward the circle of crimson-hooded guards at the black pyramid.

On the pyramid face, a translucent green stone dagger handle protruded from the center of a horizontal line two yards from the pyramid base. *The dagger.* Again Ereben inserted his hand into the pouch of munu, and aimed Hobart's dagger at the handle in the pyramid. He struggled to focus his mind on the releasing spell Ailantha had taught him. A vast surge of power passed through his body. For a moment, the black stone surrounding the inserted dagger glowed yellow. Then it changed to dull brown and began to slough from the pyramid as countless brown worms emerged from the stone and slid to the pavement. The dagger remained unaffected.

Ereben closed his eyes. *Three daggers. There are three daggers. How am I going to tell them apart?* Within the leather pouch, over half of the munu was gone. *It used so much!* The sounds of battle continued around him, growing closer from the North.

Menash waded into the circle of crimson robes. The first guard to oppose him was cleaved from head to groin by the massive, two-handed sword. The second guard swung his longsword into Menash's flank, but the blade glanced over the steel plate of armor. Menash countered into the guard's chest.

Corban inserted a second dagger into the right side of the portal. *If this is the wrong one...* His munu would be gone. He swallowed, grasped the munu, pointed the dagger and focused on the spell, this time mouthing the words, in the hope of excluding the growing distractions and sharpening his intention. He remembered looking over the book written in Hobart's hand, entitled "Ephesiac Fragments". Even though it was written in language he could read, he had scanned enough of it to realize he understood very little of it's meaning. Now, so much depended on his being able to make magic happen. He shook his head and scolded himself for allowing his mind to wander. Tightening his grip on the dagger, he aimed it again at the second handle and cast the evocation of releasing. Power surged through him, more difficult to control than on the previous casting. He removed his left hand from the now-empty leather pouch.

Standing beside Corban at the portal, a crimson-hooded guard threw himself to the pavement. During the casting of the spell, the guard had briefly moved between Ereben and the dagger handle. On the stone paving, the guard writhed briefly, then arched his head and shoulders backwards. Beneath his robe, the guard's body assumed a bizarre shape. His hands and face, however, swelled and split. The openings of his mouth, nostrils and eyes everted themselves. His tongue extended from his exposed jaw until it tore itself free from its attachments and fell beside him. Both eyes exploded in a vitreous gush. Ereben swallowed the bile that had risen to his mouth.

Corban turned and looked at Ereben crouched ten yards away. After a momentary flash of recognition crossed the High Protector's face, he smiled contemptuously at Ereben then drew the third dagger and inserted it into the remaining slot in the portal's margin. Corban stepped back.

The triangular portal glowed red, then slowly spread its glow over the surface of the pyramid, until the entire central pyramid pulsed with red light. The pavement rumbled beneath Ereben. Lightning flashed among the tops of all the towering stone pinnacles, then ceased. A deafening groan was followed by a low pitched sucking noise, as the pyramid lost its glow and the portal dissolved. Two crimson-robed guards who stood to either side of the portal were immediately sucked into the opening by the fierce draft of wind. Bright light flashed deep within the portal, then faded. Columns of Crotus' priests, who had been pressing closer to the black pyramid halted abruptly and stared. So far as Ereben could tell, all fighting had stopped while the forces of all three sides looked to the central pyramid.

"Dragomin!" Corban shouted with his arms raised, "I command you to come forth and serve my bidding."

Menash backed away from the pyramid. As Corban spoke his blasphemy, priests looked at one another, but they did not move or speak.

"Come forth now, mighty Dragomin." Corban touched his hands together above his head. When he spread them, blue sparks jumped between his hands.

A terrifying growl echoed from the portal. An enormous reptilian head slowly emerged from the opening of the portal. Its nostrils were the size of a man's head. Its skin glistened with tiny golden scales, as a sea of jewels. Golden tendril-whiskers drooped from its yard-wide chin. On either side of its boulder sized forehead, great snake eyes gazed out at the thousands of stunned faces. Above its eyes, a crown of golden horns cleared the margin of the portal. Seeing the size of the beast's head, Ereben could not imagine how large its body must be, nor how it would pass through the opening.

Corban stepped back. "I command you to sit upon the pyramid and await my bidding!"

The beast slowly began to emerge. Nearly everyone who had been lustily killing one another moments before turned and fled from the central pyramid, leaving only the dead and wounded. Even Menash fled from the beast. Only Corban and Ereben remained. *A dragon!* Ereben fought the urge to run.

With the pliability of a serpent, the golden dragon extracted its incredible length from the pyramid. Ereben realized that it could hardly have fit beneath even the great central pyramid. *This is a door to a much larger chamber.* Golden membrane wings unfolded and stretched to their full length. No drawings, no stories had captured the reality of so large and serpentine a creature. Whirlwinds trailed from its leathery wingtips as it drove its writhing body into the air and lighted upon the apex of the pyramid, arching a serrated loop of snake-like torso into the air between its front and rear legs. Its golden tail sparkled from the top of the pyramid to its juncture with the white paving stones. The sky over the pinnacles was devoid of all birds. Even Pelegri and Krey were nowhere in sight.

"You will obey my command and only my command," Corban shouted at the dragon.

The dragon gazed longingly at the wintry, afternoon sky. Its tail, nearly half its entire length, swept back and forth across the base of the black pyramid.

Ereben was certain that Corban would, at any moment, order the dragon to kill him. He looked about frantically. The munu grew in abundance around the Shrine, but only beyond the stone paving. The fires still burning to the West would have destroyed the munu. Words from the Ephesiac Fragments jumped into his mind. "All things are an exchange for Power, and Power for all things." *All things.* He realized that he was still kneeling before the decapitated body of a guard. Grasping the guard's remaining hand, Ereben pointed Hobart's dagger at the right handle in the portal margin, knowing that either of the lower dagger handles might be his own. He would have one more attempt before Corban ordered him slain. With his eyes fixed upon the handle, he stepped his mind through the evocation.

Agony tore through Ereben's arms and chest. The pain locked within the flesh of the dead guard became his own. Hatred and anger and horror drained from the guard into Ereben. He fought it, channeled it, forced it to pass through—forced it to leave his own flesh intact. His left arm trembled uncontrollably. For a moment he looked down at the body. Its flesh shriveled from its bones. Its exposed bones crumbled to dust. When the spell was completed, he held a complete hand attached only to a crumbled wrist. The crimson robe settled empty upon the pavement.

Ereben looked back to the portal. Corban faced him, shouting something, his arm extended in Ereben's direction. The dragon's eye met Ereben's. For an instant they shared a notion, a common knowledge. Ereben recognized that they both understood what it is to be beyond time, to see time as a distant landscape. The dragon hesitated.

Corban spun back around toward the pyramid. From the right side of the portal, an ice leopard walked toward him. *An ice leopard? The ice leopard that disappeared! An ice leopard. Two shadows within the dagger! The spell worked! It brought out an ice leopard!* Ereben slapped his cheek in amazement. *An ice leopard!*

Moving himself closer to the pyramid and his golden dragon, Corban circled the ice leopard until he stood beside the portal, fighting against the draft. "Your tricks are worthless, you foolish boy!" he shouted at Ereben.

With the ice leopard facing away, Ereben noticed that the leopard had no tail. He looked more carefully at the leopard. Its ghostly spots were missing from its snow-white fur. And the ears...the ears were more rounded than they should be. He recalled Ailantha's story about the hen's egg in the oak. His view of the leopard changed from seeing what appeared strange to searching for some resemblance to his grandfather. The elbows of its front legs were bare and wrinkled. Its gait seemed to be afflicted by Chrysanthus' rheumatism. When the leopard finally growled, Ereben began to grasp the implications of what he was seeing. The leopard's teeth were yellowed and cracked. Its skin hung limp on its aged muscles. *Like an old man!* The feeble leopard paced about, but hardly seemed capable of leaping at Corban. *Grandfather, what have I done?*

Corban laughed. "Your cat seems too tired to fight!" He looked up at the dragon. "You have no choice but to obey me. I control the daggers and the portal. Now kill the scum!"

No sooner had the words been spoken than a second dragon head emerged from the portal. Corban jumped back from the opening, accidentally catching the handle of one of the daggers in his cloak. Its blade pulled partly out of its slot. The High

Protector turned to reinsert the dislodged dagger despite the fearsome head of the second dragon, but its blade slid from the stone slot and fell to the paving. In a clap of thunder that threw Corban to the ground, the portal closed, trapping the second dragon by the neck. The dragon head grimaced, as though to roar, but no sound came from its immobilized throat.

In that moment, the decrepit ice leopard pounced onto Corban's supine body. In apparent confusion, Corban struggled to free himself. The leopard's teeth and claws seemed to cause little injury to the High Protector, but its weight was sufficient to prevent him from escaping. Corban grasped the fallen dagger and plunged it into the leopard's chest. The leopard collapsed.

The struggling of the trapped dragon increased. Its serpent eyes bulged red above incredible rows of pointed teeth. When Ereben thought the dragon's head was ready to explode, the portal began to glow red. Fracture lines spread from the portal into the black stone of the pyramid. The first dragon, perched on its apex, lifted into the air an instant before the entire pyramid crumbled to pieces and crashed into a dust filled pit. The second dragon clawed itself free of the rubble, spread its wings, and took flight.

Corban rolled the dead leopard to the side and rose to his feet. "Two dragons! I command two dragons! Kill this boy!" he shouted. "And kill the priests! Kill all the priests!" He watched as the two dragons circled overhead.

Something stirred beneath the pit of rubble that had been the black pyramid. A third golden dragon emerged. Then a fourth.

"I love it. I love it. It's wonderful!" Corban shouted. "It's wonderful!" Again he held his hands above his head and drew sparks of power between them.

In all, seven golden dragons came from beneath the Shouda Shrine. Now seven dragons, each with its crown of golden horns, soared in a great circle above the pinnacles. *Settah dragomin.* Ereben looked about. The only living things remaining within the boundary of the Shrine seemed to be himself and Corban, aside from three or four ravens which cautiously picked the flesh of slain warriors, while keeping an eye on the circling dragons. None of the Protectors appeared to have the courage to stand by their master. None of the priests appeared willing to risk the dragons in order to attack Corban. Ereben took up his spear and stood. He balanced the shaft in his hand, remembering Jasper's story of how Saikal Sahm's spear had passed through Corban's head, and how Corban had fragmented into a swarm of hornets. *I will hide beneath my leopard cloak.* While Corban still faced away from Ereben, he cast his spear. The spear flew to the High Protector's back, and seemed to strike him, but at the instant of its impact, Corban caught a glimpse of the threat.

Ereben's spear dropped to the pavement just beyond Corban. The High Protector of Dragomin shimmered briefly, then broke apart into dozens of black and crimson snakes, which dropped to the pavement in a writhing mass. A raven landed nearby. After observing the snakes for a moment, it snatched one in its beak, dropped it, jumped back, bit it again. Four such attacks, and the raven succeeded in killing one snake. Apparently satisfied, the bird picked up the dead snake and flew away with it hanging limply from its beak.

Slowly, the remaining snakes coalesced and rose from the stone pavement, forming themselves once again into the shape of Corban. The High Protector staggered. When he turned to face Ereben, his right eye and right cheek were missing. Only skull and teeth showed in their place. "I cahuahh yoah," he screamed at the dragons, but his gaping face prevented him from forming the words. Saliva sprayed with every sound he attempted.

One dragon drifted to the plaza before the destroyed black pyramid and landed in front of Lord Corban. It tipped its massive head at the strange sounds spewing from Corban's face. The dragon's nostrils dilated repeatedly.

The form of Corban shimmered, then became solid again. His face was now whole, but the fingers of his left hand were missing. He drew his longsword, pointed it directly overhead and fired a bolt of lightning into the sky. "I command you to obey me!"

The dragon lifted itself up on its hind legs, spread its wings, and drew in a great breath.

"Kill the priests!"

Flame erupted from the dragon's mouth. The image of Corban shimmered into a cylindrical pillar of bricks, blackening in the dragon fire, but remaining undamaged. Enraged, the dragon dashed its great tail into the brick pillar, launching bricks across the plaza. Before each brick struck the paving, it transformed into a wisp of steam, which rose in the winter air to a height of five yards, where it solidified to the form of a small black bat. Hundreds of black bats swirled into a dense, rising column above the rubble of the destroyed pyramid. The swirling column shot upward, arched over, then streamed to the pavement before the confused dragon. There the fluttering mass of bats swarmed into a shifting, pulsatile figure of Corban, six yards tall, not quite solid, not quite corporeal.

A hollow echo of a voice boomed from the pulsating, manlike swirl of bats. "You will obey me!"

The dragon glanced briefly to its six circling companions. Serrated arches of its back tightened as it drew its head farther from Corban. The dragon sprang with lightning speed into the enormous swirling likeness of Corban, striking what would have been Corban's chest. Its reptilian jaws slammed shut on dozens of bats. The swarm collapsed, coalescing into the standing body of Corban. The High Protector looked down at his chest. There, open to the sky, his lacerated heart dumped gushes of blood onto the pavement. Corban's body shimmered momentarily, but did not change. As his knees buckled and dropped him to the blood-covered paving, a fountain of flame exploded from the dragon's mouth. Before Corban's dying body had come fully to rest, it burst into flame.

Where Corban had stood, only a charred corpse remained on the blackened paving stones. Even the longsword and the blade of Ereben's spear had been reduced to puddles of slag.

The dragon's gaze fixed on Ereben. Its tremendous tail swept back and forth across the rubble of bodies and stone. The dragon tensed its muscles, as though to pounce, then lifted into the air to join the others. Seven golden dragons spiraled upward, and flew off to the North.

Ereben ran to the partly burned body of the leopard. He saw something familiar about the leopard's rheumy eyes. He pulled the dagger from its chest. It was not his dagger. He tucked it into his belt. The leopards claws appeared more like toenails than catclaws.

Menash rode up on the keplie, Kehlibar. "Ereben go now. Priest come!"

Ereben looked up to see thousands of black-robed priests swarming toward the northern margin of the Shrine. He rushed to the pile of crumbled black stone. Where the portal had been, he dug into the rubble with his hands. There, lying a half-yard beneath the surface he found a dagger with a small notch at the base of the blade. He retrieved it and inserted the knife into its sheath, in place of Hobart's dagger, which he tucked into his belt.

"Now, Ereben," Menash shouted.

Ereben took Menash's hand and vaulted onto Kehlibar's back. The kelpie galloped toward the onrushing tide of black robes, sprouted wings, and rose into the air as the priests engulfed the center of the Shrine. Kehlibar climbed steeply, curving to the southern foothills. Ereben looked back. Among the pinnacles and columns of smoke, the movement of something white reflected the late afternoon sun.

ഇന്ദ

What seemed a goal served only to mark the beginning of greater trials.

Ereben Leaf: Chronicle of the Counterspell

Ereben sat cross-legged on the bank of the Clootie River, puffing coltsfoot in his applewood pipe and thinking of how much he missed Titus. He had not seen the great gyre falcon since the Battle of the Black Pyramid. Titus had been the only living tie to his family.

He drew the dagger that had changed his life, and studied it. Its handle was no longer translucent green stone. The translucency remained, but its color was milky white, almost the same white as the stone of the pinnacles. Ghostly green circles, like leopard spots, were distributed evenly over its surface. When he had focused his mind into the dagger yesterday, he had seen a single shadow within its crystalline substance. Turning the dagger over in his hands, Ereben considered what might emerge if he were to cast the releasing spell now. He could sense the presence of his grandfather bounded by the limits of the dagger's physicality. His plan now was to study the books and scrolls in his possession. Perhaps then, he would again attempt the spell of evocation.

He thought of Ailantha. She could surely help him. When they had stopped at her house, in route to the farm of Liddie Burn, the old woman was gone, as were her chickens and goat. So she might be alive somewhere. More likely, he thought, she had died.

Phaena approached him at the river bank. Ereben patted the ground beside him and sheathed his dagger.

She sat silently for a while, tossing tiny stones into the shallow water. "What was Father trying to do with the dragons?"

"I'm not really sure," Ereben answered. "Hobart said that, from some of the ruins your father explored, he learned about the power of Dragomin being locked in the black pyramid of Shouda. It seemed like he expected the dragon to come out, but I think he was surprised to find more than one."

"Did he think he could control the dragon... or dragons?"

"As long as all three daggers were in the portal, he seemed to have some control over the first dragon. Once one of the daggers came out, the dragons did whatever they wanted." Ereben recalled two of the dragons looking into his own eyes as though they knew him. They didn't fear him, but they hadn't obeyed Corban's order to kill him. He had felt a sense that they were waiting for another day, another place.

"Ever since I can remember," she said, "he talked about the power of Dragomin as if it was something religious. It's so hard to believe that he ended up in a war against the priests of Dragomin."

"I think Crotus started all that."

"Why?"

"The priests have always taught that magic didn't exist except as an evil. I guess they never figured out that the fireball they make at the end of every service is magic. They call it a miracle. Well, with your father using magic to make all those birds bigger, and control the wolves and all, Crotus decided it was heresy. Or else, he just used it as an excuse to grab power."

"I don't understand," Phaena said.

"I heard from Otah Kadeef that, as soon as the battle was over, Crotus announced it was the power of the True Faith over evil. He sent out word that he had ordered the dragon to kill your father in the name of The Redeemer of the True Faith. Doesn't sound very religious to me."

A musical clang sounded from Liddie Burn's house. She stood by the door of her mound house, turning an iron rod inside an iron triangle. "It's all ready!" she shouted. "Off yer duffs and over tae the table!"

A calf had been roasting on a spit all morning. Liddie and Barrow had set up a table outside the house, while Yarnish and Minkar had improvised benches. Jasper came with Bahsa from the mound house, carrying pots of beans and potatoes.

"The news all sounds worrisome," Blen said, as he served up slices of meat. "The priests have been ordered to capture any Protectors they find."

"That sounds good to me," Jasper said through a mouth full of potatoes.

"And," Blen continued, "they're looking for anybody else who committed the sin of magic."

"And we're supposed tae believe," Barrow interrupted, "that all the fire those bloody priests used tae skaith the Protectors was the holy miracles o' Dragomin?"

"I hope that none of us has the opportunity to debate that with them," Minkar said.

"Do you think Menash and the others will be okay?" Jasper asked.

"I doubt Crotus even knows about the tunnels under the Shrine," Ereben said. Mufta Ibrah had given Ereben only vague reasons for wanting to go down there. But the Mufta, Menash, Otah and Amal had led the surviving Shouda into the labyrinth after the Battle of the Black Pyramid. They had allowed the two giant doves, Fantas and Pneuma, to fly away together. Menash's kelpie stallion, Kehlibar, had carried Ereben and Phaena to Liddie's cow farm.

After the meal, Liddie Burn stood by the outdoor fire with her arms folded, shaking her head. "Yer appetites werna up tae the task. I've got half a rostet calf goin' tae waste. It'll be spoilt by the morn."

The ground began to rumble.

"The coos!" she shouted. "The coos are stampedin'."

A shadow crossed the ground. Ereben looked up to the sky. The enormous silhouette of a bird spiraled out of the sun toward them. Ereben's heart leapt. In a maelstrom of wind and dust, a great gyre falcon landed on one leg beside a startled Liddie Burn. *Titus!* His other leg was held off the ground.

"Titus! It's Titus!" Jasper shouted, shaking Ereben's shoulder.

Bahsa grinned and clapped his hands with glee.

"I don't suppose yer hungry," Liddie said, looking up cautiously at the huge falcon.

Titus turned his head toward Ereben, blinked, then hopped toward the leftover, roasted calf. He snatched the carcass, spit and all, and flew with it to the far bank of the Clootie River, where he set about consuming it.

Liddie Burn smiled with satisfaction. "That taks care o' that."

THE END
of volume one

Appendix 1: The Ephesiac Fragments

Compiled by Hobart from anonymous scrolls discovered within the labyrinths of the ruined city of Ephesia. Their original sequence is unknown. They appear to have been ordered by Hobart according to the progression of their arguments. Words of unknown meaning have been translated by comparison to fragments of other contemporaneous scrolls, though their authenticity has been questioned by some scholars.

Ereben Leaf: Chronicle of the Counterspell, Documents

1. All things exist within the Ether.
2. The Ether without conflict or stress is uniformly void—nothing exists.
3. Matter exists as the conflict of Power.
4. Power is an uneven distribution, or stress, of the Ether.
5. Uniform void may be visualized as the flat surface of a quiet pool of water. The water, the Ether, has no stress and is void. If the water is disturbed by the dropping of a tiny pebble, it becomes disturbed or stressed. That state of stress is Power. The stress creates ripples which we may identify as distinct objects, even though the ripples are nothing more than the void of the still pool which has been stressed. That the ripples appear to exist as distinct objects is a product of conflict between two stresses. The first stress is that of the pull of earth, which, though hidden, has transformed the pool from its native state. That native state is as a ball. The pull of earth has stressed the ball to assume a flat surface. The second stress is created by the pebble. This second stress attempts to drive the water from the pool. The result is a conflict of stresses, which result in ripples. One product of that conflict, that is, one ripple, may be named a tree, another a pig. But all are of the

same origin. The pig and the tree differ only in the attunement of conflict and stress within the Ether. As a particular ripple progresses across the pool, we may continue to identify it as a persistent object, even though the substance of the ripple at one instant is never the same as its substance in the previous instant or the next instant. Only its form seems to persists. And even that changes, progressing slowly from the crisp newness of creation to the blunted feebleness of senescence, until it vanishes once again into the pool. All matter is impersistent and illusory.

6. Matter only exists in the conflict of opposing stresses.
7. Diversity has its basis in unity.
8. Unity is manifest as diversity.
9. All things are an exchange for Power, and Power for all things.
10. Power exists by consuming and transforming itself from one apparent form of matter to another.
11. Power can be partly released from matter as in a fire, which transforms wood to vapor.
12. The greatest Power is released when matter is completely extinguished, becoming pure Power, pure Stress of Ether.
13. The diminishing of conflict increases Stress.
14. The diminishing of Stress increases conflict.
15. Matter and Power may be considered as unity of the Ether or the diversity of objects. When seen as unity of the Ether, there is no wonder that a pig may become a tree. But since men see not the unity of the Ether, but only the diversity of objects, they are incredulous that a pig may become a tree. So they ascribe such a transformation to occult mysteries.
16. If men do not seek the unexpected, they do not find it.
17. The Upward Path is the transformation of conflict, which is matter, to stress, which is Power. This is the extinguishing of matter. The Downward Path is the transformation of stress to conflict. This is the creation of matter. The Paths of the Horizon are the transformations from one conflict to another conflict.

These are the transformations of one object into another.

18. The Upward Path gives off warmth. The Downward Path draws warmth from its surroundings.

19. The Paths of the Horizon follow one of two courses. It is the Light Path by which conflict is altered in its conformation, though not its magnitude, transforming matter directly from one apparent form to another. This is in contrast to the Dark Path, by which conflict is annihilated to produce incorporeal Power which, in turn, regenerates conflict of a different conformation, transforming matter of one apparent form to Power and thence back to matter of a different apparent form.

20. The Light Path, if uncontrolled, may transform matter to unanticipated forms. The Dark Path, if uncontrolled, may dissipate its Power as a cataclysm.

21. The Light Path is witnessed in the transformation of an acorn to a great oak, and in the transformation of honey to meade. The Dark Path is followed by the Sun, which forever consumes itself while rebuilding itself.

22. Within the Light Path, there is perfect attunement between the Upward Path and the Downward Path. Within the Dark Path, the attunement of Upward and Downward Paths is imperfect, first displaying a preponderance of one then the other, in turn. As the string of the lyre is stretched to one extreme, only to rebound to the opposite extreme, in turn.

23. The true nature of matter and of the Ether is well hidden. Those who see its truth laid out before them for the first time are as confused as those who have not seen it.

24. All matter is God's creation out of the void of the Ether. To Him, all His creation is satisfactory. To men, some of God's creations are called good, and some called evil.

25. Those who study the true nature of things touch upon all issues of matter and the Ether. To other men, those who study the true nature of things are called good or called evil, in relation to the labels men have affixed to the issues studied.

26. All Paths—the Upward, the Downward, and the Paths of the Horizon—and their hidden attunement to one another, comprise the universal law or Logos. Men may recognize the Logos and accept it, or they may rant against it, manifesting their ignorance in attempts to punish those who truly see.
27. Most men can not see how that which is in conflict exists nevertheless in attunement according to the Logos.
28. The One is always many, and the many are always One. Opposites are inseparable.
29. All things come into existence and pass away through conflict.
30. Knowledge is to know many things. Wisdom is to know the Logos by which all things are steered through all things.

Appendix 2: Knurlish Dictionary of Yarnish Blen

Date Unknown. Found among the collected documents of Hobart. Ereben Leaf: Chronicle of the Counterspell, Documents

a-gley	awry
aa	all
aff	off
ahin	behind
aik	oak
ain	own (adj)
airt	direction
alang	along
amang	among
an'	and
ance	once
aneath	beneath
anither	another
argy-bargy	dispute
arselins	backwards
aside	beside
atween	between
auld	old
awkwart	awkward
aye	yes
ba'	ball
baillie	magistrate
baith	both
ballats	ballads
barefit	barefoot
barley-brie	ale
barlyecorn	barley
beastie	small beast
belang	belong
beuk	book
bid	ask
bide	live
billie	comrade
birl	whirl
bizzard	buzzard
blastie	damned thing
blaw	blow
bleeze	blaze
blether	chatter
blin'	blind
bluid	blood
bluidy	bloody
bow't	bent
breid	bread
brither	brother
broo	soup
buff	bang (v)
buit	boot
bum	buttocks
burn	brook
burnewin	blacksmith
bu'	but
caa'd	called
cam	came
camshauchle	distorted
cartes	cards
cauld	cold
cauldron	caldron
caup	cup
chamer	chamber
chitterin	shivering
claithin	clothing
cleuch	gorge (n)
clishclash	gossip
cloot	hoof
clootie	devilish
co'or	cover (v)
coo	cow
coof	dolt

corbie	raven
cou'dna	couldn't
couthie	comfortable
craw	crow
creeshie	greasy
croon	song
dae	do
daft	crazy
darena	dare not
dinna	do not
dochter	daughter
doon	down
drap	drop
drouthy	thirsty
duff	seat (n)
duffie	water closet
e'e	eye
e'er	ever
eas'lan	eastern
easy-osy	easy going
een	eyes
eerie	fearful
efterin	after
eldritch	haunted
endweys	forward
fae	foe
fallowt	followed
farl	oat-cake
fau't	fault
feardie	coward
fecket	waistcoat
fell	dreadful
fend	defend
fit	foot
flee	fly (v)
flinder	shred (n)
fother	fodder
fou	foul(drunk)
frae	from
frien'	friend
fu'	full
fugie	runaway
gae	go
gaed	went
gaen	gone
gairden	garden
gangrel	vagrant
gate	road
gath'rin	gathering
gear	money or goods
geck	gawk
gemme	game
gie	give
gied	gave
gien	given
giftie	gift, little
glamour	spell (n)
glower	stare
golach	earwig
gowd	gold
gree	prize
groff	coarse
guid	good
hae	have
haein'	having
hale	healthy
haly	holy
hame	home
han	hand
haud	hold
hed	had
hersel	herself
heuk	hook
hill-tap	hilltop
himsel	himself
hings	hangs
hornie	devil
houlet	owl
houss	house

hoyse	hoist
hunder	hundred
huvna	have not
i'	in
ill-theif	devil
intae	into
ither	other
itsel	itself
jauntie	short trip
jink	dodge (v)
kail	cabbage
kelpie	river demon
ken	know
kintra	country
knaggie	knobby
lad	boy
laird	landowner
lammie	lamb, small
lan'	land
langer	longer
langth	length
lap	leapt
lass	girl
leddy	lady
len'	lend (v)
licks	beating (n)
loch	lake
lowp	jump
lowse	untie (v)
lum	chimney
mair	more
maist	most
maister	master
maistlins	almost
mak	make
maun	must
may't	may it
maybes	perhaps
midden	dunghill
mirk	dark
mither	mother
nae	no
naething	nothing
nane	none
neebor	neighbor
needna	needn't
neest	next
nigh	near
nirly	nearly
nocht	nothing
noo	now
norlan	northern
o't	of it
oot	out
oursels	ourselves
outlan	outlaw
parritch	porridge
pat	pot
pinkie	finger(5th)
pit	put
plenisht	stocked
pou	pull
pray'r	prayer
puir	poor
quean	queen
ramfeezl'd	exhausted
randie	obstreperous
rase	rose up
raw	row (n)
reave	rob (v)
remead	cure
rig	ridge
rin	run
rive	split (v)
roosty	rusty
roun	round
rung	cudgel (n)
sab	sob
sae	so
saft	soft

sairly	sorely
saul	soul
saut	salt
scowder	scorch
scriechin	screeching
sech	such
see'd	saw
selt	sold
sen'	send
set	sat
shae	shoe
shaird	shard
shaw	show
sheuk	shook
shoon	shoes
show'rs	rain
showther	shoulder
sidelins	sideways
siller	money
siller	silver
simmer	summer
sin'	since
skaith	damage
slade	slid
slidd'ry	slippery
sma'	small
smiddy	smithy
snaw	snow
sodger	soldier
sonsy	buxom
soom	swim (v)
soor	sour
spak	spoke
speet	spit
stan	stand
stane	stone
stang	sting
stap	stop
starn	star
stick-an-stowe	completely
strak	struck
strath	valley, wide
straught	strut
studdie	anvil
sune	soon
suthron	southern
swall'd	swelled
sweert	sworn
swick	cheat (v)
swirlie	twisted
sybie	onion
ta'en	taken
tae	to
tak	take
tap	top
tapmost	topmost
tassie	goblet
telt	told
tether	rope
teuk	took
tha'	that (p)
thae	those
the day	today
the morn	tomorrow
the night	tonight
thegither	together
thir	their
tho'	though
timmer	timber
tinkler	tinker
tither	the other
toop	top
tousie	shaggy
trewsers	trousers
turn'd	turned
'twad	it would
upo'	upon
vera	very
vittle	victual

wad	would
wad'a	would have
wadna	would not
war	where
wark	work
warl	world
warlock	wizard
warse	worse
wast	west
wat	wet
weanie	baby
wee	little
wer	were
werna	were not
wes	was
westlan	western
wha	who
whaizle	wheeze
wheen	wind
wi'	with
wifie	wife
willcat	wildcat
wilna	will not
winze	curse (n)
wonner	wonder
woo'	wool
wraith	ghost
wrang	wrong
wrocht	worked
ye	you
ye're	you're
yestreen	last night
yon	that (adj)
yonder	those

Counterspell:
THE SECOND LAW

Volume 2 of The Counterspell Chronicle

Chapter 1 Preview

In less than half a year, The Redeemer and his disciples rose from obscurity to near absolute control of the eastern lands. Centuries of peaceful relations among the races of man were swept away in the reign of religious terror which ensued.

Ereben Leaf: Chronicle of the Counterspell

"The priests appear to be heaping branches around each of them," Minkar Jarad observed.

Ereben Leaf closed his eyes at the thought of what he was about to witness. He had heard rumors that heretics were being burned alive, but he had not expected the well armed dwarfs of Zink to allow such a thing without a fight. He looked down into the market square again. His view from the earthen wall of the city made it difficult to recognize the thirty dwarfs tied to posts. One, he thought, was the Baillie of Zink. Several others seemed to wear the uniform of the Baillie's guards.

"Is there nothing we can do?" Minkar asked. The words of the brown Shouda warrior were filled with sadness.

"No more than all of them," Ereben answered, indicating the hundreds of dwarfs standing about the market square in cowed silence. "If the Baillie had fought the Knights instead of trying to appease them, this wouldn't be happening." The Knights of the Redeemer, Ereben had decided, were nothing more than opportunistic thugs. They surely would have avoided the walled city if there had been any chance of a battle.

"May Elloh forgive me," Minkar whispered, "for not lifting my spear against this."

The great mounds of twigs were set afire. Frightful screams rose from the market square. Ereben could not watch. He turned his backside to the wall and skidded down the long, grassy embankment, then up over the outer wall of the dry moat.

Barrow stood waiting at the bottom. "We hed better move oursels away from the city," the dwarf said. Barrow leaned on the handle of his great, golden battle-ax as he watched Minkar follow Ereben down from the earthen wall.

"It's true," Ereben said to the dwarf. "They burned them all alive."

"Aye, lad," Barrow replied, "I was telt as much by a farmer escapin' tae the norlan brae. I couldna find the courage tae climb the wall and watch. He said that the Baillie was one o' those tae be burnt, the poor bastard."

"I think I saw him there," Ereben continued, "and some of his guards."

As Minkar reached the base of the wall, he ran toward them, urgently waving an arm. "I believe one of the knights has seen me. Four of them are climbing the inside of the wall in this direction."

They ran to the cover of the heather mounds, then wove their way along a game trail to the gully where Jasper waited with the kelpies and two dwarf ponies. Ereben had decided it would be safer if they were seen on natural appearing mounts rather than the giant birds. Four ponies would have been ideal, but dwarf ponies were so small that Ereben's feet dragged the ground. For Minkar, keeping his knees off the ground would have been difficult. At least full size horses had become a more common sight in Knurlan since the Knights of the Redeemer had gained the upper hand. Although the kelpies, Dantel and Kehlibar, were sometimes difficult to control, in their current form as horses, they appeared to be natural so long as they were not coaxed to sprout their wings and lift into the air.

"What did you find out?" Jasper asked.

"It's true," Ereben answered. "They're burning heretics."

"It'll be us they burn, if we stand around tradin' stories." The dwarf climbed onto his pony and tied his ax to the rear of the saddle.

Ereben hoisted himself onto the broad shoulders of Kehlibar. As Jasper mounted the other pony with the aid of his carved wooden staff, it was plain from the expression on his face that the boy would have preferred to ride "his" kelpie, Dantel. Minkar, for his part, was not happy riding a river demon, but had agreed to it with the understanding that the arrangement was temporary. They headed south at a deliberately innocent pace. Ereben hoped that they appeared as simple travelers, even though Minkar's dark brown skin, pointed ears and extraordinary height raised eyebrows wherever they went, especially here, in the dwarf land of Knurlan.

Gentle ripples on the Clootie River cast sparkles of late day sun into Phaena's eyes. Her golden hair danced in the breeze of early summer. Ereben longed to reach out and touch her cheek, kiss her lips. But she had built a wall about herself. She seemed to desire his company, but not his affection. Since the death of her infamous father, Lord Corban, High Protector of Dragomin, she had been transformed from heiress of privilege to loathsome criminal. She still expressed confusion about her father's aims and his posthumous disgrace. Now, all Ereben could offer was his steadfast love. He was grateful to the dragons for sparing him the responsibility for Corban's death.

"Where did the dragons go?" Phaena asked.

"Some people say they flew north, to the Nether Reaches," Ereben answered, "but I don't think anybody knows for sure."

"Do you think they'll come back?"

He knew they would, eventually. "I hope not. Yarnish is trying to find out what's happening with them." The tinker, Yarnish Blen, had left them two weeks earlier for Valand. Barrow had suggested the trip, since Blen was not known to the priests of the True Faith, and most of Corban's Protectors, those few that had survived the recent spate of burnings, were in hiding and not likely to cause Blen any problems. "Barrow says that it might not be safe here for much longer. He's heard that Crotus is nearly beside himself over not being able to find us."

"I'd like to go somewhere else," she said. "Living on a cow farm in the middle of nowhere gets pretty boring."

"But nowhere is about the only place we can hide. The priests and those Knights of the Redeemer are crawling all over the cities and towns. Where else could we go?" He didn't care what Phaena's answer would be, transfixed as he was by the subtle, pouting movements of her lips.

"Oh, Ereben. Anywhere else. The mountains or the forests or the sea coast. Just somewhere with something to look at besides grass and cows. Somewhere that we could fly without worrying about priests and religion."

"I don't know too many places where a bird five yards high wouldn't cause a little curiosity." A scent of wildflowers wafted from Phaena's hair, distracting his logic. "Or winged horses."

Phaena smiled. He loved to see her smile. It reminded him of the days so long ago when their lives were predictable and peaceful. Since the death of his family at the hands of the Protectors, everything had become more complex, more dangerous. Just surviving required concerted planning and constant vigilance.

Minkar Jarad's five year old son, Bahsa, wandered toward them from Liddie Burn's mound house. The handsome Shouda boy seemed to grow taller by the week. Since witnessing his mother's death in the Shouda massacre, he had not spoken. Bahsa seated himself in the space between Ereben and Phaena, and leaned his head against Phaena's shoulder. She stroked his tight, black hair and kissed him on the forehead, playfully pinching the points of his ears. Ereben considered how normal the dark brown skin of the Shouda seemed to him now. Before his flight from Rippleton and beyond the borders of Valand, he had never even heard of people with brown skin.

"You are so handsome," Phaena said to the boy, "and you're getting so tall. In another year, you'll be taller than Jasper."

Bahsa smiled and took her hand. When he looked at Ereben, his smile seemed to reveal a satisfaction at being able to hold the hand that Ereben could not hold. Ereben found the boy's manner and behavior much more engaging than he would have expected from a five year old. He remembered Minkar's endless stories about Bahsa filling the arduous journey through the Broken Mountains.

"Did you do your letters?" Phaena asked the boy. Phaena had been teaching him to read and write.

Bahsa squirmed a bit, then shook his head.

"You have to have them done before dinner, or no sweet bun for you."

The boy's demeanor assumed one of consummate hardship, as he stood and headed back to the house. Ereben found it hard to understand why Bahsa would not talk. He listened well, and expressed his thoughts well without words. It seemed as though it would be a simple thing for him to just talk. But he didn't. Minkar had tried all sorts of incentives and tricks to get him to say even one word, but to no avail.

"Ereben," Phaena asked, "when are you going to do that spell thing with the dagger?"

"Pretty soon, I think."

"Do you really believe your grandfather is in there? I mean alive?"

"Yes."

"That's all so strange."

"It's... It's strange and scary. The ice leopard that came out of it looked different than before."

"What do you mean?"

"It was old and feeble, like Grandfather. And its fur was all white and brittle, like Grandfather's hair. The leopard's eyes were tired and kind of cloudy. And... it had no tail."

"Ereben! You mean your grandfather might have a tail?"

"I don't know. But I'm pretty sure he'll be different. I'm not sure that bringing him out is the right thing to do."

"And you're going to do it anyway? Maybe he wanted to go into the dagger and stay there."

"When he went into the dagger, it caused something like a fire ball. I saw a burned body, but it was someone else. That means that somebody else was there. It was probably one of the Protectors trying to steal both of the daggers—Grandfather's and mine. So I think Grandfather went into the dagger to escape, and to keep them from getting both daggers. It seems like he would want to come back out."

"I hope you're right, Ereben Leaf."

At dawn, Ereben sat alone in the misty paddock beside Liddie's mound house. He had stacked three large sacks of potatoes on the ground two yards away from where he sat. The blade of his dagger stood embedded in the upper sack. In his left hand, he held munu, the praying hands mushroom, which would supply the power for the spell. The potatoes, he hoped, would channel the counterspell. Ereben's right hand gripped Hobart's dagger to focus the casting of the evocation.

Both hands trembled at the thought of what he was about to do. If he failed, then his grandfather, Chrysanthus, Guardian of the Ruins, would be lost forever. If he succeeded, his grandfather might emerge with unspeakable deformities. But Chrysanthus must have learned more about the dragons than either Hobart or Ailantha knew. Hobart was now merged with the rock of the great canyon, and Ailantha was probably dead. And his own inadequate understanding of all of this left him with no choice but to try to release his grandfather from imprisonment within the forged layers of steel.

"Oh, Grandpa, I hope I'm doing the right thing."

"Are you going to do it now?" The sound of Jasper's voice startled him.

"Yes."

"Why so early?" As usual, the eleven year old's sandy brown hair stood out in several directions above his dirt smudged face. He carried his carved wooden staff, attempting to twirl it in one hand the way Minkar twirled a Shouda spear. "Nobody's up yet." The staff fell. Jasper retrieved it with a forlorn sigh.

"I couldn't sleep last night," Ereben answered, "so I decided to do it now." He had hoped to be alone. That thought seemed so silly when he considered the tens of thousands of priests and Protectors surrounding him the last time he had tried, during the Battle of the Black Pyramid.

"Can I watch?"

"Well... I suppose so."

"Is your grandfather real old?"

"He was when he went into the dagger."

"Does he like kids?"

"If you're going to watch, you'll have to be quiet."

"Sorry."

Ereben took a deep breath and silently reviewed the details of the evocation. Ailantha had spent only that one night teaching it to him, but he had turned it over in his mind a dozen times a day for the past five months. He knew what she had taught him, but he was not certain that it was the correct evocation for what he needed to do. The scant discussion on evocations he was able to decipher from his paltry library of magic only added to his uncertainty. While he continued to have difficulty translating the ancient Shadae, in which many of the materials were written, he was convinced that they dealt with other, unrelated subjects. He had to admit to himself that one of his motivations for releasing Chrysanthus was that he felt incompetent. *I'm the last Guardian of the Ruins, and I don't know any magic!*

"How long does it take," Jasper whispered. "Sorry." Jasper placed his fingers over his lips.

Ereben returned his attention to the dagger perched atop the sacks of potatoes. An unsettling thought crossed his mind. *What if Grandpa doesn't recognize me? What if he's changed so much that he attacks me?* He laid Hobart's dagger on the ground and drew the third dagger from his belt, the dagger Corban had used to kill the ice leopard. Hobart had said that three of the daggers placed in a certain arrangement would create a field of power. It was just such an arrangement which had opened the portal in the face of the black pyramid. Ereben envisioned the distances between the daggers when they had been inserted into the slots of the portal. *About two yards.* He stabbed the third dagger into the dirt on the far side of Jasper, then seated himself again, equidistant from the two daggers. When he lifted Hobart's dagger again, he sensed a thrumming of power within it. Waving the dagger slowly through the air, he was able to feel a point of consonance, a point at which the three daggers seemed to be attuned. The handles of all three daggers glowed softly. His heart raced. He knew that he was tampering with powers which he did not understand—powers that could change the attunement of nature, that could consume him in an instant.

"Ereben?" Jasper whispered

"Shhh."

"Ereben," Jasper persisted, "look at my staff."

Without moving Hobart's dagger, Ereben turned his head toward Jasper. The munu, the praying hands mushroom Jasper had carved at the head of his staff so many months ago glowed a soft red, pulsing subtly with the palpable thrum of the power field. Its carved menagerie, which spiraled from one end of the staff to the other, seemed alive. The animals and birds and fish remained in their assigned places, but each of them moved a head or legs or fins. Jasper held it by the smoothly carved grip above its center. The boy's hand trembled. His eyes stared wildly. As the red glow of the carved mushroom extended down the staff toward his hand, he released it, allowing the staff to tip into the triangle marked out by the three daggers. The head of the staff came to rest at the center of the triangle. By then, the entire wooden staff glowed red. Jasper sat immobile.

Ereben sensed power and control resonating within his body. It did not flow from the munu gripped within his left hand. It echoed in harmonious play with all that surrounded him. His vision grasped a gossamer connectedness that reached from dagger to dagger and from within himself to all things. His ears heard the melodies which played from fair to foul and back again. The odors of growth and decay swirled about one another as opposite poles of the same message. Sour and bitter, sweet and salt extended as dimensions of a solitary sensation. In an instant, he understood that all things were connected—that the daggers and potatoes and the earth itself were all expressions of the same substance. Everything was connected by resonant strands to everything else. He recalled his journey within the rock of the great canyon. He knew the weave of matter through time. Tendrils of each connection reached into the past and into the future. It was those connections, those relationships that he wished to alter. With their dependencies and paths now visible, Ereben understood what he must change and what he must not change. He stepped his mind through the evocation of releasing, confident that he would succeed.

Within the triangle of daggers, a mist of matter began to condense. As it grew more solid and opaque, the sacks of potatoes sagged. Ereben's dagger descended toward the ground as the sacks collapsed. When the figure within the triangle had become completely substantial, Ereben moved Hobart's dagger beyond the point of attunement. The field of power subsided.

Jasper gasped. In front of them stood a man without clothing. His skin was covered in short white fur, stippled with ghostly spots. About his head flowed white hair and a full white beard. Little white tufts rose from the tops of slightly pointed ears. He blinked. A feline quality about his green eyes revealed confusion and caution. Massive muscles rippled beneath the surface of his chest and arms. From each finger grew a dark, metallic claw. Ereben's eyes followed sleek, powerful legs to fur covered feet. Most remarkable of all was a leopard tail swishing nervously behind.

Ereben looked at the unmistakable face of this leopard-man. "Grandpa?" He asked, tentatively.

The man opened his mouth as if to speak. White leopard's teeth glistened in the light of dawn.

www.ingramcontent.com/pod-product-compliance
Lightning Source LLC
LaVergne TN
LVHW091044080826
845145LV00002B/618